HOUSE
OF
HEARTS

HOUSE
OF
HEARTS

House of Jewels, Volume II

Amber Jakeman

Lorikeet Press, 2021

This is a work of fiction. Similarities to real people, places, or events are entirely coincidental.

HOUSE OF HEARTS
First edition. May 5, 2021.

Copyright © Amber Jakeman.

ISBN: 978-0-6454625-8-6

Written by Amber Jakeman.

Also by Amber Jakeman

House of Jewels series (ISSN 2653-0384)
House of Diamonds
House of Hearts
House of Spades
House of Clubs

www.amberjakeman.com
www.lorikeetpress.com

To all good men.

To those who remind us we always have choices.

To the power of love.

Chapter 1

Lisa patted Rossco's rough brown fur as he blinked at her and tried to lick her hand.

"See you tonight, old fella," she said, as she opened her car door and slid in.

"January 4," said the dashboard calendar. Eighteen months to the day since she'd fled west with just Rossco and a few boxes of possessions. Eighteen months of professional fulfilment. And a ton of personal guilt.

She must phone her parents again, remind them of how happy she was in her new life, how she hadn't meant to hurt them. She didn't blame them for what went on between Art and her. What *hadn't* gone on, more like it.

Lisa loved this part of her commute. Once she'd left her peaceful Boulder City home and then the outskirts of Vegas, she passed the garish towers of Downtown and slipped into the lower-rise, older blocks, where the 1950s neon signs never failed to cheer her. She congratulated herself once more on her escape, on the fact she'd been able to study while Art had tended the samples in his lab and devoted himself to his research. She'd finished one degree after another, then found her dream job and perfect career – counselling.

As she pulled into the clinic, Lisa opened her glove compartment and put her name tag in her pocket. It still gave her a thrill.

Dr Lisa Bakker. Group Counsellor and Diversion Therapist. The Peters Clinic. She loved to encourage others to better understand themselves and their behaviour, to recognize and act on better choices, to grow and thrive.

With its palm trees and curved, 1930s style white facade, the front of the clinic and health retreat always made her heart lift. She parked next to Dr Peters' "Reserved" sign.

The receptionist's parking spot was still vacant, the one dark moment of her morning. At 8.50am, unless Mindy had caught the bus or walked, she'd either be late or absent all day – again. Lisa would have to lodge an official complaint with Dr Peters.

She checked her hair and lipstick in the rear-vision mirror, flicked a dog hair off her slim grey skirt and entered the side door of the counsellors' suites.

Normally, she loved this part of her day. She'd have a few moments alone in her consulting room to center herself and review her notes, but with Mindy AWOL again, she'd have to sort the clients' folders herself. She'd end up running behind all day.

And with Dr Peters away in Europe for ten days, she had more appointments than ever. She'd asked her to stand in to welcome a couple of her new clients – the ones who'd join her group sessions later in the day.

She headed into reception, and sure enough, there was no Mindy. Nothing prepared. Lisa reached for the folders just as Dr Peters' first new client arrived. She glanced at him again. Was there something familiar about him?

He sized her up with a cheeky half-smile.

Distractingly good-looking, he wore a tight white t-shirt and faded jeans. Eyes the color of faded denim. Nice teeth, chewing half of his bottom lip. Was he staring at her? At her legs?

Damn Mindy for not being here to do her job! Especially with this extra case load.

Lisa gathered up the folders – in a hurry now – and dropped them. They skidded all over the floor. Disaster.

In a flash, the man was down on his knees, scooping them up. Thank God. Her skirt was a bit tight for bending over. So, he was a gentleman. *Why did that bother her?*

"Thank you," she said, accepting them and disappearing to her room to sort them as quickly as possible. She slipped on her white coat, positioned her name tag, glanced at the front of the top folder, and reappeared in reception.

"Will Huntley, please," she said. Why was her heart beating so hard? Lisa smoothed her hands down the side of her jacket.

He stood, that grin in place, as if he knew he could make her blush.

"Welcome to The Peters Clinic," Lisa said. She held out her hand, her smile professional. "I'm Dr Lisa Bakker, part of the team. Dr Peters has asked me to get things started for you. Follow me, please."

...

On her way home at the end of the day, Lisa called in at the grocery store for fresh vegetables and pasta. Jilly, her old friend from grad school, in town to visit her mother, was coming for dinner and a talkfest. Wonderful, outspoken Jilly, Jilly who'd told her about Vegas, who'd shared her love of skyrunning with her back in college. Without Jilly, none of her new life would exist, this patch of sunlit color in a universe of gray.

When Jilly arrived, she didn't waste a minute. She hugged Lisa, dumped her hot-pink handbag on the couch and followed her into the kitchen, where she washed her hands and helped prepare the meal.

"So, Lisa, hooked up lately?"

Good old Jilly, fast and fearless. Love-life front of mind. Maybe growing up with her mother had made her believe it was the only sensible topic of conversation. Scoping stepfathers, matchmaking, how to avoid her mother's mistakes ...

Lisa slid the chopped tomatoes into the steaming sauce as the silence stretched.

"Come on, Lisa," Jilly said. "You've got to get out there. Eighteen months? And we both know it's been longer than that. Look, Art never even gave you a love-life. If that's why you left him, maybe you should have just stayed."

Lisa stared at her old friend. No wonder that tech company had snapped her up for their human resources team. Jilly nipped any nonsense in the bud, called a spade a spade, and she was usually right. Jilly might be outspoken, but she was also wise. There was always some truth to what she said. Even if Lisa rightly accused Jilly of always having too many boyfriends, it wouldn't change the fact that Lisa had never had enough.

She'd had a husband, instead – Art. Straight out of school. And how was she to have guessed that a fine family friend wasn't necessarily good husband material? He'd been as disappointed with her as she'd been with him, no doubt, not that they'd ever spoken about that. In their eight years together, they hadn't spoken about much at all.

Lisa sighed and twisted open the lid of a jar of tomato paste, then dumped the contents in the frypan.

"I don't know," she said. "There isn't much time for romance, Jilly. I work flat out with people all day, and when I come home, I go for a run and then I'm tired. Besides, Rossco gives me all the love I need right now."

"Evidently. But I didn't mean 'love.' I actually meant 'sex.' How's your sex life?"

"Not everyone requires hot, uninhibited sex every night, Jilly."

"Okay, but *no* sex? None at all? You don't realize what you're missing. It's not natural. Physician, heal thyself."

"I suppose you're right," Lisa said, hiding her face in the cutlery drawer, clattering and jangling as she searched for matching forks. It had been a while. Maybe since never, if she was honest. Had she ever had proper sex, sex you read about and heard about where your lover knows what they're doing and cherishes every part of you and you're both in ecstacy? Had she ever experienced sex beyond the rapid, embarassed fumbling in the dark which Art had attempted? Sex with Art had never improved, no matter how much she read up on what should be happening. In the end it had been easier just to avoid it all.

"It doesn't have to be about sex, even," said Jilly, picking up on Lisa's hesitation. "How about a simple date? Just one. Give yourself a chance. You know, we're both twenty-eight. In fact, I'm willing to bet you've *never* been on a date. I just worked it out, Lisa! You married that old creep straight out of school."

"Jilly!"

As the high school principal's only child in a conservative small town, Lisa might as well have had "do not touch" tattooed on her forehead. Marrying Art straight after her high school graduation seemed the perfect solution at the time.

Born shy, with parents who wanted to protect her from the evils of the world, she'd grown up with fairy tales and books as her best friends, only

10

to discover that "happy ever after" didn't necessarily follow the white wedding.

Tertiary education broadened her mind and gave her the qualifications to make her own way professionally and financially. But it wasn't possible to study "Perfect Relationship 101" or even "Elementary Dating." Well, sure, eventually she learned about the Gottman Institute, but she'd committed to addiction therapy as her specialty by then, and her own love-life had never been a priority.

"Okay," said Jilly. "All that's in the past. You escaped. All I'm trying to tell you is that the sky won't fall in if you go on a date or three. It's not like you have to go out there and match up with Dream Lover or Mr Right straight away."

Jilly helped herself to a stray piece of uncooked pasta and crunched on it.

"It's just about having fun," Jilly said. "Playing the field. Call it what you want. It's all very cosy here. Now don't get me wrong. I love the way you've decorated this place." She waved her hand at Lisa's blue-and-white kitchen. "And I couldn't be happier that your career's going so well. You've got a great job, by all accounts, and we all love Rossco, though he does need a bath, just between you and me…"

Lisa inspected the pasta and dumped it in the colander, steam rising in a cloud around her. Now her cheeks were pink for two reasons.

"Fun," Lisa said. "Yeah, dating. I get it. I'll think about it. Now, what about you, Jilly? Been on any dates? Had a night at home lately? That'd be new and different. I suspect you enjoy enough excitement for the two of us." She selected two big bowls from her wooden dresser.

"In fact, Jilly, here's a challenge. I'm willing to bet you've never been on an actual date, either. You just have to meet a man and he falls for you. They're all putty in your hands. I've known you for seven years, and in all that time you've never once been on your own. Men adore you."

Lisa pointed at her friend with the cutlery she'd selected. "One smile and they're yours," Lisa said. "It's different for me. Men don't go for me. Maybe they worry I'm analysing them all the time. Maybe I am!"

"Lisa, you're gorgeous! You might be the world's best addiction therapist, but you don't even notice when men find you attractive. You're a beautiful human being."

"That's so lovely of you to say, but not everyone wants to date a giant."

"You are *not* a giant. Okay, you're tall. So? *Models* are tall. You know what? I'm willing to bet that if a man looked at you like he wanted you, you wouldn't even notice. Open your eyes. Let yourself thaw out a bit. You're a long way from that conservative home town now."

"Maybe." Often it was easiest just to agree with Jilly. "So come on, how's your new job? Your mom must love it now you're only one state away. *I* love it. Thanks for the visit."

…

Lisa brushed her hair as she got ready for bed. Had Jilly been right? There was no way Lisa wanted a life like Jilly's. But a little bit of fun wouldn't go astray, now that everything else was so stable in her life. The thought scared her. But did she really want to hide away forever?

And that bit about her not even realizing guys found her attractive? Maybe Jilly was right about that, too. Only that morning, there'd been that new client, Will Huntley, the handsome Australian. The way he'd scooped up those folders and handed them over. Chivalrous. Had he been giving her the eye? Had he been thinking of her in *that way*?

Brush mid-air, she stopped and studied herself in the mirror – caught herself smiling. Because he really had been looking at her. At her ankles, and then into her eyes, for just a second too long. Long enough to notice her blush.

She put down the brush and stared into her own eyes. Jilly was right. She was tall but she wasn't exactly ugly. Why did the thought he might find her attractive please her so much? Because it did. A sudden thrill gave her cheeks a fresh, healthier glow, and her eyes sparkled.

And then in her consulting room, he'd been embarrassed to have mistaken her for the receptionist. She laughed, remembering how he'd done a double-take.

Earlier, in reception, he'd been so self-assured with her, so at ease in his own body. Arrogant, in a casual way. Lean and effortlessly handsome in that t-shirt, which sat tight over his pecs and biceps. Show-off.

She grabbed the brush again and swept it through her hair, finished the job, threw it on the dressing table, and jumped into bed.

In fact, for Will Huntley, being so handsome was a big part of his problem. Everything came too easily for people like that, and when the going got tough, they were lost, with alcohol and gambling a major temptation. It was why they ended up coming to therapists like her.

Lisa turned over and plumped her pillow. Well. Jilly might be sad to hear it, but there was no risk she'd ever get involved with Will Huntley. Bad-boy Will was strictly off limits. She was a professional. No clinic client could ever be dating material.

Her job was to focus on their minds and their behavior, not their bodies. Though his body had, in fact, been spectacularly distracting. And his eyes. They'd been so curious, so alive. And his smile. It seemed genuine. He'd laughed at his mistake about her role. She liked that in a person; a sense of humor.

And then he'd had the grace to admit he hadn't been looking forward to the treatment. That he'd actually only agreed to it because of the food at the retreat, not because of the clinic's reputation for helping people stop gambling. Cheeky.

So yes, he did have some appealing qualities, but that was literally no business of hers. Completely irrelevant.

Dating someone like Will Huntley would be ridiculous. Not only was he an addict, he was a client. So, even if they were attracted to each other, the American Psychological Society code of conduct forbade such relationships for two years after therapy ended. There. It was utterly impossible. Easy. She was a good girl. Professional. She'd never broken a rule in her life.

Rossco whined and nudged her knee, desperate for a last pat before he settled in his basket. She tickled his ears and had his tail wagging in no time, thumping against the side of the bed. She and Rossco were happy. Happy enough. Well, maybe she should take a risk now and then. Okay. Maybe one date. With somebody. One day.

Chapter 2

Will felt lucky.

The clinic in the Vegas health retreat his mother had lined up for him had a receptionist with legs to forever and beautiful, honey-brown eyes. Bonus!

She was avoiding his gaze as she fussed about near the counter, sorting folders.

Coming in here twice a day for three weeks would be no hardship after all, Will decided. Yes. It was better than watching fish in a tank or rifling through a stack of tired magazines. He could do this.

He took a seat on the white couch, which was plush, tasteful; the exact opposite to the pavements of outer Vegas. Not that sleeping rough was a choice.

From check-in last night to "show up for treatment," this retreat was like a five-star hotel. Not bad. Not bad at all. He linked his fingers behind his head, leaned back and gave her a little smile. Not a full-on flirt. Just some encouragement ...

It backfired.

Suddenly the folders spun out of her grip, dropping and sliding across the tiled floor like gambling chips shoved towards a winner.

In her tight skirt, she hesitated, staring at the chaos.

"Allow me," Will offered, dashing across from the couch and scooping them up with the speed and dexterity of an athlete.

"Thank you," she said, flustered. "So sorry. Back soon."

He chuckled. Had he rattled her with his chivalry? Good. Despite rock-bottom poverty, he hadn't lost his touch.

She retreated down a corridor and returned several minutes later in a white lab coat, more composed, folders neatly stacked and presumably in some kind of order. When she resettled them on the corner of the counter, she selected the top one and called out to him.

"Mr Will Huntley, please."

He stood and followed her down the hall and into another white room. There was an abstract painting in pastel colors, a low table with a box of tissues and a cactus in a white pot. Beyond the window was a courtyard with more cacti.

"I'm Dr Bakker, Mr Huntley," she said, closing the door, her smile tight. Professional. Warm yet distant.

"Oh." Will barely hid his astonishment. He studied her with renewed interest, embarrassed to have underestimated her. She was so young. He wasn't sure whom he'd expected. Someone older, for sure. Not this Dr Bakker, with her straight blonde hair pulled back into a neat ponytail and those caramel eyes; kind eyes. Delicious.

"Yes," she said. "Our receptionist appears to have been held up this morning."

Although she clearly refrained from saying the word "again," Will noticed the shadow of annoyance. It vanished as she turned her professional face to him once more. She gestured at the couch, a twin of the one in the waiting room, and Will targeted it. He waited for her to sit before he did, in the armchair opposite. She checked the wall clock, and set a little timer on her watch. He sat up straighter, suddenly nervous in this unusual habitat.

"So, Mr Huntley. You're actually Dr Peters' client. She's asked me to welcome you on her behalf. She's on her way back from a conference in Europe. You'll see each other twice a day for three weeks, while you're at our retreat." Will nodded.

"And you'll be part of my therapy group. I'm also a diversionary therapist, so depending on how things go, we might take part in some other activities together, too, while you're with The Peters Clinic."

Will sat forward. He'd pictured psychologists as middle-aged men with thick glasses and paunches. He ran his eyes over Dr Bakker. Better and better. Tall, on the lean side. Healthy; not much makeup. Outdoorsy, despite the professional outfit. What did his grandfather say? "A sight for sore eyes." *Ah, Jim.* He winced. He missed him. He smiled, then frowned, then studied her again. This therapist was wholesome. More than that, she was classy, though maybe a tad serious. Would she know how to have some fun? Wouldn't he love to show her …

15

Several more seconds went by. Jim. What would he think of this? Was he aware he was here, at a clinic? Did Will even care? He thought of the old man; his blue eyes, that twinkle. Jim had always had a smile for him, a connection. Not that Will had ever given him much in return. Jim had the knack of catching his eye as he was dashing out the door. How was Jim, he wondered? Maybe he should give him a call. He hadn't called him in months.

It had been Jim's idea he go away. He'd forgotten until now. It was after that last family business meeting in their staff room, back in Australia. Will had been late as usual. At least he'd managed to show up.

Jim had called the meeting off soon after he'd arrived, and saved him from another of James's rants and Nicole's disgust. She'd sneered at his crumpled shirt, about to roast him again for appearing like that in the shop, about to give him another serve regarding "branding" and "image" and "reputation,"., as if he hadn't heard it all before, as if Nicole herself were perfect. Her idea of style? Peculiar. He could swear his sister was colour blind, and there was always something weird about her makeup. Maybe he didn't try hard enough, but there was something to be said for not trying too hard.

And James, perfect James, clenching his fist when Will had had nothing to add to proceedings. Will hadn't exactly applied himself to the task, whatever it had been. He'd thought James was going to go off, chest heaving, staring at him as if he might finally have the answer to the mystery of life. But self-control wasn't one of James's problems. He had the full quotient, to Will's zero.

"What exactly do you think you do for Huntleys?" James had asked.

"Fucked if I know, bro," Will had managed. Why did James have to speak so loudly? Couldn't he tell Will had a hangover?

"You're not a teenager anymore, Will."

There'd been a big silence then, mercifully. Will had lunged for a coffee while the rest of them had just stared at him with eyes like fury, and at each other with pity, frowns and sighs.

The coffee had been cold. Disgusting. He'd spilled it a bit as he'd banged the mug on the table.

It was Jim who'd brought the meeting to a close. Usually James ran it all.

"We're done here, James, Nicole. You come with me, Will."

He'd thought twice about following Jim, but what could it hurt. Let Jim do his thing then skip out. The surf might be up. He'd go get a bacon-and-egg roll and see what the day might bring.

"You," Jim had said, and had pointed up the spiral staircase. "Give me ten minutes. Clean yourself up. You make sure you turn up. On time. I've something to show you."

Ah. A special session with Jim. In his lair.

Will had been up there over the years; not very often. James loved it up there. Not Will.

It was a tiny space, too hot in summer and an icebox in the winter. There was barely room for Jim and his ancient workbench and all those tools, let alone a visitor.

He'd checked himself in the mirror. He couldn't see what Nicole was complaining about. He didn't look too bad for someone who'd only gone to bed at dawn. He'd pushed his hair into place, smoothed his hands over his shirt, then nicked back and nabbed one of James's jackets from the staffroom cupboard and put it on over the top. It wasn't his style, but it covered up the wrinkles. Not bad now. Even Jim could call him "ship shape." He'd get this over with and go get breakfast. His stomach was rumbling.

The old man wasn't at the bench, however. He was pacing back and forth with his subtle limp. Unusual.

Jim glanced at his watch, looked Will up and down, and nodded. "Good," Jim told him. "You're not stupid. You put on a good show when you want."

Contempt? Whatever; Will just wanted this over so he could go get that roll.

Suddenly, Jim had grabbed his wrist with his gnarly old fingers, and turned over his hand. He thrust something hard into his palm. What was this? Show and tell?

Will didn't want a lecture. He wanted breakfast. The thing was small and hard and kind of ugly, but he couldn't study it. Jim pinned him with his eyes. The least he could do was return the old man's attention and listen.

"You think I don't know what it is to be lost?" Jim said. "I've watched you, Will, since before you were born. Watched you grow and charm everyone and run away and do exactly what you want and get away with it year after year after year because you are so loved nobody's ever said 'no' to you." Will wondered how long the old man would keep him there.

"And maybe it was cute once," Jim said. "Will, our scallywag. Will, the rebel without a cause. Will who lost his father … Well. James and Nicole lost their father, too. I lost my only child. We all got on with our lives. Sure, we grieved. We still do." Jim's shoulders slumped. He stared at the floor.

"I lost my Eleanor too soon after. Died of a broken heart. More grief." He looked up sharply, caught Will tapping his foot, and pinned him with his blue eyes till the tapping stopped.

"Do I sulk and bludge on everyone else? No. I contribute. I do what I can. But that's my choice. And listen to this, Will. I don't blame you. And I'm not even angry with you. Not disappointed. Not yet." That was new. Will pricked up his ears.

"I'm going to tell you something I've never told anyone else. Not because I trust you. I don't. Not anymore. Not because I hope it'll make a difference to you and your life, because it might, or it might not, and it's your life, not mine. God knows I've lived most of mine. Almost done. But I owe you this, before I die. Because what I see in you? That was me, Will. That was me in 1953 and for years after that."

A war story, at midday? In a stuffy little room in the top floor of the family business? How long was this going to go on? Will was hungry, dammit. What was Jim going on about?

"You listening, Will? You've never been able to stand still. Always on the run. I know it. Because that was me, until Korea. Lost my best friend. We were there together. Could have been me. All I got was shrapnel in this ankle. He got it in the head." Jim went silent. Swallowed.

"He was the better of us. Should have been me that got that bullet. You don't need to worry about any of that … What you need to know? I came back empty. Hollow. Hollow man. Nothing inside. Two arms, two legs, a buggered ankle. No more running, but I wasn't there anyway. Nowhere to run, but always running." Jim was on a roll.

"Aimless, Will. Smokes. The grog. Hunger didn't matter so much. I hurt all the time anyway. That ache. Aching was good. And then I met Eleanor, and she saw something in me. Maybe she put something in me. Put something back. Found something that had survived and made it grow. My Eleanor."

Jim groaned. "You listening? Young man in a hurry. To who knows where. To everywhere, or nowhere. Well, I need to tell you. I've been there."

Jim pointed at Will's fist. "Go on. Have a look, then you can get on your way."

Will opened his fist. An oily pink stone, smaller than a pea.

"Ever held one of those?"

Will shook his head and poked at it with one finger, rolling it over. When he pinched it and held it up to the light, it was a bit translucent.

"Pretty ordinary, isn't it?" said Will.

"That's a rough diamond," said Jim. "Argyle. Pink. Nothing much to look at now. You'd never guess the beauty inside of that, until you cut the thing, let the light into it. That's all I'm saying, young Will. Now you give that back to me and go." Jim waved him away, but he still hadn't finished.

"Go away. Get out of here and see what happens. God knows you don't want to be here. It's obvious. Go visit your mother. Go find some new suppliers. If you can clean yourself up, you can drop our name around the place. What is it Nicole calls it? 'Grow our branding.'"

Will nodded.

"Go on. Go see your mother in France. Go to the US. I met some great guys back then in Korea. Probably mostly dead now, but they had some stories, alright. Beautiful country, so I hear. So, you give me that thing back. And you get out of here, hollow man."

"Yes, sir." Will couldn't describe Jim's expression. Face like that, eight decades of flesh and joy and sorrow, and it was hard to tell whether he was laughing at him, or envious, or about to cry. Maybe all of that.

Will handed back the diamond. Jim stood in front of the stairs, so he couldn't go even if he'd been ready. Was he ready? Hell, yes. "Hollow man." What kind of insult was that? Or had Jim been telling him he was a rough diamond who needed some edges knocked off?

Jim looked him up and down. Was he remembering when he'd been off to Korea, off to explore the world?

Will held out his hand, and Jim shook it, his grip firm from decades of wrangling gold and fire and gemstones.

Jim broke into a grin and slapped him on the back.

…

So, what was it Jim had said to him the last time they were together? Up in his lair at the top of Huntleys, up where the magic happened. With the smell of the torch, behind his rounded jewelers' bench surrounded by the spikes of files and pliers, Jim had pushed up his magnifying spectacles, thick as bottle glass, and locked eyes with him.

"Going away, then?"

"Yeah, Jim. Find some more suppliers for you."

"Got plenty here."

"Better ones, maybe. New gems. Premade settings."

"*Premades*," he spat. "Over my dead body."

They'd just stared at each other, Will desperate to get to the airport, longing to explore, to escape; and Jim, hunched and shrinking from seven decades at his work bench. Jim stood, came around and put his gnarled old hands on his grandson's shoulders.

"You think I don't understand. I was like you. Only fifteen. So desperate to get away, I lied about my age. They took me. They took anyone at the end. Saw more than I bargained for, that was for sure."

"I'm not going to a war zone, Jim. I'll go see Mother, like you said, then head to the US. Pretty civilized."

Jim had nodded, but wouldn't let him go.

"Will," he'd said. "Little William. Your father, my Jimmy, and I; we had such high hopes for you."

"Sir?"

"Will I see you come good? Before I die?"

Hell of a way to say goodbye. How was he supposed to reply? A few cold beers at the airport and he'd forgotten all about it. Until now.

…

Minutes had gone by. Sweet Dr Bakker waited. Patient. Serious.

"Mr Huntley? Would you like to tell me why you're here?"

Will exhaled noisily through tight lips and stared at the corner of the room. No cobwebs. Clean, clean, clean. Unlike his soul. This was awkward. It reminded him of being at school, desperate to escape. He could still stand up and walk out.

He ran his fingers through his long fringe and tossed it back, pinning her with his gaze as he seriously considered "doing a runner."

He'd left school a decade ago. So what was he doing here? Good question.

He smiled. "Dr Bakker. I'd like to know why you're here." He gave her his smoldering look, the one that acknowledged the whole of her, mind and body, the look that suggested the two of them should be anywhere else but here, maybe at a bar.

"We both know I'm here to listen to you, if you're willing to talk to me."

"Am I willing to talk to you?" He said it slowly, emphasis on "talk," as if it meant something else.

"Talk. Share your thoughts. Explore things. Like what brought you here?"

Will remembered the phone call with his mother. She'd insisted he come to this retreat, pleaded with him, begged him in the name of his dead father.

"I made my mother a promise," Will said, wondering why a grown man, especially one like himself, would keep such a promise. "... in the name of my dead father."

Something flashed in smooth Dr Bakker's eyes. A flinch, quickly covered up, but Will noticed it. Pity for him? Or sympathy? Could she guess he usually broke his promises?

He studied the carpet. Spotless. Then tossed back his head to narrow his eyes and study her again. Yes, he'd prefer to have this conversation in a bar. With a whisky fling and the cover of darkness, with background music pumping, bridging the silences, and the inevitable gentle lean, closer and closer, till they found the comfort of each other's arms.

Come to think of it, maybe he'd been having this conversation for more than a decade already, with one beautiful woman after another. Not with this Lisa, though.

He sat straighter, noted the tissue box on the table between them, and Dr Bakker, pen poised at his folder on her lap, patient.

"Your father," she prompted. She waited, with those big, gentle eyes, warm and brown as maple syrup.

"So, why *are* you here, Dr Bakker?" His question was genuine.

21

"I'm here to listen," she said, leaning forwards. "I'm here to listen if you want to discover more about yourself, to understand more about behavior, to make some changes. Are you here to change, to grow? What might you want to be different about your life when you leave this place?"

Will shrugged.

"Are you willing to find out more about yourself? Are there things you'd like to change about your life, Mr Huntley? Are there things you're doing now you'd prefer not to do in future? Here, you have the time and space to consider how your life can be different. That's what this retreat offers – a chance to change."

"Well, that's the thing, Dr Bakker, isn't it?"

"What's that?"

"My mother might want my life to be different. But is it my life or is it my mother's? And you can call me Will, by the way."

"Thank you, Will. You're absolutely right. That's an important question. Only you can make these decisions."

What would she know? Sitting across from him, all clean and wholesome and believing in change for the better. He was willing to bet this Dr Bakker had never known anything but teacher pleasing and straight-A grades all her life.

Will gave her a slow smile. "How about you? Ever been bad?"

"What do you mean by 'bad'?"

"Like skipping school, like taking the first piece of cake, the biggest piece, like …"

"Most of us know what it's like to disappoint our parents," she said. "But I also understand that sometimes the people who love us most are the ones who notice things we can't, and they love us enough to tell us that. How would your mother live your life, do you think? What changes might she like to see?"

"Oh, she's told me. Says I'm wasting my life, drinking and gambling. Says I can't see further ahead than the next bar or casino. Thinks I waste my time, waste my advantages, waste my family's hard-earned money and my inheritance; says my father would be rolling in his grave to know I was stuck in Vegas, no thought beyond the next win."

"And what do you think?"

He looked at her, at the cactus, all spikes in the air-conditioned room. Looked out at a distant mountain ridge.

An image of Dr Bakker beside him in a bar hovered between them. He sat forward, elbows on his knees, fingers linked.

"Me? I want to get out of here. Don't you want to get out of here, Dr Bakker? I'd like to understand why you're here. Why you're actually here, now."

She met his gaze, matching his posture, leaning forwards, linking her fingers, folder sideways on her lap, pen clipped into the top of it. She was sincere alright. Convincing, even.

"I love my work, Will. I love it when my clients discover what might be driving their behavior, when they become more aware, and make better choices. I love to empower them."

Was there some passion there when she'd said "empower"? Her eyes had lit up. So, she believed in what she was doing. Now she gave him the polite smile again.

"And I'm here because I want to guide you, Will; to help you make the changes in your life you want to make. Do you agree with your mother? If you answer some of my questions, then maybe I can answer some of yours. Reasonable?"

He held her gaze. Stroked his thumb and forefinger down either side of his chin, felt his three-day stubble.

"You want to do a deal with me, Dr Bakker?"

"You could say it like that."

"Alright, shoot. Question number one."

"Do you agree with your mother that you're wasting your time?"

"Not right now I don't." He tilted his head and gave her a slow smile.

She rewarded him with a small smile of her own, then dropped her eyes to his folder and added a note or two. "And before you came here?"

"No. If I'd done anything differently, I wouldn't be right here, with you, Dr Bakker, would I?"

"You're skirting my question."

He stared at her skirt and nodded. She pressed her knees together.

"What I mean is, thinking about the past six months, or even the past six weeks, or even the past six days, are there some things you'd like less of in your life? Or are there some things you'd like more of in your life?"

Will considered. Six months ago, he was in Europe. After that Italian shemozzle, he'd dropped in on his mother in the south of France. But talk about the pot calling the kettle black. She hardly had her own life together, did she? Wandering around raving about French antiques and spending the family fortune on things she didn't need.

Then he'd had an affair or two on the Riviera. They'd been starlets, English, identical twins. They'd picked him up and shown him a good time. A bit of fun for all of them. He'd bought the drinks; no hearts broken, easy. Though the French beaches were overrated. No surf, and full of stones; hard on the feet.

But what a playground! The night life. Casino Royale. All the lights and colors and sounds and smells came back to him now, in the blank room of the clinic. That first big win! He shook his head and laughed. All those gambling chips, then all that money when he'd cashed them in. There'd been women hanging off him all night, not just the twins.

Next day, the three of them went shopping together and he bought them everything they wanted, almost, plus a few things for himself. Some white trousers and shoes, a flashy Italian belt and a couple of pale-blue shirts with sleeves tight enough to show off his muscles. The twins chose them for him. He remembered them beside him in the mirror, all three of them as attractive as movie stars. He'd had half a mind to show up at the next audition with them and try for a role, for a laugh. Maybe he should have.

But then James had called. Talk about a downer. His big brother wanted to know how he was spending the company money and when he'd be going on to the US, because there were some suppliers he needed to see.

"Scoping the competition," he'd told James, and it was true there'd been plenty of jewelers on the Cote d'Azur and plenty of rich people wearing lots of jewels. He'd had no shortage of excuses for hanging around, with or without the twins.

They'd been happy enough to accompany him to one casino after another, and when they were tired, they'd crash on the floor of one of their acting friend's tiny old rented apartments.

Will had slept half on the balcony in the heat of the summer nights, French doors open to the faint whisper of a sea breeze, cushioned on a rolled-up rug, getting high on admiring the moonlight over the Mediterranean. What a life.

But he'd been burning through his winnings. He always got another win, though, often enough, just as he was almost out of cash, and he'd be so pumped up then, the twins fussing all over him again. He'd loved it.

It had all come crashing down. Most things did. He'd had a bit too much to drink one night, and got a bit cross at losing at roulette, the fifth or sixth time. No one liked to lose. And no one liked a loser, and sure enough, those two little starlets were whispering and pointing, and they'd simply left him. Picked up their little purses and swung their hips in their short skirts, off to the other side of the floor, where they'd latched onto a trio of tall young Germans. Game over.

Will thought about going after them, but in truth they'd started to bore him, so he'd just walked out, walked straight to the airport in that gentle night air, with just enough money for the plane ticket to the US.

Next time James had phoned, he'd been in LA, still broke. James wouldn't give him any more money till his pay cheque was due, so he'd rung his mother. She'd come good the first time. And the second time. She'd transferred enough so he could get to Vegas and activate his private plan to win some more.

Except he hadn't won; not in a while, a long while. Long enough so he was sleeping rough, outside with the drug addicts and the prostitutes, in the heat and the dust. He hadn't exactly stooped to living in the sewers yet, nor to the drugs, but he'd been tempted.

The third time he'd rung, his mother had booked him into this retreat.

"You're a grown man, Will, and you should know better, and so should I," she'd said. "Too many loans, never repaid. When are you going to grow up, son? I'm your mother and I love you, but it's time for some tough love, isn't it?" There'd been a silence, which she'd filled.

"God knows I should have been tougher with you sooner, but you always had to do things your own way, didn't you? Isn't this a wake-up call for you? Don't you see what you're doing to yourself, what you're becoming? Is this the way you want to live your life?"

He'd kept listening, because he'd needed the money.

"You've had every advantage, Will, darling. We couldn't have loved you more. Now listen. Are you listening? I'm giving you more money, but not the actual cash. I'm booking you into a clinic. You'll get a roof over your head and food for three weeks, and you can sort yourself out."

"A clinic?" He was so broke and so hungry, it was her mention of food that really caught his attention. Food mattered once you hadn't had it for a few days. Will knew he'd try anything once, especially if it included free meals.

"They have some good therapists, Will, apparently. Excellent. The place should suit you. It's unconventional. It has a great reputation. But I refuse to bail you out again, do you understand? You've got to make these three weeks work for you. Make the most of it, Will, 'cause God knows I can't help you and you've never helped yourself."

She'd given him the address, and he'd hitched there with the help of a soda truck supplier, all the bottles clinking and chinking in the back of the van making him thirsty.

So here he was. His intro session with Dr Bakker, before Dr Peters arrived, the big guns. Though he couldn't imagine anyone he'd prefer to be treating him than this cool Dr Bakker, sitting there in silence, waiting for his answer.

He clapped his hands together and laughed.

"Come on! Let's lighten it up a little, shall we? We'll never get through this if you're going to be prim, and I get all gloomy. Nice place you've got here. Let's have some fun."

Lisa had looked down. Had he annoyed her? She'd taken a breath then met his eyes again.

"'Fun,' sure. You tell me what you enjoy, Will. What's your definition of 'fun,' then?"

"Okay. A big win. Ever had a great big win with everyone watching?"

"A big win."

"Yes! Who doesn't like a big win? All the lights and bells. Against the odds. And there you are. On top. A winner, alright."

"'A winner...'"

"Exactly. Everyone's watching and you know you can buy every single one of them a drink. You ever get that winning feeling, Dr Bakker?"

"I do," she said. "Sometimes, and it feels good."

This would be alright. He'd got her onto a bearable subject. Get her talking about herself a while and they'd be through the hour in no time, free of this nonsense. He'd go and explore the place, then bang. Another free meal.

"So, tell me about *your* wins, Dr Bakker." He gave her his own "I'm interested, I'm learning" smile, the one he'd used in school before skipping out.

Dr Bakker smiled back with those beautiful brown eyes. Caring eyes. Will had the impression she genuinely cared about him, and a little cog in his cynical heart ticked over. He was used to women caring about him when he was winning, caring about him any time, really. So what was different about Lisa's smile? What wasn't she telling him? What was her power?

She was a therapist, dammit. She was paid to care. And she was good. This clinic had a top reputation.

"What's a 'playboy,' Will?"

"Someone who likes to play?"

"What else might that mean?"

"Playing the field. But it's not just me leaving them. They leave me, too."

"Any idea why they leave you?"

"Because I like to play?"

Chapter 3

He gave her that smile, the smile that suggested everything, that he appreciated her, that he could …

Lisa inhaled and turned away. Suddenly, the room was too small. Will's personality was overpowering her. It was unusual. She was professional, dammit. Now, where was she?

"Would you like them to stay with you?"

"Not if they're no fun anymore."

"What makes them no fun?"

"They nag," Will said. "They want to control me. They don't like this and they don't like that. They want promises. They expect too much."

"What do they expect?"

"They want me to settle down. Why would I settle down? The world's a big place."

"It can also be a lonely place."

"Can it now, Dr Bakker?"

This wasn't about her. Why did he keep doing that? Trying to distract her, and avoid answering her questions. Why did she feel like he was suddenly the therapist and she the one with problems?

Was she lonely? That wasn't the point. She was in charge here. She'd been entrusted to help this man, goddammit, and he wasn't about to wriggle away from her. *Cheeky.*

She held her tongue, keeping her expression neutral. "I'm asking you, Will."

"Yeah, it can be lonely out there. The sidewalk's not great. I'm not proud of that."

"No."

"It's not lonely in here, though, with you listening and nodding." He flashed her a smile. Was this a flirt?

"Good," she said. "Tell me about your friends, your family."

"Oh. My family's pretty sick of me, I guess," Will said. He shrugged. "They can't get away, though, unlike girlfriends, eh?"

"Hey, now. Not everyone wants to get away from you. You're the one who's travelling. What brought you to this part of the world?"

"I'm supposed to be doing business, finding suppliers, selling my grandfather's rings," Will said. "He's a jeweler."

"'Supposed to be?'"

"I got a little sidetracked," Will said. "Stuck in Vegas."

"Sidetracked gambling?"

Will nodded, then ran his fingers up the side of his chin.

"Do you want to talk about that, Will?"

He was quiet once again, nodding slowly, looking her in the eye. A lot of clients pretended they hated gambling. They knew how to lie. Years of borrowing money from friends and family had taught them to say what others wanted to hear. Was Will one of them?

28

She'd treated plenty of big boys who never grew up. In their thirties, their indulgences gathered at their necks and girths, where, fleshy with too much good food and alcohol and bad choices, they started to sag.

She glanced at Will's file and back at him. Twenty-nine – he was young. Athletic. In his prime. Could she save him?

"Yeah," he said. "I guess. Sidetracked. I never planned to be a gambler. Never planned anything, though. Much."

"That's okay. Not everyone has to plan everything out. I see some people who worry they plan too much. There's a spectrum for every kind of behavior. We're all different, and our impulse control varies. But gambling's a big one, a major addiction, and notoriously difficult to beat. But it is possible. That's why Dr Peters set up this clinic."

"Do you gamble, Lisa?"

"Never."

"Why not?"

"So many reasons. A lot of people believe gambling's all about luck. Are you one of them?"

"Yeah. No."

"You understand odds?"

Will sighed. "I reckon however much I win, I lose more," he said.

Lisa nodded. "That's all you need to know," she said. "So, why do you keep doing it?"

"I already told you. I like to play."

"All the time?"

"Maybe," he said, considering her question. "I don't know."

"What else do you enjoy?"

"Eating. Winning, talking to beautiful women."

He did it again; undressed her with his eyes.

She rolled hers and looked away once more. She'd had her share of clients who flirted. Some of those movie stars, it was all they knew how to do. They had one trick and they used it well. But she knew her business, and she'd been successful in helping many of her clients to get back on track. They'd thanked her for helping them find their longer-term goals, rediscover the joy of motivation and achievement, and she would help Dr Peters do the same with Will Huntley.

"I like talking to you," he said.

"Thanks, Will, but it doesn't really feel like you are talking to me. Your answers to my questions are short, which makes it difficult for me to understand where you're at." She needed to move him along.

"Yeah, right. Thanks for the compliment."

"Did you know everyone likes to win, Will?" she asked. "Not just you and me. Do you know what happens in your brain when you win?"

"It feels good."

"Exactly. You get this rush of dopamine in your brain. It's the same part that lights up with certain drugs. That's why the drugs are so addictive, and it's one of the reasons gambling's so addictive."

"Dopamine, huh? You calling me 'dopey,' Dr Bakker?" He was interested. This was new. She'd caught his attention.

"No more than anyone else, Mr Huntley, Will. No more than I am. We're all prone to addiction. In the right circumstances, dopamine keeps us alive. Helps us learn the behavior that finds our food, keeps us safe, helps us find a mate. Of course these things are very complex, and we're only starting to understand them." He was listening carefully now, considering her words, so she kept up the stream.

"Apparently, oxytocin and serotonin are also important for helping us stay safe. They settle us down. There's research now that indicates we boost our levels of these hormones by showing compassion, even to ourselves."

...

She'd got him there. Slightly off track, the most interesting place to be. He narrowed his eyes and considered her – her legs now carefully crossed with those beautiful long shins, parallel, as if she'd learned etiquette. That was it. His mother, who'd never cared for any of his girlfriends, would approve of Dr Bakker's manners.

"But as humans, we've made our worlds so complex that dopamine is far too primitive to rely upon. We need our rational minds as well."

"Tell me."

"Humans aren't always so nice. You'd be aware of that, Mr Huntley. We lay traps for each other. I make no secret of the fact I loathe and despise the gambling industry, but never its victims. It's why I'm here."

"You're a crusader?" More and more interesting.

"You could say that. The people who make those gambling machines with the bells and lights you described? They're my colleagues, I'm ashamed to say. They use their research skills to find just the right lights and just the right bells, to make you play and play and play and play. Have you heard of Skinner?"

"Skinner boxes? Yeah. Something. I had a girlfriend once who studied psychology. 'Rats and stats,' she called it. I remember something now about a bird that starved to death. Cruel, I reckon."

"Yes," she said. "Skinner was American. A radical behaviorist, philosopher and educator."

Will stifled a yawn. A real win would be to get out of here. He pulled out his phone to check the time. Half an hour to go. Murder. A new message had popped up, a "free bet" opportunity. That was more like it. He rested it on his lean thigh, in view while he pretended to maintain eye contact with this therapist.

"Oh?" He feigned interest in Skinner. "An educator?" He knew how to repeat the last few words to keep a conversation going. Easy as pie. He didn't even have to think.

"I'm glad you've got your phone out. Is that a free bet? Skinner would call that a stimulus. You'd know that already, I imagine. So, Skinner would say that if you ever click on that, and if you get a reward from it, even once, you're more likely to click on it again. The only way you can beat that kind of stimulus is to totally ignore it."

"'Ignore it.'"

"Exactly. Which is a lot easier said than done. I'm willing to wager you can't resist clicking on that, Will. Either now or later."

He drew his eyes up from the screen to hers, saw her amusement and felt like a child caught stealing.

If he clicked on it, she would have won, and he would have lost. Clever.

"Don't put it away," she said. "You could use it to read up on Skinner. Try that now, if you like, if you've had enough chat. Or we can talk some more."

"Talk some more. Isn't that why we're paying you?" Ouch.

"You like to win," she said. She wouldn't take the bait. She had a job to do here; wanted to get through to him. "Tell me about your first win."

31

Will sat for a moment, remembering. Remembering. His father. Down there for him, on his haunches, arms out, with the biggest smile. Acres of green lawn. James and Nicole behind him on the swings, swinging, back and forth, back and forth, and his mother there on the picnic rug, with treats in a basket.

"Cynthia, look, look. He's walking. Will's walking! You can do it, Will," he could hear his father's voice, see him so clearly, waiting for him to toddle across.

On the soft sofa, with the harsh light of the desert sun softened by blinds, in this neutral space, with Dr Bakker, her legs crossed – quiet, waiting, listening – Will closed his eyes, inhaled and held his breath. He pressed his fingers to his eyes.

The tissue box. If she nudged it towards him he'd crush it, dammit. Throw it at the wall. Winners never cried. He looked at the clock. *Tick. Tick.* Good. It must only be another twenty minutes to go. Torture. Whose idea was this? What was this ache at the back of his throat?

His father, his father. Always there. Always there for him at the finishing line, at the awards ceremonies. So proud. So bloody proud of him. The Will and Jimmy show. He'd known his father had loved him best. And even towards the end, on those rare days when his father would get up out of bed, it was Will's room he'd visit. He'd admire that line of trophies and pat him on the back, and laugh. "Once you started running, Will, you never stopped."

So, well might Dr Bakker sit there, so wholesome and fresh and professional. And well might she have her theories about what Will should or shouldn't do. But was she there when his father was dying? Was she there when he was gone? When he no longer turned up to his matches and races? When winning became a bit ordinary, the point of it lost. And that pain. Deeper every time. However hard he ran, and however far, his father would never, ever again be there at the finish line. Never witness him score a winning goal. Never …

Will swallowed and tipped his head to the ceiling. He avoided her eyes. What would she know? What had this Dr Bakker ever lost, in her perfect white coat? Why would she care, but for the squillions it cost his mother to send him here? They could talk or not talk for the hour. She'd still get her money.

32

Free bet, his phone flashed at him from his knee. *Free bet. Free bet. Free bet.*

Free bet he wouldn't come back. Free bet he'd keep running. What would his mother care? He could still leave. It wasn't a jail. He'd broken no laws. He was managing okay, wasn't he? Evolution. Dopamine.

He'd get out of here. The door wasn't locked, was it?

But when he met those eyes again, he was shocked. She was with him, as if she'd been inside his brain. Those honey eyes, undemanding. Not dismissing him. Not laughing at him. Just there for him.

Of course. That's what they paid her for. That's why she was here.

"How can you stand this?" he asked.

"I can't always."

"That's honest."

"I'm human, too, you know." Was she human, sitting over there, legs uncrossed now, knees and ankles together?

"Do you like to win?" he asked.

"Don't we all?"

He shrugged. "So, what else do you like to do?"

"I like to run," Lisa said.

"Run away?"

"I have, actually done that." She nodded, holding his eyes. The grief in his chest eased a little. This Dr Bakker. She was something. Her fingertips joined as she waited for his response. Measured. Neat fingernails. No polish. No jewelry. Maybe the shadow of where a wedding ring might once have been.

Had he ever studied a woman so closely before? Not that part of their anatomy, anyway. This Dr Bakker in her white lab coat. Cool. Calm. Quiet. Classy. Maybe he'd come back for more.

...

Will couldn't believe he'd given Dr Bakker his phone. She'd held out that clean hand at the end of their session and offered to keep it for him, just till the afternoon, to help him keep their bet that he wouldn't succumb to temptation.

He missed it. Kept feeling for it, needing to check the screen. The colors. The lights. The possibilities.

33

Reaching for it again for the tenth time, he slapped his hand hard against his thigh. Was he really so pathetic? No. It was just a habit. A meaningless one. It wasn't something he'd ever chosen to do, to answer to a small rectangle of metal and glass and circuits.

What had Dr Bakker asked – what did he want more of? What did he want less of?

He went exploring.

There was an indoor pool with a few people doing laps and the smell of chlorine. There was also a heated spa, a sauna, and a well-equipped gym behind a glass wall. Attendants in black trousers and white shirts stacked towels or made marks on clipboards or iPads. He'd definitely try that out. All of it. Maybe now.

Then there was the dining area, with the largest salad bar he'd ever seen, and several yards of domed silver lids. Bacon, sausages, mushrooms, eggs. Baby hamburgers, chicken and rice, spring rolls. Everything. The spread made him hungry.

There was even a colorful dessert bar with more than a few fancy cakes. So, sweet things were okay, even if there was no alcohol. It was a resort, this place. Shame about the lack of a bar. His stomach rumbled. Sleeping rough had made him lean and hungry. He'd enjoy this part of the retreat, no question. Eat his fill, then work it off. That was a plan, something to tell Dr Bakker.

Surely there'd be a spare bread roll for him for now, or some nuts or a cheese plate. He could just cruise in for a closer inspection, maybe snatch a cracker or two, but he was stopped short on a small chain at thigh height. Oh. Not feeding time at the zoo just yet …

He wandered on, then pushed open a door to a stairwell, and in four multi-stepped climbs, he was up on the next floor, emerging into a reading gallery. A long picture window the full length of the room faced east.

Taking in the view, he was amazed at all that space. Low-rise Old Vegas buildings in the foreground with their art deco masonry and classic signs, but in the distance, sky and desert and mountains.

For an instant he was homesick for Sydney, with its green street trees and harbor and heavy humidity. Vegas was a long way from the coast. He was stranded. Dr Bakker was right. Had Vegas ever been part of a plan? Had there ever even been a plan?

The south of France hadn't been too bad, but how had he ended up here?

His thoughts were scattered, attention span shot. Mountains. Could he escape and go up there? Get some perspective? Dr Bakker had asked him what he'd like to do more of. Maybe go explore some mountains.

He scanned the room, with its tasteful clusters of armchairs, arranged so people could sit close to others without really engaging. Magazines on the side tables. Something on fly fishing, a boating one with the prow of something sleek and sexy, a luxury international real estate magazine, and a couple of glossies on cooking and handcrafts.

He wandered past a chess set, the armies peaceful, the battle yet to come. There were jigsaw puzzles on tables against the wall, and he placed a piece or two in one with boats in a harbor. The masts made it easy, but there was far too much blue sky.

Would being "healed" involve a partial return to childhood, to a time of fewer computers, with good, clean hobbies? He almost snickered.

Without his phone, he might have to return to this space and find a book. Would the librarian have censored everything? Maybe he could read about vice if he could no longer engage in it.

The constant air conditioning was making him thirsty, and he closed his eyes, imagining a decent head on a glass of beer, condensation beading the glass. Fat chance of that. If there was anyone around, he'd ask about contraband. Where was everyone? Meditating somewhere?

He remembered the minibar in his room and bound away up the corridor, buzzing the door with the card and flinging it open. In one movement he'd yanked open the fridge, but was disappointed. Sparkling mineral water, tomato juice and orange juice. Not even an energy drink.

He found a "natural" lemonade and downed it in three gulps, the cold citric acid burning his gullet. Not ideal, but a sensation at least. Maybe he'd go mad here. What would Dr Bakker think of that?

For the first time, he noticed a pencil and pad on the sideboard. He could make a paper plane, maybe write "rescue me" on it, but the windows didn't open.

Three weeks? How could he bear it? He'd have to hatch a plan. Maybe write some goals. That would be impressive. He lay back on the bed, pencil in one hand and pad in the other. Wrote "1." Underlined it. Wrote "eat."

Chimes and a well-modulated voice announced lunch. He was down there in a flash, first in line, first to open all those gleaming lids and pile his plate high. He'd put a check next to that first goal in no time flat.

…

"Finding your way around okay?" Dr Bakker asked. Will had surprised himself, turning up seriously early for the four o'clock group session. He'd hoped to see more of Lisa; had a hunch she'd already be there, and he'd been right.

"You should know. There's not actually that much to see." He winced at the tone of his own voice, petulant, sulky, childish.

"Sorry," he said. "Actually, the food's really good. I haven't had a feed like that in a while. I'm just … Actually, Dr Bakker, it's four o'clock. What I'd really like is a beer."

"That's perfectly normal, Will. Well, maybe not at four pm, but there are consolations."

"Oh?"

"This is only Day One, remember," she said, smiling. "You've got to expect some challenges."

"No pain, no gain?"

"In a way. And definitely no drinking, though I can assure you there are plenty of other things to do here, not all of them painful. Did you find the music bar?"

"No," he said. "But I found the library. Nice room. Great view of some mountains. What mountains are they?"

She sat up, more interested. "Beautiful, aren't they! It was probably Virgin Peak. They're even better up close. There are actually mountains all around Vegas. Vegas is in a valley."

He nodded. "Okay, Dr Bakker. You got me. What's a music bar?"

"It's a bit like an old-fashioned juke box, but you wear earphones, and the choices are phenomenal. I recommend it. You create your own playlist and then listen while you're working out, if you like, while you're on the exercise bike or the running machine. It's fantastic."

"You sound like you've tried it?"

"Yes. And some of our clients have discovered passions for whole new music genres, like opera or heavy metal. In their evaluations, a majority of our clients say the music bar helped them get out of old habits and find

36

new interests. When you're not gambling anymore, you'll find you have a lot more time for other passions."

"Passions," he repeated. He could still do it. Set something to smolder between them.

Dr Bakker smoothed her hair then tapped her pen on her folder. If it had been awkward for a moment, a tad more interesting, it was all back to business now.

"So, apart from looking around, have you had a think about my questions from this morning."

He smiled at her. She was trying so hard over there in her upright armchair. Apart from her rush of enthusiasm about the mountains and the music bar, how could she stand it? Wasn't she tired of people like him in here, day in and day out? The department of lost causes. He pitied her.

"Want to share your thoughts?"

"You said this morning you'd answer some questions if I did, Dr Bakker."

"Yes."

"You got some answers. You probably know a ton about me you wish you didn't, over there in that folder. So, can you at least tell me your first name?"

"This is a space for honesty, so I'll tell you. It's Lisa."

"Lisa." Now he gave her his attention alright. He uncrossed his arms, gave her half a smile and ran her name across his tongue again and smiled. "Lisa."

...

His Australian accent. Her eyelashes dipped as she studied her notes. Would they make any progress? Maybe this was a mistake. The man knew he was attractive. She'd done her homework on him. She'd thought she'd be fine. Forewarned was forearmed. She was experienced, dammit. He was a client, that was all. And the other clients would turn up shortly.

She sat up straight again, knees together, pulled the lapels of her white coat close around her chest and repositioned her folder across her lap. Gave him the professional smile.

"And there's the tea bar." Back to the facilities. A perfectly safe topic. Okay.

37

This time he laughed, and it was pure joy, the shadow of loss lifting, hovering, gone.

"You're kidding."

"No," she said.

"Well, I found the salad bar. Does that count for something? You going to note that?"

"I am, actually. Did you enjoy it?"

"Hell, yeah. Not much salad out there on the streets of Vegas. A baby spinach leaf lasts about six minutes before it shrinks to nothing. I timed it once. But the salad here is brilliant. I'm still digesting it. Not too sure about your tea bar, though. Where I come from, it's a device on the ski fields for getting you up the mountain. I worked them hard when I was a kid. You got 'em here?"

"Sure do," she said. "And pomas."

"Pomas …"

"How about you tell me about your first T-bar and then I'll tell you about mine." She could do this. Build rapport. They wouldn't get anywhere if they couldn't communicate. She wanted to make progress with Will Huntley. Get him better and get him out of here. Out of her life. Out of that couch where he sat like God's gift to lonely therapists.

"Deal. I must have been about four years old. One of those kids in an all-red suit on tiny skis. James and Nicole would have been five and seven. The instructor paired up Nicole and me because we were such similar heights. Told us to wait at the top for the rest of the class." Will settled into telling the story.

"We'd been doing it all morning. Up this little slope on the T-bar and back down again, snow ploughing. Up, down. Up down." His hands pointed up, then down, as if they were tiny skis.

"This time, Dad was at the bottom watching, waiting, that big, proud smile on his face. Was I going to wait at the top like I was told? Nup." He shook his head. "James was with me at the top, telling me, 'Wait, Will! Wait.' Why would I wait? I skied straight down that time, first time parallel, zooooom, straight down and in between Dad's skis. And he laughed! Picked me up right there and held me up, skis and all." Will's face was alight with joy.

"I can still feel him holding me up like his bright-red trophy, his skis below him, the white of the valley, the blue of the sky, still giving his great, big laugh. He was so proud of me. James was furious. He got down eventually with the rest of the pack, ploughing those S-bends." He nodded, remembering.

"I was having hot chocolate with Dad by then, with extra marshmallows. Sweet and steamy. Dad took me up with him next time, T-bar at the back of his knees."

She could imagine it all. Will, the speedster. Will, the rebel. Will, the favorite.

"You miss your father."

"'Course I miss my father." His tone was abrupt. He was still hurting, still angry. Betrayed, even.

"Do you want to tell me about that?" She used her gentlest voice.

"Oh, it must be almost a decade. But he started leaving us much earlier than that. You know, you're a kid, but you can sense something's wrong. Something changed in the house. Mum and dad talked about different things, went quiet when they noticed us nearby. 'Test results' and 'try this,' 'try that,' 'second opinion.' They held hands more often. Sad faces. Earnest conversations." Will stared at his feet.

"It wasn't overnight," he said. "It got worse over two or three years. Even the teachers looked at me differently, let me get away with more. Towards the end, I hardly bothered with school. If I got up and walked out, they just let me. I was still winning on the sports field, still getting all those medals for the school." He cleared his throat.

"Dad didn't turn up at the comps anymore, but the kids all cheered. Teachers cheered. Home got a bit grim. We boarded for a while, James and me, and Nicole. Dad would make an effort on Sundays. We'd have a meal together once a week, cringe at how much he'd shrunk. The house smelled like medicine." He gazed at the cactus on the coffee table.

"By then there were drips and oxygen machines. Mum was devoted, now I think about it. Didn't have a lot of time or thought for the rest of us, and we were getting older, becoming independent. James was at uni by the time Dad died, and I was old enough to leave school."

Silence. Acceptance.

39

"This is the first time I've talked about this. I still miss him. Never really said goodbye."

Will breathed, stared at the edges of the room and back at Lisa. She gave him a gentle nod.

...

Will rested his elbows on his knees and held his forehead in his hands. The ache in his chest kept building. The dam could burst in there and it would be okay.

He wasn't sure how long he sat that way when just as suddenly, the ache began to lift, to dissipate, like mist in the valleys of the snowfields. It left his body more relaxed and his mind clear. Good.

He sighed and sat back. Sweet Lisa across the room was still there, ready to listen.

"You know we sold the house? I guess I understand it. Too many hard memories for mum, and we were hardly ever there together anymore; all going our separate ways."

Lisa nodded.

"Mother built a new house in Moss Vale, in the country, south of Sydney, but in the end she moved to France. Created a whole new world for herself. I guess we were lucky. We joined the family business, James, Nicole and me, and worked with Jim, our grandfather, who set it up. Huntleys House of Diamonds."

"You enjoy your work?" Lisa asked.

Lisa listened so well, those big brown eyes, full of understanding.

"Yeah. No? That's why I'm over here with a gambling addiction getting counselled by you, Dr Lisa Bakker." Sarcasm, but with a smile. Honesty. Was this progress?

Lisa gave a big nod.

"So, what would you rather be doing, Will?"

"Well. This, right here, right now? This is okay. You're okay. You're good. I've never talked about that stuff, Dad dying, how it feels when your hero's not there for you anymore."

He sat straighter and looked Lisa in the eye. "Those British twins, and all the others, they didn't care. It was all about what we were doing, you know? Where was the next party? Who was buying the drinks. That kind of thing."

"Sounds familiar," Lisa said. "Living in the moment. That's not all bad. Have you heard of Existentialism?"

"Exist … what? I'd look that up, but you've got my phone."

"Want it back?"

"I get it back?"

"Only if you really want it," she said. "It's up to you what you do with all of this. You can lie to me about your phone and what you do with it. But you can't really lie to yourself. Well, you can. Plenty of people do. All their lives, in fact. But it's you who ends up stuck with the consequences."

"Consequences." Like shrivelling up on the pavements of Vegas like a piece of lettuce. Not ideal.

"Are you ready to get your phone back, do you think?"

"Ready for 'free bet,' 'free bet?'"

"Exactly," she said. "You know yourself better than I do."

"Yeah. But what's exist …?"

"Existentialism." Lisa stood, opened a drawer in the sideboard, and handed Will's phone to him.

He punched in the letters and read it out. "'A philosophical theory or approach which emphasizes the existence of the individual person as a free and responsible agent determining their own development through acts of the will.' So, you're saying I can choose to choose."

"You could say that."

"Free bet" coaxed him across the screen. Incredible. He'd had the thing back for less than a minute. He tossed it back to her. Dr Lisa Bakker was far more interesting. She was even a good catch.

Just then the others trailed in.

Chapter 4

Rossco whined at the door by the time Lisa arrived home. She turned the key in the lock and dropped to her knees to hug him, dear old thing.

His shaggy coat was rougher than ever. She really must wash him, like Jilly said. And brush him more often.

He licked the back of her hand slowly as she rose, and he followed her to the kitchen, where she opened a can of Wuffles, his favorite. It was probably full of salt and sugar, but the vet had told her his time was limited. At this stage, she gave him what he wanted.

His tail wagged as he slurped the soft food slowly. Hardly any teeth were left.

"Good day, Rossco? Did you sleep all day?" He turned his head towards her voice, then swung it back to the food and finished most of the plate.

She changed into her runners and shorts and singlet top, and grabbed a light puffer jacket. It was almost dark.

"You coming, old fella? Will we go for our walk?"

The tail wagged some more and she clipped on the leash, rubbing the back of his ears as he opened his mouth and panted with joy.

"Beautiful boy." How she loved him. He was the very best part of her failed marriage, the only thing left.

It was a slow walk. She let him stop and sniff and pee as long and as often as he liked, his determination as pure as his pleasure, sniffing out the poochy news. She studied the gardens as she walked, then up at the mountains, silhouetted against the darkening sky. It was time she went again, up into the peaks. It had been too long, and she'd had too many shifts in a row. All work and not much play.

She listed her clients, then Dr Peters' new clients, and tried to push them out of her mind. She needed a break, knew it wasn't healthy to think of work all the time.

One of her neighbors approached, clutching a fresh carton of milk. It was Mrs Benedict, recently retired. They were civil, but not best friends. Mrs Benedict disapproved of her black exercise wear, considered it a bit tight – "revealing, dear" – but refrained from mentioning it this evening. It was a bad sign. There must be something more important to complain about.

"Lovely evening, Mrs Benedict."

"Certainly is. Well, I've had the grandchildren all day, and they drank all the milk! They grow so fast!"

"I'm sure they do," said Lisa, smiling, waiting for the point of the conversation.

"That dog of yours."

"Rossco."

"Yes," her neighbor said. "He howled all day."

"Perhaps he wanted to be with the children, Mrs Benedict."

"Mmm."

"Would they like to play with him next time they visit, do you think? He's very loving and he's good with children. You're welcome to come into my yard next time they're over, whether or not I'm home. Rossco would love that. He'd love the company. I'm sorry he barked so much today."

"Yes. Well." Mrs Benedict wasn't convinced.

Rossco lifted his head and walked on.

"Have a good evening!"

It was beautiful as the sun went down, golden in the west. As she enjoyed Rossco's own satisfaction with the smells of the pavement and the edge of the road and the stumpy, hardy Nevada grass, memories of Will, Dr Peters' client, made her chuckle. What a rogue! As their session ended, he'd tried to persuade her to take them both to a bar. As if!

"Not happening," she'd said. "Surely that doesn't surprise you, Will. You know that can't happen. Technically you're not my client, but you're at my clinic."

43

"What if I promise to just drink juice. Would you come with me then? Hand-on-my-heart pledge. No booze. Yes?"

"No," she'd said. "We must uphold professional boundaries."

"Man! You ask me for my goals and I just start to share them with you and you close me down straight away. Break my heart, Dr Lisa Bakker!"

She'd flashed him her "don't you dare go there" warning. She'd needed to distance herself from him, and vice versa, fast. Clinicians were there to serve their clients, not make friends. There were no prizes for blurring that line.

"Sorry, Lisa," he'd said. "Sorry, Dr Bakker. I didn't mean to offend you. Backing right off now. See that? I'm out of here. No more invitations to bars. I was just joking, you know. Keeping it light since we have to get together again tomorrow for your group session." He gave an exaggerated sigh.

"Guess I'll have to go think up some more goals," he'd said. "Some 'acceptable' goals. But I won't let you down. It's been good today. You've been good. You've made me choose to come back and see you in the morning. No bar. Maybe the music bar. Maybe the tea bar. But no actual 'bar' bar. I've got it."

He was cheeky. Like a kid. Like he got stuck in his teens when his father got sick and died, and never finished growing up. A charming troublemaker. She laughed and shook her head. Her job fascinated her. She adored it.

Rossco was done. They padded slowly home, and she opened the gate and led him in. He was lapping carefully at his water bowl as she headed out again, this time on her own, running down five blocks to the park where the baseball players were training. She ran in laps around them ten times or more, until she was tired and the cool night air chased her home.

Rossco lifted his head off his padded mat in the kitchen as she entered, grinned at her and placed it back on his paws. He thumped his tail on the floor once or twice. He watched her cook some dinner. Steamed vegetables with a pasta reheat. He was snoring by the time she sat down to eat, and she smiled at him sadly.

"Yep. Best thing, old Rossco."

He twitched in his sleep.

She turned her phone on to "do not disturb," ran a bath and picked up a book. She read it till the water turned cold.

When she slept she dreamed of skiing.

…

"You never did tell me your T-bar story, Lisa," Will said as he turned up extra early again for the group session and flopped himself down on one of the white chairs opposite her.

Bad-boy Huntley was shaven this morning. Clean. Attentive. Privately, she'd given him less than a fifty-fifty chance of showing up for the group session, let alone promptly. She'd tried to treat his type before, people who thought they knew better, those who'd never toed the line, so used to doing their own thing they defied treatment.

She was quietly pleased to see him there, legs out, arms folded, eyes on her nametag.

Despite his compliance, he reminded her of a lanky colt, trapped. Edgy. If she didn't do this right, he could still flee at any moment. She mirrored his posture, made her voice casual, and took them both out of that neutral room.

"Okay," she said. "Since you turned up, I'll tell you. I grew up on flat land, lake country, midwest. Plenty of snow for snowballs, but the only way to ski was cross country. Long, flat miles. For anything like a hill, we had to drive an hour and half." Her hands mimed the geography. "My parents never bothered, so we took ourselves, my friends and I," Lisa said. "We must have been about fifteen. Just got our licences. We thought we were so cool. All of us bound for the winter Olympics or something."

She snuck a glance at him. When he gave her a half-smile, she continued.

"The first time I used the T-bar I had no idea. I tried to sit on the thing."

"Tsss." Did Will know what was coming?

"It swivelled sideways and caught a belt loop in my brand-new jeans. I was halfway up that hill when the thing ripped and I slid back down, backwards, skis getting further and further apart, till my nose was flat down against that cold snow."

Will laughed.

"Not cool," she said. "Not cool at all. I couldn't even get up. And of course the kids below in the line came straight up at me and everyone

45

yelled. Quite a tangle, I can tell you. Oh, the humiliation! Have you ever done that?"

Will seemed entranced. "Can't say I have." His face was dead pan.

"Really?"

He broke into a huge grin. "'Course I've seen that on the beginner hot slopes. Everyone's done it! Don't worry. You're not the only one, Lisa. I was just teasing. It's an Aussie thing. You Americans never understand our sense of humor."

"Well, I'm glad you're happy," Lisa said. "So how're you doing today, Will? How was your evening?"

"Two goals. Eat. Swim. Check. Check. I hit the salad bar again, and the hot food. Pretty good. Very good. Great establishment. Shame about the lack of alcohol. But I didn't let it get to me. I wanted to please you, Lisa."

Now he stared at her. Directly. Like she was his next goal, target, next game, next win.

She sat up, crossed her legs, cleared her throat, and checked her notes. She'd had clients try to flirt with her before. She'd be fine. She never went there. She was experienced, professional.

"So, Lisa ..."

She gave a prim smile and nodded for him to continue.

"I swam instead. Swam till I could swim no more. I lost count of the laps. At least an hour, maybe two. Got out staggering. I'm still a bit spent, but I slept like a baby. I hit the breakfast bar hard again, and here I am, existentially, all yours."

He appeared pleased with himself. Excellent. She loved it when clients came to her in good time, before their addictions were too entrenched. Will was making progress, in her estimation. She flicked the pen out of her top pocket, opened her folder and made some quick notes.

"What're you writing? Am I ten out of ten?"

"You can make your own notes, Will Huntley. What would you give yourself?"

"Definitely ten out of ten. I don't get much better than this. I've complied for a full twenty-four hours, which is unheard of."

"Against whose criteria?"

"Yours."

"But what about against your own?" she said. "What do you hope to achieve here? Ultimately, it's not about what your mother wants for you, or what I want for you. It's about what you want for yourself. Have you thought about that yet, Will?"

"Lunch."

"And?"

"I'm not allowed to take you to a bar ..."

She narrowed her eyes.

"I remember," he said. "I haven't forgotten. But what about ... the mountains? I've been in Vegas for weeks. Can't understand the attraction, to tell you the truth. I've thought about that. I've no idea why I'm stuck in Vegas. Can you believe that?"

She nodded. This was good. She trusted him, shared his reflections.

"There might have been a plan. I told you about all my wins in the south of France. I had this idea I was a winner. I'm meant to support our family jewelry business here in the US, meet suppliers, find outlets for Jim's rings."

Lisa raised her eyebrows in a question.

"Jim, my grandfather," Will said. "Founder of the business. He makes the rings. He's a great guy. I miss him. Miss Sydney. I feel like I've been travelling for years, Lisa. Maybe I have. I've been restless all my life. I ran away from school and I've never stopped running."

"And you want to stop running? You think you might want to 'settle down'?"

There was a long pause as he considered the carpet, considered Lisa's ankles.

"Maybe," he said. "Dunno. 'Settle down'... I've never really thought about it. I could settle down ... with the right person."

Chapter 5

Settle down with Lisa? Now *that* was an idea. Will smiled. There she was, all cool and collected over there in her white coat, relaxed today, with her big, brown, understanding eyes and the occasional nod, giving him all that attention. He flashed her a smile. A genuine one, free of artifice.

Lisa hastily made more notes. Did he unsettle her?

"The right person," she repeated.

"Hey, that's my trick."

"What's that?"

"Repeating the last few words," he said.

"You do that? Therapists do that, too. It's called *active listening*."

"That's ridiculous. You're kidding. Active listening?"

"Yes."

"I only do it when I'm not actually listening. What do you think of that!"

"Ridiculous."

They both laughed. He loved to make her laugh. She didn't do it often enough. Dr Serious.

"So what's your plan for today, Will?"

"I still want to get out of here," he said. "Don't you? The air conditioning's driving me crazy. How about you take me to the mountains?"

"Not today."

"Maybe another day?"

"Maybe another day."

"Maybe another day – you repeated it! You're caught now, Dr Lisa Bakker. That's almost a promise."

"Almost a promise," she said.

"A promise!"

"Do you keep promises, Will?"

He was quiet.

"No," he said. "Actually, not generally. Why do you ask?"

"Because you're so charming. I think you're used to getting your way, Will Huntley. I think things come easy for you, and when they get hard, you take the easy way out. I don't blame you. Am I right?"

"Harsh," he said. "But correct. You're sharp, Dr Bakker. I could lie to you, but …"

"You'd be lying to yourself. We've been through that."

"We have. I got it. I'm not stupid. Sure, I take the easy way. My brother, James? He does it the hard way. He's honest, trustworthy. He's a slave. He took on the whole business when our father died. Imagine that. He'd been having a ball at uni." Will shook his head. "Having the time of his life. And he swapped it all for duty. Had to learn to read the books, pay the wages, order in stock, work out the taxes. He never stopped. He still works all the time. Sucker."

"You despise your brother?"

"You could say that. He makes me feel so guilty every time he phones. He does so much for all of us. James keeps the business alive."

"You're not grateful?"

"I think he's a fool," Will said. "I keep letting him down."

"Why do you think he keeps bailing you out, Will?"

"Dunno. He told me he promised Dad. He was always the good one, James. I was the larrikin. My father loved me for it. He encouraged me."

"What's a larrikin?"

"ADHD. Not that I was ever diagnosed. I was a wild child."

"You could grow up, though," she said. "You could choose to grow up."

"Doesn't sound like much fun."

"Being down and out in Vegas doesn't sound like much fun, either," she said. She held his gaze.

"Right again, Dr Bakker. You've got a point."

"So how about you think about that? How might a grown-up Will Huntley behave?"

"Behave?"

"What would you choose for yourself? You do set goals, Will, but they're all short-term ones. Children do that. They want instant gratification. They snatch the toy that fascinates them, then toss it away and are on to the next big thing. Ever spent time with a toddler?"

"No. Are you saying I'm childish?"

"No," she said. "I'm saying your behavior shares characteristics with that of children. It's all short-term thinking. I'm interested in what you'd do if you set longer-term goals, and what those goals might be. We know you're competitive, Will. You like to win."

He nodded slowly.

"What goals do you feel might really be worth winning? You've got time to find out while you're here at the clinic. You say you don't like Vegas. So, where would you prefer to be? Where else would you want to be?" She held out her hands, as if to hold infinite possibilities.

"Where might you want to live if and when you were to 'settle down,' Will? And you say James makes you feel guilty. You say you don't like James telling you how much money you should get from the business and why or why not. Do you have to stay with the business? How would you like to make your own living?"

Will was silent, as if the thought had never occurred to him before.

"What might that look like?" she said. "How would you support yourself? These are questions all adults can ask themselves at some point. And they might not get all their goals. For example, I wanted to be a ballerina. I did alright until I kept growing. At five feet ten inches, I had to accept it wasn't possible. And I've already told you about my ambitions for the winter Olympics. That didn't end too well, either."

"But you picked yourself up and dusted off the snow."

"I did. And my new jeans were a write-off. Tragic. But I've faced a few more setbacks than that, and made a few mistakes before I got here, Will Huntley. That face-plant in the snow? I was a teenager. I was so ashamed. Thought the whole world was laughing at me. You know what it's like at that age."

"Laughing with you, I'm sure," he said.

"No, *at* me!"

"Hang on. Who's the therapist here? I'm the one with the problems."

"Oh, of course. I'm sorry, Will!"

"Are you going to tell me how to solve them, Lisa Bakker?"

"Maybe. How about you think about some long-term goals, and I'll share some more about myself."

"Okay," he said. "Bargain. Would you come to the tea bar with me, Lisa?"

"I don't get a break today, I'm sorry. Dr Peters is still on her way back."

"So you get her clients as well as your own?"

"You don't need to think about any of that."

"Sounds a bit rough," he said. "What if we meet at the tea bar at four pm instead of here? We can keep talking. That's all we're doing, isn't it? You can bring your folder and pen, your clipboard. How 'bout it?"

He gave her his winning grin. He almost had her. Like a fish on a line.

"Maybe next week," she said. "We do have a lot of freedom at our clinic. But it's very early days for you, Will. We've only just started to understand what you need, to maximise what we can offer you, for the greatest benefit."

"Oh, come on, Dr Bakker! The therapy here is supposed to be 'unconventional.' I've had a bit of a flip through the brochures in the room. What's the point of having the freedom to be 'unconventional' if you never exercise it? It's all very well you telling me to have goals and so on. What about you? What are your goals, apart from listening to people like me for eight hours a day?"

"Our group session is about to begin, Will."

"It is. More clients. Back to back. All day. It must drive you crazy."

"It's nice of you to care, thank you, Will."

Lisa stood as two more people entered, and then a third. She moved to the door, checked the corridor and her watch, and closed it.

A skinny woman in her late teens, all in black, sat in one chair, pushing it sideways to avoid eye contact with Will.

"Morning, Sam," said Lisa, beaming. "Glad you could make it. Beth. Chase. Welcome. Thank you all for being so prompt. We never like to waste each other's time."

The door opened wide and a man Will's age burst in, staggering a bit. Will recognized that kind of walk.

"Yo!" He was laughing, as if group sessions were hysterical. The biggest joke. So, this place was dry and drug free? Probably not.

Lisa narrowed her eyes at the newcomer. "Connor?"

"Yo!" He laughed again.

"You're in high spirits, Connor. You have thirty seconds to settle or you're out."

Connor waved at the teenager and pulled a sad clown face at her, mirroring her expression, then laughed again.

"Excuse me, everyone." Lisa stood. "I'll be three minutes. Thank you, Connor. Come with me."

"She won't take any nonsense," said the older woman, nodding, her soft hands clasped in front of her. "She gave Connor a chance last time. Looks like he blew it."

Lisa swept back in, cool and in control. "Right. Thank you for waiting. Will, Sam, Beth, Chase, I'll take this moment to remind you all that everything we say within these four walls remains completely confidential. This is a safe space. We listen. We respect each other. We grow in understanding; about ourselves and about others."

Everyone nodded.

"This morning we'll talk about relationships," she said. "This is because there are a number of theories that say our behavior, including addictive behavior, is influenced by our relationships."

Will guffawed.

Lisa stared at him. She wasn't amused. "Would you like to share your thoughts with us, Will?"

"What? Am I in trouble, too?" he asked. The others laughed. Lisa shot him a warning glare. Okay. He didn't want to upset her. Class clown came so naturally.

"I'm sorry, Dr Bakker. I was just thinking I'd come to the right place to talk about relationships. I've had a few. They call me 'Huntley heartbreaker' in the tabloids."

Lisa nodded slowly, as if trying to understand what that might be like. To be labelled a heartbreaker publicly. Until he'd said it out loud, he'd never really thought much about it himself. Never questioned it. Never

52

wondered what effect it might have on him. He sat quietly, reflecting. It was clear he could stay if he settled down. He wanted to stay. This could be interesting.

"There are many relationships in our lives," she said. "Some theorists say that patterns are established very early within our families. Would anyone else like to share something about relationships?"

Lisa scanned the circle. She encouraged participation, and Will got to know the others better.

The young woman was Sam the Goth, too skinny in black, shoulders slumped. She sat to one side and pushed her chair back to avoid eye contact. She chewed her black-painted nails and studied them, displeased at what she saw.

Beth, plump and smiling, was a widow in her sixties, anxious to please. Beth's gambling problem sounded worse than his own. She'd been on the verge of losing her home when her children had stepped in and insisted she attend the clinic. They'd witnessed her gambling grow and become more than a hobby. She'd done it all her life, but when her husband had died, to hide from her loneliness, she'd turned to it non-stop. It rapidly became all she ever did.

Chase, "not my real name," was at the clinic on the recommendation of his agent, who would drop him otherwise. Chase's life mirrored that of the character he played in a long-running soapie. He'd been written out of the last series due to a problem with alcohol, but his fans were clamoring for him to return, healed and "hot" once more. He and Will had paced it out together on the treadmills, competing for distance and times. Chase was beating him on the weight loss, but Will was younger and had been in better shape in the first place. He didn't have a lot of spare fat after living on the streets. Meeting Chase in their first session had given him a wake-up call. He didn't want to be lost and looking like Chase in a decade.

The hour flew by. Lisa gave them time to think, and time to share their thoughts, to name the people who'd had most of an influence on their early lives, and to describe the quality of those relationships, the high points and low ones. Will nodded as Chase, an actor, spoke of the auditions his mother had taken him to as a child, of the pressure to perform, and how his mother's expectations might have encouraged his challenges with substance abuse. Sam barely said a word, but she listened carefully. Beth was more open.

"My gambling addiction is directly related to the death of my husband," Beth said. "No mystery there."

It made Will wonder about the loss of his father, and about the ongoing bad-boy role he played in his family. Was he tired of it? Lisa said he could choose a different path. A conversation he'd had with Jim, his grandfather, just before he'd left Australia leapt into his mind.

But time was up.

"Thank you, Will, Beth, Chase. Sam. You might like to think some more about your relationships before our next session."

Lisa stood and moved to the door, and Will followed everyone out. He wasn't sure he wanted to think so much, beyond the fact that Lisa smelled fantastic. Fresh. Wholesome. Now there was a relationship which would interest him. How long until their next group session? Twenty-two hours?

Just as well it was nearly lunchtime and the salad bar was a perfect distraction.

…

The memory of his final conversation with Jim wouldn't go, not even with the all-you-can-eat pasta bar and another two helpings of salad. All the swimming made him hungry, but eventually lunch had to end.

Without his phone, Will was at a loss. He swam again, ate again, tried out the gym. On the running machine, he sifted through everything Lisa had said. He'd never talked so much in his life; not about himself, and had never thought so much. Maybe coming here was a good idea for lots of reasons; not just for the food. Though if he kept exercising like this, he'd be hungry again soon.

What had Lisa asked him? Was he sidetracked by gambling? Yes. Big time. Even he could tell it wasn't where he wanted to be. Broke and on the sidewalk. He hated asking the family for money. Being in their debt. Being here wasn't just about the food. He could admit it. He could do with the help. He might not know what he wanted to do with his life, and he might not have a plan, but at least he knew that gambling wasn't enough. He stepped off the treadmill and wandered around the gym.

Goals? Existentialism? Philosophical concepts. Instead, all that came to him was Jim's face.

He straddled an exercise bike, adjusted the torque and started pedalling. What had Jim called him, in his gravelly voice? "Hollow man."

What had he meant? Was it about grief? That shock and ache of loss? Will knew it too well. So, Jim had copped it, too. And got over it.

And his grandmother. Eleanor. She and Jim had been inseparable. Will would never forget her, all soft and powdery, and so generous with her smiles and pocket money. She'd had a tin of lollies she would share with him. Barley sugars. He'd hang around till the tin appeared, grab one, then shoot off, barely managing a thankyou.

Will swung off the exercise bike, muscles aching. He swigged some water and headed for the shower, but as the water rushed over him, he kept visualizing Jim's face. And his grandmother's.

Jim must have missed her when she'd died. Not that Will had noticed at the time. A pang of shame shot through him. The realization that he'd been so blind to the pain in his own family. He'd been preoccupied with his own. Lisa was right. He'd behaved like a child for too long.

What had Jim said? About losing his friend in the war, and wandering around lost. That Eleanor had seen something in him?

Here in the clinic, surrounded by blank walls, there was too much time to think. He couldn't block out the questions that kept forming like clouds in his empty mind.

What had Jim been like back then? How had he and Eleanor met? And what had he meant about Eleanor?

He wasn't used to thinking. Wasn't sure he liked it.

He wandered back up to the library. Maybe he could find someone to give him a game of chess, or have a go at one of the jigsaw puzzles.

There was no one there. The wide window called out to him, drew him across to peer into the car parks of neighboring buildings and a beige sky, mountains obscured behind dust or pollution.

There, on the window sill, someone had left a slim book. The man on the cover looked a bit like Jim, and Will picked it up and riffled through it, for want of anything better to do. It was poetry. A few words caught his eye. *The Hollow Men.*

Wasn't that what Jim had called him?

Will laughed out loud at the coincidence. The air conditioner hummed back. He read the poem. This would be something to tell Jim about.

He read it again. There was nothing else to do.

The words tumbled through his mind, haunting.

Is this what Jim had meant? Did he think Will's life was so meaningless? Was he so lost? So blind? So wasted?

He stared at the man on the cover again. Hair slicked back and parted. Wrinkled brow, staring off to one side. No, he decided. He was nothing like Jim. He hadn't Jim's sense of humor.

…

The sudden need to talk to Jim again was urgent, and Will bolted back to his room, still holding the slim book. What time was it in Australia? Morning? Something like that. If Lisa hadn't taken his phone, he'd be able to find out.

He grabbed the phone by his bed and called Huntleys.

"Huntleys House of Diamonds, Jim here."

"Grandfather."

"Will?"

"What time is it?"

"About eight o'clock," Jim said. "Where are you?"

"Nevada."

"Everything okay?"

"Fine, sir," Will said. "I needed to ask you …"

"Money? You want money again?"

"No, sir."

"Good."

"That last time we spoke. You called me a 'hollow man.'"

"I did. But only because it takes one to know one. What is it?"

"I found a poem, *The Hollow Men*, by T S Eliot."

"Ah! Good. Yes."

"I never asked how you and Grandmother met. Can you tell me? Have you got time?"

"I've got time for you, Will, if you've got time for me."

"Now?"

"Your grandmother," Jim began. "Most civilized woman I ever met. And I was the opposite. I fell into her. Literally. Fell off the tram outside Huntleys. Plenty of hollow men about back then, from World War Two, not just Korea. Being hollow involved a lot of drinking and not much

56

talking. Plenty of pubs in Bondi Junction." Will waited for the gravelly voice to continue.

"This woman was about to get on the tram and I'd been a bit slow getting off, with my ankle still a mess, and I was none too steady after all the grog. I bumped her pretty hard, knocked off her hat. She was all dressed up. Beautiful woman, your grandmother. She was a vision. Knew how to dress. How to talk. How to behave. I was mortified. You still there?"

"Yeah, Jim. Go on."

"I retrieved her hat, a bit dented, a finely woven thing in beige and white. Expensive. Quality. And now it was grubby down one side. I apologized. The tram bell was ringing. But she wasn't angry, just gave me a sad smile. It wasn't pity. It was dignified. That lady; she gave me dignity."

"Dignity."

"Yes, Will. Don't knock it. It was the first time I'd felt human in years. She was humane. She thanked me and gave me that beautiful smile and the tram left and I stood there and stared after her. I was ashamed, Will. That I could have behaved like that, slamming into her, out of control."

"Yeah?"

"Well, I imagined how she saw me, this wreck of a man, feeling sorry for myself, shuffling about," Jim said. "It made me feel sick and I told myself right then I wouldn't do that anymore. It had been too long. Years."

"So …"

"So I cleaned myself up. Got a job. Storeman. Trolley boy. I was still young and strong. It was hard work on my ankle, but that spurred me on. But I had to do something with my hands and my brain if I wanted to get off my leg. So I started going to night school. Workers' Educational Association, WEA. Met some good people there; got a few breaks. It's still a going concern, if you're ever interested. Good organization. Well, I studied a few things, like economics and English literature. I had to write an essay on *The Hollow Men*. Saw myself in that poem, alright. Another wake-up call."

"Yeah."

In the moment of silence, the distance between them stretched out to half a world, half a lifetime. Yet Will had never felt closer to the old man. Joy surged in him as the voice continued.

"So then?"

"That crumpled hat and that beautiful sad smile," Jim said. "They haunted me. I wanted to make it up to her. I'd cut down on the drinking. Didn't have time for it anymore with night school. And I saved some money. No more living hand to mouth."

"Go on," Will said.

"So I caught the tram back to Bondi. Must have been a year or so later. I had this idea that I could buy the lady a new hat. Montgomery's was the place in Bondi Junction back then, a department store that even the Queen had visited in 1954. She'd been at the beach, anyway. In my mind, I'd fused the two of them. Our young queen and the woman whose hat I'd ruined."

"So what happened?"

"As I said, it was a year or two later, and I didn't really have much of a plan. I suppose I hoped history would repeat and I'd find her right there again when I got off the tram, but of course, once I got there, I looked around, but there was no sign of her. But I noticed Montgomery's and decided at least I should buy the hat, so if I ever found her again I'd have it ready." Will tried to imagine Jim fifty years younger, walking into the shop. It rang a bell somewhere in his memory. About how meeting his grandmother had changed his grandfather's life.

"I'd cleaned myself up, as I said. I was wearing a suit this time. Had a few certificates from night school and a bit more self-control. I'd got interested in making jewelry and had bought a few tools. You still there? Haven't you heard all this? I thought all of you knew this story backwards."

"You probably told James and Nicole, and I probably ran away and didn't listen."

Jim laughed at that. "You never could sit still," he said. "How are you managing now?"

"Spent," Will said. "Sitting down for once. Swam a few miles in the clinic pool and tried out the gym for a few hours. Nothing much else to do, here, except read poetry. You know where I am? Vegas. Mother got me into this clinic. I only agreed because of the food. But it's okay. Getting on top of … the gambling."

"No. No idea where you've been and why. Good. That's good, Will. A great sign. There's nothing hollow about improving yourself. Nothing hollow about naming the problem, then beating it."

"No, sir." A little glow of pride lit up inside Will. Ridiculous. How old was he? He wasn't a child. Still, it felt good; better than hunger, better than losing. Maybe a bit like winning.

"The hat?" Will prompted.

"Plenty of hats in Montgomery's. I walked into the store and headed straight for them on the ground floor. Everyone wore hats in those days. I remember the display, all of them hanging off central poles on little wooden nubs. Men's on one side of the store and women's on the other. I'd never seen so many hats, before or since. Hardly anyone wears them these days."

"And?"

"All of them were perfect," Jim said. "Some with feathers. Some with little bits of mesh that covered the eyes. Black and navy and cream and pale blue. I had no idea which hat to buy. Maybe they came in different sizes. We all wore hats back then, and I was turning mine around and around in my hands, just standing there, and up comes the sales assistant ..."

"Grandmother?"

"You *have* heard the story."

"Must have. Not all of it. So what happened?"

"Well. She wasn't the sales assistant. She was Eleanor Montgomery, and I worshipped her. She looked even better the second time I saw her, there in the shop. She was older than me. She had real grace, real style. Her sweetheart had died in the war. I still don't understand what she saw in me, but we just clicked. She actually remembered me from that time I'd knocked her hat off."

In the white room, Will smiled, imagining the moment.

"When I asked her which hat she would like as a replacement, she laughed and told me she already owned them all. Her father owned the place. But it wasn't like a boast. It was hilarious. We laughed till we were both in tears. We never looked back."

"Good story."

59

"I thought you knew our story, Will. That's what I'd wish for all of you – for James, Nicole and you. That trust. That partner in life. Not that everything was always perfect. We had plenty of challenges. But we faced them together. Good luck to you, Will."

"Thank you, Grandfather."

Chapter 6

The following day, at the group session, Sam, Beth and Chase had all shared stories before Will spoke. Lisa started probing.

"Tell us about your relationships, Will. Are you ready to talk about this?"

"What 'Huntley heartbreaker'? The whole world talks about my relationships."

"Why do you think that is?"

"Because I'm one hot lover." He couldn't resist. There she was, in her white coat, trying to ignore the effect he could have on her. He slid down on the white chair, legs splayed, hands behind his head, and fixed her with his bedroom eyes. Yes. She blushed. Then rolled her eyes. Sighed. Pursed those lips. Tapped her pen on her folder.

Will sat up straighter. He didn't want to be expelled, like Connor. He actually enjoyed Lisa's sessions.

"Sorry. Just joking. I don't mean any disrespect. Look, it's a long story."

"That's fine. We have as long as it takes, if you're ready to talk about this."

"All my 'conquests'? It's not as bad as the media makes out. Never has been. My problem? I dated the wrong girl. Well, actually, she dated the wrong brother."

"Want to tell us?"

"James was meant to go," Will said. "To the school formal. Our sister, Nicole, she's in the middle. Two years older than me, two years younger than James. We were at separate schools, private schools. James and I were at the same school our father went to, but it was just for boys, so Nicole was at the girls' school down the road." Everyone was listening, even Sam.

"You Americans don't do that so much," he said. "Boys' schools and girls' schools. Builds up a kind of mystique about the other sex. We'd flirt at the bus stop, that kind of thing. Do you ever flirt, Lisa?"

"This is about you, Will." Was she warning him? She shouldn't get mad. Sam was listening. Chase was relating. He'd already shared how his manager tried to keep the tabloids off his case. Chase was up to divorce number three. Beth was cool. She wanted to hear more.

"Just asking," he said. "Hey, don't get offended."

"Not offended, thank you for checking. So ...?"

She was nodding. He'd made her laugh. Good.

"Well, with Nicole, we got to see both sides of this huge 'formal' thing," Will said. "I'm telling you. Her school formal? Major dress drama. Shoe drama, hair, nails and makeup drama. But the biggest drama of all? Who to invite. In some ways, we Huntleys had it easy. Nicole had already been to James's formal, on the arm of James's best friend, Scottie. She didn't care much for Scottie. She just used him to get into the place so she could flirt with everyone else. Poor Scottie. Nice guy; but that's another story." He didn't mind this. It wasn't quite as good as holding the floor at the pub, but it would have to do.

"So, Nicole's formal? James was supposed to go with one of her friends. James, he was hot property. Two years older. We were Huntleys, the big-time local jewelers. Formals were good for our business."

"Why's that?" Beth asked.

"Plenty of Nicole's friends and their mothers came in to check out James on Saturdays when he was working. He got six or eight invitations that year. It was the one bright point in our lives, with our father so sick. He was really ill by then. Dying. But every evening he'd want an update on the formals. Who was asking whom, where. Whether James agreed to this invitation or that. He'd have a bit of a chuckle. Maybe he remembered his own early days with Cynthia, our mother." Will went silent. Everyone waited.

"Maybe Father encouraged James to accept this date with Nicole's friend, but she turned out to be poison, I can tell you," Will said. "Bad choice alright. Penelope Simpson, 'Pen.' Her father was a big wig in the media. Maybe Father thought it might win us some good media coverage or something, or maybe he had nothing to do with it." Lisa and the others looked confused.

"The thing is, James was supposed to go," Will said. "We had his tux. Bow tie the same color as Pen's dress. Corsage all ordered. He'd had the big haircut, polished the shoes. He even had those fancy studs down his shirt and some cufflinks, courtesy of Huntleys, of course, and he had this little pearl on a chain for Pen. Bonus gift. Again, no guessing where that came from and why." Will laughed, remembering.

"Mother had shown James how to waltz," he said. "We kept telling her it wasn't like that. Just really loud music so no one could talk, and so we'd all have an excuse to grope each other in the dark. Maybe that's all a waltz is anyway, eighteenth-century groping." Everyone had a chuckle, but no one interrupted, so Will continued.

"Well. James got sick the day before. Seriously ill. Probably food poisoning."

Sam looked down.

"We both ate anything and everything back then," Will said. "Mother was preoccupied with father and we were hungry all the time. Still growing. Plenty of takeaway meals and leftovers. But James was still crook come five o'clock. There was no way he was going to get to that dance. More drama.

"And then, Mother looks at the tux on the hanger, looks at me, and says, 'Will will go, won't you, Will?' Me? Party? Fancy food. Chicks? Hell, yes. I hadn't had the big haircut, but by the time I'd got in and out of the shower, stolen a bit of James's aftershave and put on all that clobber, I looked mighty fine if I say so myself. Rakish. I was tall for my age. Not that much younger than Nicole and her friends. I was in."

Chase was nodding, his smile wide.

"Pen didn't care that she'd pulled the stand-in. A Huntley was a Huntley, and we practically look the same, James and I. I hadn't had the waltz lessons, but it didn't hold me back. I remember Pen." Will smiled and shook his head. "Pen was on the scrawny side back then. Backless dress. Shoes so high she could barely walk, let alone dance. But we had fun. Danced every dance, and by the time her mascara was running we were holding hands and pashing in the corner, and when it was over and time for the after-party, I was in, no questions asked, free grog, cigarettes, fallen shoulder straps, ooh yeah."

Chase was still nodding. Even Beth was enthralled.

"Pen's family hosted. They had this big house. Even bigger than ours. They didn't even realize I wasn't James. We were all underage. Legal drinking age is eighteen in Australia, but we were all at it. A bit of puking behind the shrubbery. Pretty standard, really. So, at the time, it was no big deal." They waited for him to continue, Lisa making a little note or two now and then in her folder.

"Down the track? It backfired pretty badly. Mainly because Pen and I were an item for a few months. Inseparable. Every afternoon after school. She was keen. Why hold back? Mother and Father had no idea. Nicole and her friends were jealous. That was supposed to happen at formals, after all. True love, then sex. It was every school boy's dream. Sure, my school work suffered. I wasn't getting a lot of sleep. Not in my own bed, anyway, but nobody noticed. Then dad died."

Will was silent, remembering. Lisa was still sitting opposite, looking at him with those honey-brown eyes. So accepting. The others were quiet, waiting, watching him.

"I don't really remember much about that time." Will sighed. He didn't want those memories coming back. The huge black hearse, shiny as a grand piano. The only music the infernal organ in the church. Weeping music. Being back in a suit. Shaking so many hands. Pen's father's among them. And Pen, in the choir. The whole bloody choir was from Nicole's school. Whose idea was that? Pen with her great big sad eyes. It wasn't her father that died.

"I went a bit wild after that," Will said, eyes on the carpet. "Didn't want to be anywhere, so I was everywhere, if you know what I mean. Wagged a lot of school. Used to go up on the headland and stare out at the sea, for some sort of comfort. All that space."

Lisa nodded, and Will's eyes returned from far away to meet hers, to explain.

"The sound of the waves crashing into the cliffs, one after another," he said. "They eased my mind. So yeah. I smoked a bit more. Drank a bit more ..."

He looked at Lisa, Sam, Beth and Chase. They weren't laughing now. They were listening to him, taking him seriously. Accepting, understanding.

"No one noticed, busy with the business, dealing with their own grief," he said. "I just stopped going to Pen's. I remember this big argument with her. She said I should at least tell her, discuss it, let her down a bit gently. But I had no idea. Grief? God. It was this savage beast inside of me. I was so angry at my father for leaving us. For leaving me. I took it out on everyone else."

Will stopped. His fists were clenched, arms across his chest, whole body tense, head bowed. Gradually he unfolded and looked across at Lisa.

"I've never talked about this before," he said. "Not like this. I can see it now, from Pen's point of view. I was cruel to her. When she sent me a card, I ripped it up. When she came to the door, I just closed it in her face. I guess I can't blame her for what happened afterwards."

"What happened afterwards?" Lisa asked.

"I didn't get much schoolwork done. The only thing I really turned up for was sport. I loved it. I could put all my aggression into that and win. So many winning tries. So many records at athletics. The school loved me. Oh, there might have been a parent-teacher meeting or two where they tried to read the riot act, but Mother was hardly coping herself. And Nicole was mad at me about Pen, her friend. 'Just talk to her,' she kept saying. What would I have said? I had no words then. Not for anyone."

Beth pulled out a tissue and dabbed an eye.

"Pen made me feel guilty for breaking it off. I just didn't want to go there. Maybe I was ashamed. I don't know. There was so much I couldn't say. I didn't have the words; still don't. I was all action. Action man. I didn't care how hard I ran and tackled, and scored those tries. The school loved me enough to turn the other way when I failed my exams. Sport was the only thing that eased the pain. I was a bit of a hero. Not so good when I think of it now. There were girls on the sidelines. Sisters. Girlfriends. Pen with her long face …

"One game, the whole lot of them were there. Nicole and her bunch of friends, with Pen half looking the other way. They cornered me after the match. I was on a high, king of the mountain, man of the match – all that glory – before the pain set in as usual. They'd lined themselves up where

I had to walk off. What's that expression? Looking daggers? 'Cept there was one of them, on the side, tall, cute. And she was just laughing. She slipped me a note. I liked the look of her. Elke, she turned out to be. Exchange student. It was simple. She liked me. I liked her. Pen never forgave me."

"Pen never forgave you?" Lisa prompted him.

"Pen had our future all mapped out. Nicole kept bringing it up. Said I broke her heart."

"That's not unusual in first relationships," Lisa said. "Black-and-white thinking. All or nothing."

"I was barely eighteen."

"And grieving," she said.

Good. Lisa wasn't piling on the guilt. She just nodded. She was with him.

"There's a theory," Lisa said, her voice gentle. "We use it in relationships therapy. I'll tell you about it. It might help. You loved your father. Your father left you. That hurt so much that you never wanted to expose yourself to that kind of loss ever again. So you broke off your relationship with Pen before she could break up with you."

"Yeah. Maybe."

"And Elke was a perfect choice for you. You knew in advance she was going to have to go back to her own country at some stage. No need to commit to a future. And after Elke?"

"Callie, Nettie, Lydia. Man. Those days."

Will remembered the first time he'd gatecrashed a party, taking the fence instead of the gate. It hadn't been difficult, though climbing with a bottle of rum in a paper bag in one hand had added a layer of challenge. When he'd landed on the other side, they'd all been ecstatic, especially Rosetta, the host, who'd just turned eighteen. Ah, that garden. The perfect place for a hot kiss behind the stand of camellias or whatever they were, until her father came looking for her, calling her for the birthday cake. Rosetta, Rosetta, fresh and thrilling. The torch. The fury. The scramble back over the fence. The freedom. It helped to be an athlete. There was no way Rosetta's dad would catch him.

"Those days?" said Lisa.

"Well. Lots of parties. Then Pen got a job with her father's company. She went from cadet journalist to gossip columnist. She still went to the same parties we all went to, for years, but now she'd bring along a photographer. If we were at the same party, I always got a mention. 'Bad-boy Huntley.'

"I made Pen's career," Will said, staring back at everyone in the group. "She still won't let me go. She's got media networks all over the world. She doesn't even need the facts anymore. One photograph of me on the arm of someone new and she's off, recounting the history of all my failed relationships.

"At first I thought it was funny. Then I got defensive. Then guilty. Thought I must have brought it on myself. Maybe I owe her an apology? But I do love women. And they like me. So why shouldn't I have relationships with them?"

Lisa sat back. Beth was smiling at him. Chase, too. Even Sam gave him a half-smile before she sneered.

"I'm with Pen," Sam said.

Everyone sat up.

"Why couldn't you just explain it to her? Apologize?" she said.

"I said. I tried, but I didn't really know what was going on."

"Back then maybe," said Sam. "I'm talking about now. You say she still hates you. Why don't you email her? Explain it to her now that you understand better. You men never take responsibility when you break our hearts. What did she ever do to you before you went off and slept with her friend? Of course she's bitter!"

Chase sat silently, arms crossed. Beth and Lisa were nodding.

"You think I'm spinning a tale?"

"There are several things happening here," said Lisa. "What Sam says is right. You have many choices to make. You could choose to apologize to Pen, even now. You could also choose to recognise how it is that you've formed this pattern of having multiple relationships. And you can continue to have lots of relationships, if you want. But some clients want to break that pattern at some stage. Settle down."

"Yeah?"

"You can go around and repeat that behavior for the rest of your life, or you can accept that that's what happened, see it for what it is, and be ready to question yourself next time you start going down that same path."

"Breaking it off?"

67

"Yes," she said. "There's a theory we use in relationship counselling, couples counselling, that might be useful for you. It suggests that clients who can't hold down a relationship are frightened of getting hurt. They break off a relationship before it gets serious because they're worried the other person will break it off. They don't want to be the one who's hurt. Sound familiar?"

"Yeah," Will said. "Maybe. Yeah."

"This has been a very positive session," Lisa said. "I'm very pleased with the way you are all sharing, all listening, opening yourselves up to learning. The main thing is that everyone has more choices than they realize."

"We do?"

Beth nodded. Chase sat up. Alert.

"If you're in a relationship, and you recognize you're about to break it off, you can think about what's happened in the past, remember you have choices, and push through that fear that the other person will desert you. Why not find out what could happen?"

Did she mean that? Sitting there, smiling? Find out what could happen? With Lisa? Hope shot through Will, rattled his bones and exploded through his solar plexus; made his fingers tingle.

"I look forward to seeing you all tomorrow," Lisa said.

…

Chase started it in the next group session. Talking about cast parties. Chase explained the dynamics, the temptations, the highs and lows of emotions when, at the end of a show, cast and crew threw caution to the winds. After working together as a tight-knit group to create a show day after day, they were about to become individuals again, scattering around the globe, trying to pick up work in other productions.

So they would party like there was no tomorrow, because there wouldn't ever be a tomorrow anything like it had been, with that set of people. Add to that the power imbalances, the mix of stars and starlets, directors and crew, the hustling for future work, and returns of favors, real and perceived – the parties were legendary.

"You like parties?" Lisa asked the group.

"Who doesn't?" Will weighed in.

"I never did, not much," Lisa said. "The music's too loud. Can't have a decent conversation."

"Come on," said Will. "Don't you like to dance? All work and no play, Lisa?"

"I don't know."

"You've never been to a real party, then!" Will was incredulous. "Everyone likes a party. All that bad food. A few good slugs of grog and you're in the zone. The music? It's all about the beat. Check out the talent. Have a bit of a flirt."

Will would never forget his first real party. Not that he'd actually been invited. Up over the fence with the contraband in a brown paper bag. He'd been popular alright.

"So come on – where's your sound system in here, Lisa? Group therapy party time! What's all this tinkley relaxation music? Crank it up, I say. New kind of therapy. Worked for me."

"Did it?"

"Well, yeah," he said. "For a while. Maybe."

Had it? Waking with a dry mouth and headache, wondering where he was. Fights with girls who thought he owed them something. Melanie. Stacey. Penelope. Pure poison. Then Melanie again. Yeah. That hadn't been great. All that emotional angst. Even on the beach he wasn't safe. Kept running into them.

"Thank God for the gap year," he said.

"What's a gap year?" Beth asked.

"Chance to find yourself before you go to uni — college — not that I actually got to uni, given that I totally blew my final exams. Not proud of that, but the gap year was great. Chance to go see the world. I did my time in Huntleys. Saved up. Bought a one-way ticket. It's a big world out there. Vietnam. Power lines all over the place. Thailand. Spice. Beautiful women; petite. And a whole bunch of backpackers like me. Youth hostels, beaches, traffic chaos, crazy motorbikes, Tuk Tuks, bicycles everywhere, Thai beer, Thai whiskey. And after dark? Anything goes. Non-stop parties."

Will's face lit up.

"And Bali!" Will said. "More beautiful beaches. Tattoos. Spicy food. A kind of freedom in the heat. Polite local people. Meditation. Too many

Aussies, maybe. Can't understand why the whole world doesn't migrate to Bali."

Chase pricked up his ears. "Bali?"

"I thought about running a bar there," Will said. "Had half a plan, with one of the guys in my basketball team. We talked a lot, but he went and got married and moved back to Oz. Piker. 'Course I ended up back home, too. But Sydney was so bloody boring after Asia.

"Asia was exotic, alright. The spirits and gods go to sleep after dark in Thailand, Chase, Beth, Sam, Lisa. Did you know that? Anything goes if the spirits aren't watching. No one's offended. Bloody brilliant. Have you done much travelling, Lisa?"

"A little."

"It could help you loosen up," Will said.

"Travelling can broaden the mind," Lisa said. "There are many choices we can make about how we spend our time."

"You love to talk about choices, Lisa."

"It's important. So many people don't realise we all have choices we can make at any moment."

"Existentialism?" Will asked.

"A lot of my clients are impulsive," Lisa said, nodding. "They don't realize they don't have to follow the first thought that comes into their head. It all comes back to setting goals and following through. Self-control. Controlling their impulses. Not giving in to every temptation. You don't want to get out of here in the next week or two, spot the first casino and walk straight back into it, do you?" She looked around the circle as they all shook their heads, even Will.

"Ever watched a puppy in a park?" she said. "They're all over the place. They smell this and bite that, and rush from one place to another, chasing their tails. They have no agency. No plan."

"What's wrong with living my life like that?" Will asked.

"Nothing," she said. "As long as you understand that not making a choice is also a choice. If you choose not to choose, you're still choosing. We all need to ask ourselves, do we like the results of our choices?"

There was silence as they looked at each other and considered her words.

70

"Because if we don't like the results, we need to remember that we have the power to make different choices." She smiled. Will sat straighter. They all did.

"Now," she said. "I'd like you all to consider the power of choices, until our next session. Please be ready to share some examples of choices in your lives. These can be little choices or big ones. As small as deciding what to wear or whether to make use of our gym. Or as big as looking at options for your future.

"For example, you, Chase. Would you audition for a new show, or movies? Sam, will you try out for art school? And Beth. Have you given more thought to having a fresh start, or going to visit your daughter in Miami for a month or two next winter, like you were telling me?"

Will stayed back again to check a point.

"Lisa?"

"Yes, Will?"

"You say I'm too impulsive?"

"Possibly. It depends on the circumstances."

"Exactly," Will said. "You see, what I think is that some people aren't impulsive enough. Maybe it's true I've had too much fun ..."

Lisa waited.

"But maybe you ..."

"Me?"

"Yes, you, Lisa. Maybe you haven't had enough." He fixed her with his best bad-boy smile.

"Maybe," she said. She ignored her heart as it skipped a beat. "But this is about you, Will. What will you do next time you're tempted?"

"Oh," Will smiled, "I know all about temptation, Dr Lisa Bakker. Maybe I'm being tempted right now. Question is, do you know about temptation?"

"I'm not sure what you mean, Will."

"Do you choose not to understand?"

"Our session is up," Lisa said.

He stood back so she could exit ahead of him, but he kept speaking.

"Do you sometimes have clients who, you know, are not impulsive enough?"

"We see a whole range of people, Will," Lisa said. "Everyone is different. What are you asking?"

"Well, you reckon all I ever say is 'yes, yes, yes' when I'm tempted."

"It's a common problem among people who struggle with addiction," Lisa said. "They tend to go back in for more, without thinking twice, without realizing they have a choice and can actually control their impulses — that saying 'no' is a valid option. Everyone benefits when they consider the consequences of their choices."

Will nodded. "Well, Lisa. All I'm saying is that some people say 'no' all the time, without realizing they have choices, too."

"Correct," she said.

"And consequences."

"Correct again, Will."

"Such as not having much fun, or being lonely. A bit too much 'no, no, no' if you know what I mean."

Will helped Lisa straighten the chairs. When they bumped elbows, Will felt as awkward as a schoolboy.

"I'm glad you stayed back, Will."

There. So easy. Will's confidence surged. This Lisa was just like the rest, putty in his hands. He gave her one of his half smiles, with seventy per cent bedroom eyes.

"There'll be no more of that," she said, suddenly Miss Prim.

"What do you mean?" Surely she wasn't freezing him out.

"I remind you, my relationship with you, Mr Huntley, is purely professional and nothing but professional. Every time you look at me like that — and you know exactly what I'm talking about — you do me a disservice, and you do yourself one. I didn't study for nearly a decade to be treated like your next lay. What you do with your own life, does interest me. And I do care about you. But don't you insult me like this. You're not welcome in my group sessions unless you're here for the right reasons. If you turn up early again, I'll send you away. Stay there. I haven't finished."

Will drew back, wary.

Lisa reached into her pocket, all business.

"Now, Will. It's time I gave you back your phone, but before I do, I want you to take a few moments to remember exactly what it is that you love about gambling. I want you to visualise everything that you love about it, the way it affects your body — the sounds, the colours of the lights, the feel of the phone, everything it does and everything you do in response. Afterwards, if you wish, you can tell me how it really was."

He stood there, sizing up Dr Bakker. He had to fight to ignore the temptation to see the woman behind the therapist. He listened to her words, clenched his fist as if it could already feel the phone in his grip. His lips parted. His pulse was racing, his heart quickening, a sheen of sweat breaking out over his skin, a flush coming to his face. He closed his eyes and visualised the dollar signs, heard again those sweet jingling melodies and the ringing jangle of an almost-win, followed by all the bells of a big one.

She held out his phone. He wanted to snatch it from her, right now, but held off. He licked his lips. Was she chastising him with those big brown eyes? No. He stared into their depths, while the phone hovered, dark and shining between them in the blank room. Her white coat covered her curves.

He swallowed, bowed his head, held out his hand, palm up.

When she handed it over, the phone was warm from her touch.

...

Lisa. White coat. White room. White hallways.

Back in his room, he'd barely closed the door before he pressed the phone back on and took the first free bet on offer. Damn sexy Lisa Bakker in her ice white coat.

Will played and played, his body crouched on the edge of his bed. He played until his back ached from slouching.

Yes. Again and again. More money. More bets, More chances, last chances, final chances, extra chances — oblivious to the fading light, to the beauty of the sunset, to the need to pee, to the growling hunger and the ache in his neck. The tension of his arm was the throb of wanting to keep on playing, without distraction. That there was no money was no problem. He swapped sites, searched his messages. There was always another free bet, and another. He ran out of power, moved to the other side of the bed, plugged in the phone and played again. If his mouth was dry, he ignored it. Was he grunting, swearing at it? No matter. He slammed his thumb on the prompts, his throat dry.

Now the sun was coming up. His shirt stank and still he hung over the shiny black rectangle, betting like the best of them, like the worst of them, the wins never big enough, and always another bet and better win just out of sight, just within reach, if only he kept on at it.

He looked up. Was it really three o'clock in the afternoon? He'd missed dinner, breakfast and lunch. His arm was so cramped his fingers refused to move. He let the phone fall to the floor and stared at it, head in his hands.

When he stood, he could barely unfold his body. The phone lay there on the white carpet, daring him to pick it up again and continue.

He covered it with his foot, and shot it out sideways so it skidded across the blank expanse and ricocheted off the wall.

He stood, peeled off his clothes, dragged on his bathing costume and white robe, and headed back to the oblivion of swimming laps.

Propelling himself through the tepid water, he swam faster till all his muscles burned and he struggled for breath, each gasp for oxygen a relief.

The rhythm of the swim did little to lull him out of his memories. Worse was the screaming revelation he was wasting his life.

He'd rushed from one experience to the next so fast, he'd never stopped to savor the moments.

If he'd thought he could lose himself in alcohol and women and bets, to escape the pain of being abandoned by his father, he'd been wrong. It was all still there, that agony, coiled up deep inside of him, right next to the ecstasy of losing himself inside the frenzy of discovering sex with Pen and all the guilt-free fun he'd had with Elke, the raspberry smell of her lip gloss, then Lachlan's insane parties, the stereo so loud they'd been deaf for days. How dare Lachlan die in that car crash, in that little red convertible his father had bought him.

Turn and splash and kick and breathe. Lachlan. More bloody loss still there inside him, however hard he tried to forget it.

As he towelled himself off, the pain of loss still burned in his chest and he limped to his room, drank some water and crouched back on the end of the bed. The phone was still there on the carpet, begging him to pick it up and play again.

They stared at each other, the phone and Will, and he picked it up, turned it on so the lights would talk to him and take him away. Free bet. Always there for him, unlike Lachie.

He kept it in his hand, but this time, he bowed his head and let himself cry for Lachie, the great sobs erupting through his spent and hungry body.

They'd stood there in the church in their best blazers, and tried not to blubber. They'd been men by then, their wrists poking out of the sleeves, biceps too big for the armholes, school shoes barely holding together, the end of school so close they could all taste it, the crowning glory of their final assembly, with all those smaller boys envying them their freedom, still condemned, and that emptiness afterwards. Except for the parties. They even called it "getting wasted."

If there'd been any plan for Will's life after school he couldn't remember what it was. Maybe he was supposed to be an Olympian, but he'd never stuck at any one sport long enough to do more than show extraordinary potential.

A careers advisor had encouraged him to think about sports scholarships in the US, but he'd never followed up. There was always another party, or something Huntleys needed him to do. Serve customers. Count the coins into bags and stack them in the safe. Unroll the packs of small change into the tills. Vacuum. Polish the cabinets. As long as he cleaned himself up after the latest binge, no one really guessed how hard he was partying. He'd bought his own little red convertible. Fuck Lachie totalling himself. He'd never do that.

Well, maybe he had. Slowly. Where was he a dozen years later? Thirsty as hell on a hot Vegas sidewalk. Then swimming till his arms fell off at a luxurious health retreat, and staring at a dark phone on a pale carpet as if it were a grenade.

...

A day later, Will shaved and ironed his shirt. He turned up bang on time for the group session, and handed Lisa his phone.

"You keep it, please, Dr Bakker. I don't want it and I don't need it. It's not what I want any more."

She nodded, cool as a cucumber. Professional. Keeping it professional.

Chapter 7

Apart from that frisson of discomfort Will always left in his wake, and the fact that Chase and Will had talked up the allure of wild partying a little too much at the start, Lisa was pleased with the group session.

Sam loosened up, clearly listening, more comfortable to ask questions. Beth was going strong, and Chase was still on the wagon. As for Will; he was smart. He was making good progress. And his case had been mild to begin with. No suicidal thoughts. No self-harm beyond the tendency to addictive behavior, lack of impulse control.

But when Lisa reached the privacy of her own consulting room, she smoothed her hands over her coat. Her heart was still pumping – too fast. He kept doing that to her. Flipping it. It was as if Will had become *her* therapist.

Partying with Will Huntley? Saying "yes" to Will? How would that be? Well, that would never happen. Self-control? She was an expert at it.

Was she lonely? No. She had a life. Her marriage hadn't worked, but she'd made a fresh start here in Nevada, and she had her faithful old dog, Rossco; and her work was demanding. Dealing with people in such depth day in and day out, she didn't need a busy social life. No, thank you.

Besides, the consequences of saying "yes" to someone like Will "heartbreaker" Huntley? Pretty damn obvious.

So why did she feel like a prude back there, like she was missing out on something? Like she was the one with the problem; the one who always said "no," the one with too much self-control?

She shook her head and picked up the folder of her next client.

But that evening, she could still sense the pull of the man. She remembered this restlessness. It had invaded her life with Art. Back then it hadn't been about wanting another person. It had been about needing to be with herself, to escape her stultifying marriage, even for an hour.

They'd been married almost a year. After all the excitement of planning the wedding, the careful guest list, the dress her mother had made for her, the solemn ceremony, so traditional, Art had been unwell. She'd nursed him through their honeymoon, confident that the joyous future she'd expected would unfold in time.

There'd been the thrill of starting college, almost daily visits from her mother as she settled herself into Art's house and existence, Sunday dinners back at her childhood home with Art in the same chair he'd always occupied, and her parents' mock sadness when she'd leave to go home with him. But if they'd imagined she'd been happy, they were wrong. She wasn't exactly sad. She'd just been blank.

Art at home was the same as Art anywhere. Controlled. Considered. Polite. Highly disciplined and well informed; a man of ideas, if not of action. An older man of long-formed habits, with a very young wife. An esteemed microbiologist, a world expert on what went on in cells, and no clue what went on in her heart and soul.

She'd worked so hard to inject some sparkle into their marriage. She studied recipes and created elaborate dinners. The seafood paella had taken all day to prepare. She'd made a special trip to the next big town to source the ingredients, and taken all afternoon to peel the tiny shrimp.

And when she'd brought it all out in triumph that night and served it by candle light, all Art could do was complain about fish bones. He went on and on about the dangers of swallowing one. He clearly preferred the simple meals he'd once cooked for himself.

She experimented with makeup and different hairstyles to try to catch his attention, but he remained indifferent.

She even ordered some fancy negligees online and tried some perfumes with seductive titles, like "allure" and "enchantment," but Art barely noticed. He still preferred reading his books.

When it dawned on Lisa that the one and only thing that excited him in life was his research, she finally understood she must plan her escape – to make the most of her situation. She studied hard and achieved the best grades possible, and applied for the placement with Dr Peters, as far away as possible.

Only then could she position herself to head out into the wider world without him, able to support herself, secure in her own career.

…

Lisa joined the runners' club in her final year. It was the first time she'd stood up to Art and insisted on something for herself.

She often thought of the irony of that. She'd been an expert in human behavior but had failed to recognize her own repression. Her conservative upbringing made it hard for her to tackle Art's prudishness. He hadn't just been uninterested in sex; he actively avoided it.

"I have to balance all my study with some exercise, Art. Please."

He'd disapproved, but he hadn't been able to stop her. All it took to go for a run was to put one foot in front of the other.

There were arguments. Some of the other runners were his students. He'd thought it "undignified" that his wife should be seen wearing tiny shorts around the campus. She'd stood her ground.

"So you want me in our house, all day and all night when I'm not in the library or in lectures, even when you're not here? Do you really think that's reasonable, Art?"

He'd sulked while she cleaned up the dishes. She stared out above the steamy suds as the others sprinted past one day, and made herself a promise.

And the next day, when they trained on the oval, she simply joined them. In her long pants, to mollify Art. That freedom. She hadn't felt so high in years. She'd needed her own space. After years of inertia, she revelled in the mindlessness of simply moving her legs, launching herself through space.

And if Art thought his sulking silence at dinner that night would bring her into line, he was wrong.

"I need this exercise, Art," she'd said. "Running doesn't cost anything. Nothing else happens. You've seen what we do. We run. I have to get out sometimes. And it's safe this way. We're all together. No one's going to jump me when I'm in a pack like that."

"And we talk," she'd failed to add, as she cleaned up the dishes that night. Put the salt and pepper shakers back where they'd been for thirty years. Maybe that was what Art was most afraid of.

And we think. We question. Best of all for her. Worst for him.

There was no obligation to talk as they ran. In fact, it was difficult, once they got going. Too much puffing. They were all fitter than she was, many of them long-distance champions from their school days. A couple were even at the college on athletics scholarships, and kept up their fitness by running in the club.

Lisa found company again for the first time since school. Simple companionship. A couple of them were aware she was married to a researcher, but it was no big deal.

She heard about their majors, their favourite lecturers, their hometowns. They opened up a world for her she'd barely known existed. Their stories fed into what she learned about human behavior, about the wide variety of choices out there. Hardly anyone led a life like hers. Protected. Coddled, even. Sheltered.

Lisa knew her parents loved her, but their love meant barriers, not freedom. Things were done the best and only way. Her mother washed the clothes and shopped on Saturdays while her father washed the car and gardened. They'd eaten home-made hamburgers on Tuesday nights for as long as she could remember. She thought everyone ate hamburgers on Tuesdays. And on Sundays? Roasts. With her father's best friend, Art, in the fourth chair. They doted on Art. And Art doted on her. It had only occurred to her in her second or third year of matrimony that theirs had been an arranged marriage.

Compliant, sensitive, so ready to please her parents, she'd simply gone along with it.

Resentment grew slowly. With her life with Art had come the excitement of living on campus and the thrill of her studies, a wider world, no question. But by the time she joined the running club, the strictures were more than obvious. These became the first heady steps of her escape.

Sometimes they ran on campus, and sometimes cross country. Anyone could lead the pack. The time Jilly led was a revelation. Jilly wore hot pink. She was loud and fearless – the opposite of Lisa – and Lisa admired her.

The club was popular enough to form splinter groups which ran at different times. One group took a minibus out of town on Saturday mornings, into local national parks.

A few months in, when Art had accepted Lisa would never give up running to please him, she announced her plan to go with a group to run in their local ski fields, out of season.

"We'll leave really early. I won't even disturb you. I'll leave your breakfast out, and your lunch will be in the fridge; and I'll be back by nightfall. This is good for me. For us. It's healthy, Art, for me to have different interests."

"I'm not happy about this, Lisa."

"I understand, Art. But it'll be fine. You'll barely notice I'm gone."

If running on the flat had been good, running up an incline was sublime. Lisa's soul soared ever higher as they climbed, every few yards of elevation yielding a better and better view. When they reached the summit she knew she was on top of the world.

They'd sat for ages up there, taking in the view from every angle. Jilly pointed to the west.

"Hello, Vegas!" she'd shouted. Then all the others had pulled up Google and pointed at their own home towns.

When Lisa pointed at her own, right there below them, Jilly had been incredulous.

"You didn't want to go away? Explore the world?"

"It never occurred to me."

"Whoa!" Jilly was tactful enough not to probe, but Lisa got the message. Jilly pitied her. So, she wasn't the only one questioning her life. It might have been one tiny comment, but it gave her courage.

The campus was tiny, but the world was big, and at every step of their descent, her conviction grew. She knew what she would have to do; once she had her doctorate and could make her own living.

Her parents wouldn't like it. Nor would Art. But she couldn't waste the rest of her life merely half alive.

She and Jilly liked to run early in the day. She didn't exactly keep their friendship secret from Art. He simply never asked.

Jilly had grown up in Vegas. Like her mother, she'd worked in casinos. From Jilly, Lisa learnt about the world of gambling, the terrible bind of guilt and hope and the elation brought on by an occasional win, the way gambling could trap a person, separate them from everything in their lives but the quest to win again. It fascinated her. Here was a subject worth studying, a specialization worth doing.

The job offer from Dr Peters, where she'd done her internship, had been everything she'd hoped for. And everything Art had feared.

Well might Will accuse Lisa of hypocrisy. In her heart, Lisa knew she'd hurt her parents and Art when she escaped west with just Rossco and a few boxes of possessions. For all the elation she'd felt at making good her escape, she knew the weight of guilt. Apart from a phone call to her parents every month or so, she hadn't been back. The fact her father would never speak with her was a tragedy of his own making. At least her mother would share her good news with him, or so she hoped.

Chapter 8

Will was pleased to run into Lisa at the door to her consulting room as he emerged from his four pm session with Dr Peters. But something was wrong. She was on the phone, hunched over, nursing the receiver as if it were a broken bird.

"Rossco!" Distraught, she slumped against the wall, face ashen.

Will leaned forward and grabbed the top of her arm, gently steadying her. "Lisa, what is it?"

"Rossco. My dog!" Stricken, her face crumpled. He saw the howl behind her eyes before she doubled over.

He ducked back to the waiting room. No receptionist. He dashed back. Considered interrupting Dr Peters, but the next patient had already gone in and the door was closed. He could do this. Whatever was needed. Thank God for some excitement. He'd been so good he bored himself.

"Lisa, tell me what's wrong."

She straightened, searched his face.

"Let me help you, Lisa," he kept his voice steady. "I can help you. This is my goal right now. I want to help you."

As she considered her options, he was glad he'd ironed his shirt, shaved, and looked respectable. He'd been making the effort.

"C'mon. I just finished with Dr Peters. I've got nothing else happening here." It was the clincher.

"Yes, please. Thank you. I ..." She entered her consulting room again, shook a key, unlocked a cupboard, grabbed her handbag.

"Where am I taking you, Lisa? Where do we need to go?"

"Boulder City. You can drive. You're licensed. You have all your faculties, all your capabilities, no police record. I wouldn't normally ask, but ..."

"Unconventional treatment. I offered. I want you to know you can trust me ... and it's good for me. You need someone to help you, and I need to be trusted to help. Win, win. Okay, which way?"

"Boulder City. Oh, Rossco. He went under a car."

...

Will amazed himself. He stuck to the speed limit in Lisa's little shiny blue Ford Fiesta. Every time he glanced across, she was pale, anguished, agitated.

"Mrs Benedict's grandchildren," she was saying.

"Uh-uh," Will encouraged her.

"They left the gate open."

"The gate."

"Rossco!" She gripped the edge of the car seat, hard.

They were just ahead of rush hour, and making good time.

"Turn left here again. Now right. That's good. We're nearly there. The white house."

There were tire marks on the road. Lisa rushed out of the car, leaving the car door open. Will turned off the engine and ran after her, around the back of the house. There was a porch. An old dog. Blood.

"My baby," Lisa keened.

The dog was still alive. Just. Lisa squatted and cradled the old dog's head in her hands. She smoothed the fur of his nose, his jowls, his forehead.

The dog whined. The tail gave a thump.

"Rossco, brave boy. You're still here." The dog licked her hand, breathing rough. Left blood on it. "Brave, brave, Rossco. My beautiful boy."

"How about we get this fellow to a vet, Lisa? Does he have a bed? We could use it like a stretcher."

Will still had the keys. She pointed at the back door. "Yes. Yes. In the laundry."

They eased Rossco onto the canvas bed and Will hefted him into the back seat of the car before he took the wheel again.

"The best dog," Lisa said.

83

"Mmm. Where's your vet, then?"

"Yoo-hoo!" Just as Will was about to pull away, someone waved at them through the windscreen.

"Oh God no," said Lisa, cringing. She ducked down low, closer to Rossco. "Mrs Benedict. I really can't do this. Can you find out what she wants, please, Will?"

"Of course."

He sprang out of the car and maneuvered himself between Mrs Benedict and Lisa's window.

"Mrs Benedict, I'm Will Huntley. Pleased to meet you."

"Mighty sorry. That dog okay?"

"We're on our way to the vet, Mrs Benedict."

"Oh. I'm so sorry. I would've taken him to the vet, but, all the children … It's awful. I hope she doesn't blame me …"

"No, I'm sure Dr Bakker understands it was a terrible accident. No, please don't worry. These things happen … No. Now's not the time to apologize in person. Maybe just leave it a few days, if you could. Time is crucial now. We need to get Rossco to the vet, please, as I'm sure you understand. We'll be fine, thank you. Yes. Goodbye for now, Mrs Benedict."

Lisa's head was still down low as she cradled Rossco in the back seat. She looked up as he closed the car door and ignited the engine.

"Thank you, Will. Mrs B likes a long chat. You handled that so well."

Pride hit him like a lightning bolt — better than a win. "I'm glad to be here, Lisa."

"Such a good dog, Rossco. You came west with me, didn't you?" She spoke in a monotone, as if to herself, looking down at the old dog, still smoothing his ears. "Always here for me. My faithful Rossco. My rescue dog. We'd rescued Rossco, but we couldn't rescue our marriage."

Was she talking to the dog or to him? Will had to focus on the journey. He'd driven on the right before, but it always took concentration, particularly with Lisa so distressed in the back seat. He needed to be careful. And quick.

"Art. Hopeless. I thought I loved him. I was far too young. But I got my degree, and my job, and I still have you, Rossco, don't I, boy?"

It was rush hour at the veterinary clinic. Had every dog, cat and hamster gone under a car?

"Rossco's hurt pretty bad, ma'am."

"I'm sorry, sir. We see our clients as quickly as possible."

Every time Rossco whined, Lisa reached for Will's arm. He placed his hand over hers, gently. Had he ever sat still for so long? He'd sit there all night if he had to. Next to Lisa, steadying her, being still, solid, dependable. He'd never known he had it in him.

Opposite, a mother held a cat cage on her lap. Her two children crouched, peering in, whispering. From time to time, she'd smooth her hands over their heads, hushing them, comforting them.

Finally, Rossco's turn came. When Will stood back, Lisa grabbed his arm and pulled him into the examination room with her.

"This one's had a good, long life," the vet said and Lisa nodded, beyond words, fraught. Will explained about the car accident.

"We'll have to see what's possible," the vet said. Again Lisa grabbed Will's arm, and he laid his hand on hers again. This was becoming a habit. A good one.

"He's had a big shock, but there are no broken bones," the vet said. He'd given Rossco an injection and completed the check. "There may be internal bleeding. We'll need to keep him for a few days. We'll keep a close eye on him; make sure he's in no pain."

Lisa nodded, moving forward to cradle Rossco's head softly against her chest. Something in Will's own chest turned over. He placed a gentle hand on her shoulder. She didn't object.

As they walked to the car, she let him keep her close. It was nearly midnight.

"I'll take you home now," he said.

"I should drop you at the retreat." Lisa's voice was flat. "But security closes up at eleven." She stared out the window as he pulled away from the curb.

"I'll just take you home first, Lisa."

"This would be totally against retreat policy."

"You think I don't know how to bend a rule? Extenuating circumstances. Common sense."

She let him drive her home. Let him walk her inside. She was acting like a zombie. What could he do to help? If he was famished, surely she was hungry, too. He was no chef, but he knew a few basics. Two, anyway.

"How about some tea and toast," he said. "Scrambled eggs or baked beans?"

Lisa stared down at her pale suit, blotched and smudged with Rossco's blood and hairs, then back at him.

"Oh, thank you, Will. I'd like to shower. You're right. I'm starving. Scrambled eggs, please. You're very kind."

The kitchen light was too bright, but the contents were predictable. Will had no trouble creating the slap-up meal, though he struggled when he saw the cold bottle of white wine lying there in the fridge like a tempting green torpedo. That would be pushing his luck. He didn't want to jinx a thing. He wouldn't even mention it.

He took the toast and eggs into the living room and set it all on the coffee table with a couple of mugs of tea. Perfectly harmless.

When she emerged, steamy and fragrant from the shower, her head was wrapped in a towel and she was in warm pajamas, a dressing gown and some chewed pink slippers, one with a pompom, one without.

"Rosscoed," she said, wiggling her toes, laughing and crying at the same time. Will handed her the plate of steaming eggs.

He glanced at her as he ate his own. He was being so good. Lisa looked warm and perfect under the robe. What wouldn't he love to do. But he wouldn't. He didn't want to put a foot wrong. Never. Not with Lisa. This woman was an angel. It hurt him to see her troubled.

"You're so kind, Will. This is exactly what I need."

"It'd be better with vegemite."

"Pardon?"

"Aussies have vegemite on toast for meals like this," Will said.

"Oh. That black stuff?"

"Magic."

"I'm not too sure about that. This is perfect. Thank you. Thank you for everything."

When they'd finished eating, she gathered up the plates and mugs and took them into the kitchen.

Will leaned his head back on the couch and closed his eyes. He couldn't remember feeling more content. He wondered at himself. This was the kind of responsible thing James would do, to put someone else first. What a discovery, to find it felt so good.

He was glad to help Lisa. As the baby of the family, he'd been indulged. He'd been given every comfort. He'd always been the one to expect special treatment, yet never given it to others. There was a lot to be said about the joy of giving. He was astounded at what he'd been missing. It was a revelation. If anyone had told him, he'd never have believed it. He rested his head against the back of the lounge. Comfortable.

...

Lisa washed the dishes quickly. She should call an Uber for Will. Maybe if she phoned security they would let him in. Of course they would.

But when she returned to the living room, Will was fast asleep on her couch, head back. She leaned closer and peered at him, at his eyelids and dark lashes, the eyelids strangely vulnerable.

Maybe he was just pretending. But his breaths came softly, rhythmically, like old Rossco's when the sun went down. She stood over him, taking in those strong arms and long legs, crossed at the ankles. He was totally relaxed, as if he belonged right there.

She pushed her foot against his shin, to test if he would wake. Nothing. A soft snore. Well, it was nearly one am. He'd been so helpful, and incredibly kind. She placed a blanket around his shoulders, gingerly admiring his body as she tucked it around his thighs. He was so fit; lean. If something stirred in her, she tried to ignore it and jumped back away from temptation.

She turned off the light, then flicked the lock on her bedroom door and fell into bed, bone weary, and slept.

The sun was rising when Lisa stirred. The ache of grief and worry for Rossco twisted deep in the pit of her stomach as she remembered the rush of events. The accident. Her sudden decision to trust Will. It wasn't like her at all to pull a client into her personal life, even if, strictly speaking, he was someone else's client. It wasn't one hundred percent professional.

She'd have to tell Dr Peters about this. Was she losing her judgment? But Will had been fine. Perfectly behaved. She'd been right to trust her intuition. They'd been working on that, she and Dr Peters. She'd told her she was learning to read her clients better than ever, that her experience was adding up. "We're not robots," Dr Peters said. "We're human, too." Still, she doubted she'd condone this.

She dressed quickly, eager to be up and in control before Will woke. When she tiptoed past the living room, his breathing was rhythmic. Still asleep. It was a strange comfort, without Rossco at her heels. She closed her eyes and replayed the horrors of yesterday evening.

But it was okay now. Rossco was with the vet and likely to pull through. Thank God Will had been with her, been sensible, helped her not to panic.

But this. Will. She must savor these moments. This must be totally against the rules, even Dr Peters' unconventional ones. These were stolen moments, while the world turned slowly in the dark before the dawn, while delicious bad-boy-come-good-Samaritan Will Huntley slumbered on her couch.

Her mind whirred in the darkness. Nothing in her personal rule book allowed for this; nor in her professional code of conduct; nor in the clinic's. To be with Will Huntley like this surely broke Rule Number One: "Never get involved with clients."

Would she lose her job? A little stab of panic hit her, but she pushed it away.

She wondered if Mrs B was aware a strange man was in the house with her right this moment. That technically they'd been "sleeping together." Mrs B would be horrified.

She mustn't laugh or she'd wake Will. They could laugh about it later.

No. They couldn't laugh about it later. There could be no "later." He was a client at her clinic, dammit. This was dangerous ground. They'd warned her about this kind of thing at college. It was completely against the rules for so many reasons.

She must put her client's recovery ahead of her own desires.

Will was vulnerable, even if he never acted that way. She must be totally committed to his pathway to a better future. If she allowed this kind of entanglement, she'd sell him short.

Theirs was a client and therapist relationship. They couldn't even be friends. They certainly couldn't become lovers. *Lovers* ... that whole other realm ... Her rational mind told her it was impossible. Her body wanted otherwise and was already rebelling.

Well, that idea was laughable, wasn't it? He was her client. But wasn't love supposed to be kind? And selfless.

Too often, she knew, love was a bind. She remembered her parents and their careful expectations of her. Small-town school teachers, they could only dream of a love for her the same as theirs. It wasn't for herself she married Art, the famous professor. It was for them. For her? It'd been stultifying. Wrong. She would never want to do that to Will, this free spirit, to pin him down as she had been trapped.

Anyway, this attraction? It wasn't love, was it? It was more like lust. The way he looked at her, so cheekily. He knew he was gorgeous. Knew just how to …

Again, she almost laughed. What would her parents think if they knew a renowned playboy was here in her house; had spent the night with her.

No. In just an hour or two, it would be over between her and Will. It had to be.

Chapter 9

Will awoke to a feeling of lightness; then of loss. He was somewhere unfamiliar. Not that that was unusual.

This time, though, there was no hangover. No fuzzy tongue. He was clear-headed. There was the sound of a kettle. Someone was tiptoeing around him, placing a mug on the coffee table. He opened his eyes slowly and studied her. Graceful. *Lisa*. In her own space, moving quietly around the furniture as she let him sleep.

She brushed last night's crumbs from the coffee table and into one palm, efficiently, then tiptoed back to the kitchen. She returned with her own steaming mug and placed it beside his. Nice. She adjusted the blinds, let in the sunrise, retrieved her mug, then sat on an armchair to one side.

She sipped, her legs curled beneath her. She reached out and took a cushion, hugging it to herself.

Will's heart ached for her. She clearly adored her old dog and must be worried about him. He would comfort her again if she would let him. He studied her brow. Even in repose like this, she was beautiful. There was so much care in those features, and intelligence. Lisa Bakker was one interesting woman.

Her gaze shifted from the front gate to Will's face, and her own eyes widened. She'd caught him staring at her.

"How long have you been watching me?" she asked warily. She pulled her housecoat around herself more securely.

"Only a moment or two. Thanks for the coffee." Will stood, stretched and looked out into the neutral space of the yard, giving her privacy, then sat again.

She sipped her coffee. Finally, she spoke.

"I've done the wrong thing by you, Will."

"What's the right thing in an emergency? I was glad to help. Nothing but glad. You've done me a favor, Lisa Bakker. Reminding me there are others' needs that are more important than my own."

She still looked troubled. "I've broken the therapist-client code of conduct."

"What about the code of conduct of looking out for other people's needs?"

"But you came to us for help. Not me to you."

"What about reciprocity and the law of kindness? We're hardly human if we can't help each other out now and then."

"This has to be 'then,' Will," Lisa said. "We need to put this right behind us. I'll have to let Dr Peters know about this and suggest you join another group."

"Meaning?"

"I can't continue to work with you."

"Well, that's a great way to repay my kindness! What if I don't want to be cancelled? What if you're my favorite group therapist, and I promise to misbehave in some other group? What if I go on strike?"

"This is exactly why I've done the wrong thing, Will. I've jeopardized your treatment by putting my own needs ahead of yours. It's not done."

"But you're the first person to say your clinic is unconventional," Will said. "What if you've just discovered another kind of therapy? Call it 'help your therapist therapy.'"

"Very funny." Was she biting her lip? Yes. He'd almost made her laugh. Good. She didn't laugh very often, this beautiful woman. Surely someone as good as Lisa deserved to be happy.

"Honestly," Will said. "I'm only too pleased to help you, to help me. I thought about that last night. You remember I told you about my brother, James? I always pitied him, the way he martyred himself worrying about everyone else. Turns out he was onto something after all."

Will stared at Lisa. Was she following?

"Taking some responsibility by helping you last night?" he said. "That felt good. I've never done enough of that, to be honest. It actually feels good to be responsible! So what else can I do for you, Lisa, while I'm here? Since we're not even at the clinic, anything goes. Pillow fight? More coffee? I make great toast. You already had some last night. More scrambled eggs? Need the lawn mowed?"

Two could play this game. Ignore the currents running between them. He was good at this. He could banter with the best of them, and still have them wanting more. Ace playboy.

But when he stood with his mug and approached her, touching her arm, she jolted away as if stung.

The rejection hurt. He wasn't used to it.

"How about you use my shower," Lisa said. "Let me find you a t-shirt. I have a couple of large ones I use when I'm gardening that should just about fit."

She disappeared down the corridor and came back with a towel and a pale gray t-shirt.

"First door on the right," she said, all efficiency. Back in control. Telling him what to do.

As the hot water ran over his body, Will reflected on her change in attitude. Last night had been different. She'd been happy enough with him then. She hadn't flinched when he'd gone close. She'd allowed herself to be held; let him comfort her; had welcomed his embrace.

So why this sudden shift?

He turned off the water, hung the damp towel neatly over the top of the shower door, and dressed meticulously in her soft-as-a-whisper, too-small t-shirt, and inhaled deeply at its freshly laundered fragrance. He returned to the living room.

He astonished himself. He wasn't known for waiting for what he wanted, but if that was what it would take to impress Dr Lisa Bakker, that was what he'd do. Play the long game. Carefully. For as long as it took. Lisa was worth it.

…

How tempting, watching him there, handsome as could be, hair curlier when wet, leaning against her kitchen doorway, smelling like fruity shampoo. *Charmer.* Will looked good there, dammit. When he'd offered her a hug, she could so easily have stepped into those arms.

92

If only Will knew how long it had been since she'd had a man in the house, let alone a playboy. Wrong. Wrong. Wrong. To allow a client to even learn her home address, let alone inviting him in like this. *Wrong!*

She'd normally take Rossco out for a walk about now. He'd follow her around the house for a pat, tail thumping, and whine a little to be let out. Her forehead creased. She bit her lower lip. Rossco.

She squeezed her eyes shut lest the tears begin again, pressing her fingers into her brow. She must banish all these thoughts right now, get her act together, ignore the anguish gathering again. She forced brightness.

"Right, Will!" she said. "I rang the vet. Rossco's still with us. Not better, but no worse. That's something."

She looked at Will's chest, then turned away, hiding her longing.

"I mean it, Lisa. I'm here to help."

She caught her breath. He really was convincing. She closed her eyes. She was grateful, she really was. She was also scared. What had she done, allowing a client into her life like this? She absolutely could *not* allow it to go any further.

This man might be the most interesting person she'd met in her whole life, let alone the most desirable. How unfair! Tough. He was a client, first and foremost. Keep it breezy. That was the answer.

"Pancakes, coming up!" she said.

As she stirred the batter, Lisa counselled herself. She would get Will back to the clinic. She'd speak with Dr Peters straight away, before their first clients showed up. She'd done the wrong thing, but it was salvageable.

If her eyes took in Will's perfect torso, encased just right in her tight t-shirt, she couldn't let on, couldn't let her eyes linger there on the biceps that swelled just a little as he took his plate. He smelled so clean, his combed wet hair slicked back like a sun-kissed Elvis. And that devastating half-smile made her heart flip like a pancake.

"Maple syrup?" she asked, her voice bright, as if it had only ever been just about the food.

"Sure." His Aussie accent mimicked her American one as he pinned her with his eyes and flashed her another smile. He knew the effect he was having on her, damn him. She'd better get this timebomb out of her house, back to the retreat and out of her life. Fast.

Vegas appeared gradually as they left Boulder and the empty desert country, with Lisa at the wheel. Gas stations and auto repair shops, low-rise cheap apartments and laundromats, and a symbiotic mix of chapels, wedding-dress shops, divorce attorneys and pawnbrokers.

"Strange place, Vegas," Lisa said. "I'm still not entirely used to it."

"Yeah," said Will. "I never expected I'd be here. Glad I came, though, now. " He turned sideways and gave her that half-smile, eyes half closed. As they pulled up at the clinic, he radiated a quiet joy.

An answering flare ignited in her chest as she glanced across at him and met his gaze. She squashed it down. Warning. *Boundaries*. She must raise them higher and maintain her guard.

"I've got to see Dr Peters," she said, facing him as she turned off the engine. "You are doing very well, Will. Now, I am enormously grateful for what you've done for me. It was so good to have your company. I don't really know how to thank you, but we won't talk about that now."

"Pleasure was mine, Dr Bakker." His voice was a monotone. Did he realize what she had to do? She hoped she hadn't offended him, or worse, set back his treatment. This was why she shouldn't be falling for him. It was exactly why she had to retreat from him now, push him away, put up that professional barrier again, quick smart.

His next question startled her.

"Give me some homework, Lisa?"

So, he was keen to learn after all. She couldn't ignore that. Alright. She considered him. She really did believe in her profession. Will Huntley might look like the perfect man, right here in her car, but she knew better. She knew he was still vulnerable, and still a creature of habit – bad habits.

It was her calling to ensure that this man left the retreat better and stronger, more centered, more capable.

"Long-term goals, please, Will," she announced. "You're making excellent progress. Maybe do some research, up in our reading room. There are some great books about goal setting, and about motivation. Our retreat has a well-deserved reputation for helping clients develop insight into their behavior."

Will nodded.

"Knowledge is power, Will," she said. "When we understand ourselves, we have greater control over our choices in life. I tell all my clients they can keep on gambling without considering the consequences. *I* can't stop them. Only *you* can change your own behavior, Will."

He nodded again.

"So think about why you might want to behave differently," she said. "Imagine what you'd like to do instead of gambling. Consider the rewards that might come to you longer term, if you change your behavior now, and every time you find yourself about to gamble in future.

"How would you prefer to make your living, for example? Imagine some scenarios. Then, if your family does cut off your allowance, it won't be all bad, will it? You're so young, Will. You have many talents. You would finally have the chance to stand on your own two feet. You'd be fully grown, then, fully capable. No longer a child in any sense of the word."

"A playboy no longer?" He gave her that flirty half-smile. "What about a playman, Lisa?" he asked.

Lisa blushed and looked down. He must have guessed she was attracted to him. But she was no fool. She could trust her professionalism, her self-control, couldn't she?

Lisa quickly found her train of thought again, though she fussed with her keys, rather than risk looking at him.

"You've been gambling and forming relationships without considering the consequences," Lisa said. "Short-term thinking. Sometimes it's called 'going for low-hanging fruit.' Do I make sense, Will?"

"You do, Lisa."

"So, why not do some deep thinking about your motivation," she said. "Why do people do what they do? Why do you behave the way you do in certain circumstances? Consider what might make you behave differently. Think about the future, beyond today, beyond next week, beyond next month, beyond a year or two. Imagine what the rewards might be if you learn to think twice, and delay gratification."

"Delay gratification?" Will said, voice low, eyes hooded.

What was he insinuating, saying the word like that, as if he'd be grateful to undress her? She swung her head around to him in anger, pinning his eyes with hers.

"Have you even been listening to me, Will?"

"Oh, yeah."

She must get away from him, get out of the car, take her body elsewhere, away from his, immediately. How easily she could just lean towards him and be held again, explore the shape of his jaw with her hand and run her fingers through the hair at the back of his neck, brush her lips against his …

She snapped her gaze back, away from his. He was far too good at seduction. He was doing it to her, gazing at her with those half-closed eyes, leaning in … *She had never really felt this kind of longing. This Will* …

She opened the car door, sprang out, dropped her keys. He matched her. He was by her side. Handed her back her keys, then, like a gentleman, he held up her fresh white coat and helped her slip it on, so close to her she could feel the warmth of him, but refusing to touch her like she ached to be touched.

Lisa knew she should be suspicious of his motives. But he was so smooth. He knew just how far he could step without making her angry again, and she was grateful for the care he showed her, deeply grateful. She stared at her feet.

It was there between them. He was about to ask her something, something she'd have to refuse, but maybe he saw the warning in her eyes. He bit the side of his lip and stayed silent.

She stepped away and did up one button. The transformation was complete. Dr Bakker gave him a two-dimensional smile and turned her back on him, all efficiency.

She would have to tell Dr Peters about what had happened, straight away. How in a moment of panic she'd let Will help her out. How he'd ended up staying the night, how nothing had happened, how torn she felt about that. Professionally? Relieved. Personally? Maybe a tad disappointed. Maybe Will didn't find her attractive.

"Stop it!" she counselled herself. Will was a clinic client. Strictly off limits.

Chapter 10

Will returned to his room, smarting a little. He wondered at Lisa's change in attitude. It wasn't entirely unexpected. Of course a woman like Lisa Bakker wouldn't want to get entangled with him, a client. A playboy. A loser.

He'd paced all the corridors, done the calculations. He was just one of up to thirty clients. For all he knew, they were all in love with her. Who was he, anyway, to imagine he might be able to offer her anything for the future, beyond his ability to comfort her when her dog was injured?

She'd needed him then, alright, when she was so distressed she could barely function. But now she'd pulled herself together, he was back to being just another client.

Except he wasn't just any client. He was Will Huntley. Yes, he was a recovering gambler. Maybe he was a recovering playboy as well. But he was a hell of a lot of other things, too. They'd been exploring that, in their group sessions. Who was he, when he wasn't just acting on one impulse after another, giving in to his addictions to parties and women and gambling? What did Will Huntley stand for, apart from Fun 101?

There was Lisa, leading the group, so cool in her white jacket. Now there was someone with a purpose, committed to her calling, devoting her talents to helping others. While he'd been gadding about for a decade, her head must have been deep in her books and glued to her computer screen. What kind of discipline must that have taken? And here she was at the clinic, studious, accomplished, and impressive as hell.

What had he achieved in the same time, apart from a few thousand hangovers? A lot of laughs. Plenty of fun with people who'd come into his life and drifted out again just as quickly. The thought was enough to make him want another drink.

The vision of Lisa studying bothered him. She was serious, but sexy, too. Did she realise how attractive she was? Did she ever have any fun?

The gym equipment called out to him as he traversed the retreat for the fourth time that morning. He paced its confines like a caged dog.

He booked a session with one of the retreat's personal trainers. He vowed to try out every device, to push himself to do a few more than his targets each time. There was a goal. Personal Best. He'd had a sports teacher once who'd told him about the power of PBs. How had he forgotten? It must have been about the time his father went to bed, never to rise from it again. Well, he'd remembered now. He'd be sore tomorrow, but he didn't care. No pain, no gain.

After a savage session in the gym, he launched himself into the pool and swam till he could barely lift his arms. He stumbled up the steps and took a long, hot shower.

Under the jet of water, he closed his eyes and remembered the sensation of showering in Lisa's space just that morning, in among her little stock of shampoos and potions, her pink razor, her toothbrush, and her shower cap with a pineapple pattern, hung so neatly behind the door.

Lisa's home had been domestic, and strangely appealing. So different to the places he usually stayed – his bachelor pad back in Sydney, and, during his Huntleys travels, the succession of hotel and resort bathrooms, with their marble and mirrored walls.

Following his nose around the world on the company payroll, he'd cared most about the contents of the bar fridge and the reactions of his guests to the fancy decor. Now, when he contrasted them with the sheer homeliness of Lisa's place, he knew those neutral spaces bored him.

Glamor had its compensations, but it was impersonal. How odd. The crumbs on Lisa's coffee table and the chip in the handle of her simple blue mug held more value to him than any of those designer showcases.

Still, he could go some beer nuts right now. All that exercise left him famished. Dinner was an hour away. He might have to hit the reading room again.

This time, he pulled open a drawer and discovered some letterhead and envelopes. Why not?

Dear Pen,

I'll bet you never expected to hear from me, since you're the one who does all the writing (joke). But seriously, I reckon I've owed you an apology for a very long time. This is a decade late, but it's sincere.

I'm sorry I hurt you back when we were still at school. My father was dying, and it messed me up more than I realised to lose him. It's no excuse for the way I treated you, but it's an explanation, and now that I'm old enough to understand better why I behaved so badly, I know what I should have done. I should have been straight with you, and explained to you that I was hurting too much to give you the attention you needed. I wasn't mature enough to be in a proper relationship.

I understand now that what I did to you was cruel. I didn't mean to hurt you. I apologise.

I hope life is working out well for you. Whether or not you can forgive me, please know that I realise you deserved someone who treated you properly.

Thanks for the good times.

Best wishes,

Will Huntley

He sealed it in an envelope and sent it care of James. James kept in touch with the old crowd. He'd know how to find Pen. It was just the kind of helpful thing he'd do, to pass it on to her.

Will took the letter to the receptionist to be posted. Heading off to the tea bar, he smiled and punched the air. Two good deeds in twenty four hours! Unheard of.

…

Without Rossco, Lisa's home was far too quiet. *Rossco*. It rose up like a wail inside her. The loneliness. Nothing greeted her. No more jingle of his collar. No tapping of his paws on the tiles. No wheezy snoring, nor barks, nor whimpers. No crazy grins with his tongue lolling out …

She grabbed the phone and rang the vet.

Though they reassured her Rossco was doing as well as could be expected, all evening the ache grew. What if Rossco died! No more Rossco to lick her hand and tickle her with his old, gray whiskers.

Stomach tight and tortured, Lisa collapsed on the couch. She scarcely believed the turn of events. Had Will really slept here all night? The vision

99

of his head and shoulders in slumber on her couch hovered. She could sense again that hum of warmth between them, if not the buzz of something more compelling.

Stop it, she counselled herself, but she couldn't resist replaying events again, the whole previous evening, night and morning. She stood and walked to the window, suddenly doubting her sanity, chilled. What if Will had attacked her?

Hadn't they had it drilled into them at college, never to have a relationship with a client? They were vulnerable. It would be taking advantage of their trust. Moreover, as students, they'd read and presented to each other a litany of tragic cases, when therapists had thought better of all the advice and found themselves trapped with lunatics who'd injured or killed them.

So why had she let Will into her private life like that? What had been different about him?

Apart from Dr Peters' client notes, two full weeks of therapy with rapid improvement at every session, she still didn't know Will from a bar of soap. Many of the clinic's clientele were excellent liars, manipulators, conmen. It was a simple fact. They lied to themselves and to everyone else. Why on earth should she imagine Will would be any different?

Yet he hadn't made a move on her, despite those bedroom eyes. He'd done no more than comfort her. He'd driven Rossco to the vet then taken her home and held her. Exactly what she'd needed and no more.

She'd spent all night in her own bed, with Will asleep on the couch and he hadn't done a thing to compromise her sense of safety with him.

Maybe the media had it wrong and he was gay. That would explain it. All the best-looking men were gay at college. Maybe he'd made up those stories about the twins in the south of France. Come to think of it, had he said they were female twins? Well, yes, he had.

So maybe he just didn't find her attractive. A little part of her heart folded in on itself at the prospect. She'd always felt too tall. Art had never cherished her body. That had been a big part of their problems. Maybe she was destined to be alone.

Without Rossco to ground her and remind her of the joy of every moment, Lisa was utterly alone, quite abandoned. Depressed. It wasn't like her to feel this way. She pushed open the back door and stared up at the evening sky, still soft mauve towards the horizon. The stars began to appear. She let the cool of the night creep into her fingertips, felt her chest rise and fall with each breath, and listened for night insects.

As she drifted off to sleep that night, she remembered the warmth of Will's arm around her. They'd fitted together so perfectly. Her drowsy mind flirted with a silly fantasy that Will would actually recover fully and become a part of her life. She wanted him back here. No question.

Nonsense. It must just be the shock of Rossco's accident, the fact that he was still at the vet and the house felt empty. Was it possible to fall for a person on the rebound from a relationship with a dog?

If her eyes were open, she would roll them at herself. She needed to sleep, to turn off her mind.

The fantasy wouldn't go away, however. Rossco had been her rescue dog. Could Will become her rescue man?

The idea was insane. The man was Australian. There was no point dreaming of a man like that. Next thing she knew, he'd be back on a plane to Sydney.

...

The next evening, Lisa visited Rossco at the vet. Amid the smell of disinfectant, Rossco was barely recognisable, with large sections of his scraggy body shaved. He wore a huge conical collar to prevent him tearing out his stitches and eating his bandages. Deeply sedated, did he even recognize her? Could he have brain damage?

"Rossco, old pal?" She held her fingers to his moist black nose, behind the bars. It twitched a bit. He whimpered, opened his eyes, sort of smiled and panted. Then she left him to sleep.

At home, still worried about him, still lonely, Lisa tried to rally.

"Quit moping and get yourself out there!" she counselled herself. She pulled on her running shoes and set out. If it took fifty laps of Boulder City track and field to quieten her mind and let her sleep tonight, so be it, she determined.

She ran first along the route she usually walked Rossco, then on to the park. The baseball team was just packing up. On the spur of the moment, she took herself over to the coach. Whether or not Rossco recovered, she must fill in her spare time more productively. She always advised her clients to reach out and find friends after a loss, didn't she? Now it was time to follow her own advice.

"I'm Glen," the coach greeted her, face shiny with good will.

"Lisa." She panted, hands on hips, and smoothed back her loose strands of hair.

"You new in town?"

"Not exactly," Lisa said. "Maybe I could train with you all sometimes? I run a bit. I could cover the outfield; send the ball back."

"Sure, we'd love to have you," Glen said. "Tuesdays and Thursdays, six o'clock to seven-thirty. See you next Tuesday?" His smile was a bit too insistent, but maybe it was just what she needed.

"Sure. Thank you, Glen."

"Thank you, Lisa."

If Glen reminded her of a younger version of her school-teacher father, she tried to suppress the thought. *Nothing ventured, nothing gained.* She jogged back home and tried to forget the image of poor Rossco with tubes in every orifice, fighting for his life.

Suddenly, it was Will who leapt to mind; Will in her t-shirt, Will in her shower, Will here at home with her, offering her scrambled eggs. She must banish this ridiculous sense of longing.

She pulled out the vacuum cleaner, a tried-and-tested method of calming her down. And then she found it, down behind the couch. A soft gray jacket. *Will's!* She pulled it out and gave it a shake. Dogs' hairs rained down. There were black stains on the sleeve and on one side. Rossco's blood. She must soak it in cold detergent.

She hesitated above the bucket. She couldn't help it. No one was looking. She held the jacket in both hands, so warm and soft. She pushed it against her face, closed her eyes and inhaled, long and deep. Smells of Rossco and of Will. Oh, *yes.*

Then she plunged it down into the cold water to soak and set off back to finish the vacuuming.

Later that night, she tossed and turned in the dark, unable to sleep. At one o'clock, she sat up, dragged her computer to her lap and pulled up the International Skyrunning Federation page. She needed something realistic to fill her mind, a new dream. What was it she told so many clients? It was time for her to revive some interests, seek out new challenges, plan a holiday.

She clicked on a few links and found the events page. If she could find a competition in Europe, she could plan a training schedule for herself. This was more like it.

The screen was bright in the darkness. She let her eyes adjust and scroll through the options. That was it! A Mont Blanc skyrace, in early August. She'd always wanted to go. Why not this year? She could look forward to it, start training, to make the most of it. She wondered if Jilly might want to join her. This was a plan.

Chapter 11

Dr Peters had taken Lisa's group sessions for a couple of days when she'd told her about the turn of events. She declared Will's progress fine, and cleared Lisa to take the group again.

Lisa's heart performed a tiny tapdance as she walked to meet the group, but she kept her face calm.

Will was the only one there when Lisa arrived. He greeted her with a big smile she couldn't help but return.

"Any news about Rossco?"

"He's okay," Lisa said. "Not home yet. Still recovering. Thank you."

Home. The word triggered memories and they exchanged a glance. Lisa turned away first, her cheeks coloring.

"Are you excited I haven't asked for my phone, Lisa?" Will said. "Excited I've turned up again? Excited to find out I've doubled my salad bar intake and sped up in the pool and on the running machine?"

"Of course, I am. Yes. That's great, Will. Really good. Do you feel better for it?"

"I do actually," he said. "But you're hiding something, I can tell. Something good. Fess up."

Why did he do this to her all the time? He acted like he actually cared about her. It made her shy, as if she were a child once more. She peered down and opened his folder.

"Oh, no you don't, Lisa," Will said. "Come on. Didn't you tell me this clinic was a safe space for honesty?"

She glanced at him and smiled. It was lovely of him to care. Unusual. Most of the clients were fixated on themselves. Many were famous movie stars and musicians, happiest as the center of attention. It did them no favors.

"Okay, I'll tell you, since you insist," she said. "I've planned a vacation. In Europe."

"Not Monte Carlo or the casino coast, I assume. Could give you a few tips there, you know ..."

She loved the way he joked, but flashed him her "I'm warning you, bad boy" smile.

"Just as well we both know you're joking, Will," she said.

"Well done! You'll be able to treat any Aussie soon, Lisa. I've trained you. I can give you the accreditation. Write a review for the clinic. New market for you and your Dr Peters. Plenty of drunken gamblers in Australia. We're the world's biggest losers."

"Very good."

"It's true! I read all about it, up in your reading room. Italians are the next biggest gamblers, after Australians. Honest. You do have some interesting stuff up there, but not as interesting as your holiday. Come on. Give us some details. Where're you going? Skiing? More T-bars?

"No. Not this time. Running. Skyrunning."

"You love those mountains," Will said. "It must be about time you showed me your local mountains, Lisa. Show me this 'skyrunning.' I love a good run. I could run with you."

Her eyes snapped to his, alarmed. She'd love that, out in the wild, out on a track, just the two of them, free of the walls of the clinic, free of all restraint.

No relationships with clients. Full stop. *Danger*.

It shut down their easy banter.

She stared at her folder, flipped a few pages. Cleared her throat. "So," she said, changing the subject. "Do you have your goals ready to share with the group, Will?"

Suddenly, Will stood. He clenched his fist.

Lisa stood too. She was closest to the door, could press the hidden alarm if necessary.

"Will?" She kept her voice calm.

"I won't hurt you. I don't do that. But you might like to be aware, Lisa. You're hurting me."

"Oh?" She could still do it, be at that door and out in the corridor in a flash.

"You told me you could help people make changes in their own lives, didn't you?"

"I did."

"And do you believe in your own ability?"

"I do," she said. "I have the evidence."

"But do you believe it thoroughly? In your heart?"

"What do you mean, Will? What is this?" She'd never noticed him so serious. Gone was the veneer that life was a joke and he was the star joker. This Will was strong. Determined. With no trace of disorder. A man who knew his own mind and purpose in this world.

"Because if you don't, then you're a fraud, and so is Dr Peters," Will said. "And in that case, you're wasting your time, and you're wasting mine."

"Oh?"

"I'm here to change, Dr Lisa Bakker. With Dr Peters' and your guidance. And when I walk out that door for the last time next week, I intend to be a changed man. No longer a bad boy. No longer a playboy. No longer just a boy who lost his father too soon and never grew up. A man. An adult."

Lisa made a note in his folder. This was excellent progress. It gave her a chance to dodge the power of his attack.

"This clinic's done great things for me, Lisa. You've helped me understand a lot, and fast. You've changed my life alright, and for that I'm grateful. Always will be. But I need to ask you something."

She glanced up from the page.

"I've seen the way you look at me. You're wary. I'm going to come out and say it, because it's true. I sense something between us. Something good."

Lisa stared at him. Panic gripped her chest.

"Are you fighting your feelings for me?" Will said. "You're doubting yourself, but most of all – the way this is coming across – you're doubting me. And that's actually a bit insulting."

Lisa stayed silent.

"I can handle rejection as a lover, for example," Will said. "But if you were to reject me as a human being, as a person – if you believed I would always be damaged, and could never fully recover from addiction – then you never should have welcomed me to the clinic that first day, Lisa."

Lisa flinched at the word "lover." What was this flash of longing at her core? She held the folders close, like a shield.

"You believe people can change, and you devote your life to it, but you don't really believe people can change, because you worry I'll relapse," Will said. "Think about that. It would make you no better than a charlatan. And how do you reckon it would make me feel?"

Again, Lisa had no words.

"Subhuman," said Will. "And that would be offensive."

Lisa pulled herself to her full height, hiding the impact of his words. He was dead serious. Savage. What was he saying? His eyes were pure blue, in pain. His hand was out, reasoning with her. Had she inflicted suffering on him? She couldn't breathe – could only watch and listen.

"I'm coming to the end of my time here," he said. "I'm still hoping you'll take me out skyrunning with you. Show me your world. Why not chat out there in the fresh air, doing what we both love?"

When his eyes locked on hers, she ducked his gaze. She didn't want him to guess the possibilities running through her mind, of what might happen between them, out there on the mountain, alone together. Her thoughts were inappropriate. She dragged her mind back to the room, the walls, the carpet, and Will's words.

"I want to trust you, Lisa," Will said. "I want to trust that you truly believe that when I finish here, I will be as capable and in control of my life as any other person in this world. On an equal footing. And I'm walking out of this room now, and asking you to think about that. You can make a note in your folder there. I showed up in good time for my group session, and then I excused myself. And you know why."

Despite the obvious tension in his body, Will kept it in check. Lisa had treated violent men before. Relieved, she trusted that Will wasn't one of them. His display was dignified. He nodded politely at first one and then another two clients, who entered as he left.

The instant Will walked out, Lisa was busy with the group session. She pushed his accusations out of her mind – cleared the slate – so as to be fully present for Sam, Beth, and Chase.

It was only afterwards, as she wrote up her notes for each client, that she allowed herself to dwell on his words.

She opened Will's folder, clicked the pen off, then on, then off again. His demeanor had been active. Angry? Not exactly. He'd stood his ground, defended his position politely but firmly. This was rational behavior. Mature. Excellent, really.

But he'd called her a fraud. The criticism stung. If he'd tried to hurt her, he'd found a chink in her armor. She only wanted what was best for all her clients, didn't she? He'd made her feel she was letting him down. Was she? Was she a fraud?

Will was a puzzle. She flipped through his notes. At first he'd tried passive resistance and had tried to get her to take him to a bar, even the tea bar. He'd been sulky, typical of all her clients who had been given what they wanted all their lives.

But then he'd become interested and engaged. She'd been so pleased with his progress that she'd taken that huge professional and personal risk and invited him into her private life to help rescue Rossco. She'd benefited most, yet he'd insisted it had helped him, too. Of course she'd had to raise her professional barriers again to help his treatment. He was a client, not her friend. Was a client "subhuman?"

Nonsense. He was just manipulating her because she hadn't agreed to take him to the mountains with her. Clients did that sometimes. Insulted her or attacked. They acted out something they'd experienced themselves, or tried out some new kind of behavior in a safe space, aware their therapist was unlikely to reject them.

To be a sounding board was part of her power. So why did it hurt her so much that he'd walked away? Because he'd rejected her. And it stung. For all the polite delivery, it was a slap in her face.

She wrote that he'd turned up and then excused himself from their session, then slowly closed the folder and tidied the arrangement of chairs for her next group, still mulling over his words.

Her previous clients. Did she truly believe they were fully recovered from their addictions? She understood that relapse was a normal part of addiction recovery, but that each time, the time in the wilderness was briefer, and the time back on the straight and narrow, longer.

Lisa was no fraud. She took her job seriously, didn't she? Was she treating Will any differently to her other clients? This was an unconventional clinic, and a successful one.

There was the man who'd rediscovered his love of chess. He and Lisa would have their discussions in the reading room over one of the retreat's boards. At first, she could easily distract him, and even win a game or two. But by the time three weeks was up, he was back and showing the promise he'd shown in school. When he'd claimed victory in five moves, she'd known he'd recovered his earlier love of the game, and about a year ago she'd received a thankyou card from him saying he was competing on the global circuit again, making his way back up the ranks.

Then there'd been the woman who confided her long-held wish to decorate cakes. The retreat chef had been only too keen to take on a fresh challenge, and a number of staff and clients had joined in the classes. Lisa herself had learnt to make frangipanis out of marshmallows, and marzipan roses, slightly wobbly, but recognisable. She smiled now, remembering.

Will was right. There was every reason she should take him skyrunning with her. There was no chance she'd be tempted to do anything with him other than run and talk. She was a professional. She respected the rules.

She made a note in Will's folder, to raise his request with Dr Peters in their weekly debrief. Dr Peters had insisted Will stay in Lisa's group and told her she had full confidence in her professionalism. Still, she'd double-check the skyrunning would be okay. She returned to her own consulting room, more relaxed. Resolved.

She was about to put down Will's folder and reach for that of her next client when there was a tap at her door.

Was it Will again? She patted her hair into place and adjusted her white coat.

When she opened the door, though, it was Mindy.

"Phone call for you, Lisa."

"Who is it, please?" Lisa couldn't keep her annoyance out of her voice. Had the exchange with Will rattled her more than she expected? "Mindy, I really need you to take their name and details in future. You should know that by now. And if it's a supplier, please ask them to just email."

"You should be free right now, because you just finished group," Mindy sulked. She shrugged, mumbled an apology and headed back to the waiting room.

"Dr Lisa Bakker," Lisa said into the phone, closing the door.

"James Huntley here, Dr Bakker, Will's brother."

Lisa's heart jumped. He sounded so like Will she wondered if Will was playing a prank. Then she remembered Will's conversations about James; James the older brother, the one running the business, the one about to cut off Will's allowance.

Dealing with friends and families could be fraught. She was well aware that many gamblers burnt their loved ones. They let them down again and again.

"One moment please, Mr Huntley."

She checked her computer. The Huntleys appeared to have settled Will's account ahead of time. No problem there. Will had been booked in by his mother, Cynthia. James was named as a relative, as was Will's sister, Nicole. He wasn't a member of the press looking for an inside story. Everything added up.

"Yes, Mr Huntley," she said. "I can confirm Will is still with us. In fact, he's almost completed his treatment."

"Is it possible to visit him there, please?"

"You'd like to visit? Our visiting hours are two o'clock to four o'clock every day, on the premises. We prefer it if you don't take the clients out while they are in treatment. Certainly during the first visit. Which day are you planning to come? You're calling from LA? Tomorrow? I'll let you know." Lisa began an email to Dr Peters about James visiting.

"I have to inform you of our visitor policy, that you agree to message our clinical staff should anything trouble you during your visit," Lisa said. "And in some cases, our clients don't wish to meet their visitor, even when they've travelled quite a distance. That's always a possibility, due to the nature of their situations. I hope that's understandable under the circumstances. And you'll need to sign a confidentiality agreement before entering. Do you still wish to visit?"

He did.

"And you'll stay in Vegas for a few days? Yes? Multiple visits are acceptable as long as the client responds well. We'll have to confirm that

110

after your first visit. Some clients become upset. Others insist upon total privacy until they've completed their treatment. We need to give them the power over decisions about visitors, you understand.

"We'll contact you again this afternoon after we've raised this with Will," Lisa said. "Thank you. Yes. We'll let you know, either way."

Lisa lifted the phone again.

"Mindy. Would you ask Will to come and see me, please? Any time before two o'clock would be fine."

...

Will turned up twenty minutes later with a sheet of paper. Lisa was relieved. Impressed, even. It was true he'd made excellent progress.

Will seemed serious. Sincere.

After Will's accusations earlier in the day, it was more important than ever that she receive him respectfully.

"Thank you for turning up, Will," she said. "I have some news for you."

"Okay." His tone was guarded.

She could sense a change in him, imagine their relationship from his point of view. He'd taught her something, this Will Huntley. Quite apart from his generosity of spirit, and the way he'd comforted her after Rossco's accident, Will held himself with a new maturity. He stood taller. He looked well. Fit. If only there were no barriers between them. She shook her head.

"Please take a seat," she said. "Firstly, I heard your question this morning. You asked if I thought you were subhuman, and I need to tell you straight that that is not the case. Our relationship is a formal one here at this clinic, Will. You are a client and I am a therapist."

"I am a man, Dr Bakker. And you, Lisa, are a woman. And beautiful."

"I've been flattered before by clients, Will, but thank you for your kind words." If her heart hammered a little louder, she doubted he noticed. She kept her voice neutral. "Now, you've expressed an interest in running with me, in the mountains, and I want to reassure you that I'm taking your request seriously and will raise it with Dr Peters."

He'd leaned forward, elbows on his knees, hands in prayer position, fingertips at his lips. While he gazed straight at her and nodded slowly, it was hard to concentrate.

"Secondly, the reason I called for you is that I need to inform you that your brother James has contacted us. He's in LA, and he plans to visit you

111

tomorrow, here at the clinic, between two and four. I need to ask you how you feel about seeing him."

Tension struck his body. He sat back, stared at the ceiling, ran his fingers through his hair. Exhaled through tight lips.

"Old James, eh. Come to cut off my pocket money …"

Lisa remained silent, listening, waiting.

Will breathed again, looked across at her. "Well. I'm ready for him," he said. "So sure. I'll meet him. Tell him 'yes.'"

Will took his piece of paper and laid it on the coffee table, next to the cactus, fingers wide, hand flat. Lisa read the heading.

"Goals?"

"Goals," he confirmed. "I'm sorry I didn't stay for your group session this morning, but I feel strongly about this. It's important to me that you see me as … fully human, Lisa." He let the words sink in, eyes on hers, his gaze intense.

"Anyway, I thought you wanted to follow up on my goals," he said. "Check I'd done my homework."

Lisa nodded.

"Number one. No gambling. I don't do that anymore. Dumb idea. Not sure how I got into that in the first place. Been there. Done that."

"You know we can help you test that, Will," Lisa said. "Now that you truly don't want to gamble, you're ready for our desensitization test. You might remember we charted your baseline arousal, in your first week."

Will's eyes locked on hers at the word. Her blush spread, hot on her cheeks and chest. She felt it deepen, ashamed. She was a grown woman, not a schoolgirl. She was a divorcee, for heaven's sake. It's not like there were many mysteries. Or were there? What would it be like to make love to Will? She dropped her eyes, horrified at her lack of professionalism. Had he noticed? It was his eyes, dammit.

Will looked away, giving her a break. He nodded. "Desensitization testing," he said. "I'll do that. Nothing to lose." This time he made her laugh, releasing some of the tension between them.

Relief bubbled up through her. She took a deep breath and let her shoulders relax. Grown-up Will was every bit as appealing as his playboy self. More so, with that sense of fun still lurking under the new veneer of maturity, just beneath that newfound gravitas.

"Goal number two," he said. "Be less selfish. I didn't realize, but your letting me help you with Rossco the other day was a turning point for me. I've never had that Mr Reliable reputation. But you trusted me to help you. And I wanted to."

Lisa nodded, smiling.

"I'd never really understood that giving is receiving," Will said. "And I want to do more of that. I finally get it. I've thought a lot about this. Swimming a lot of laps, running miles on those boring machines, I've been training on the inside. Buff outside? Buff in here." He flexed a bicep and then pointed at the side of his head, and they shared another laugh.

Lisa had to turn away. She needed to dial down the currents running between them.

"Goal number three," Will said. "Go skyrunning with you. Now, while I'm in here, I know that part of this is up to you, and maybe up to Dr Peters, and I'd prefer to go with you this week, before I leave. But I'm willing to wait."

He gave Lisa a confident smile. "I've been good," he said, slapping his thighs. "I've been a model client. Didn't even nick a bread roll, and that's saying something, the amount of kilojoules I've been burning. But seriously. If you won't take me with you one day this week, there's always next week. And the next week, *Lisa*."

She sat straighter, paid attention. No one had ever said her name like that. With such longing. It was more than the Australian accent. It was a prayer. As if he cherished her. All of her.

Will leaned forwards and opened his hands to her, softly. An entreaty.

"Next week, when I'm out of here, I will ask you as a free man, a better man. Because dammit, if you don't believe in your power to help me make the changes I want to make in my life, I sure as hell do. And you have no right to take that belief away from me."

She admired his resolve.

"When I stand up and leave this place, your influence will go with me, no matter what you believe," he said. "So really, it will be over to you, and what your own goals might be. You don't have to give me an answer about that right now, by the way. Or ever. That part will be up to you."

Lisa inhaled as he flashed her the challenge.

113

Over to her? Her own goals? Was he serious? Her heart leapt. It pulsed in her ears. Was Will intimating there might be a future for the two of them. Together?

Will pointed at his sheet of paper.

"Goal number four," he said. "Support myself. This one's a bit complicated. But I've had some time to think. I've worked in the family business since I was a kid. Retail. Jewelry." As he smiled, Lisa could imagine him as a child, with slightly messy hair, always on the run.

"I used to have to assemble the fancy bags, from when I was younger than I can remember, put stickers on the ring boxes, that sort of thing, polish the tops of the glass cabinets after trading, vacuum after busy sales days."

Lisa smiled.

"Then, when I was old enough, I helped out with customer service. I greeted them at the door, helped with trade around Valentine's Day and Christmas," he said. "I remember my grandmother, Eleanor. She showed me how to count out change at the big old till."

When she met his gaze again, confidence beamed out of him.

"I've got retail in my blood. I just never owned it before. I thought everyone knew this stuff, but I can do it with my eyes closed. And I can clinch a sale."

"I just bet you can, Will."

He rewarded her pun with a laugh.

"So," he said. "I just need me a store." He'd put on a crazy American accent. "James visiting tomorrow is perfect timing. I'd like to convince him to buy into my shop; give me some kind of advance. This is achievable. We need to explore Boulder City. Check out what shops are already there, scope the competition."

Will placed his hands on his knees and leaned forward. "I have a suggestion," Will said. "Maybe you take James and me skyrunning with you. He was a runner, you know. At school. Cross country. Pretty fit. He won't cark it on us. And after that, James and I can explore Boulder City together. Check out what's there, and what's missing."

Will opened his hands to her. "So, I could use your help to get to know Boulder City better," he said. "But if you're not willing to give it, I can do it alone. I can do this. I trust myself. And whether or not you want to be involved, well, that's up to you."

Will sat back, and put one hand on his heart. "Me? I feel good," he said. "Haven't been so healthy in years. Good food, no alcohol, and plenty of exercise, day in and day out. I like feeling good. This place has been the best. I'm willing to admit I only agreed to come here 'cause the food was free, but Dr Peters — and you. I've sorted a few things that needed sorting. You've turned my life around, Lisa."

Lisa reached for the folder of her next client and tried to ignore the excitement clamoring at her chest; that Will might not go back to Australia after all, as she'd assumed.

Clients' plans at this stage in their treatment could be all over the place. Her job was to listen and encourage and not become involved. She'd do Will no favors if she started to make assumptions about his plans and probe too deeply. None of this was about her.

. . .

Out in the corridor, Will squared his shoulders. That had gone alright. His time would soon be up. He'd be out and "recovered," a free man, free to date Lisa. Free to approach her as an absolute equal, not a gambler, no longer one of the clinic's clients.

That was his fifth goal, but he wouldn't risk sharing it with her yet. It was the one that excited him the most, out there on the horizon, like the gleaming prize after a long, long quest. To love Lisa, that was the biggest goal of all. The one worth fighting for. Every other distraction? He'd say "no." To win Lisa, he'd need to do this right. All of it.

Chapter 12

Will met James in reception.

"Bro! Can't believe how good it is to see you, James!"

"Bro."

"Graying at the temples a bit, James... You know, you almost remind me of ..."

"Dad?"

Will nodded, laughed and clapped him on the shoulder. Had they ever discussed their father? This felt good. More equal.

There in reception, they gave each other a quick embrace – more of a pat on the back. Will sensed respect in James's glance. The new Will was toned, terrific, healthier than he'd been since school. This clinic was something. By contrast, James looked tired. Maybe the financial worries were taking a toll.

"Maybe you should book yourself in for a few days, James," Will said.

"Tasteful, alright," James said. He took in the white theme. "Seems to be working for you."

Will gave James a quick tour. His heart leapt when they crossed paths with Lisa in an upstairs corridor, carrying the usual bunch of folders.

"James, I'd like you to meet Dr Lisa Bakker, one of the clinicians," Will said. "Lisa, James."

"Lovely to meet you, James," Lisa said. "I believe we spoke on the phone yesterday. Welcome to our retreat."

"Thank you, Dr Bakker. Impressive place you have here."

Lisa smiled. "Thank you," she said. "Well, enjoy your visit, Mr Huntley. See you in our group session as usual, Will?"

116

Will nodded as she headed past, away from them.

The brothers rejected the library and tea bar and settled instead in a corner of a large meeting room on the ground floor, their conversation made more private by the subtle splash of an indoor fountain.

"Looking good, Will," James said.

"Feeling good. You look a bit sick, mate."

"Thanks, mate. Jetlag. Plus, you know why I'm here. This won't be an easy conversation."

"I guessed that," Will said. "Mother warned me. Said you're on a cost-cutting mission; got the knives out for me."

"It's not easy," James said, "to cut you off the payroll. To clip your expenses. It's not like I want to leave you in the lurch. I promised Father I'd look after you."

Will studied James. Had Will himself caused those worry lines? He cleared his throat and sat back. *Guilty.*

A tinkle of ice cubes against glasses brought him back to the present as a waiter walked past with drinks on trays. Visitors and clients in other corners of the large room looked up. Visiting-time refreshments. Very civilized.

James reached for a sparkling mineral water, and Will did the same.

"Bet this impresses you," said Will. "Me drinking water. Told you I'm a new man."

"Off the hard stuff?"

"No other choice in here," Will said. "But guess what, James? I've never felt better. Never gave myself the chance to try life without it. Might be the first time since my teens I've actually been sober for more than a week. Highly recommended."

"We all tried to tell you that, Will, but you never wanted to listen."

"No," Will said. "Guess I never did understand why you should tell me what to do."

They stared at each other. Would they fight after all, like old times?

"You're too smart, Will."

"What do you mean?"

"You know if we fight, it just makes it easier to cut you off."

"Bro! You're hurting me. You don't think I'm genuinely glad you showed up?" Will held up his glass. "Cheers. You thought I'd tell you to fuck off. But I actually need to thank you for bankrolling this place. It's been incredible. Really worthwhile. Straightened up a few things for me."

"Really? Forgive me, but how long do you reckon this is going to last?"

"What?"

"No booze. Good behavior. Fit and fabulous."

"Yeah, thanks, mate. Not. For having so much faith in me." Will rolled his eyes at James and looked away.

"Sorry," James said. "You didn't deserve that. You've obviously made some fantastic progress. We all want you to make a go of it – to find health, wealth and happiness on the right side of the law. All that."

"Yeah. Well, come on. Out with it. Say what you've come to say."

"It's not all about you, actually. I'm forced to do this. Business is going broke. We're fighting it, and we're getting some wins. We put a few new things in place; new ideas, revamped the website, made Jim a bit of a star. And the trend is good. Excellent. But you know how it is; how it's always been in retail, I guess. The competition never stops. So we've all got to be on our toes. Everyone in the business has to contribute. Actively. You can't imagine how hard it's been for me, this trip. Having to confront Mother and you."

Will stared at James and took a swig of water. The bubbles burned the roof of his mouth.

"Worst thing is, I kind of understand why you took the path you did," James said. "Father adored you, and I was jealous. It's true. The way you won trophy after trophy. You couldn't put a foot wrong. It killed us all, the way he went, wasting away like that. But you took it hardest of all. Even I understand that now."

Will was silent. He spun the ice cubes in his glass, and watched them settle. "Yeah well."

"Yeah," said James. "So, we all have to grow up eventually. If the business dies, we'll all be left with nothing."

Will snorted.

"What's up?" James asked.

"Oh nothing," Will said. "Just contemplating poverty. What the hell, James. What do you think's up? Unlike you, I know what it is to be broke. I know, and I never, ever want to go back there, back on the sidewalk, watching what food people are tossing in the trash can, and you're so hungry you want to grab it."

The brothers stared at each other.

"No money, eh?" Will said. "Easy for you, MD of Huntleys, wage assured. It sucks to be the second son throughout history, eh. Maybe I should have joined the military. Isn't that what second sons did back in the day? Or joined the church. Become a preacher."

They both laughed at that.

"We'll work it out," James said. "I'm just saying no more handouts. You've still got your car. I try to give it a run once a month, even though it's unreliable. Bloody Italian lemon. You should sell that. And your apartment. Is that still empty? At least rent it out. You're hardly destitute. So no more loans. No more expenses. And if you're working for Huntleys, we need to see the evidence."

"Yeah. I got it."

James stared at him, bracing for a fight, but Will just smiled.

"Told you this place was good, bro," Will said. "Look at that! You cut off my income and I'm so bloody together I'm not even going to fight you!"

"Miracle alright," James said. "So tell me. How come you've grown up all of a sudden?"

Will shrugged. "This place happened at the right time for me? Dr Peters is a world expert. I guess it's a bit like getting the best Olympic coach. It can't hurt. And staying sober. Having time to think between one party and the next."

James raised his eyebrows.

"Even old Jim," Will said. "We had a couple of chats on the phone. First time ever. Did he tell you? And that Dr Bakker you met? Lisa. She's amazing. I only ever get to see her in group sessions, but she got me wondering, alright. About choices. And goals."

Will looked at the fingers of his right hand, remembering the goals he'd shared with Lisa the day before.

"I was never into self-reflection," Will said. "I avoided all that mind stuff until now. But I know I never meant to be hungry and on the street. I know I never planned to be a gambler and all that playboy thing. You know how the media gets hold of something and won't let go. Ever since Penelope. Penelope bloody Simpson and her poison pen."

"Pen," James said, twirling the ice in the glass, then placing it down. "It's bad luck having your first girlfriend become a gossip columnist! She clung to you like a liana vine and lashed out when it was over. Her career would be nothing without all those bad-boy stories about you. I still can't believe she had you followed in Italy!"

"Wasn't all bad, bro," said Will. "It gave me kudos. Celebrity status. Got me into better parties!"

"Yeah?" said James. "At what cost, though? A decade of bad press? Bad for the Huntleys brand. Bad for you. Still, you say you're on the mend now? On the up and up?"

"Yeah," said Will. "I even wrote Pen an apology. I'm hoping you'll deliver it for me. I posted it home. If I'd known you'd show up I could have just handed it over. And I helped rescue a dog; Lisa's dog, as it turns out, the clinician we met in the hall. She's incredible, and no, I'm not just talking about her looks. She gave me the big welcome while Dr Peters was still away. So, right from the start, she got me to think – about behavior. Choices. Goals. She's made me really understand about short-term rewards and longer-term thinking."

Will took another sip of his water and sucked on an ice cube. "This water's alright, you know. No hangover." He savored it. "Man, I just let things happen for years. One thing after another."

"You sure did."

"But hey, let's talk about the future! I'm making plans. And yeah, it's time to rent out my apartment or sell it. Get some other income. I'm going to need it because I've got a plan or two. So, you caught up with Mother? How is she? How did she take your special news? You cutting her off, too?"

James nodded. "Actually, visiting Mother worked out well. I take it you've met Emile, the Belgian boyfriend?"

"Yeah, Emile the handy Belgian boyf. They still in that 500-year-old place in Provence? I stayed with them for a few days, before I headed for the Riviera."

"He seems to make her happy," James said. "Emile the vagabond handyman. Turns out he's got all sorts of skills. Did Mother tell you they

120

want to open a branch of Huntleys in that place; in the front room? Did you see that huge chandelier?"

"Couldn't miss it. It was the only thing in the room when I was there. Huntleys in France, eh? I like that idea."

"Our family!" James said. "Mother ends up settling in just the right kind of fashionable tourist town, on a corner in the main street, with windows all along both sides, and that chandelier …"

"Yeah, well," said Will. "I've got a theory now about Mother and her obsession with French antiques. Turns out it's not so bad. Diversionary therapy. She's been comforting herself in the wake of Father's death. I went for women. She went for French furniture."

"On Huntleys' payroll."

"Well, she probably earned it," Will said. "Back in the day, if not now."

"Unlike you. How's the brand building going? Isn't that what you're supposed to be doing for Huntleys right now?"

"Yeah," said Will. He stared at the bottom of his glass.

"And you managed to get the Huntley name out there again with those twins from the Riviera," James said. "Great coverage. Wrong key messages but great placement. Tabloids went wild as usual."

"They got it wrong again," said Will. "Those twins dumped me, not the other way around."

"The point is …" James began.

The waiter came back with the big silver jug and topped up their glasses. Will saw him stare at James's phone. Maybe the staff were paid extra to check the visitors. It must be an ever-present danger; visitors bringing contraband and breaking rules. Why hadn't he thought to ask James? Nah. Just as well. The straight path. That's what Will had his eye on now.

Actually, Will was looking at James's photo of his mother's chandelier, and then the Google map of her property, in prime position in the village. It really was retail gold.

"Yeah. Good one." Will nodded. Had James ever spoken with him for this long? Ever included him in strategic decisions about the business? This felt good.

"So Emile's making the cabinets, and Mother's doing what she's always done best, trawling for treasure at the markets, collecting stock," James said. "They'll display some of Jim's best rings, and I hope we'll also be able to run a line of affordable contemporary jewelry there, designed in Australia. There's this line called Stellar. Long story. Anyway, I want there to be something for everyone who comes in."

"That's good." Will nodded again. "It's funny. I never realized it's an advantage, being a shop kid. Not everyone grows up with it like we did. I've been thinking about that a lot. Making plans. Imagining what should sell and why."

James narrowed his eyes.

"You probably think I'm scheming, wanting to rip you all off," Will said. "But being here, it's made me grow up. I've got choices. And I can make them with or without you. I want to make something of myself. Make Jim proud. First time for everything, eh?" Will stood and strode to the window.

James stood too, stayed silent, then joined him at the window.

"Yeah, I've had a few schemes," Will said. "Maybe even a scam or two. I'll admit it. A few more excuses to party."

"You gave us the runaround alright," said James. "High distinction in making excuses."

The weariness in James's eyes hit Will in his gut. What was this? Was this regret?

"Yeah, bro," said Will. "Too many excuses, I know. But now, I realize they did no one any favors. Least of all me. Short-term thinking. Well, I'm changing that. I'll prove it to you."

Will looked James in the eye. "You've come a long way to visit me, and I appreciate that. And I reckon I've never thanked you for all you've given me so far. So this can go two ways, bro. We can fight, or we can cooperate. Yeah, I could fight you, and I might yet. Get some lawyers involved. Force you to sell Huntleys and just split the profit once and for all."

James stiffened. Glared at him.

"But I don't want to do that. Give old Jim a heart attack. Cut you all off for good. Have Father's ghost spooking me all my life. That's no way to go forward. No. What I'm aiming for is cooperation. Collaboration. Mother's French branch? That's a great idea and I reckon she'll make it work."

Will waited until James nodded.

"And I want the same chance," said Will. "I want to open a shop here in Nevada, and do it my way. There's plenty of people who come to Vegas and hate it. Hipsters. But there's a lot more to this place than casinos. I can't wait to get out of here and explore the place. Not just deserts. Plenty of reserves, parks, beautiful wilderness."

James leaned forwards.

"Ever heard of Boulder City?" Will said. "Hear me out, bro. There's no gambling at all there. It just doesn't exist. Never did. Something to do with the past, from when they built the Hoover Dam. Prohibition and all that. Yet Boulder City thrives."

When James gave a nod, Will continued.

"And that's where I want to open my shop, my own Huntleys. It's not jewelry I've got in mind, though. I want to do my own thing. Gotta do more homework. Soon as I get out of here, that's where I'm going; away from all these casinos and out into some fresh space for a change. Yep, that's my plan."

James nodded again. "Mother was right to book you into this retreat. You've actually changed. I like the new Will." He clapped Will on the arm.

"You don't have to like me or my plans. I can raise all of the capital myself. Sell my Sydney apartment. Prices have skyrocketed over there, haven't they? There's plenty there for me to invest. And I really mean 'invest.' Not lose, for once in my life." Will shook his head and smiled. "Do you know how that feels? To actually accept some responsibility, to have a longer-term plan? You do, don't you? You were born that way, the eldest, the sensible one, trustworthy. James Huntley the third."

Will smiled at him, then shook his head. "I could never have that place in the family," Will said. "You took it. So now I see that's part of why I went the other way. Irresponsible little Will. A bit mischievous. I had the time of my life. I loved that freedom. All of it. I pushed it for what it was worth, didn't I? And bugger the consequences."

He took another ice block and crushed it with his teeth. "But you know what? I reckon it would have killed me. Just a few weeks ago, I was sleeping rough. Can you imagine? Gave me the fright of my life. Rock bottom."

They wandered back to their chairs. James stared at him over the top of his water glass. "Well, you're different," he said. He placed his glass on the coffee table. "You're stronger. Confident in a new way, a better way. Maybe you needed that fall so you could pick yourself up."

The brothers nodded at one another.

"We all want you to lead a good life, Will, a better one. Jim wants it. Nicole. Mother. Father would have wanted you to find your feet. Although you always had better feet. Faster ones, anyway. And I resent that, Will Huntley. Never did get over the fact that you could beat me in the two-hundred-metre sprint, even though you're four years younger. Unfair."

They laughed.

"I need to thank you and Mother and Jim and Nicole for this chance you've given me," Will said. "When I get out next week, it's like I get another chance at life. I'm not planning to waste it this time."

Will gave James a steady stare. He meant what he said, and James was listening, taking him seriously.

"I actually like the sound of your Boulder City shop," James said. "You were always our best salesperson, when you actually turned up and put your mind to it. Customers loved you. The way you could clinch a sale! I envied you. Until you turned your back on serving. What happened? Did you just get bored with it? You were so good."

Will shrugged.

"You could make anything work, once you decided on it," James said. "You just kept changing your mind, though, wandering off after some new adventure or another. So I really hope you make your dream a reality. You know there's a lot of work between an idea and making it happen? What if you wander off track again?"

"I'm done with that," said Will. "Going to really give this a go. Keep my eye on the prize."

Would James know what prize Will had in mind? It was too soon to divulge the whole Lisa dream.

"Well, that always worked for you in sport, anyway," said James. "You've got it in you. We all want you to come good. And if you can do it, really make it work, there might be something in it for Huntleys. With the French branch, it will make us global. We could have branches on three continents. Father would be glad we're keeping the family together, thriving."

"'The family,'" said Will. "Believe it or not, I've missed you. For a day or two there, anyway. Tell me about Nicole."

The brothers talked for the full two hours and embraced when the time was up. Will accompanied James to the door, felt the Vegas afternoon heat gush inwards as it opened. He watched James walk away with one of the free clinic notepads and pens in his top pocket. Good. They'd written a list of questions about Boulder City to explore. Looked like James was onto it.

...

Lisa could see the entrance to the clinic from her consulting room, and observed James depart. Both men were wildly attractive, their likeness stunning. When she'd first met James, upstairs in the corridor, she'd wondered if she was seeing double.

James was older, a little taller, his hair a little darker and more neatly cut, and he was dressed more formally, in a suit, his expression serious.

She was pleased that even after their altercation, Will had introduced her with respect. Then, he'd even given her just a hint of that bad-boy smile, and with James turned the other way, followed it with a look of desire so loaded it had smoldered.

She passed them, shook her head and counselled herself as she made her way back to her room. "*So* not getting involved," she whispered to herself as they headed in the opposite direction. Yes, it was time to discuss Will with Dr Peters again. Check her feelings weren't straying into dangerous ground. Thank goodness she was such a sensible person.

...

Lisa stopped in at the vet on her way home. Rossco was still in the wars, shorn and bandaged; an alien with a collar like a lamp shade. He jerked his head up off the floor of the cage and whined with joy as she fondled his ears, licking her hands and wrists.

"Hi, Rossco. Good boy. You being good?"

"He keeps pulling his stitches out," said the assistant. "We're sedating him to help him rest and recover. He's not quite ready to go home yet, unless you're able to give him the antibiotic injections? We'd really like to observe him a bit longer. It could be the medications, but he's still not eating much."

"Rossco, my baby? Off your food? That doesn't sound like you. Get better! You can do it!" His tail thumped on the floor of the cage as he closed his eyes and let her stroke his head. She hated to leave him, but knew he was in the right place for now.

With a heavy heart, Lisa returned to her empty house.

A phone call from Jilly lifted her spirits.

"How are you, Jilly? How's the job?"

"Just as well I love being run off my feet,Lisa. You know me. It's a ton of fun. I still can't believe they pay me. They've just given me the professional development portfolio — team building exercises, all that kind of thing. I ran a survey and you wouldn't believe all the ideas that came back. I'm planning a scavenger hunt around Seattle for all the new graduate recruits, next Tuesday, with a harbor cruise that night."

"Jilly, you're bad. Not another harbor cruise. Didn't you end up throwing someone overboard last time?"

"He asked for it. I threw the life buoy in straight after."

"Wasn't that Ryan? You were together for months, weren't you? Before Luis. Who's the latest again?"

"Still Carlos. His mum doesn't like me, so it won't last. So, how's your own love life, Lisa?"

"Not a lot of water in Nevada."

"Ha ha." Jilly's laugh was a joy. "Seriously."

It felt good to share her news. Jilly had always been a great listener.

"Oh no, Lisa. Poor old Rossco. How did that happen?"

Lisa told her the whole story in a rush.

"Hang on, who's this Will? I should phone you more often. Is there actually a man in your life? This is big, Lisa. Tell me everything. I told you, you're ready for love."

"Oh, it's nothing like that. He's just a client."

There was silence, as deep as if a bomb had gone off. Jilly was rarely short of words.

"I mean," Lisa said into the silence. "He's not actually my client. He's Dr Peters' client. Well, I see him in group … Jilly? You still there? So, this Mont Blanc trip. I've booked our accommodation. It's a kind of bed and breakfast. Looks really quaint on the outside, very 'Heidi,' but the inside looks great. Comfortable. We'll be able to rest up before the big run."

"Oh no you don't," said Jilly. "You do *not* change the subject so fast. You're not going to tell me more about this *client* who was at your house? *At your house*, Lisa? How old is this guy? If he's not actually your client, surely you can share a few details."

"Confidentially, of course, he's twenty-nine. Australian. Kind of an heir to a jewelry fortune. Except not much of a fortune anymore. A real womaniser. Playboy, actually. Are you interested in this guy, Jilly? Don't you have enough men in your life?"

Damn, Jilly. That would be just her luck. That Will would fall for Jilly. Every man did. Funny the thought had never bothered her before. She must be really ready for a vacation.

"So you had a hot Australian at your house," said Jilly. "Hot and kind. This is good."

Lisa looked over at her couch, where Will had slept. It was true. He had been hot. And he had been kind. Was still hot. Yes. It had been good to have him at her house.

"He wants to go skyrunning with me," Lisa said.

"*And* he's a skyrunner? This guy sounds perfect for you."

"He's not a skyrunner, but he's a bit of an athlete."

"So where will you take him? Up Virgin Peak?"

"Are you teasing me? I haven't decided whether or not to take him at all. He's still at the clinic. I need to check it's okay with Dr Peters. He leaves at the end of the week, so we might go in a day or two while his brother's in town. He ran cross country at school, apparently."

"Chaperone."

"I hadn't thought of it that way," Lisa said. "I've taken other clients skyrunning. Diversion therapy."

"Uh-uh. Maybe this 'Will' can be *your* diversion, Lisa. This is good. Better and better."

Their easy banter halted.

"No, it's bad," Lisa said. "I know you said I should just have some fun, and this Will is a ton of fun. Mr Mischief. But you and I are both aware of the rules. And I'm pretty sure he's still out of bounds. So technically, he could be 'worse' for me."

"Don't tell me that." Jilly groaned. "You've already had 'worst.' You had Art, remember?"

"Oh God, Jilly. Maybe I'm doomed."

"No. You can't think that way about anything. Remember? It's called 'catastrophizing' and when our clients do it we show them how ridiculous it is."

"But that's exactly it, Jilly. Our profession. My whole reputation. I know I shouldn't have brought Will to my place. I never break the rules. But I got the phone call just before my last session for the day and I needed to go to Rossco. I was just so shocked. I wouldn't have been able to drive safely."

"Go on," said Jilly. "Spill."

Lisa shared the basic details.

"He stayed overnight?" Jilly said.

"Well, it's not like we actually did anything. Not like you're thinking. He just stayed. On the couch. And nothing happened, so that was okay. You've gone silent. You still there?"

"I'm still here. So, what's the problem?"

"Well, you know, Jilly. You're aware of our clientele. Addicts. Gamblers. He's a gambler. And you know how they can relapse. And Will's resolve has yet to be tested back out in the world. But so far so good, and he's agreed to the follow-up program. I believe his outcome will be excellent. Even in his short time with us, he's made many changes. He's really lovely. He seems to have his gambling under control. And his drinking. He doesn't do that anymore."

"You've fallen for this guy, Lisa."

"But that would be wrong, wouldn't it?" Lisa said. "We're not allowed to fall in love with clients. It's forbidden. It's like Counselling 101. We can't go there. Power imbalance. Misuse of professional trust. Vulnerable clients, blah blah blah. It's impossible. Am I a fraud, Jilly?"

"That's ridiculous, Lisa. I don't know anyone who works harder than you. You're an excellent therapist. Isn't that why you got both those promotions, and you already told me about all those positive evaluations? You kick goals."

"Thanks, Jilly. But I checked it again on the internet. In case the American Psychological Society had updated their policy, but they haven't. No sexual relationship with former clients for two years."

"Just because there's a rule, doesn't mean it doesn't happen," said Jilly. "It happens all the time. That's why they had to make the rule, right?"

"But ..."

"You do follow the rules, Lisa. It's endearing. But it's not that common, believe me. Now let me finish. Why shouldn't you fall in love? I already told you it's time you had some love back in your life."

"So I'm not crazy?"

Chapter 13

Will arrived early for the group session. He'd swum again, and thought about what to wear. Though he'd hauled on Lisa's freshly laundered too-small tee-shirt, he didn't want to embarrass her. No. He added a soft denim shirt, buttons undone, sleeves rolled up. Lisa's shirt was only just visible beneath. Perfect.

In the circle of white chairs he chose one opposite where Lisa would sit, and a little to the left.

The others wandered in, Sam, Beth and Chase. When Lisa entered, her eyes halted at his chest. Did she recognize her t-shirt? Then they lit on his own for a fraction of a second. Alarm? Excitement. A little jolt ran between them.

She sat down and greeted them all without a hitch. Good.

"I'm so pleased with all of you," Lisa said. She gave each of them eye contact. "Dr Peters tells me you're all making great progress in your one-on-ones. But in this session, I want to find out how much you each believe *you* have changed." She opened one hand to them, to invite their participation.

"I want you to share, just among ourselves, and confidentially as always, the changes you've noticed in yourselves since day one, the realizations you've come to, about the reasons for your past behaviour, and how you expect you will behave differently in future, when you go back out into the world," Lisa said. "Would anyone like to volunteer to begin?"

"Sure," said Will. "Unless anyone else wants to go first?" Sam looked relieved, Beth smiled and Chase gave him a "be my guest" wave.

"Stage all mine, Chase?" There was a general chuckle. "I don't mind admitting I was lost when I came here," he said. "I was like tumbleweed, blowing any which way. Well, to be specific, if there was temptation, I took the bait every time without thinking. Alcohol, women and gambling? I could never get enough."

Chase gave a nod. "Yeah. I've been there, man."

Will continued. "Being here is the first time in more than a decade I've allowed myself to think about all that, to accept I have choices. That I don't need to swig down every last glass of beer or wine in sight. Being sober is great. I haven't been this fit in years, and I'm planning to stay that way." He flexed a bicep and hammed up his strength. He made the others laugh.

"Fit and sober," Will said. "Being sober helps me think twice about everything else. And I can't see any sense in gambling. Not going there again. No way. As for women?"

Lisa crossed and recrossed her legs. Will sat up straighter. He wanted to appear decent, like James. He was ready, wanted to show Lisa how much he'd grown; changed for the better.

"Well, I don't mind admitting I was a playboy," Will said. "Internationally acclaimed. But I realize now, I don't need to behave that way for the rest of my life. Don't get me wrong. I love women. I love everything about them. Their eyes, their bodies, their generosity, the way they dance. But that doesn't mean I have to have relationships with them all."

Sam glanced at him as if considering him for the first time. He gave her his half-smile and she sneered, but Beth beamed at him.

"Say, Beth? Date?" Will said. Everyone laughed. "And I want you to know that I'm not as bad as the media makes out," he said. "All that 'Huntley heartbreaker' stuff? That was partly just bad luck with my very first girlfriend, the gossip columnist. Not that I blame her. I took up your suggestion, by the way, Sam. That apology letter is on its way."

"That's great, Will. It's often easier to blame others than to examine our own behavior," said Lisa. "But to make choices about the future, we need to learn to reflect."

"You're right," Will said. "I'm not denying I've been a playboy. But the poison Pen made me out to be worse than I am. Most people've had a few relationships. Often they're not sure who broke up with whom. From Penelope Simpson's point of view, it was always me doing the breaking up. And somehow she's found out about almost every relationship I've had since. And written it up, making me out to be the heartbreaker every time. I guess I played up to that reputation, but I don't want to do that anymore."

Sam stared at him again, as if to dare him, but he shook his head. The old Will? Definitely would have given her a go. Maybe skipped a session or two with her and had some fun.

The new Will? No way. Indiscriminate shagging was out of the question. Big boys didn't do that. He sat up a little straighter, and flashed her a little smile of regret. Nothing personal, he would say to her, if it came to that. He moved his glance to Lisa then flicked it away again.

"I'm not done with women by any means," Will said. "But I'm done with jumping in without thought. The future is all about self-control. I'm getting my act together. Planning. Long-term." He sat up straighter. "I want to settle down now. I do. Never thought I'd be the one to say those words. Being here, with Dr Peters and Lisa; their expertise? They've helped me grow up. My father died when I was still a teenager, but I'm over that. Maybe I blamed him for leaving me. I loved him; hated him leaving me. But when I think about what he wanted for me? It wasn't the life I've been leading and that's for sure."

"Yeah, man," Chase said. "Same for me. In my case, it was my mom who left me. I was just a kid. I wanted to punish her. But I was using that as an excuse. Still drinking at midday twenty years later? That was just hurting me, hurting my own career." He shook his head. "I'm with you, Will," he said. "I'm a changed man, too. I'm just sad we don't have another full week here, man. I was about to beat you on that treadmill."

Everyone laughed.

"Dr Peters reminded me how there were better things I could do with my time," Chase said. "Motorbikes. I loved my first motorbike. Spent day and night making that thing run properly. Gonna buy another one." He raised his hands to imaginary handlebars and gave a rev.

"Yep. I've got the money now," Chase said. "So any time I've got free time in the middle of the day, I'm gonna head out on the highway. *Big rev revival*. What d'y'all think of that? Can't wait for that high again, eating up the miles. Gonna pitch to my agent I do a doco. Maybe Route 66. Fans might go for it."

Sam shared next, explaining she'd taken cooking lessons with the chef. As if on cue, the chef came in with a bunch of melting moments "fresh out of the oven," he said, though he confessed he'd been the one to sandwich them together. But he'd used the mix Sam had made.

A waiter came in with tea and coffee and juices, and they took a break. Will noticed Lisa was pleased to see Sam eat a whole melting moment.

"These are seriously good," Will announced.

"I added extra lemon juice," Sam said self-consciously, then opened up. "I found the recipe in the library. I'm going to do a catering course." It was the longest string of words she'd ever uttered. Will gave her a high five.

As they sat with their beverages, Beth looked around the circle as everyone nodded. "The loneliness was the worst," she said. "Ray and I'd been together nearly 40 years. I didn't know how or what to think with my Ray gone. The club staff always had a smile for me. Cooking just for myself made me so lonely, I stopped doing it." There was anguish in the silence.

"I'd just go and eat at the casino," Beth said. "The staff would bring the food to me on a tray so I could keep playing. I had my favorite slot machines. I felt sure they would pay up if I kept feeding them, the way the stewards were feeding me. And when I won, then I'd have something to tell the family." Everyone nodded.

"But I lost more than I won. Everyone does. I know that now. At first I thought I was just unlucky, and that made me depressed, so I'd go gamble some more and forget my worries. I'd have a little win and feel encouraged; like maybe my luck would turn in life. But it never did." More nods.

"Those machines ate up all Ray and my savings." Beth's voice had dropped to a whisper. "And then I got a loan based on the value of the house. It only takes a year or so to lose everything. Makes my blood run cold how close I came to that." Her expression was grim. She sighed and looked around at everyone.

"So don't you dare take up gambling again, Will, you handsome young man," Beth said. "I've lived a great deal of my life, but you have a whole life ahead of you. Don't you waste one more moment in a casino. You promise me, promise Sam and Chase and Lisa. You be my witnesses and let us be yours, Will."

"I promise you, Beth," said Will, hands out, empty, innocent. "And I promise you, Sam and Chase. No more gambling." He moved one hand to his heart and gazed at Lisa. "Hand on my heart, Lisa."

"Man," said Chase, breaking the silence as Lisa fought to hide a blush. "Steamy. We could get you a part in my TV show, Will."

Everyone laughed, tension dissipating.

"Can I ask a favor?" said Beth. "Can one of you young things show me how Facebook works?"

Sam came to life.

"Piece of cake," she said and everyone laughed again. "I'll help you. But you might prefer Instagram."

"Thank you, Sam," said Beth. "I want to keep in touch with my kids and grandkids better. They nagged me, but I just never got around to it. I want to impress them. I want to be 'techno grandma.' I've proved I can spend time on a machine. I just want it to be productive time in future. Send emails. Oh. And I'd like to downsize. That'll keep me busy. Find a smaller place. Pack up. Move. Make some new friends."

"I love the way you offered to help Beth, Sam," said Lisa. "And I love the way you're all finding something new to turn your time and attention to. Reviving old passions. Finding new ones."

Will's eyes bored into hers. Did she catch her breath before continuing?

"But you need to recognize you can still say 'no,'" Lisa said. "We all have choices. If your new behaviors become obsessive, you'll need to remember to step back and think – think twice. Remember what you've learned about addictive behaviors. Ask yourselves if you're being honest with others and with yourself. Ask for help. We're all human."

...

Will stayed back to help Lisa straighten the chairs. She was glad. She'd missed him that day he'd walked out. Missed their chats. His shoulders were relaxed and his demeanor optimistic. Good. Meeting relatives could be fraught, Lisa knew, though he'd appeared more together than ever in the group session. Did he have something on his mind?

"Seeing James, that wasn't so bad," Will said. "Not half as bad as I thought it might be. Maybe it helps that I've realized James didn't get the greatest deal either, with Dad dying early. He's actually a good bloke. Takes things seriously."

Will stood for a moment, hands on either side of the back of the final crooked chair. Once he'd straightened it, he'd be out of excuses to linger.

"James promised our father he'd look after me," he said. "I haven't made it easy for him, that's for sure. But that's changed. Maybe we're on the same side now. Life's a gift, sure, but you've still got to make it work. James saw the changes in me."

"You were ready to change," said Lisa.

"Or maybe Lisa Bakker is a 'miracle worker.' Nice tagline?"

She laughed then, a rippling one that caught her by surprise. Where had that come from? She'd thought she was immune to flattery.

"I'm sure it was Dr Peters. She's your therapist. Besides, I'm suspicious. You're buttering me up. What are you after?"

"Sprung. Well, I still want you to take me skyrunning. Had a chance to think about the weekend? C'mon, Lisa. I was even good in group session. You saw how good I was."

"I did," Lisa said. "And in fact I *have* considered your request, but it's Dr Peters who makes decisions about clients' diversion therapy, not me."

"I've asked Dr Peters. James is keen, too. Take us both. James said he's travelled so much he could do with stretching out. Cross-country running was the only thing he was good at, whereas *I* was good at all sports." He made a Hercules pose.

Lisa shook her head and gave him a smile. She was fond of him. She'd miss him when he left.

"Sibling rivalry," she said.

"You know about that?"

"Only from textbooks. I was an only child."

"Oh. So how was that?"

"Lonely."

"No wonder you're so serious! No one to play with. No fights. No need to share. Nothing much happening for little Lisa."

135

Why had she told him that? Now he looked like he wanted to comfort her again. Well, she didn't need anyone's pity. *He* was the one who'd come to the clinic to change, dammit. Still, he hadn't said it unkindly.

"Anyway, this is not about me," she said. "So you'd like to take your brother with us?"

"Yes. Tomorrow?"

"Like I said, Dr Peters will make the call. But I'll ask."

"Thank you! Stunning."

...

Dr Peters was busy at her desk when Lisa popped her head in the door. "Ready for our debrief?"

"Of course, Lisa. Come in. Come in. I'll be right with you. Water?"

"Yes. Thank you. I'll pour yours, too."

She joined her a minute later, and they raised their glasses to each other, part of their weekly ritual.

"How are you?" she asked.

"Excellent, thank you. And they're all doing well but Connor."

"Ah yes. Connor." They discussed Connor's expulsion from the group and some strategies Dr Peters was trying with him, before moving on to Beth's progress, then that of Chase and Sam, and finally, Will's.

"Will," said Dr Peters. "It appears his brother's visit is going smoothly. Do you agree? We have an unusual opportunity for you to do some diversionary therapy."

"Is this the skyrunning? With his brother, James?"

"Exactly," said Dr Peters. "I see Will has raised this with you already?"

"He did. After group, just now. What do you think? Would James be a good influence? Will's remarkably calm about James's visit, given his earlier comment about James cutting off an allowance. Do you think Will's bluffing?"

Dr Peters took another sip of water and considered Lisa's question. "I don't believe Will is bluffing, no," she said. "I had a follow-up call with James. He can't believe the transformation. I don't believe Will has an inherent disposition to addiction."

"I agree," said Lisa. "Environmental; the early loss of his father, then the complicating factors of that first girlfriend making his consequent relationships so public which exacerbated his problems – he played up to his bad-boy reputation."

"Agreed," Dr Peters said. "Will and I have discussed this at length. He has a much greater understanding of his motivations and his choices now. It's as if a veil has been lifted, giving him power over his choices. It's excellent. He's responded very rapidly. I believe he'll be ready to leave us next week, with minimal follow-up."

"So, would you like us to go ahead with the run?"

"Yes, please. If you don't mind, Lisa. In my view it's an excellent opportunity; one we shouldn't pass up, if you're willing to go with them both. I had James checked out before we agreed to his visit. There are no criminal records, nothing at all. And Will says you've already met him?"

"Only briefly, in the corridor," Lisa said. "The brothers' physical resemblance is extraordinary. All seemed well, not that I had time to delve deep. I'm glad you've checked out James. Dr Peters, I actually believe that a run would be just the right activity for him at the right time. Will's made it clear from the start he'd love a run."

"Let's call it a reward for the fact he's stepping up," Dr Peters said. "He wasn't always so compliant. He certainly didn't take his schooling seriously."

"No," said Lisa. "Oh, and just now, in group, Will volunteered that his meeting with James went well. He shared some insight about the way their father's death influenced James's own life. I was impressed."

Dr Peters finished her water and plonked the glass down on the coffee table. "I can't see any reason not to go ahead with this, as long as you're happy to take them both," she said. "Yes?"

"Yes," said Lisa. "I've been open with you about how I find aspects of Will's personality quite attractive. His sense of fun, for example. He can be quite mischievous. I don't think it's a problem, though. After all, James will be with us, and he gave the impression of being perfectly sensible. Your call."

"I trust you to keep your professional distance," Dr Peters said, locking eyes with her over the top of her glasses. "You're among our best clinicians. And as you say, James will be there." Dr Peters smiled, sat up and drew their meeting to a close.

"Good. Thank you, Lisa. Oh. Are you aware Will's making plans to stay in Boulder City? Said he wants James to explore the place with him while he's in the area. Would you mind touching base with them both next day, please? Don't worry about your schedule. I'll arrange subs."

"Pardon?" Lisa asked.

"James has put in a request to take Will to Boulder City on Sunday morning for brunch while he's in the area," Dr Peters said. "Something about scoping business opportunities for the future. It'd be good if you could join them, since you live there, just to check all is well. If you could file an online report, I'll review Will's notes before we release him next week."

"No problem, Dr Peters." She loved her job.

Chapter 14

It was his day of escape – out with Lisa – with big brother James in tow. Thank God for diversionary therapy. If he saw another white wall, he'd climb it.

Will met James at the clinic reception and took him to the carpark, as arranged, where Lisa transferred her running shoes from the back of her small car to one of the retreat's white vans. He'd feared she or Dr Peters might cancel it, but here they were, about to head out. His heart was already on top of the world.

"We'll drive north-west towards Mount Charleston and the Spring Mountain Range, in Toiyabe National Forest," Lisa said.

Will couldn't work out what excited him more; freedom from the confines of the retreat, or the fact they were barrelling along in the white van bound for the mountains, Lisa at the wheel.

She'd removed her white jacket. He was in the front passenger seat, with James in the back. Will looked across at Lisa and just drank her in, her beautiful profile, fine hands on the wheel, and those long legs. A little of her hair had escaped from the tight ponytail and danced in the slipstream in the morning sunshine.

She glanced across at him once, gave him a private smile, then focused back on the road.

Beside them, desert slid past while the range steadily approached.

She and James talked about skyrunning, discussing how it differed from cross country; how it emerged in the 1990s and became more and more popular.

"It's essentially cross country across mountain ridges," Lisa said. "Mont Blanc would be the most famous international comp. Then there's ultra running and vertical running, in the stairwells of skyscrapers. Crazy, huh? That's the only way some people can train."

Lisa gestured at the peaks. "I've been doing it since grad school. I love to get out here as often as I can. I was born in the Midwest. I grew up on flat land, so all that high terrain still fascinates me. The views are spectacular. You'll see. You're practically flying."

"Maybe I'll take up skyrunning," said James.

"It's the perfect antidote to an office job," Lisa said. "In one run, I burn up fat from a week of lethargy. Counselling's sedentary. You sit there listening, day after day. And it can get pretty intense, with no easy way to let off steam."

They turned off the main road and headed for higher ground.

"I try to go for a run in the evenings, around Boulder," said Lisa. "I'm thinking of training with the local baseball team, but there's nothing like the freedom of skyrunning. I absolutely adore it."

"It's so good to be back out in the world," Will broke in. "Man. No joke. I feel like I've been indoors for weeks, not counting the night—"

"So you still run, James?" Lisa cut him off. Okay. She might not want James to know he'd spent a night at Lisa's, even though it had been totally innocent.

Will vowed to be more careful. He wanted to get this right. Lisa was like no woman he'd ever met before. If he wanted a future with her, he'd need to consider his actions, do some planning. No more jumping in and ignoring the consequences. That Will was the Will of the past.

"Yeah, but not nearly enough," James said. "Retail's busy. Long hours. Not much time off. I would have been fittest when I was eighteen. I'm into my thirties now and I'll probably never be as fit again. But I'm really looking forward to seeing something other than the inside of airports, I can tell you. I've been travelling for too long. Getting a bit homesick for Sydney, in fact. Ever been there?"

Lisa's hair whipped back and forth as she shook her head. It shone in the sunlight that slanted in through the open window. Will studied her and fell into a reverie as she and James talked about the Sydney Opera House, the harbor, and koalas, and the Blue Mountains and the Great Dividing Range.

At the reserve, Lisa parked and threw them each a water bottle. She locked the van and they did some stretches, then took off on a slow warm-up jog. Squirrels scampered. The smell of sagebrush and cool fresh air smelt better than Christmas.

As they began to climb, Will pointed at a lone eagle circling. "That you, bro?" Will asked.

"No, mate. Thinking of settling down." James told Will about Stella, the Australian jewelry designer who had stolen his heart. "Can't wait to be back with her again. What about you? Are you really getting back on your feet? Out of that crazy maze of casinos? So far, so good, right?"

"Looking good, bro." From here, the Vegas skyline was tiny. No temptation at all. Here in the sky, with Lisa beside him, Will had the whole world at his feet.

They came to a fork in the track.

"Loop track," Lisa explained. "Another four miles. Everyone up for it?" James shook his head.

"Gotta make some calls," he said.

Up ahead, Lisa and Will fell into a steady rhythm, their paces well matched. Will was glad he'd trained hard in the gym every day, even though balancing on the rough path was nothing like running on the treadmill.

The freedom was incredible, the views even better. Lisa was right. He was flying.

They ran together so easily, side by side in the wider parts of the trail. They effortlessly alternated the lead as the trail narrowed between boulders or along narrow ledges.

Will picked up the pace at one steep stretch, but Lisa easily caught him. The next time, she sprinted out in front, then he accelerated to join her side. Their pacing was perfect.

They ran downhill for a while, into a saddle, when she stumbled for a moment and he caught her arm. She felt so warm. Precious. He didn't want to let her go.

Two more strides, and she stopped and perched on a rock. Will pulled up beside her, panting.

"Pebble," she said, puffing a little.

Will stood beside her, hands on his hips. He caught his breath as she fiddled with her shoe for a few moments. She extracted the culprit and re-tied her laces.

Up here, the air was even fresher, chilly; much colder than Vegas. Some clouds had gathered. They were at altitude, high on the Fletcher Trail Peak. Snow had settled on the peaks above them.

It was pure exhilaration to be surrounded by nature, with Lisa warm and beautiful and so close. In the far distance he caught another glimpse of the Vegas skyline. From here, those fancy buildings were smaller than the stone that came out of Lisa's shoe.

"Sure helps you keep things in perspective," he said.

"Oh?"

"From up here, the retreat's invisible. And I can't imagine what I thought was worth doing on the inside of all those casinos. They're so tiny from here. You've done that for me. Lisa. Helped me realize I could stop, and think, and make a choice. Every time."

Lisa took a few sips of water, took in the view, turned her face to him slowly and smiled.

"I'm proud of you, Will; proud of the progress you've made."

He let the compliment sink in as he ran one foot over a loose stone on the path. Her words made him glow. He'd always wanted to please her. More than that, he wanted to remember this moment, up here, in the clear air, away from all the temptations that had entangled him for too many years. On impulse, he stooped, picked up the stone and slipped it into his pocket.

Maybe it would help him to remember her belief in him. There may be tough times ahead, building a real living, making long-term plans and sticking to them. It might not be easy. He wanted to be able to draw on this sense of immense wellbeing for ever, to look to these mountains, or tumble this stone back and forth in the palm of his hand and draw on this strength.

"I love it up here," Lisa said, into the sound of the wind in the pines. The sky darkened as more clouds formed, the wind freshening. "It's so … free."

Did Will dare make a move, to show her how he felt about her? He'd blown every relationship in his life so far, except with his family, and even those he'd taken to the brink too many times.

Dr Peters had spoken with him about that – how, according to Dialectic Behavioral Therapy and attachment theory, some people broke off relationships before they were in danger of being hurt. She'd called it "commitment phobia" – an inability to form long-term relationships. It had rung true for Will.

He'd never looked deeply at what he wanted in a relationship, beyond sex. It was easier to move from one relationship to another than to risk once more that savage pain he'd experienced when his father had left him for good.

But now? A long-term relationship with Lisa Bakker? There was nothing he wanted more. Inside the clinic, Lisa stood out. She was impressive. Purposeful. She shone with something no makeup could create. The women he'd dated in the past, even the movie stars, had nothing on her. In her home, he'd felt welcome. The domestic disarray was endearing. More than that, he wanted to be back there with her, day and night. Could see himself in her life.

And now, up here in the mountains, with no distractions but that crisp breeze blowing ever stronger, like his feelings, swirling around them, he was sure of it. He wanted to be part of her life in every way. Lisa brought out the best in him. Beyond that, she was the sexiest woman he'd ever met. Even her ankles were sexy.

But how could he let her know?

"How free are we?" Will said. Maybe a general question would do it. Dammit. He was clumsier than a schoolboy. So much for his womanizing reputation.

"What do you mean?"

He looked from the distance to Lisa, to her shoulders, the grace of her neck, that soft patch of skin below her ear. Would she want him? A man with a bag of problems? A history of nothing to show for his time on earth? He'd never lacked confidence with a woman before. What was happening to him? The clinic might have stopped him gambling and drinking, but this. This was the hardest thing he'd ever done. Wooing Lisa Bakker.

Yes. That's what he wanted to do.

What the hell. He had to start somewhere.

"You taught me I said 'yes' too often in my old life," Will said. "I had to learn to say 'no' more often. But there are people. I'm sure you see them in your practice."

"What people?"

"They have the opposite problem."

"They do?"

"I'm no psychologist, but we've already spoken about how some people say 'no' all the time. So, up here, alone together, just days before I leave the clinic for ever, safely on my path to recovery, I ask you again how free we are."

"How free," she echoed, her eyes on his as she stood. She didn't move away.

"Yes," he said. "Are we this free, for example?" He leaned towards her and tucked a stray lock of her hair behind her ear. Her warmth. Her pulse at her temple. The smell of her shampoo

In less than a heartbeat, Will had moved closer, to brush with his lips the silky softness of that patch of skin beneath her ear. When she didn't pull away, he followed the line of her throat, as gently as a butterfly. And she let him. Time stopped.

Softly he brought his hands to her waist, then down to her hips. Nothing existed but this slow exploration, his hands running the trails of her body, so slowly it was as if it wasn't happening. Was Lisa giving him permission? Will stayed gentle. Controlled. It took every ounce of his willpower. Now above all, he must not frighten her away.

It was only when cold drops of sleet began to fall, steaming on their hot skin that she broke away, embarrassed.

"Oh no!" Lisa sprang back. "I can't! I mustn't. Oh God. What have I done?"

"You didn't do anything," Will said. "It was me. The only thing you did was to give me a gift. It was me who started that, not you, and no one ever need know about this but the two of us. A gentleman never tells. I won't tell a soul. Ever. But don't you ever doubt my new self-control. You're beautiful."

She stared at him, a thousand unspoken thoughts in her eyes racing like the clouds in the path of the wind.

"Have I done the wrong thing?" Will said and reached one hand towards her.

Lisa took another step back. "Better get back to James, don't you think?"

"No?" He risked it, and she rewarded him with a rueful smile. She understood him. Appreciated him. He knew it. But could he ever convince her to accept him in her life?

No matter. One step at a time. He followed her down the mountain, warm with a new hope, buoyed by the promise of possibilities he'd only dared to dream.

Chapter 15

Lisa dressed carefully. The woman in the mirror was different. Radiant; alive like never before. At the last minute, she pulled a red ribbon out of her drawer. When was the last time she'd worn something so bright? It made her feel like a schoolgirl again.

Why not? Red was a happy color – the same color as the tiny flowers on the cactus in her consulting room that had started to bloom for the first time. Red matched her mood; joyous. She was going out to breakfast. Her vacation approached. And Rossco was recovering steadily, due home in a day or two.

She found some lipstick to match the ribbon and paused at the mirror, her heart stopping. She brushed her fingertips against the soft patch of skin at her neck where Will had almost kissed her. Her body glowed, the wonder of it stilling her breath. The shadow of his touch still played about her hips and waist – an echo, soft as a whisper. Had she ever felt so alive?

Luckily she was professional. If they'd been testing their boundaries, they'd found the limits. They'd stopped, hadn't they? She hadn't let it go any further. And she wouldn't let it go any further.

It wasn't unusual to identify more with some clients than with others. After three weeks at the clinic, some began to feel like close friends. Many would send her thankyou cards. A couple of them still emailed her from time to time, and she would reply. They were all human after all. That was Dr Peters' philosophy.

She was fond of Will. She could admit it. He'd been a lovable rogue to begin with, and then he'd helped her out with Rossco, which she'd appreciated, and his new maturity was admirable.

She looked forward to seeing the brothers for breakfast. It would give her an extra opportunity to check James wasn't being a bad influence. The last thing Will needed was to be pulled off the rails just as he was getting his life in order.

Family dynamics could be complex. She'd have breakfast with them, then head into work. And Will would leave the clinic in a day or two. Good. He'd probably move on, out of her life, and she could put those moments on the mountain behind her. She'd mention the incident to Dr Peters, of course. It was verging on irregular. Wrong, really. She'd play it by the book.

Her vacation! Mont Blanc. A dream come true. And Jilly had agreed to join her. They'd both started their training regime.

Yes. If Will was turning up for himself now, the least she could do was turn up for him this morning.

The cafe was bouncing, full of young people in colorful exercise gear in fancy new fabrics, and young couples with baby strollers with big wheels.

Will jumped up as Lisa entered the restaurant. He pushed in her chair like a gentleman. Lisa noticed James size her up and glance from Will to her and back again.

Apart from the showy welcome, true to his word, Will kept his distance. What would happen if she touched his thigh? She found herself letting her fingers stray as she adjusted her napkin on her lap.

Will grabbed her hand beneath the table, their gestures hidden. He squeezed it, wouldn't let her fingers go, teasing her, and her heart ricocheted all over her chest. What had she started? Mistake? But poker faced, Will let them go just before James would have noticed, and she relaxed again.

There. Just a bit of harmless fun. Will was like that. A prankster. Thank goodness she'd established sensible boundaries.

There was plenty of banter between the brothers, and they included her. She wondered again why she'd been an only child. Perhaps her life would have been different with a brother or sister. Certainly less serious.

When she went on to have her own family … What was she thinking? She grabbed the menu and busied herself making a selection.

James asked her about Boulder City, the history, the current population, the makeup of tourists from month to month. He and Will exchanged

147

glances now and then. Will wasn't wasting a moment. His plans to set up shop in Boulder seemed serious. Her heart gave a little thump. Too much pancake.

...

Dr Peters had given Will permission to explore Boulder City and the Hoover Dam with James, who would drop him at the clinic on his way to the airport.

As Lisa drove herself in, she found herself singing – something she hadn't done in a long time. She'd enjoyed the brothers' breakfast banter. Will was lucky to have James in his life, and a loving family. Not all of her clients were so fortunate.

Back home again later that afternoon, Lisa found her house was too quiet without Rossco. She ventured into the spare room, vowing to make a dent in the stuff she'd retrieved from her failed marriage. Box after box was full of things to remind her of Art and her barren hopes of happiness. He'd been as devoid of fun and life as his textbooks. On a whim, she hefted six unopened boxes into the back of her car and drove them to the welfare collection depot.

She threw open the windows of the cleaned out spare room, revelling in the extra space and fresh air. She pulled down the curtains and washed them, along with the bed linen and bed spread, then sprayed all the surfaces with cleaner and scrubbed the wooden floorboards. The room glistened when she was done, and she was exhausted.

When she slipped into bed that night, her whole body hummed with quiet joy.

...

When Will turned up for his final biometric test the following day, Lisa gave him her best professional, confidence-inducing smile.

"Okay," she said. "Let's get this final test out of the way. We have the reading from your first day, and from last week, and then we compare it with today's results; examine any trends."

"Okay."

Lisa opened the wall cabinet, extracted the device and unwound the cords. She peeled off some fresh sticky patches for attaching the electrodes.

"Remember how this works?"

"I could hardly forget," Will said. "I've still got those bald patches on my chest from the last time. But how you think you can tell what makes my heart race, I just don't know."

Lisa smiled at him as she pulled up the program on her laptop. It lit up a display on a big screen on the wall.

She'd explained it all before the first test. The test was a retreat invention. It exposed the clients to gambling and alcohol stimuli and measured and graphed their responses. If the test showed that the measure of a client's excitement levels could drop as they tried out new thought processes, it showed they were exercising control over their initial impulses, and demonstrated their progress.

"Once again, I'll need to ask you to pull up your shirt, please, before you lie down."

"That part's easy," he smiled and pulled off the denim shirt. "I actually need to give you this back," he said, fingers under the edge of the soft, gray t-shirt beneath – again the shirt Lisa had lent him at her house. At ease with his body, he hauled it up over his torso.

She supposed he'd had plenty of practice undressing for other women. All the more reason for her to turn the other way. But she couldn't.

All that swimming. All that bench pressing. Will should be proud of what he'd achieved. He had nothing to hide. The opposite. Mercifully, he slipped the denim shirt back on, buttons undone, before he lay on the couch.

Lisa was as professional as ever as she approached him with the device. She was adept at using this machine. It was a standard part of her day, measuring the progress of one client or another. No big deal. So why was her heart pumping harder than usual?

Horizontal now, he tried to catch her eye as she held the little sticky pad towards his chest. The heat of him drew her closer, and something else. An aroma? Like something she was missing in her life. He flinched when she touched his chest. One sticky pad down. Five to go.

Will's eyes were closed as she placed the fourth pad in position. Thank God. She'd done this a hundred times. Why did this time feel so intimate? Her fingertips were trembling.

Will's eyes opened and searched her face.

Third pad.

Second one.

Final one. Gently, Will's fingertips settled on her own, just above his heart. She paused.

"Uh, I think this one's loose," Will said.

"No. It's fine."

"Me. I'm a loose canon."

"Ha-ha." Lisa straightened, ready to return to the computer.

"Uh," Will said. "This other one. On the side. I think it's come unstuck. Needs adjusting, please."

She leaned across his chest to take a closer look, too close. Her sigh was faint, an "oh" of longing so intense she couldn't tell if it was his or hers, or just their souls, opening one to the other.

Will's voice was soft and low, his breath soft on her ear. "If you think something, can you make it happen?" he asked.

Lisa's eyes searched his. She was in new territory. She'd never felt this way about a client. Whatever Jilly had said, she knew this shouldn't be happening. She'd thought about Will's move up there on the mountain and was prepared to put it behind her.

But this? Now she was risking her whole profession. Everything she stood for.

She also knew – in a great rush of certainty – that she'd never wanted anything more.

So this was what it was like. Desire. Will smelled divine, this pure, powerful man, a man who respected her, who wanted her, who was waiting for her consent. She knew it, as surely as her own blood was pumping in her veins – far too fast, dangerously fast.

This man was nothing like Art. Art who lived for his research, who had no idea what a woman might want.

This man was in his prime. He lay there, promising her everything that was missing in her life. All she'd have to do was …

He cupped his hand over her fingers again, so gently, a caring touch, the tiniest suggestion. And his eyes, steady, willed her to bridge that distance between them, between their lips.

As his fingers squeezed her own, her sigh was a whisper, just above his bare chest. When he squeezed her fingers again, she moaned, her longing impossible to hide. Lisa closed her eyes and let her head drop, slowly, slowly, closer and closer until he almost caught her lips in his.

Time stood still. *Almost*. Will's welcoming warmth. Deliciousness. She knew it in her whole being. There would be an intense and utter delight, and then a fall, a plunging, an all-consuming hunger, an unquenchable thirst for more ...

Lisa whipped her lips away from his, snatched back her hand and stumbled back up onto her feet, gasping.

She pressed her fingers to her lips, shocked at what she'd almost done, appalled by her need for him. She'd never behaved like this.

"I'm sorry, I ..."

"We both wanted that, Lisa," Will said. "It's the nicest thing that's almost happened to me for a long time, maybe ever. Why apologise?"

"There's a rule against that. I ..." Lisa sprang away, busily buttoning her lab coat. Every button. Embarrassed. Stricken.

"Lisa. Listen to me." Will's voice was almost a whisper. "I've always broken rules. And that was beautiful. And you can't tell me that something that feels so good can be wrong. I'll never believe you."

Heart hammering, Lisa looked at him, astonished at his new maturity. This time, she didn't doubt his smooth talk. There was a different kind of confidence – a decency. A new sincerity. This wasn't sweet talk. This Will Huntley was utterly convincing, reassuring. She was the one who was a dithering mess, rattled, adrift.

"Oh, but your test."

"Come on, then," Will said. "Let's get this test over and done with, shall we? But, like I said, I can't promise consistent results. How you think that thing can tell what makes my heart race, I don't understand. Anyway, my heart's no longer my own. My heart belongs to you."

She flashed him a look. How many times had he used that line?

The machine. She had to get this over with. Electrodes all in place, she retreated to the safety of her chair, operating the laptop.

Up on the screen, the stimuli flashed. Gambling chips, the ace of hearts, a lit cigarette, some dollar bills. Whisky on ice. A full glass of red wine. A frosty beer. Some blinking lights, like the screen of a poker machine, the tinkle of bells and little tunes.

Each time, Lisa took a reading. Nothing much was registering.

A few neutral stimuli. An electric kettle. A ping pong ball. Calm. Calm. Calm.

"Told you so," Will said. "Mind over matter. I'm doing well, aren't I? I'll conquer this. I'm all over it."

"You are. You're doing well."

Then a roulette wheel. Calm.

A "free bet" offer. Calm.

A croupier at a table. Calm.

Two cards. A queen of hearts and a joker. Suddenly the machine went wild.

"Lisa, that's us! Tell me that's not us. I'll never believe you." He sat up, whipped off his shirt, pulled the electrodes off his chest all at once, hauled her t-shirt back on, and shrugged the shirt back on over the top.

"I'm more in control of my life," Will said. "Womanizing? Gambling? I don't do that anymore. This clinic? It's given me some tools. I understand the triggers better, and I'm making long-term plans."

Will smiled at her. She was lost for words. What he said was good. Excellent. But she remained stunned at her own behaviour.

"And now, I want to focus on the things that matter," Will said. "Before I leave, I'm showing you my full hand. You are center stage, Lisa. You're my Queen of Hearts, queen of my heart, that's for sure. And I aim to prove it to you."

Will stood there respectfully, super real. His vitality, his personality, the attention he'd given her – as if she were the only woman in the world. As if he really cared about her.

Lisa kept her face blank as she let Will out of the room. She dodged those blazing blue eyes, gave him a curt nod and closed the door. She leaned against it and closed her own eyes.

She inhaled, steadied herself, then opened them again. In a daze, she packed up the equipment, grateful for the routine, going through the motions while her brain raced and tumbled and panicked.

Had she really almost kissed him? Kissed a client? Not just any client. Will. The pure thrill of it ricocheted through her. And she'd wanted more, so much more.

Lisa sank down onto the couch, its surface still warm from Will's body. What had she done? Her elation plummeted into horror.

Blinded by her own need, she'd failed this man. Failed herself. Failed the clinic and all it represented.

A great wave of regret rose up in her and tumbled over as she held her head in her hands and covered her eyes with her palms. There could be no undoing her intention. And no matter what Will said about not telling, there was no way to erase the truth.

How could she have been so foolish? Why had she not seen this coming? All the while she'd thought herself immune to Will's charms, perfectly in control. Instead, she'd welcomed him right into her life and dreams, as if he belonged there. Wrong, wrong, wrong.

Yet still her body longed for his. Were he to walk back in that door, she'd go to him again. She knew she would.

The solution? Lisa saw only one option.

Lips tight, operating on auto, she made a note of Will's results, snapped his folder shut and marched herself to Dr Peters' office for their weekly debrief.

She hesitated at the threshold, one hand on the door frame. Dr Peters was preoccupied, staring at her desktop computer. She glanced up at her and waved her in, eyes back on the screen.

How she'd loved her career, and this job. That all those thousands of hours of diligent study; that every judiciously chosen word of counsel with every person in her care should lead to this; that her whole world should spin and topple …

Grief seized her throat. To step into Dr Peters' office was to step over a cliff, to hurtle through space to a personal ground zero.

Chapter 16

"**G**ood week, Lisa?"

"Good week, thank you, Dr Peters." Her voice was hollow. The words formed themselves out of habit. She owed her more than this. Her dream boss. No! It was all over.

"Pretty much," Lisa said. "Well, no. It was. Till about five minutes ago." Was this really happening? She looked around Dr Peters' consulting room, the white walls, the abstract paintings. She loved it here. Wanted to stay. Should she tell her? Should she stay quiet? What was she doing?

"'Pretty much?'"

"Will Huntley," Lisa said, her voice a whisper. She laid his folder on the table between them. She could scarcely breathe. Time creeped as Dr Peters opened it, studied the results and snapped her dark eyes to hers, framed in the characteristic tortoiseshell glasses. Eyes that got to the point immediately, that saw through clients' excuses and lies and reflected them back, till clients learned to pull themselves up on their own behavior.

What theory, textbook or method could pin down the effect of one therapist's eyes? Dr Peters was gifted. A genius at addiction therapy. Lisa was in awe of her opportunities to work with her in her internship, awe-struck at the job offer, and devoted to her work right here, with her, at this clinic.

Bringing her problem to her now, like this, risked everything in her life that was going so well. This would be worse than leaving Art, when at least she'd known she had this job to come to. She would need to rebuild her whole world again. She took another deep breath. Her fingers were tingling. She knew from running she was hyperventilating. Almost panicking. It wouldn't help.

"But these results are excellent." Dr Peters sat back, removed her glasses and swung them in her characteristic way. "Will has been a model client. He's set to leave in a day or two, isn't he? Is there some problem?"

"Well, no," Lisa said. "Not with Will, anyway. Strictly speaking, he's done everything we've asked of him, as far as I understand. Though according to him, it's been a struggle. Will's been excellent in group therapy. Supportive of the others. Honest. From my perspective, he's giving every indication he's well on the road to recovery, Dr Peters."

"Well, what's the problem, then?"

There was no point delaying this. No point wasting their time. She had to do this.

"The problem is with me." Her voice shrank as if she were a child who'd done wrong, tiny, dwarfed in the face of a world of wrath and trouble brought on by herself.

Dr Peters pinned her with her eyes. This was so hard, but she was no child. She must get on with it. Own up.

"I didn't realize," she gushed. "I'm sorry. I should have seen this coming, but I was blind. I should have spoken up sooner. It's just I've never had this happen before."

Dr Peters was silent, waiting.

"Well, I've had clients hit on me before," Lisa said. "I've told you about them, too. Remember that guy from Idaho? Dawson, the Tire King, with the ego. He kept propositioning me, and you swapped him out to Stephanie for me.

"And I would have done the same with Will," Lisa said. "But I thought I was immune. I thought I could handle it. It's not as if I wasn't forewarned. If you read his notes, that day I welcomed him, it all came out. How he's an international playboy. I should have been more on my guard."

Lisa scrunched the hem of her lab coat with both hands. Looking down, she tried to smooth the fabric with her palms, force out the creases she'd just made. She glanced up at Dr Peters again. She remained silent, her face unreadable. The face that had heard ten thousand confessions.

"But it's too late now," she rushed on. She hated her words, the high tone of panic. "You can't swap him out, because he's ready to leave anyway.

He's due to leave on Tuesday. I should have spoken up sooner, about what happened up on the mountain, when there were just the two of us."

Dr Peters looked up sharply.

"I thought I was in control, but I wasn't," she said. "I was fooling myself. Because … because …"

She waited, eyes drilling into hers.

"Just then, back there, in the testing room," Lisa said. "I … Oh, Dr Peters. I almost kissed him. I'm so ashamed. He was on the couch and I was adjusting the tabs. It's not as if I haven't used that machine a hundred times." Lisa squirmed on the couch, full of regret.

"And he could have grabbed me," she said. "I'm always conscious of that. I've usually got one hand near my pocket, ready to press the alarm, but I never thought *I* could be the one to do the wrong thing. It wasn't Will. He didn't do anything wrong today." The memory of his hand on her hip, up on the mountain, came searing back. What kind of a fool was she that she hadn't noticed what was happening, and prevented it?

"I was the one who made the first move in there just now," Lisa said. "Every single thought just went out of my head. This was my body on autopilot. It took over. I broke away before anything actually happened. As soon as I could. As soon as I realized what I was doing."

"What did Will do?" The glasses had stopped swinging.

"Oh, he wanted to kiss me. He's made that clear. And when I pulled away, he just smiled." Lisa pressed her fingertips to her lips. They were still burning. Blazing. Pulsing; betraying her rational mind – branded by Will Huntley. Lisa sat on her hand, and flashed her eyes to her boss.

"Will said he wouldn't tell," she said. "But I can't lie to you, Dr Peters. I'm sure I've done the wrong thing. It's major, isn't it?" She stuttered, garbling and panicked, and Dr Peters just sat there and stared back at her.

"It's … it's against our code of conduct, the American Psychological Association, and your clinic protocol, I know," Lisa said. "I'm jeopardizing everything. What if he sues? I'm so sorry. I'll have to leave. I'll have to resign now. I've loved my work here. You won't even be able to give me a reference, will you?"

Dr Peters remained calm, her expression unreadable.

"And there's more," said Lisa, staring at the floor. "When we were skyrunning, James stayed behind at one stage to make some calls. We ran on ahead. I guess that's when this whole thing started, though I didn't realize it at the time. Now, I see I was fooling myself; I wasn't taking this mutual attraction thing seriously."

"Maybe I shouldn't have sent you off together," Dr Peters said.

"Well, it shouldn't have been a problem. I've taken other clients skyrunning with me, for their diversion therapy. There was Lucy Stringer. And the man from Maine. I could barely keep up with him. Both of them went well. Last time I analyzed the longitudinal study they were both still running and both still controlling their addiction."

Lisa's pulse was a bass drum. The room expanded and contracted. What would Dr Peters say? She interlaced her fingers in her lap and considered her.

"How do you feel about Will, Lisa?"

Will had accused her of not truly believing he could change. He'd called her a fraud, for treating him as if he were subhuman. Well, that wasn't true. She respected all her clients. She cared deeply about their progress. It was the reason they responded so well.

"I'm not sure," she said. "Will was a rogue when he first arrived, but then, he changed. He's very likeable. He calls himself a joker, yet he accuses me of not taking him seriously. And now this. I've never lost control like that before."

Dr Peters waited, in silence.

"Yes," said Lisa. "Well, I didn't admit it to myself till now. I'm attracted to him physically. Very. And his sense of humor. He's fun. He makes me happy. He respects what I do. He's thanked me for guiding him onto a better path. But, I realize I should never have let him help me with Rossco. Should never have let him stay over. And now, this ... kiss. I still don't understand what came over me. I'm so sorry."

Dr Peters' expression was inscrutable. The second hand of the clock ticked in the silence. "We're clinicians," she said eventually. "We're psychologists. We're professional."

Lisa nodded slowly, her lower lip trembling. She stared into her eyes. "I'm so sorry, Dr Peters," she said. "I've let you down. I've let Will down. It's disgraceful."

Dr Peters held up one hand to hush her. "But we're also human," she said. "And humans are fallible."

Lisa nodded again, waiting for her to continue. Could there be a ray of hope, a life line?

"There's not one human walking this earth who hasn't made mistakes, Lisa," Dr Peters said. "The whole point of psychology is that we learn to control our behavior and make better choices."

"But that's just it, Dr Peters," said Lisa.

"What's that?" she said.

"I didn't feel like I had any choice."

"But if you did have a choice, what would you have chosen to do?"

Heat rose in Lisa's cheeks. "I didn't want to break away. I wanted …"

"But you did break away," said Dr Peters.

"It was wrong of me to want to kiss him, though, wasn't it?"

Dr Peters drew a deep breath and looked away to the corner of the room. There was a statue there. A figurine. Of a woman dancing, or skating, nymphlike, arms up, one leg back, weightless, carefree.

"We live, Lisa," she said. "And if we are lucky, we love."

"We love?"

"My husband was a musician. He left me for another musician. It nearly killed me. I couldn't work out what I'd done wrong. We were still students. I threw myself into my studies. I was lucky love found me again. You've met my Nancy. Nancy made everything possible."

Dr Peters balled one hand in a fist, and held it with the other, before releasing both and holding them out, to encapsulate her world. "Nancy is the reason for my success," she said. "More precious to me than this clinic. Nancy's the balance in my life, and I still can't resist her."

"Are you saying it was all right to almost kiss Will?"

"It's wrong, Lisa, but it's happened," she said. "And now we have to deal with it."

Black dread in the pit of Lisa's stomach took hold and grew in the silence.

Eventually, Dr Peters spoke again. "Two years," she said, then thought some more. "You know about the power imbalance, the vulnerability of clients."

Lisa nodded slowly. She wanted to disappear. Why couldn't she turn back the clock and undo those moments? But it required more than that. How could she erase her impressions, the way Will's smile lifted her heart, the warmth of his care the night he helped rescue Rossco, the way their bodies fit together up on the mountain. She couldn't undo Will Huntley. She didn't want to.

"Like many of our clients, Will's problems stemmed from the fact that he was abandoned – by his father," Dr Peters said. Lisa forced herself to focus on her words.

"For you to reject Will right now when he's almost ready to leave, well, that could be just as harmful as if you were to fall into a full relationship with him without thinking."

Lisa frowned. Did Dr Peters condone their relationship?

Dr Peters sighed. "You're aware of the dangers, Lisa," she said. "You're the one who's brought it to me."

"Yes." She nodded.

"Well, you could have hidden it. Lisa."

Was she saying she shouldn't have owned up to the incident? Her eyes grew wide. Double disaster.

Dr Peters shook her head, stood, walked to the window then turned to her. "Do you realize how rare it is to find a colleague so truthful?" she said. "Why would I punish you by firing you? Where else could I find someone as good as you to replace you? Every colleague is human, just as I am human."

"You mean it's alright?"

"No. It's never alright to kiss a client."

"But what will we do?"

"I need to consider this, Lisa. There might not be an easy answer. People and relationships are infinitely complicated. That's why the APA created the code in the first place."

Dr Peters stood, walked over to the figurine. Turned it in her hands. Placed it down again, facing the other way. "You say you stopped before things went any further?"

"I did," she said. "I didn't want to stop, but I did."

"That's good. That's excellent."

"But I could barely trust myself not to kiss him just then, could I? He calls me his Queen of Hearts. I didn't take it seriously earlier or I would have told you sooner. I thought it was just him buttering me up to help pass the time," said Lisa, relief starting to bubble up, to ease her chest and free her tongue.

159

"He's a flirt," Lisa said. "Everyone falls for him. Even Sam and Beth. And they're totally different people to me. They'd all kiss him if they could."

"What's this about the Queen of Hearts?"

"Will says he's no longer a gambling addict. And now he jokes that he's addicted to me."

Dr Peters stared at her, and then she laughed, a huge, pure, roaring laugh that filled the consulting room. Lisa laughed too, nervously at first, and then relief rocketed through her, relief that she'd done the right thing to tell her everything, relief that she might not be dismissed.

"Lisa. Love can be like an addiction in the early stages," Dr Peters said. "And a good one in the right circumstances, if it's reciprocated."

"I told you how Will helped me out when Rossco was hit by a car," Lisa said. "How we spent the night together at my place. He fell asleep on my couch. He was perfectly well behaved. A gentleman. He helped Rossco, helped me get him to the vet, and then he made me tea and scrambled eggs. He was so sweet, and there was nothing sexual. That's why I thought there was no problem."

Dr Peters waited for her to continue.

"But there's definitely a problem now," Lisa said. "I can admit it. I'm so attracted to him, it scares me."

"You're not seeing someone else, Lisa? You don't have to tell me."

"I'm happy to tell you. There's no one else in my life, that way. I left Art when I joined the clinic eighteen months ago. The divorce came through earlier this year."

"Well," said Dr Peters. "As you must understand, this situation is far from ideal."

Lisa nodded. She could still lose her job. Hope nosedived. The clock ticked.

"Technically, Will Huntley is my client, Lisa."

"But he's mine, too. None of the clinic's employees are allowed to fraternize." She stared down into her glass.

"You haven't initiated this Queen of Hearts idea, have you?"

"No, but he's vulnerable, isn't he?"

"Lisa, my consultations and these results tell me Will Huntley is well on the path to recovery."

"But if we were to have a relationship, just say we went down that path, wouldn't it be illegal for two years?"

Dr Peters looked at her. Then she took Will's folder, flicked through it and sat back.

"He's my client, not yours. Sure, you welcomed him to the clinic on my behalf, but I took over after those first couple of sessions. Technically, he's more my client than yours, but the media wouldn't see it that way. The wellbeing of our clients and reputation of this clinic are paramount. This is a serious matter."

Dr Peters looked over at the figurine again and pursed her lips, exhaling through them. "I'm taking Will off your group and diversion list, and you are not to see him for any follow-up sessions. Do you understand?"

"Yes, Dr Peters."

"Now I know you've got plenty of leave up your sleeve," she said. "You've taken the Easter, Christmas and New Year shifts since you arrived, and we're all grateful for that. It hasn't gone unnoticed. But maybe it's taken its toll and your professional judgement has been compromised. You can't abdicate control like that again, Lisa. Not in my clinic."

"No, Dr Peters." Shame rose in her like bile. It pulled down the corners of her mouth, and made her shoulders slump.

"I'm giving you a serious warning, Lisa. You'll need to do the six-month APA Boundaries course. You can do it online. Email me evidence that you've enrolled as soon as possible."

Lisa nodded.

"And I insist you take time off, starting now. I don't want you and Will running into each other again while he's still here, do you understand?"

Lisa nodded. "I understand."

"You're lucky you have so much leave owing."

Dr Peters slipped her glasses back on and stood. Lisa jumped up. Case dismissed?

...

Lisa retreated into her consulting room and sat on the client's side of her coffee table, face in her hands, still in shock. She had to grab her bag and take some leave. Thank God her boss was so understanding. She'd look up that course she mentioned and start in on it the moment she got home. How could she have allowed herself to stray like this?

161

Just then there was a knock on the door.

Lisa stood to open it, admonishing the receptionist. "Mindy, what did I tell you about interrupting me?"

"He says his name's Art and insisted I put him through to you or he'd sue me," Mindy said in a sing-song voice and looked at her nails.

Lisa looked up at the ceiling. She remembered Art's superior way of bossing people around and actually had some sympathy for Mindy.

"Art," she said when she picked up the phone, "this really isn't … what? But … you … How long have you known about this? No, no, I'll come."

She felt the colour drain from her face and sank down onto the edge of the couch.

Chapter 17

Lisa threw some warm clothes in a wheelie bag, grabbed her winter coat and ran back into the waiting taxi, grateful for once that Rossco was at the vet's. She wouldn't have to find someone to feed him.

Her whole being focused on going east, and she caught the very next flight. She got as far as Chicago, her quest urgent. She ran through the terminals to catch her connecting flight, but when she arrived, her gate was full of people and baggage going nowhere.

"Snow storm," the ground crew told her at counter after counter. "No one's flying anywhere for at least five hours. The last flight left an hour ago."

"I have to go home. My father's dying!"

"I'm sorry, lady." They just shook their heads. People in queues lined up with their backs against walls. There simply weren't enough chairs.

Lisa ran to the car hire section and insisted on taking a van.

"I always drive vans in snow," she told the official. "Better visibility. I'll be fine. It's got chains. Yes, I grew up in snow country. I know all about black ice. I need to get home now."

Lisa signed all the paperwork, raided a sandwich shop and grabbed some fruit bars and drinks. Then she turned her phone to silent to avoid any distraction, pulled out her thermal gloves, beanie and scarf, threw her bag and food in the passenger seat and headed out into a swirling world of white.

It was slow going, the visibility poor. She longed for night to fall so at least the truck lights might help show the way.

There was plenty of time to think, out here on the highway, to think about her father and mother and Art, and the way she'd left them as soon as she'd got her degree, and how her father hadn't spoken to her since. Is this why he'd been so silent? How long had he been ill?

Lisa'd had no idea her father had been unwell. She'd stayed in touch, phoning them every month. She couldn't help it if he never wanted to speak to her. She'd sent them birthday cards and anniversary cards. If they'd been hurt she'd moved away, she couldn't help that.

With Art, she'd been slowly dying of boredom. She'd chosen life and freedom, freedom from all the expectations, and especially freedom from her esteemed but wooden husband and sham of a marriage.

She was still angry at Art. How typical of Art to phone her out of the blue like that, to leave it till practically the last minute! Why couldn't he have told her? She would have made time to visit more often, taken some leave.

Eighteen months had been too long to stay away. It made her feel cruel. Selfish. She'd known her parents loved her. That she'd found their love constricting had not been their fault. Perhaps if she'd stood up to them all sooner, tried to explain …

There was no point reinventing the past. What was done was done. All she could do now was hope to reach her father in time, to reassure him she'd always loved him, and had appreciated the warm home he had provided, and all the education he'd shared with her so generously.

Her time at the Vegas clinic had exposed her to all kinds of different childhoods; relationships she would not have wished upon anyone. Her own constrictions were mild in comparison. Her parents had loved her too much. It seemed trifling to criticize them for it, ungrateful even.

Carefully she drove and drove, panic rising at the amount of time it was taking. How long had Art said she might have? Her father had been drifting in and out of consciousness for days already.

How she hated Art. Perhaps he'd done this deliberately to manipulate her and punish her for leaving him … To ramp up the guilt.

Thank goodness she'd turned off her phone. Any distraction would be suicidal. She couldn't risk taking one hand off the wheel or half an eye off the treacherous highway. It would be too easy to lose control.

She pulled off at a truck stop after a few hours, to suck on juices and munch on sweet fruit bars, and she stopped twice to fill up with fuel and stamp her feet on the winter cold ground. The hours were punishing, but gradually she conquered the distance. Too late each time, she remembered she should check her phone, but as her concentration started to fade, her main aim was to see her father before he died. If the call was to tell her she was too late, she didn't want to hear it. If not, the matter would just have to wait.

Towards dawn, she headed into town. Covered in shoulder-high snow, it was as beautiful as a *National Geographic* photograph, except for the dirty slashes the snow ploughs had left at the edges of the road.

Maybe Art had shovelled her parents' driveway, or one of the Brunker brood from the corner house, more likely.

She parked in the drive, opened the car door and stepped out, stiff from all that time in one position. The quiet of the suburban pre-dawn street was shocking. Her body still hummed from the vibration of the engine, hour after hour after hour through the long night.

As she slid out of the seat, there was a sharp shattering of glass. Her phone! It must have been caught in her scarf and the layers of clothing as it lay in her lap. It had speared straight downwards, smashing on one corner onto the frozen concrete, the glass splintering to smithereens, indistinguishable from shards of ice.

So much for all those messages. She retrieved the tiny card, fingertips burning with cold as she pushed it into a pocket, then gathered as many remnants as she could into the bag with the empty food wrappers and threw it all in the trash. Her parents still stashed it right there, beside the house. She shook her head. It was a stupid way to end the long night. She'd be disconnected from everything in Nevada.

At least she'd made it without any other incident – finally – but had she made it in time?

Carefully, she made her way up the ice and snow-covered steps, remembering from childhood the need to lower her center of gravity to reduce the likelihood she'd slip. She still had her key.

This was not how she'd imagined she'd return. In her mind, it would have been Thanksgiving, or spring, a hopeful time. Instead, it was dismal.

The house exuded a strange fragrance of cinnamon toast and disinfectant. She called out quietly, unwilling to wake her parents, nor wanting to frighten them.

Her mother emerged, padding up the hall in her dressing gown and slippers, face drawn, simultaneously happy and sad. She took off Lisa's gloves and held her cold fingers to her soft, warm face as she'd done ever since Lisa was a toddler coming in from the cold.

"Love you, Mom," Lisa said. When she enveloped her in a hug, it was as if her mother had shrunk. Lisa felt even more like a giant than she did as a teenager, when she'd just kept growing.

"Lisa, Lisa, Lisa! You've come, my baby girl! The radio said planes are grounded. When I heard the van pull in, I hardly dared hope it was you. Dad's sleeping. He'll be so glad to see you. Are you hungry? Coffee?"

Lisa was so weary she could barely stand. It was so strange to be here. Nothing had changed and everything had changed. She tiptoed along the hall and peeped into her parents' bedroom, with its tangles of medical equipment beside her father, a slumbering lump on his side of the bed.

"You didn't tell me, Mom. How long has he been unwell?"

"He didn't want to worry you. You had your own life to lead. You made it clear."

"But this was dishonest, Mom. Not to tell me something so important!"

"Hush. Let's not argue straight away, dear. Your father's so proud. He always intended he'd just get better. Let's enjoy our time together. You look so well. Tired, but healthy. Are you happy, honey?"

"Oh, Mom. I've driven all night in heavy snow. I couldn't feel less well. But I'm glad to be here. Let me take a shower. I'll have a snack, then I might take a nap and get some energy back while Dad's still asleep. But I want you to wake me if he wakes up, okay? I've come a long way to see him. I want to see him. Understand?"

"Yes, dear. Let me get you a fresh towel and take your bag to your room. Lisa, honey. Thank you. Oh, darling, it's been so hard."

Chapter 18

All his gear back in his rucksack, Will sat in a daze on the white couch in reception. He'd asked for the fifth time to see Lisa, and been told she was on leave. How could she have left without even saying goodbye to him? Did their newfound intimacy mean nothing to her? Would he only ever be just "a client" to her? He was a man; a man with a future.

Mindy brought him the exit forms, the evaluation. Food, "tick," gym, "tick." There wasn't a category for how his heart was feeling.

He looked up from the clipboard, remembering his run with Lisa up in the clear air of the mountains. Vegas had been minuscule from that altitude and distance. Insignificant. What was he, after all, but one tiny dot on the surface of the planet; a swirling, random dot?

No, that wasn't true. He had agency. If she'd given him nothing else, Lisa Bakker had given him a sense of his own sovereignty, his own ability to make decisions at every turn and to follow them through. This wouldn't be the last he'd see of this woman, his Lisa. He wouldn't let that happen.

Mindy collected the clipboard and told him to keep the pen. If Mindy made eyes at him, he barely noticed. It was Lisa he cared about, his Queen of Hearts.

He didn't expect it to feel like this, leaving the clinic, like part of him was missing. In his whole life, had he ever looked back?

Acres of hot desert and all the temptations of Vegas towered up, not so far to the south. Out in the hot, bright day, Will stopped and thought, hitched his rucksack onto his shoulder and deliberately headed towards Boulder City. Let Lisa do what Lisa needed to do. He had a goal alright.

167

He couldn't lose sight of it, would never let it go. He'd show her. Will Huntley was still a winner.

A mile along the road to Boulder, Will turned on his heel.

Steadily, he made his way back to the clinic, stood in the cool blast of the reception air conditioning for a few moments and helped himself to water from the cooler before enacting his plan.

For once Mindy was there, and there were no other clients. Good. Now was the time to use a little charm.

"Couldn't leave without thanking you, Mindy," he said. He gave her a big smile and held out his hand for her to shake.

She smiled, coy, and giggled a little.

"You must get all kinds of famous people in here," he said, to put her at her ease. "Do you collect autographs! Here. Want mine?"

"Are you famous?" she asked. "I just love your accent."

"Infamous, maybe." He smiled again, giving her the full thousand volts.

She handed over a small notepad and a pen, and he signed his name.

She was so pleased, he pressed on.

"I wanted to ask your advice, Mindy," he said in a lowered voice, his gaze intent. "Before I leave for good, I really want to thank some of the staff, like you, who've been so helpful. Can you help me with their names, please? Are you too busy at the moment?"

Clearly not. She'd been filing her nails.

"No. I'm okay."

"Ah, thank you. Well, first, who's the chef. Food here's sensational. Do you get to eat here, too?"

"Yeah, staff eat for free. Amazing!"

"Amazing!"

"That's Leroy da Silva. Anyone else?"

"Yes, I had a personal trainer for a while. Shelley, Sheila …?"

"That'd be Shelly Rodgers. She's my friend. Sometimes we train together."

"Sensational. And the other one's Lisa. I know she can be a bit difficult about the phone and so on, but to tell you the truth, Lisa's saved my life. I really wanted to say goodbye to her, but apparently she's on leave."

Mindy nodded.

"Would you have her phone number, please?"

"Sure."

Mindy took a post-it note off the side of her computer screen and handed it over. He photographed it with his phone and handed it back.

"Thanks for that, Mindy."

"Mr Huntley?"

"Yes, Mindy."

"Would you mind if we take a selfie together, please? I shouldn't tell you this, but Shelly loves celebrities. She wanted to ask you herself but she didn't get a chance. She'll be so glad I caught you."

"No problem. Want me to come around there, or do you want to come here?"

Mindy checked her lipstick in the reverse photograph function of her hot-pink phone, and was on his side of the desk in a flash.

Will smiled obligingly as she snapped their heads, close together, the waiting room magazines behind them on the trendy table. Before he could react, she took another, this time of her giving him a big kiss on the side of his cheek.

"Hey, what's that?"

"Shelly and I have a competition going. Thank you, Mr Huntley. I'm definitely winning now."

It seemed harmless enough. Mild compared to some of the pictures he'd taken in his time, not to mention the paparazzi's efforts. Besides, he was feeling generous. He was a free man.

"You can call me Will."

"Really? Thank you, Will!"

"Thank you, Mindy!"

…

Will was five miles back up the hot road before he stepped into the healthiest-looking fast food place he could find, ordered a tall juice and sat at a table to catch up on his messages and emails.

There was one from James, thanking him for taking good care of himself and expressing confidence in his general ideas about the US branch, but saying he'd need details before he'd consider extending any credit.

"I trust you, bro," James had written. *"Stay on the right path now. Don't let us down."*

Will spelled out his reply. *Not planning to let you down, nor myself. Thanks. For your belief in me.*

Then he set to work to message Lisa. It took him a while to find the right words. He wanted to get this right.

Lisa, I can't tell you how much you mean to me.

Too much. He didn't want to scare her away.

I hope we might catch up in Boulder some time.

Too casual. In truth, he wanted to see her right now. Wanted her in his arms. Wanted to finish what he'd started back there on the ridge; what she'd almost returned back there in the testing room. There was way too much unfinished business between them for her to disappear out of his life like this. He was confident she'd want to see him again. Most of all he worried about her; worried about what it was she might be dealing with, alone. She hadn't mentioned taking leave, apart from that trip to Mont Blanc, but that was at least a month away.

Lisa, thank you for all you've done to see me onto a better path. I'm going to Boulder to set up that store, and will train for the next skyrun at Mount Charleston. Hope to see you there. Will.

Could he wait that long? And Mount Charleston was huge. And there'd be hundreds of people there, maybe thousands. The odds of running into Lisa were pretty low.

He'd seen her twice a day for nearly three weeks. Talk about a new addiction. A good one.

A couple more "free bet" offers flashed up on his screen. He let them sit there on the diner table. He could ignore them now, completely. He smiled. He had the perfect antidote. A better goal; a real prize, if he could ever win her. The only thing that would make him jump now? Lisa. He sat and sipped on his juice, remembering the softness of her skin, the very taste of her, the way he could break her out of her professional seriousness, coax a smile. Yes, Lisa.

He pulled up her contact again and pressed it. He'd just phone her. What the heck.

"You've reached Lisa Bakker's message bank. Please leave a message."

"Uh, Lisa. Will here. Will Huntley. I've left the retreat. I want to see you again, to thank you for all you've done for me. I hope we can meet up. Soon. Ring me back."

He'd done it now. No chance to re-record his voice. So be it. Onwards.

He hitched his pack on his back again and resumed his long walk to Boulder City, hoping someone might show some heart and give him a lift.

It was so good to be out of that white building, he didn't mind the ache in his feet. The hot sun on his head was beautiful; reminded him of every childhood summer in Australia. At least this was dry heat. As long as he kept up his fluids, he'd be fine.

After the white walls of the retreat, he noticed every frond of every palm tree, every blade of grass, every speck of dust. Even the diesel exhaust smelled sweet as the trucks rumbled past. He inhaled deeply; swung his arms and smiled. Free.

Chapter 19

Lisa's father was gaunt. Same eyes, same smile behind the oxygen tubes, reflecting great weariness, but sparkling with delight to see her. She quickly began to see beyond the medical equipment, to read his mood, to save him energy communicating with her. All that mattered was being here with him.

A proud man in his striped pajamas, he let her help him sit up, let her plump up the pillows and smooth the blankets back up over his chest to chase away the cold.

He still had dignity. He'd been so tall once. Head of the whole Elementary.

Fronds of white frost climbed all over the window glass. She'd forgotten its silent beauty.

Conversation was difficult; always has been. But there were things that needed to be said.

"Love you, Dad."

He nodded. Found her hand with his and squeezed it. "Tell me about Nevada."

"Not much snow, Dad. Not in the valley, anyway. Mostly on the mountain peaks."

"Hmmph."

"High fifties. Sometimes even low sixties in the day, in the sun. I love it."

He laughed and shook his head. The laugh turned into a cough and he doubled over, eyes streaming. After a while, he slid back down into the bed, eyes closed. "And you?"

"It's a good life for me out there, Dad. I believe in what I'm doing. You always taught me the value of that."

He nodded and smiled, but his eyes drifted closed, and it became clear he was sleeping.

Lisa tiptoed out of the room, and found her mother peeling carrots for soup.

"We've got so much food, Lisa. The neighbors bring casseroles, but all he can eat is soup now."

Lisa nodded and washed her hands and began to help her mother chop up potatoes.

"How are you, Mom?"

"Oh? It's not about me."

"I'm asking about you," Lisa said.

Her mother smiled. "Glad you came," she said.

"Why didn't you tell me sooner?" said Lisa. "Why did I have to hear it from Art of all people? I could have come back and helped you sooner."

Her mother stopped what she was doing, wiped her hands on a tea towel, and came and held Lisa's face in both hands.

"My beautiful girl," she said. "Your father kept talking about coming out to visit you. He mentioned it often, going west, to surprise you."

Lisa slammed the knife into the potato, frustrated. "Well, he's certainly surprised me, Mom."

"I promised him I wouldn't let you know. I've never been able to say 'no' to him. But Art …"

"So Art called for you. Yes. You still see him?"

Her mother nodded.

Lisa had been so young when Art had proposed. All the excitement of leaving school was jumbled up with their brief engagement in her memory. All her ambitions for study were somehow tied up with his association with the college. And once the marriage had all been agreed, momentum built till it became unstoppable. She'd gone along with it. Living on campus, she attended classes, cooked his meals, washed his clothes and quietly died inside.

"Oh, Lisa, it was wrong," her mother said. "You were far too young. I realize that now."

173

"I got what I wanted, Mom," Lisa said. She hadn't meant to sound so sad, nor bitter.

Her mother drew her into a hug. "But at what cost?"

"It's alright, Mom. It's over now. I've made a good life. Come and visit. Come and stay a while."

"Nevada. I don't know about that."

"It's not like it's another planet, Mom. Just because you and Dad didn't stray far from Grandma and Pop, it's still America. It's not that different to here. It's just twenty degrees warmer. Twenty degrees easier."

"Maybe."

The soup simmered as Lisa followed her mother down to the basement to fold clean sheets. Her mother explained they'd wanted it this way, that they wanted his final days to be at home.

…

You've reached Lisa Bakker's message bank. Please leave a message.

Too bad if Lisa never replied, Will told himself, though his heart was hurting. Just a bit. Still, he had plenty to keep him occupied. First he needed to find a shop to rent in the historic part of town, preferably with accommodation above it. Then he needed to work out costs, and make that business plan James had requested.

The real estate agent showed him straight to a vacated travel agency, next door to a pizzeria, with accommodation above. The new bypass was spooking retailers. Afraid that custom would drive on by, they were breaking their leases and moving out, but Will wasn't worried and the price was right. In his view, Boulder City was a destination in itself, and his boutique business an extra reason for sightseers to stop in. At least he'd be selling goods, not ideas, and even if most young people preferred to shop online, the shop could double as his warehouse. He could ship from Boulder City as easily as from anywhere else, to anywhere in the world.

Will was already planning his website, looking forward to sharing his ideas with his sister, Nicole, who looked after branding and public relations for the Sydney business.

Bing.

Was it Lisa? His heart quickened. But no. It was Mindy.

Come to a product launch with Shelly and me? Vegas. Friday. ProFit sports gear annual product launch. We have three free tickets.

Friday was ages away. Anything could happen between now and then. Lisa might even ring back. In two days he'd left her fifteen messages, without a peep in return. He knew he'd have to stop messaging, or he'd come across as creepy.

He resolved to wait at least twenty-four hours before responding to Mindy. To head back into Vegas hadn't been in his plans, nor was spending time with Mindy and Shelly; but if nothing else was happening, maybe it would be a good test of his new resolve. Get close to those casinos and see what happened. Spend not one cent in them. Check out the roulette wheel for old time's sake, then walk on by. He could do that, couldn't he?

Besides, exercise gear was an option for his shop. And maybe he could glean a few ideas for his own opening event.

Next evening, with still no word from Lisa, Mindy's invitation beckoned. Part of him was angry at Lisa's refusal to reply. Maybe she'd only ever been interested in him just as a client. Had he misread her body language? He didn't think so, but then again, she was a total "no, no, no" person. Serious. Inhibited. Maybe they needed to be together physically for her to loosen up.

He reconsidered Mindy's invitation. Building a new life for himself meant he'd need to make new friends. Mindy and Shelly were harmless enough. He wouldn't do anything silly with them. They were so young they were practically girls. He was past all of that. He'd just keep them company for the event. He texted Mindy back.

Thanks for the invite, Mindy. Delighted to join you and Shelly on Friday night.

Super! See you there!

Nothing wrong with his phone, then. Mindy had responded immediately.

…

Will had a new kind of win one afternoon that week. He wandered into the Boulder City Library as he explored his surroundings. The librarians made him welcome. Sondra, a jolly volunteer with an afro, sixty plus, wore an "ask me" badge, so he did, and before long he was ushered into their computer lab and was shown a whole bunch of business-plan outlines.

175

Turned out Sondra Martin had been an Economics teacher at the local high school. She was passionate about Boulder City. When he shared his plans to open a shop in the main street, she was only too happy to show him how to use Excel, then how to summarize his ideas for an audience on PowerPoint.

"Cool," he said, and she glowed. "Almost as good as online gambling!"

"None of that here in Boulder," she warned.

"Just joking," he said. He gave her a winning smile. Finding Sondra had been a real stroke of luck. She wasn't above having a bit of a flirt, either. It was fun and took his mind off Lisa's disappearance. They had the lab all to themselves.

"I love your accent, Will. Tell me all about what you have in mind."

In return, as a Boulder City local, born and bred, Sondra shared her font of knowledge. She described its various festivals and visitors, the crowds who tended to turn up on weekends and special days. They pulled up a calendar and added a timeline. With Valentine's Day, Mother's and Father's Day and other retail highlights, there'd be plenty of reasons for people to visit his shop.

Will took a twirl on the library chair, then clapped Sondra on her shoulders and hooted. His plan would be solid. James had never let on that working in business could be this much fun.

"I thought I was having a ball with all that empty partying, year after year," Will told Sondra, who tried to calm him down. "Big brother James stayed sensible," he said. "If this is how it feels to take responsibility for my own future, I want more of it. Bring it on."

"So tell me again what you want to sell?"

"Strange combination," he warned. "And you're sworn to secrecy."

"Cross my heart." She smiled back.

"Exactly," he said. "I need a name. Something with 'heart' in it."

"Oh, why's that?"

He looked at her and gave her his best smile. "It's for my Queen of Hearts."

"That's just lovely! But tell me again what you're selling?"

"I'm still working it out, and you're the expert on who buys what around here and what you're all missing, but here's what I think …"

Sondra was a good listener. She had so many good suggestions, Will brought her a bunch of flowers next day. She blushed.

"Let's get this brand straight, Will," she said. "What's your value proposition? You need a mission statement. A tagline. We're not done here yet. An international branch of an Aussie iconic jewelers House of Diamonds, but it's outdoor wear, you say? So it's for people who want healthy lifestyles? That goes with Boulder. How about 'House of Hearts' for healthy hearts?"

"Sondra, you are amazing! When you come to the opening, you can pick any item in the shop."

"Ooh, I'd like that," she said. "But you'll need more help."

"I do. How are your design skills?"

"I was pretty good at creating the poster for the school musical each year. Show me the Sydney store's website?"

Sondra quickly picked up on the design elements, the colors and font, the gold lettering, and pulled up InDesign.

"We can do this, Will, my friend."

"You're on fire, Sondra. Lunch is on me. What's it to be?"

"Oh, you shouldn't."

"You've got no idea what you're worth, do you, Sondra? Undervalued, I'd say. A designer would charge thousands for this."

"I'm not done yet," Sondra said. "You go get the lunch. I'll get you some options. I love a good project. I love my job. Every day's different. And I love Boulder City. Boulder needs good businesses, a newcomer with fresh ideas. You're sure welcome, Will."

They worked flat out for a couple of days, to finalize the plans. Will settled on a big gold HoH in the same font as Huntleys, the lower half in green and the top in sky blue, with the bar of the Hs forming the horizon. All of it sat inside a heart.

They incorporated the logo into the PowerPoint summary and gave each slide a footer the color of the dry Vegas valley, with green, forested peaks on either side, and blue sky above.

Maybe he could source his own outdoor gear, and brand it House of Hearts. Or host or sponsor one of the Nevada skyrunning comps. They weren't far from the pristine Virgin Mountains. His imagination was alive with possibilities, and Sondra listed them in dot points.

"Brainstorm. This is good, Will. You would have been one of my top pupils."

"If I hadn't been wagging," Will said, then checked himself. It was no longer something to be proud of.

"Retailing's in my blood," he said. Something positive. For once, Will was proud to say it.

"Sure is," Sondra said.

Will invited Sondra to proofread his presentation while he stacked some books for her and cleaned up after the school children's visit.

By Thursday afternoon, he'd finalized his plans and sent them through to James. Will gave Sondra a wink and a high five before he sauntered out alone into the rest of the evening.

"Don't be a stranger," she said.

"No way, Sondra," he said. "You are House of Hearts royalty, my first VIP. You keep in touch." And he meant it. He was going to give that generous woman a job, even if she didn't know it yet. Why did women like Sondra think they should do things for nothing for everyone? How many other people had she helped out for nothing? He would pay her to do his books, if she was interested, that was for sure. Either way, he'd pay her for that brand work and her careful charts, as soon as he got his first thousand dollars jingling in the cash register. Would he give her cash, or a cheque, or make a transfer from Huntleys House of Hearts? Visualising the possibilities and her astonishment made him laugh out loud. He couldn't set things up fast enough. How good would it be to earn his own money and spend it any way he wanted…

He must introduce her to Lisa. Maybe they already knew each other.

Will cut past Bicentennial Park and Wilbur Square where the lights were on and a small team was practicing baseball. He considered joining in. Maybe another time.

A couple more miles and he swung west towards Lisa's street. He'd never forget the time he'd driven her home to help Rossco. His heart quickened. He'd love to tell her about his plans. Would she be home?

But no. There was nothing here for him. No sign of her car in the drive. No lights on in her house.

He headed back into town, puzzled. He hoped she was okay. He pulled out his single key and took himself up into the empty apartment above the shop. The droll puzzle of the former tenant's life amused him. He pondered the reasoning behind what was taken and what was left behind.

While Will was at the retreat, James had contacted an agent for him. With rent for his Bondi Junction apartment coming in soon, now that he no longer gambled all he had, Will had been able to pay the Boulder agent two weeks' rent in advance to secure this property, so fresh on the market it hadn't even been cleaned.

For Will, the bypass was a blessing. If it spooked the other retailers, he wasn't worried. He'd literally walked right into the best position in town.

In the residence above the shop, he opened the fridge to slap up a mystery dinner, then changed his mind. There wasn't much he could do with two empty sauce bottles, some mouldy cheese, an old onion and bad milk. He'd have to stock up soon. And he'd be able to. Having money was a relief alright. So much about his new life was so much better than the life he'd been leading.

Will was relieved to have captured all those thoughts and plans for the business and sent them off to James. He hoped he'd go for it. At least he could take a breather now while he waited for James's response. He grabbed an old takeout food bag and started to clean out the fridge.

He found a packet of cashews in the back of a top cupboard. Unopened. Bonus. Maybe the previous tenant had been too short to notice them.

Eventually, with spare clothes under his head and his coat across his legs, he curled up on the carpet. From here, he could even make out a few stars. It wasn't too plush yet, but he was out of the cold wind and free to dream. It had been days since he'd tried Lisa's number.

You've reached Lisa Bakker's message bank. Please leave a message.

...

Lisa's father was struggling to breathe, so Dr Fischer agreed to pay a house call. Lisa could barely believe he was still in practice. He'd been old when she was a child, old and wizened. He was even more stooped now, though clearly still on the ball.

"Lisa." He smiled as she opened the door. He stamped the snow off his boots and removed them, then pulled off his beret and hung up his coat.

"Long time no see! How's the big clinic out west? Plenty of custom with Vegas so close, I guess."

She nodded. It was Lisa's turn to stay with her father, while her mother got some rest. Lisa was so weary she wondered if Dr Fischer's arrival was just part of a nightmare.

He removed his gloves and almost bowed to her, as if in apology at the reason for his visit. She led him into her parents' bedroom.

Lisa's parents seemed joined by tubes, so close they could be one strange beast. Perhaps they were.

She crossed the room to join them, linking her hands with theirs. The world shrank to their hands and eyes and Dr Fischer's stethoscope, and that ragged breath, in, and out; in … and out. Perhaps they were all inside her father's lungs, willing him to breathe.

"My girls," he whispered, opening his eyes and closing them again, his fingers busy with the bedsheets, breath so faulty, halting.

"Yes, dear, we're here," her mother said. "We're both here."

Later that night, Lisa entered her own room in a daze. Her mother had insisted she go and rest. It was still all here, a time capsule dedicated to her childhood. The single bed still had all its flouncy covers, and every one of her ballet trophies was still lined up and dusted along the top of the bookshelf.

The photos of her showed her growth, year after year, captured by the school photographer. She was smiling to please everyone; no front teeth in Kindergarten, bangs and braids in the early years, big nose and braces in high school. She could recognize it all, the progression. She'd been cute, then awkward, then, finally, tall and slender, trusting, confident.

On the dressing table, her mother had placed the picture of her as a young bride, with Art beside her. She looked angelic. Innocent. Art looked like the cat that got the cream. He had. He'd taken her youth and wasted it.

Art. She shuddered. He'd worshipped her, but not with his body.

Now, as she nestled under the covers, it was only Will who came to mind, Will with his buff body and that bad-boy smile, Will leaning towards her, as if he couldn't keep away.

Chapter 20

"Jim, Nicole, I need to see you in the office, please. Two pm?" Back in Sydney, James was all fired up. "Will's plans have come through. I need you to scrutinize them. Nicole, ring Scottie, please. Find out if he's free; we need advice on trading in the US."

Will had been unexpectedly thorough, his presentation impressive, James noted. He'd never been known for his academic efforts, but the whole thing had even been branded properly. He was giving Nicole a run for her money. "House of Hearts." Nice. Perfect synergy with the House of Diamonds founding business, there in Bondi Junction. Who could have guessed Will had something like this in him?

There was even an aerial map of Boulder and the store's location, on a corner right in the center of the tourist part of town. Trust Will to wander in and secure something like that within a couple of days. The agent must have been female, James surmised. Others might have to apply, give references, and wait for landlord approval. Will would have just had to smile.

Then there was a summary of the demography of Boulder and its visitors, and a list of the annual major events that brought in crowds. There were quite a few. The town had been quite lively the day he'd visited, and clearly that hadn't been unusual.

"Huntleys in the US," said Jim, rubbing his gnarly old hands together. "By Jove!"

"Great idea to sell the exercise gear," said Nicole. "That's fresh. Great combination for hipsters."

181

"The numbers look conservative," said Scottie, their accountant. "I like that in a plan."

"So do we give him capital?"

"How much does he need?"

"I can't believe how good this is," James said. "He's modelled three scenarios. Lean, moderate and optimistic. When did Will learn to do all this?"

"Ask him."

"I will. Tomorrow morning. What's our answer?"

...

"I detect Lisa," James opened their conversation.

"What? Where is she?" Will shouted into the phone, on high alert.

"Whoa. Calm down, bro."

"Sorry, James. It's just I haven't seen Lisa since I left the clinic. She won't answer my calls, and she's not at her home. I thought you might know something. At first I was just disappointed. But now, I'm worried."

"Sorry to hear that, Will. I'm sure there's an explanation. You two seemed pretty keen on each other, to be honest. I might have made a few assumptions."

"So did I. But ... nothing."

"Sorry to hear that. Unusual for you to get a rejection."

"That's not helpful."

"I'm actually calling about business, Will; about your plan. We've looked it over, and we like it. This might sound like an insult, but did you get some help?"

"Yeah, a bit. Maybe a lot – from a fabulous black librarian called Sondra, ex Economics teacher. She's agreed to stay involved. We're working on a contract. But Lisa's my reason for doing this. Boulder wouldn't interest me that much if she didn't live here. Let's just say I've got plans, long-term ones. I'll impress Lisa yet. So, you really like the idea?"

"Jim wants you to sell some of his rings," said James. "He had some US friends in the war. He's excited about a US Huntleys branch. He can't wait."

"Well, as you saw, I wasn't going to do jewelry," said Will. "Thought I'd do my own thing. Exercise gear. I don't want to disappoint Jim, though. If things go to plan, I'll be needing one of his rings, alright. And Nicole?"

"She likes the logo and the website plans, including the online sales thing. She's off working on it already."

"You're kidding!"

"No," said James. "It might fly, Will, if you keep on the straight and narrow. Which you've never done before."

James's tone was grudging, cautious, but there was no mistaking it. It was far from rejection. Adrenaline surged through Will. He wanted to hoot. Wanted to holler. This was better than gambling. This was a real win.

"You okay there, Will?"

"Better than okay. If I can just find Lisa, I'll be set."

"We're going to need some photos to show, for then and now," said James. "Nicole said she wants to include some of these plans on our website, along with Mother's plans for the French branch. Nicole says it expands our brand internationally, under a 'House of Huntleys' umbrella."

"Not bad."

"Keep your receipts. Scottie insists. He says the tax is complicated, but he's excited. He says there might even be opportunities to float, down the track."

This was better than even Will could have imagined.

"If you're turning your life around, it's in our interests to encourage you," said James.

Will was astonished. Old Will would have taken any benefit and run. New Will wanted to make it work, to prove his worth.

"Mutual benefit," said Will. "I get it."

"Don't you dare let us down, Will. Your track record's appalling, but Father would have wanted this. Let's make it work."

"Hand on my heart, James, this is the new Will. You'll see."

"We'd better. Small steps. We can't invest much. We're trying to stay afloat ourselves."

"You won't be disappointed. No booze for more than a month, and my mind's on fire. I never realised how much fun it can be to create something like this, something big."

"Have you contacted Mother?" James said. "She and Emile could take a leaf out of your book. You're way ahead on paper. They've got half their glass cabinets made, but they don't even have a name for their store yet."

Sweet victory swelled through Will like a win, but it wasn't enough. He wanted to share the news — with Lisa.

A rush of wind through an open window flapped at a crushed and fallen poster of the Carribean on the dusty floor of the empty shop as Will reflected on the travel agent's failed dream.

He punched in Lisa's number again.

Leave a message.

Chapter 21

It was going to have to happen sometime; this test of Will's resolve. Would he have preferred to have had Lisa beside him? Yes. Was Lisa answering her phone? No.

Will had managed to hitch into Vegas in good time. He knew his way to Jupiter's and there was no question it made his heart race to walk in those doors.

The garish carpet smelled of hope and despair. There were the same tempting machines, singing their little songs to lure him into their reach, the pretend jangle of coins. Someone, somewhere, sometime had to win those jackpots, so it might as well be him, mightn't it?

Palms sweating, he stopped at a machine. It welcomed him with its lights flashing gold and spinning, just for him. He raised one hand, caressed the smooth edge of it. That visceral thrill arced through him like a lightning strike.

What would it hurt? A little flutter? Who would know?

Dopamine. Dopey, dopey, dopamine. Don't do it.

Why not? Lisa said …

Lisa who?

Lisa who never returned his calls.

The money would come through from James soon, wouldn't it? They'd never find out if he won. There'd be the original amount, plus extra. How would they actually know what went on over here, what the real costs would be? Will could win back more than he betted. That was the aim of the game.

If he was a winner tonight, he wouldn't even need their backing, wouldn't need anyone to invest in his shop. Hell, if he won big time tonight, he'd even be able to hire private detectives to find Dr Lisa Bakker and ask her a thing or two about silence. He'd show her.

The machine jingled a little comforting tune at him. It sparkled a little hopeful, "you're so lucky tonight" tune that only Will could truly understand.

He reached for his wallet and pulled out the credit card. It would be so easy. He'd just be quick. And if he was losing, he'd walk away.

He was just about to bring the card to the machine when the Queen of Hearts flashed onto the screen. The vision jolted him out of the moment and back into the white consulting room, with Lisa, his real Queen of Hearts, her beautiful molasses eyes locked on his.

Lisa had known he'd face these temptations. Maybe all his life. She'd known it and she'd almost kissed him anyway. She didn't deserve for her work to mean nothing.

He closed his eyes and tried to block out the machine's persistent tinkling tunes. Remembered again how Lisa warned them all how it might be, and the way they'd visualized how they could simply walk past; how to "walk on by." They'd practiced the self-talk. "I don't do that anymore."

He said it to the machine now, in that great hall of hope and exploitation. "I don't do that anymore." He said it twice. The second time louder.

He stepped away. His chest heaved with the effort.

A wave of nausea rose up inside of him. He'd come so close to losing it all, all his plans, all his dreams, his entire future. His heart pounded.

Hands shaking, he slid his card back into his wallet; sought a path out of the maze of machines; found a side door. Heat gushed in as he escaped.

Bile rose in his stomach. He sank to the gutter, dismayed. Was that all it took to fall off the precipice? Just one bet, and all would have unravelled; he'd be back in that free fall of failure, that downward spiral, the loneliest road to nowhere.

Had nothing he'd learned at the clinic sunk in? He bowed his head, pushed his palms into his eyes, as if they might expunge the hideous shame of what he'd almost done, but his all-night binge on the phone in the all-white room was vivid. *Despair.* If he had to cry, he would, dammit. He wasn't too proud. But betting again? That was out of the question.

186

He'd beaten the temptation of the phone, and he'd beat this. He'd go right back in there. Even in this shaken state he would test himself, tempt himself, but he would take no bait.

Will stood, squared his shoulders and chose the grand entrance. Head high, he noted the chandeliers, the sheer showmanship of the décor, as if this were a palace for the people and not some trick to lay them low.

A bar showcased all the bourbons and whiskies of the world, lit up from behind like sweet and harmless honey, the color of Lisa's eyes.

He began to salivate, hot with new anticipation. The need for alcohol slammed against the front of his skull and the roof of his mouth.

He inhaled and shook his head; steadied himself. "Walk on by," he whistled to himself. He had something better to do than gamble or drink. He was a man with a long-term plan. He was there to meet and impress the suppliers of outdoor wear and see what he might learn.

Up the grand staircase he strode. The women in high heels looked like school girls in too much makeup. Maybe they were. It didn't stop them from giving him the eye. He wouldn't be human if he didn't smile back. They elbowed each other as they passed him. He hadn't lost it. Good. Lisa might ignore him, but others still found him interesting.

In the grand showroom, ProFit had spared no expense. Had they hoovered up Junior High gym talent? Young people in figure-hugging gym clothes were up on daises in every direction, working out on black exercise equipment, spotlit. And what was this beside each black piece of gear? A matching set, slightly smaller, in hot pink? Of course. Why sell one machine when you could sell two? ProFit His and Hers.

On the machines, working in synch, beautiful bodies, males in black, females in hot pink and a few indeterminate figures in ProFit lime green. An LGBTIQ+ line? About time.

Three waiters descended on Will, each keener than the last to impress upon him a suitable beverage. Sparkling wine, bourbon and fizz; and tinkling trios of ice-cold beer with perfect heads. He took a still water, downed it in one gulp, gave a beatific smile and scanned the room for the exercise-wear display.

On stage, more perfect bodies performed a choreographed dance in skin-tight, skin-toned gym gear. Even Will raised his eyebrows. Very Vegas.

It was almost half past six when a wide man in a black suit with a ProFit green tie mounted the stage, flanked by two women in minimal evening dresses, with puffy-lipped smiles and plenty of cleavage. The man obviously didn't use the exercise equipment. Perhaps the women did.

Tech people in black adjusted the microphone, while a cluster of camera-wielding reporters detached themselves from the other displays and hustled down the front.

"Welcome, welcome, welcome," said black suit, and all the demonstrators froze and turned towards the stage.

"I'm Dave Winbourne, CEO of ProFit and we're proud to host the thirty-third annual ProFit expo."

The women beside him clapped madly and smiled like their faces would crack, prompting all the demonstrators to do the same.

"Are you loving our ProFit team; loving ProFit?"

Claps and cheers. Camera flashes.

"Enjoy!"

More applause, and the spotlights turned back to the demonstrations while teetering women escorted Dave down the stairs and into the crowd, like bulbous stick insects with a ripe piece of giant fruit and the media moved among the crowd, capturing Dave here, Dave there.

Suddenly, Will was pounced on from behind by Shelly and Mindy, in orange and white and not much.

As a photographer appeared, they leaned in towards him with their best selfie smiles, each kissing one of his cheeks.

He was dazzled by the flash. Deja vu.

"We found you!"

"You sure did," Will said, in a "down boy" tone of voice.

They were far more enthusiastic about the whole thing than he was. Was he getting old or was a lack of alcohol spoiling his fun? Too bad. He'd give Mindy and Shelly a good time, try to get some useful information about the fitness industry, then get out of there.

A big band started up on the far side of the room. Mindy and Shelly latched onto his arms and pulled him across to the dance floor, delighted with themselves. Just as they went to step onto the dance floor, Will leaned in towards Mindy's ear.

"Heard from Lisa at all?"

"Huh?"

"How's Lisa? Is she okay?"

Mindy grabbed Will's shoulder and teetered up even higher on her tiptoes to whisper into Will's ear, just as another camera flashed.

"I can't hear you."

It was pointless. Will gave up and danced instead. There were plenty of starlets here, lots of good-looking people gyrating away for ProFit; he, Mindy and Shelly among them. At least the music was okay. While dancing, he could neither drink nor gamble; and it gave him a chance to let off some steam.

He'd come so close to gambling again, he was rattled. What if he'd lost every gain he'd made in the past few weeks? It was right to dance – to dance with pure relief at his close escape.

The set finished and he offered to get Mindy and Shelly a drink. Easy. They both wanted champagne. And he only had two hands. Maybe then he'd be able to slip away, back to Boulder, back to cleaning out cupboards, which strangely appealed to him more than any of this.

He looked forward to the long jog back to Boulder. He'd enjoyed training at the clinic gym when there'd be precious little else to do. But events like this? They left him cold. He was a changed man alright.

Suddenly, a reporter appeared at his elbow. *Uh-oh. Trouble.*

"You're Will Huntley, aren't you?"

"Who? Excuse me, I'm just …" Will twisted away with an apologetic smile and the two champagnes, and hot-footed it through the crowd to Shelly and Mindy, who were thrilled. It was a good time to make his exit.

"Sorry, ladies. Gotta go. Thanks for a great night."

"Ohhhhh?!" Anyone would think a kitten had died, the way they pouted. He couldn't wait to escape.

…

Back on the road to Boulder, with the lights of Vegas behind him, Will swung his blazer over his shoulder, rolled up his sleeves and began to jog.

In the moonless night, the desert stars began to shine. The silence, apart from the swish of cars and trucks on the smooth road, was blissful compared to the blare of high capital.

He congratulated himself. He'd gone there, into the mouth of the dragon, and if he hadn't managed to find a suitable supplier of his outdoor range, at least he'd escaped unscathed.

Or so he thought. He probably shouldn't have said a word to the reporter. Even his Aussie accent might have given him away.

In his few days of freedom, Will had come to love this land, the dry rubble and vast emptiness of it as he ran each day, determined to keep building his fitness. That the hardy groundcovers survived without water reminded him of parts of Australia, parched with drought.

This was a land of contrasts. Sometimes he'd come upon soaks so green the palm trees burst out like they were having a party; a riot of plenty.

The valley was tough country alright, so flat it felt like the edge of the world, and then, those mountains, those soaring peaks and pinnacles and ridges as steep as a knife's edge, thumped across with patches of snow against every shade of brown.

And everywhere, a new discovery. Scorpions. Gemstones.

That night? A sky full of stars. He walked for hours, first flushed with relief at his escape, then glad to fall in with the rhythm of his steps. He revelled in the strength of his body, mile after mile. He kept running, beyond Boulder. Why not?

As he ran, one tiny figure in the darkness, the crunch of each step as rhythmic as his heart, his determination to make something of his life took hold. Where had he been for the last decade? Partying with strangers. He was done with that. It was high time to put down roots and see what he could achieve. Boulder City was as good a place as anywhere to make his mark.

He'd scoffed when old school mates knuckled down to their studies and gave up their freedoms for careers and mortgages and families. Now? He was envious. He wanted to make a home with Lisa, to wake up beside her every day.

When the sun began to rise, flushing out the stars, a breath of pink along the horizon, its warmth lit his heart. An optimism rose in him, pure and strong. He would make a future here. A good one.

He'd changed. He knew it in his bones. He was a better man.

Hours later he was still walking. He'd have to escape the sun. He headed down off the shoulder of the road, down into a valley, down deep among the rocks, where he found shade among the small flat rocks of an ancient wash.

He'd retrieved a complementary water bottle from the casino. It looked so out of place here in the desert, glaring with its ProFit brand. He sipped it. It would need to last.

As he sat, his fingers fell to the pebbles beside him. Absentmindedly, he tumbled them, testing their weight. They interested him, looked familiar. Petrified wood? Maybe. Was he hallucinating? These stones weren't just brown. They hinted at other colors, blues, greens and reds. He rubbed one with his thumb. Held it up to the light. Yes, he was sure of it. A translucence you'd only notice if you'd seen it before. Opals.

A memory rose from his childhood. Nicole's obsession with gemstones. She'd had a favorite. A rough opal. Uncut. She'd spit on it to make it shine.

Jim had noticed her do it at the dinner table one Sunday and promised to show her how to make it shine forever; invited her up to his lair. Will had been jealous and then lost interest, happier to run around outside with a ball, but the next Sunday, Nicole had appeared with her own stone on a long piece of leather around her neck. Even he'd had to admit it was beautiful. He'd watched it right through lunch, fascinated by the way the colors flashed and changed. How had they done that, she and Jim? Made an old stone into something precious?

Now, in the desert, Will pulled out his phone and typed in "Nevada" and "opals."

Sure enough, he found black fire opals. He read how the moisture of ancient thermal springs was trapped in vegetation and transformed with heat, forging something rotten to something so solid it confounded time and sparkled to boot. Treasure.

If he could phone Nicole, maybe she'd remember what she'd done to make it shine.

When had he last phoned Nicole? After another win, back in Monte Carlo. She hadn't been impressed. Had told him he'd just lose it all again, so what was the point. She'd been right. But that wouldn't ever happen again.

"Will?"

"Nicole!"

"Where are you?"

191

"Nevada."

"Are you alright? I'm not giving you any more money, if that's what you want. Jesus, Will. It's five am. What is it?"

"God, sorry, Nicole. Ring you back later?"

"No. I'm up now. What's up?"

"Just found some opals."

"Good for you. Is that all? I mean. Sorry, Will. What do you want?"

"How are you, Nicole?"

"Better when I was fast asleep."

"I said sorry, okay?"

"Yeah alright. What is it?"

"Remember that opal you had? The big one; teardrop shape, that you wore around your neck?"

"The one I polished myself?"

"Yeah. How'd you do it?"

Nicole yawned. He imagined her scowling out the window at a pale-pink dawn.

"God, Will. I haven't thought about that for ages. How old were we, even? I was only nine. Took bloody ages. Jim wouldn't let me use his power tools. 'Start rough and finish fine,' he kept saying." Nicole yawned again.

"Start rough and finish fine," Will repeated, revving her up before she fell asleep again.

"Alright for him with the polishing machine," Nicole said. "I had to use a knife block. Scrape, scrape, scrape. Took forever, but every time my hand got tired, I'd take another peek; and more and more colors glinted, as if all the beauty of it was in there, trying to escape and shine, and only I could set it free."

"Nice one, Nicole."

"When I'd got all the brown stuff off the outside and it started to take shape, Jim lent me a dop-stick. I remember heating the wax, then he set the stone on the hot stick, wetting his fingers first. And then he laid out a towel and brought out the different grades of black paper."

"Sandpaper?"

"Yeah," she said. "What did you think? Wrapping paper? I went up every afternoon after school, and on Saturday, he brought out a strip of leather and some brown powder, cerium oxide, I think he called it. We made a paste with some water, and then I had to rub it some more. All the while, he did his own magic across the bench, using the good stuff, extruding gold."

Will could almost smell the blow torch of Jim's lair.

"I was so proud of that stone, Will," Nicole said. "I wore it under my school uniform for years. I'm still proud of it, and it's still a beauty. I put it on a chain a few years ago. The leather strap got a bit festy. Hey, I might wear it today. Haul it out."

"Thanks, Nicole," said Will.

"So go on," she said. "Tell me. What's up with you? James said that place you were at was okay. Said you looked alright. I've seen your plans. Aren't you opening an adventure shop? Have changed your mind again so soon, Will?"

It was good to hear Nicole's voice. She'd been a grumpy big sister, but she was still family.

"I have plans alright," said Will. "Still working things out. Setting some goals, beyond the next party. Surprised?"

"I'll believe it when I see it."

"Come on," said Will. "What about you?"

"What about me?"

"James said something about you and Scottie."

"Nice guy, Scottie."

"Sure is. What about the two of you?"

"What about your own love-life, sticky beak. More headlines coming up?"

"I'm so over all that," said Will. "But yeah, I have plans. A man can dream, can't he?"

"Definitely! So when are you coming home?"

"I might not," he said. "Depending on how things go. I might stay here."

"Really!"

"Like I said, I've got some plans. Might take some polishing, you might say."

"Yeah, well, good luck, Will. You sound different. You were always the winner, till you forgot what game you were playing."

"Thanks, Nicole. All the best to you and Scottie. So. Looks like I need a knife block."

"Don't forget the sandpaper!"

Will stood, looked around him in every direction and chuckled. No hardware shops here. No supermarkets. He grabbed a handful of rubble, picked out the most promising stones, shoved them in his pocket and dropped the rest.

He pulled up his location on his phone and took a screenshot. While he didn't plan to sell opals anytime soon, it might be fun to bring Lisa back here one day; show her what he'd found.

Then he drank more water and headed up to the road, back towards civilization, back towards the future.

Chapter 22

Lisa's mother insisted on accompanying her to the little airport. She was so small, even in her black commuter coat. It looked like another whole person when she took it off in the heated interior of the airport and folded it over her arm.

Part of Lisa hated to leave her mother like this, alone; but the funeral was over and Donna was surrounded by the friends of a lifetime. She'd never been impulsive; would never accompany her out west on a whim. Maybe in time.

For now, her mother would doubtless carry on her routine, but without her father. She would donate the medical equipment and his best things, keeping one or two, then pick up her usual pastimes. Art would probably even turn up for a meal again, on Sunday as usual. Lisa shuddered.

Her mother had insisted Art join them the previous evening. He'd sat in his usual chair, with Lisa in the one she'd occupied as a child; her father's chair empty like a missing front tooth. They glanced at it repeatedly, mentioning him, filling in what he might have said about this or that; excruciating, with Art a doleful dog frowning at his walking leash, begging her to notice him. She couldn't escape fast enough.

Predictably, her flight was delayed due to ice on the wings. Frustrated business people and retirees bound for Miami and the Caribbean paced up and down, Lisa and her mother among them, prolonging their goodbye chit-chat.

"Anyone special in your life, Lisa?" her mother asked, chasing it with "maybe you'll come back and live here again."

Lisa knew her mother still hoped she and Art would kiss and make up. Now wasn't the time to spell out to her why that would never happen. She'd escaped. That was all that mattered.

Ignoring the first question, she flipped the second one on its head. "Maybe you'll come and visit me, Mom. Get away from the cold for a few weeks?"

"Maybe. Yes. I could, I guess. After a while."

Lisa smiled and squeezed her arm. Her father had been such a homebody, devoted to his hometown. Had he been the anchor? Would her mother now feel freer to explore the world?

They paced back and forth and looked at the little state souvenirs for sale, the candy shop, the dried cherries, the newsagency. Suddenly Lisa halted, curious, and stared at a magazine. A wave of pure dismay hit her. She snatched it up, took it to the counter to buy, then folded it in half and stowed it quickly in her handbag.

"What's that, dear? What a handsome young man!"

"Just something I need for work, Mom."

"Oh."

Further exploration of the topic was halted by the boarding announcement.

Safely in the air, the white, snowbound town rapidly retreated into the distance, and Lisa pulled out her purchase. It was Will alright, with that bad-boy smile, flanked by Mindy and Shelly from the retreat's gym.

"Aussie bad boy at Vegas clinic," the headline shouted.

"Serial heartbreaker Will Huntley has a new squeeze," the intro read.

"The Australian heir to a jewelry fortune is being treated at an exclusive Vegas retreat for recovering gamblers, retreat spokesperson Mindy McIntyre revealed exclusively to Your Celebrity.

"Mindy, pictured left with the Aussie heartthrob, said Will has been working out with exercise specialist Shelly Maxwell, right.

"Will leaves a string of broken hearts in Sydney and Europe, including one-time Italian fiancée Marina Giuseppa, who has links to the Italian royal House of Savoy.

"Will and his new Vegas friends were spotted in Jupiters at the thirty-third annual ProFit expo."

Lisa snapped the magazine shut and shoved it in the seat pocket in front of her. The steward arrived with the trolley, but Lisa shook her head, all appetite gone. Was Will's rapid reversion her fault? Had she let him down? She hadn't even said goodbye to him, wished him well. Dr Peters had stepped in and then, when Art had called, she'd panicked, in such a hurry to reach her father before it was too late.

"He may have only hours to live," Art had told her, stabbing her with the guilt knife as deeply as possible for leaving her parents, her state and their marriage.

She'd rushed away. But that had been about the past. Now this. Will's relapse. She'd hoped for so much more from Will.

She exhaled, deflated, hollow, confused.

Dr Peters had agreed Will's progress had been excellent. He'd responded to every aspect of treatment in record time. But human minds and emotions were fragile. Had she jeopardized Will's recovery there in the testing room when she'd almost kissed him, and by the way she'd then simply disappeared? Had she ruined his life?

Lisa gazed down at the frozen forests and tiny towns. For the first time, she doubted her choice of career. How could she ever be sure that those she treated really recovered? Maybe they all reverted; even Will, with his wit and energy and spark and sheer sex appeal.

She sighed. She shook her head when a steward offered her coffee.

No. She couldn't take on responsibility for every aspect of her client's lives. The burden would be impossible. Other therapists coped with this doubt. So must she.

The passenger on her left had pushed back the seat and snored gently, but there was no rest for Lisa. Will's handsome face stared at her from the seat pocket. She pulled it out again, reversed the fold and shoved it back in.

How dare Will ignore their treatment! How dare he run off with Mindy of all people, straight back into the jaws of his addiction. Jupiters! What was he thinking?

All that talk of settling down in Boulder? Had all of that been a lie? Had handsome Will Huntley ever planned to change his wayward ways? Probably not. He'd taken her for a fool. And maybe she was one.

This morning, when she'd gathered up her things, ready for the flight, there'd been more than a little relief and guilt at escaping back to her own life and the work she loved. After the sorrow, after the service and funeral reunions, after all the visits from friends and the many thanks for their concern and help, and the endless cups of tea and coffee and reminiscences, a part of her had hankered after her own space.

And, if she was honest with herself, the thought of seeing Will again, even in the distance, had been like a bright little doorway in her soul, in a universe of dark, dragging duty.

She'd even managed to deal with Art while he doted on her in his hurt, insipid way. Somehow she'd got through all of that, with the promise of something waiting for her back in her other life, something so much better.

Memories of Will had kept her sane, part of her anticipation at heading home to Nevada, even though he was out of bounds. She hadn't expected to fall in love with Will, or in lust with him, or whatever it was, but he certainly excited her. His kindness with Rossco had been nothing short of beautiful; an unexpected gift. Will made her feel alive.

She'd actually believed him when he'd said he'd settle in Boulder, when he'd shared his hopes to put down some roots at last and open a shop.

She pulled out the magazine again, slapped it on the tray table and flipped to the center pages, to the collage of images of Will and various stars and starlets from all over the world. A decade's worth. A quiet life together in Boulder eventually? A pipedream. Compared to Will's exciting life, her existence must be as colorless to Will as Art's was now to her. Will moved in circles inaccessible to therapists. She and Will might have had a few good chats and a lovely skyrun, but a whole future together? Doomed nonsense.

It served her right for letting herself get involved with a client. She was supposed to be there to help him change if he wanted to change, not prey on his glamorous life. Who was she to tell him he shouldn't be a playboy, anyway? Why should he ever settle down, let alone with her?

She studied the pages again; examined that bad-boy smile and those blue eyes. The worst of it was he looked like he was having fun, and so did Mindy.

It was only Dr Lisa Bakker who was miserable here. Dr Bakker with her fancy degree in human behavior, who couldn't even keep her own marriage together. What made her think she should judge and try to change the behavior of others? Miracle worker? Life saver? Fool. How could she hope to help others when she herself was miserable?

So much for being the good girl. Apart from leaving Art, she'd toed the line, studied carefully and always turned up for work on time. She was not a party girl. She would leave that life to someone like Mindy. Mindy wouldn't care when Will moved on, as he undoubtedly would; whereas Lisa's heart would hemorrhage. She and Will simply weren't compatible.

Will's charisma? Effortless. No wonder everyone loved him.

She sighed again.

So much for believing she might have held a special place in his heart. What kind of fairy tale had she been spinning?

Apart from the whole two-year dating ban for therapists and former clients, she was far too sensible to fall for someone like Will, surely, she told herself, at the announcement to put seats upright and stow tray tables. If she wanted to settle down in life, she'd be better off finding a more sensible match. Never Art. But certainly not anyone remotely like Will.

Besides, the first thing she had to do after touchdown was buy a new phone.

…

After ten days away, Lisa felt compelled to take an Uber straight to the clinic. Uh-oh. Three media vans jostled for space in the circular drive, blocking the entrance, their antennas screwed up high like strange probiscuses.

"Here's fine," she told the driver. "I'll walk the rest of the way."

The last time media vans had turned up was when they'd had country and western star David Deane staying. The news crews had camped out the front for days, trying to catch a glimpse of him.

Retreat media incident protocol demanded she go around the block and take the hidden back entrance, beside the swimming pool.

Gunther the pool attendant greeted her. "Long time no see!"

"What's going on, Gunther?" She had her suspicions, but she might be wrong.

"What? Those cameras? They still out there?"

Lisa nodded.

"That Aussie, I think. Will Huntley?" He lowered his voice, even though there was no one around. "Turns out he's some kind of bad-boy rich kid from Australia. Mindy and Shelly can tell you more, so I hear, but I don't even know if they work here anymore. Say, how you been, anyway?"

"Oh, I'm okay, thank you, but … my father, he's just … passed away."

"I'm so sorry to hear that, Dr Bakker. Well, welcome back. We missed you. Dr Peters will sure be glad to see you. Busy time."

The clinic waiting room was unattended. "Some things never change," Lisa thought, as she smiled politely at a waiting client. She wheeled her suitcase into her office, just as Dr Peters farewelled her two o'clock.

"Until tomorrow, then," she said to the client. "Keep up the good work."

"May I see you a moment, please, Dr Peters?"

"Lisa! Please."

Dr Peters entered her room and closed the door.

"Boy am I glad to see you! We're busier than ever. We might need to get another colleague. How are you anyway, Lisa?"

"I'm okay. What's with the media circus?"

"Will Huntley."

"But he checked out, didn't he? The same day I left?"

"He did."

"So what do they want?"

"You haven't heard the news?"

"I've seen this." Lisa pulled out the magazine and slapped it on the table. Will's cheeky face smiled back at her as if he were the happiest man in the world, with Mindy and Shelly equally ecstatic.

"All good publicity," Dr Peters said, nodding.

"Really?"

"It's gone international. We've had calls from potential patients in Europe and the UK. It's really put our name on the map."

"Isn't that because you spoke at that conference?"

"Maybe. No. Since this came out, there's been ten times the interest."

"Great, I guess. So how're my patients? And where's Mindy? Surely you can see my point of view now. We really need a better receptionist. And what's Shelly's story?"

"Mindy and Shelly are a bit overwhelmed with the media attention. They're just kids, all of them."

"No, he's a former client and they are current employees. Look, I know I'm in no position to be self-righteous, especially as far as Will is concerned. I'm grateful to you for your understanding and you have my highest respect, Dr Peters, but is no one else an adult around here?"

"Will's recovery is no longer any concern of yours, Lisa, and I run this clinic. I have another client now. Say, you look beat. And you're supposed to be taking more time off. Wasn't that our agreement? Have you started that boundaries course yet? Take off the rest of the month; then come back refreshed. We need you back here in top form."

As Dr Peters headed back down the corridor again, Lisa stepped into her room and sat on her couch. She closed her eyes and breathed, relishing some private time. She'd missed her blank walls, missed the routine of her client visits. She loved the profession she'd chosen, and enjoyed working with Dr Peters. So why was she still so rattled?

She ran her hand over the white leather of the couch. Oh, why lie to herself any longer? Alone for the first time in ten days, she gave in to her memories, of how much she'd loved to see Will each day, and how much she'd looked forward to his group sessions.

She pulled out the magazine, unfolded it fully and let him beam out at her. Party boy. "Party therapy." Pah!

So, he was more infamous than even she had guessed. She'd been trained to treat all her clients as individuals. All of them had stories, backgrounds, pasts. Sometimes their situations were relevant, and sometimes not. What mattered was that when they left the clinic, they felt better about themselves, more in control of their own choices, empowered to take their lives along new and healthier pathways.

Will had left. Okay. And she'd done her job as well as she could. If he'd chosen to turn around and go straight back into a casino, surely that was his decision to make.

If she'd thought he'd turned the corner and would make more sensible decisions, then that was her mistake. Who was she to pass judgement on people's lives, anyway? He looked happy enough in the photograph, didn't he? Good old short-term-thinking Will. He'd taken up with the closest, prettiest thing, or two of them for that matter. He wasn't the first spoilt heir to waste her time, and he wouldn't be the last.

She was deflated. More than that. Profoundly disappointed. Flat. She'd really believed she'd had a success story on her hands, had been certain they'd helped Will find a better path. Will Huntley was a puzzle, alright; a mystery. But if that mystery was no longer hers to solve, so be it.

Back in her car, she drove home, but couldn't let it rest, interrogating herself, over and over. She shook her head and sighed.

Hadn't he called her his Queen of Hearts? As if it had meant something? He had. Several times. And she had believed him.

So in fact, it was she who was behaving strangely. She was the one who'd taken the wrong path, while he had clearly done just as he always did, flattering the nearest floozy. Because that's how she'd behaved. She'd almost kissed him, back there in the testing room. What a fool! And to almost lose her career over him!

So now? Now it was time to put it all behind her; time to be sensible, and mark it down to experience. Refer to rule number one. "Never get involved with clients." How hard was that? Evidently, it wasn't always easy, particularly in the case of Will Huntley. But it was wise. It was the right thing. She would live and learn.

Besides, she had Mont Blanc to look forward to. She and Jilly could laugh about how she thought she might have had a thing going with Will Glitterati Huntley. Maybe she'd meet someone more suitable for herself over there.

Grateful for the time to self counsel, Lisa hauled her bag out of her car. She still felt sad; sadder than she should. Yes, sad to lose her father, who only ever wanted the best for her, even though he'd been wrong about what "the best" might be.

But it was more than that, this gloom that hung over her head. She had to admit she was also sad that her hopeful little golden dream about Will had been just a silly fantasy.

Well, she'd been disappointed in love before and survived. She must pick herself up again and keep on going; unpack her bag, go find a new phone and stock up at the supermarket. Phone the vet. Ask to collect Rossco tomorrow. She was exhausted in every way. She'd look forward to a long hot bath and snuggling into her own bed.

Easy enough.

Chapter 23

At his follow-up appointment, Will had plenty of news for Dr Peters.

"Your progress has been astonishing, Will."

"I'm a winner, Doc," he said. "I didn't spend a cent in that casino. No grog. Clean, clean, clean in every way, despite that drivel in *Celebrity*. It's you I need to thank for that, you and your team. Can't pretend I wasn't tempted. But you've totally turned me around. You and Lisa. Miracle worker."

"We need to talk about Dr Bakker, Will."

Will's antenna went up. He could sniff trouble in a tone of voice. All those fed-up teachers had taught him just how far to push the class-clown charm. One never forgot. Had Lisa said something?

"Is she okay? She never answers my calls."

"She can't answer your calls."

"Why?"

"There are professional boundaries in our profession, Will, just as there are in the medical profession. We can't have relationships with our clients."

Dr Peters locked eyes with Will. Will exhaled, stared into a corner, then closed his eyes; grasped the edge of the couch with his hands. What had Dr Peters taught him? To stop and think and recognize his emotions before he acted. Well, he knew this one, alright. Anger.

"Talk to me, Will."

"Did Lisa tell you she doesn't want to see me?"

"It's not about what you or Lisa want, Will."

"You're aware I've moved to Boulder to be near her," Will said, anger and dismay simmering. "With all this goal setting, I've planned my future around Lisa. And now you say I can't even see her? I don't believe this. Besides, how would you even know what I'm doing when I'm outside these four walls? This is ridiculous."

"I can understand your frustration, Will, but this decision isn't ours to make. It's industry policy. It's law," Dr Peters said. "It's not forever. I believe you can do this. And if you still feel the same way about her in two years, there'll be nothing to prevent you from approaching each other then. You have a sound plan. Build that business. Exercise patience. I say again, I believe you can do this. You know what you have to do."

Will grasped his fingers together, elbows on his knees and fixed his eyes on Dr Peters. "No gambling, no alcohol. No substances. Okay. But no Lisa? You realize what you're asking of me?" Will pushed his fingers through his hair in frustration, sat back, slapped both hands on his thighs.

"I do."

"And why would I do as you say?" Will tossed his head, defiant, and stared at Dr Peters.

"Because, if you truly care for Dr Bakker, you won't want to hurt her," Dr Peters said. "And if you continue to see her, she will be deregistered and stripped of her career. It's that simple."

"Jesus, Doc!" Will stood and threw his hands out.

"You can do this, Will. You resisted temptation at Jupiter's. You can do it again. You've come so far now."

"I don't want Mindy or Shelley, Doc. I want Lisa." Will sank to the couch.

"I want to show you this exercise. It's called pros and cons. Let's see what would happen if you pursued Lisa now. We'll explore what would be good and bad about that. And then we'll consider the pros and cons of you pursuing her in two years."

"But what if she's married to someone else by then?"

"It's a risk," Dr Peters said. "But there are other risks if you chase her now. Let's examine those."

...

Will pushed open the library doors. Sorely disappointed with the ProFit offerings, he had to search for alternative suppliers.

Sondra followed him into the computer lab.

"You didn't tell me you were famous," she said as she thrust *Your Celebrity* in his face.

"Oh, man! They never leave me alone. I made one bad mistake when I was still at school, and this particular journalist has never let me forget it. Every time I pop my head up anywhere, the paparazzi lurks, ready to have another go at me."

"So you're not Will Huntley?"

"Well, I am, but …"

"And you're not heir to a great jewelry fortune?"

"If only. We're jewelers, yes. But it's my brother James who inherited the business, and frankly, there's not much of the fortune left."

"And you haven't 'left a string of broken hearts all over Europe and the UK?'"

"They were all in it for the good time and were happy enough to move on," Will said. "But most of them were fabrications. It's a long story. Bad choice of first girlfriend. Gossip columnist with a bitter streak. Like I said, it's all a beat-up."

"And the House of Savoy?"

"Well, I have to admit that might have been a bit of a mistake. Everyone makes a mistake now and then, don't they, Sondra? How was I to know she'd take it all so seriously? Roman Catholic. Not to be messed with. She wasn't actually a contessa, by the way. Technically, no one is 'royal' in Italy anymore. All of that was thrown over in 1946. She was just from a hugely rich family."

Sondra was all ears.

"There was never anything much between us. A couple of wild parties. I tried to tell them early on it wasn't a serious proposal. There wasn't even a ring. I reckon it was her mother. Shockingly keen. Suddenly, there were bridesmaids and fittings for Italian suits and who knows what, but it was never my idea. I had to cut and run while there was still time."

Sondra narrowed her eyes.

"I'm not sure I believe you, Will. That's one long pile of excuses. Still, you take an exceptionally good photo. And you're famous. And you're settling here in our own Boulder City. Excellent! You are good news for our town, Will Huntley. My book club friends are going to be pretty interested."

"They weren't excuses! I don't even speak Italian." He shrugged. "There was bound to be a misunderstanding or two. And this." Will gestured at the magazine cover. "This is not at all like it looks. They take one photo and create this whole crazy story around it."

"There are more photos inside." Sondra flipped to page five.

Trip down memory lane. *Your Celebrity* must have bought every photo ever taken of Will, and now there were more. There was one of Mindy whispering in his ear, and one of him whispering in hers, and then three more of Shelly and Mindy pulling him onto the dance floor and a few gyrations. They looked like they were having the time of their lives. This proved that photographs could lie.

Will closed the magazine and turned it over so the advertisement for Pufferillo breakfast cereal was the only thing on show.

"Actually, Sondra, the reason I'm here again today is because that event was so bad. Yes, I was at that retreat, but the only reason *Celebrity* would realize that is because those two young women in the main pictures, Mindy and Shelly, work there."

Sondra's eyebrows were still up.

"They invited me to this thing, and the only reason I went with them was to check out the latest ProFit range for my shop," Will said. "Which I don't want. So now I'm back in here, to research other suppliers. And I'd love a hand if you're willing to give it again. Your business plan was sensational. The family's impressed. But I'm on a tight schedule, thanks to your project timeline. And I intend to keep to it."

Sondra sighed and pulled up a chair. "Have you done a google search? Do you want global suppliers, or only local ones?"

"Just 'outdoor wear,'" said Will. "How about we give some Australian and New Zealand suppliers a run?"

"Tariffs would be interesting."

"How do I find out about them, please, Sondra? You know I want to pay you for your help. I'm going back to Australia to settle a few things. I want you on my team. What do you say? Contract or casual?"

…

Will's head spun. That Sondra was a dynamo. There was no way he would sleep that night. Ideas and graphs surged through his brain, and always, in the background, he longed for the cool, calm, kind brow of Lisa Bakker – uncontactable Lisa, Lisa who taunted him from the sidelines, rationale, reasonable, his other half, his best half; now totally elusive. Was she even okay?

She must have seen the story. She'd be horrified.

He longed to reassure her it was nonsense. He reached for the phone again, the cool blue square of it. "Free bet." Fuck that. He flicked to messages. He'd left three screens' worth for her. No response. Same with calls. She would think he was stalking her.

What he needed was a good long run to clear his mind. He pulled on his shorts and runners and headed out, under a starry sky.

The run calmed him, the rhythmic crunch of his boots on the dry gravel at the side of the road, mile after mile after mile, the steady in and out of his breath, his body a machine that was made for this. That clinic had sure cleaned him up. Good food. Good rest. No grog. He preferred life this way. Clean. What did they call it? Wellbeing. Being well. Yeah. He liked it.

He was still walking as dawn began in the East, the whisper of light against the horizon, the fading of the stars. This big sky. He was getting used to it. He could live in Nevada – with Lisa; hell yes.

By now the mountains were bigger, their ridgetops dark against the rising of the light, some patches of snow on show as the sun rose, on those peaks that always reminded him of knives. As color seeped into the landscape, revealing the subtle beiges and browny greens of the tough groundcovers, he thought of Australia, so often in drought. Both were tough landscapes. Resilient.

But for the juggernauts that belted past several times an hour, all shiny metal and momentum and roar, he could be the only person in the world – himself and his pumping heart.

That ProFit launch had been such a circus. He didn't want his own business to be like that – all hype and sham – selling youth and sex and all that shiny training equipment most people would barely use more than a few times. No. He wanted to sell real stuff. Useful backpacks. The world's best skyrunning gear; climbing equipment – useful goods for people like him who loved to live on the edge in the great outdoors.

There was so much to explore here; so many spectacular parks and rock formations and remote peaks. He hadn't even started on the Grand Canyon, right next door in the next state. He could spend a lifetime here.

He'd been reading up on the geology. All those timescales that did his head in. Those opals he'd found? So ancient; bits of old plants and extinct animals, sitting on the floor of long-gone lakes, their water replaced by silica. Not all of it was valuable. A lot of it was soft, and flaked away. He'd been lucky with the one he'd found and was polishing for Lisa. So far so good.

He wanted to impress her. He thought about her. A lot. Funny that – Lisa was the only woman he'd truly considered marrying, and she was off limits. Mindy and Shelly had been all over him. But they were fast food. He wanted the full banquet, day after day.

Was he willing to wait for Lisa? Two years? Lisa was so cool; so controlled.

Did she realize what she did to him? What she meant to him? Not only had she brought him freedom to live a new life; she was the embodiment of all he desired. He wanted her like he wanted no one else.

What really shocked him was his willingness to consider waiting for her. He'd never had to wait before. But suddenly, all that womanizing? He was done with it. There was only one woman he wanted. And if she'd noticed that article, she'd reckon he was a loser.

...

Lisa was relieved to be home, but even with Rossco back at her heels, loneliness lurked in every dark corner.

"Stop it," she told herself as she put away the groceries. She left her new phone on the counter. "Later,' she said. "As if I don't have enough on my mind."

She needed to escape her thoughts and emotions. She knew what she had to do. She pulled on some exercise gear and ran out the door. Locked inside cars and planes and her parents' home for ten days, she was longing for freedom. Thank God winter in Nevada was bearable.

The light was just fading as she headed out, so she kept to the main streets, under the street lights. Nothing had changed while she'd been away. It was Thursday. The baseball team was training in the park. She did a few laps, then circled in just as they packed up.

Glen called out to her. "Hey, Lisa!"

"Hello," Lisa said.

"We missed you the last couple of weeks."

"Sorry," she said. "I had to go away."

"Welcome back." He beamed at her, tossing the ball into the glove repeatedly.

"Sorry I'm too late tonight, too," she said. "I only just got back."

"Hey, that's okay. You'll find we're a pretty relaxed team here. Say, what are you doing now? Can I offer you a meal? Just give me a chance to get cleaned up. Pizza maybe? Just something relaxed."

"Oh …"

He looked so decent. So safe. So unlike a playboy. But she did need dinner. And she was lonely. Isn't this what she told her clients? To reach out and take a safe risk now and then; to do something different; to connect with other people. That's all it would be – sharing a meal. Besides, hadn't Will called her a "no, no, no" person? Maybe she should become a "yes, sometimes" sort of person. Here was an opportunity.

"Okay," she heard herself saying. Even Jilly would be pleased. "That's very kind of you."

He beamed, and she suddenly regretted her decision. For him, this was probably about more than pizza. Still …

"Where do we meet?"

"How about Jeronimo's. In the old part of town."

"Eight o'clock?"

"Perfect. See you then."

She could feel Glen's eyes on her as she ran back across the park.

Even as she showered and dressed in something neutral and non-provocative, something more "girl next door" than anything Mindy or Shelly would ever wear, Lisa felt flat.

There was no question who she'd rather be having pizza with, whatever his reputation. When she closed her eyes, it was only Will's face she saw. It was hardly fair to Glen to accept his invitation, was it? Maybe she could fake a sudden headache.

"It's pizza!" she told her reflection in the bathroom mirror. "It's not a wedding, for heaven's sake."

She turned up at Jeronimo's fifteen minutes late, dragging her heels. She parked in the side street. Interesting. Someone had taken the lease on the corner shop, the old travel agency. They'd stripped back the old noticeboards and were putting in cabinets. Quick work!

The smell of pizza made her stomach growl. Glen jumped to his feet as she entered, his face shining. He wore a tie; totally over the top, totally unnecessary. She knew it. He was taking this way too seriously.

"So sorry for holding you up, Glen," she said, pulling back her hand which he'd taken in both of his. They were slightly clammy. She resisted the urge to wipe her hands on her jeans. It would be too rude. He was just a nice guy, being nice. Surely she could be nice back.

"So, what do you recommend?" Glen asked.

"Whatever you like," she said.

"No really. You choose."

"Please. You decide."

The little bell on the door sounded as someone entered.

"Takeaway?" said the waiter.

That was odd. There was no response.

Why did Lisa feel a prickling at the back of her neck? Glen, facing the door, looked slightly alarmed.

"Lisa." The accent was Australian. Was it …?

It was. It was Will, down on his knees beside her. When he clasped her hand in his. Will's touch was divine. His eyes burnt into hers.

"Where've you been, Lisa? I've left messages. Maybe twenty, twenty-five. I lost count."

"My phone broke."

"You completely disappeared, Lisa. We never even …"

Glen was up on his feet, threatening. "Excuse me. Is this person bothering you, Lisa?"

"No. No. I …"

"Oh, excuse me." Will sprang to his feet, dropping Lisa's hand. "Both of you. Please. You're busy. I'm interrupting. I'm sorry. I have no right. You knew my number, Lisa, and you didn't contact me. I know what that means. I'm so sorry I've interrupted you both." He looked from Lisa to the man beside her and shook his head.

"No, Will, I … wait!"

But Will was already at the counter. He slapped down his money, and swept out with his cardboard carton. He strode out into the night.

"I'm so sorry, Glen; I really need to finish this conversation," Lisa said. "Would you mind? It's a misunderstanding." She was up and out the door before she could think twice.

Panicking, she looked left and right. A light went on in the empty corner shop, and suddenly, there was Will's silhouette.

She banged on the door.

Will came to open it. He peered out into the dark street, and his face lit up as he recognized her.

"*Your* shop?" said Lisa.

"That's the plan," he said. "There's still so much to do. I've gotta secure suppliers, stock it. Lisa, are you okay? What happened?" The care in Will's eyes set her heart sizzling. He leaned towards her as if he really cared.

What kind of a fool must she be? She looked away. Mindy, Shelly, now Lisa herself. Could no one resist him? Did she really want to add herself to the global string of broken hearts? Yes. *Oh yes*. No! What was wrong with her? This was impossible, especially if she wanted to keep her career.

"I've been so worried about you, Lisa," Will said. "What's happened? Where have you been?"

She wanted to tell him, to tell him everything. And ask him everything in return.

"Will." She looked him up and down, every delicious detail, clenched her fists and took another step away from him.

He swallowed. "You've seen the news, haven't you?" he said. "'Course you have. How could you have missed it? But it doesn't mean anything; nothing at all. Can you give me the chance to explain? We really need to talk, Lisa."

"We do," she said. "I can't leave Glen next door. I only popped out. I'm not ignoring you, but it's too rude. I mean, I only just got back and he invited me on the spur of the moment and I needed to eat something."

"Well, hey," said Will. "You want pizza, I've got pizza. You want my pizza?"

Lisa laughed, nodding. "I do, but I have to get back to Glen. Besides, you've got Mindy and Shelly in there with you, haven't you?"

211

"No way. Thank God you can laugh about this, Lisa."

"I actually know Mindy and Shelly!"

"Lisa, you didn't return my calls."

"My father died," she said, her mouth drooping.

"God, Lisa. I'm so sorry."

"Oh!" she clapped her hand on her mouth. "I shouldn't have told you that!"

All Lisa wanted was to lean into Will's chest and feel his arms enfold her as grief welled up inside her and hot tears came. "You lost your own father."

"A long time ago," Will said, finding a clean tissue for her in his pocket and handing it over. When their fingers touched, his warmth was a comfort. Will's fingers, his hand, his wrist; she couldn't stop staring.

"It's good for you to cry, Lisa. A very wise therapist told me that. I didn't cry for years and it led to all kinds of trouble."

She nodded, then blew her nose. "But you're beating it, aren't you? Tell me you didn't gamble at Jupiter's."

"I've beaten it, Lisa," Will said. "I thought about it. It was a close thing. When you never called me back …" He shook his head. "I had this idea if I won a lot of money I could use it to somehow try and find you. God, it's good to see you. Thank you for coming back, for coming back to me."

"Thank you, Will, but …" Her voice trailed off.

"It's the article, isn't it? I didn't do anything. I was there to check out ProFit, as a potential supplier. I didn't gamble. I didn't even drink; not alcohol, not a drop. I stayed strong. You made me strong, Lisa. You and Dr Peters. I owe you so much."

Lisa fought the urge to step closer. If she could just rest her cheek on his chest, to feel his warmth and strength. She knew he'd welcome her, wrap his arms around her, comfort her after her father's death. And after that … She jerked her runaway thoughts back to Will's own needs. She shouldn't even be having this conversation, but here he was. The least she could do was reinforce his appropriate behaviour, surely.

"You stayed strong, Will," she said, and nodded. "They were all outside the retreat, too; the media."

"I'm sorry, Lisa. I didn't tell them a thing. I didn't start this."

"I can see it doesn't take much to spark a story about bad-boy Huntley. Dr Peters is thrilled because it's put our clinic on the global map. She hasn't even let on you've already left. She actually wants all that media attention. But it's tough on you."

Will's phone rang. He ignored it, but it kept on ringing.

"Maybe it's your family? I should get back to Glen."

"Excuse me, Lisa ... Hello? Sondra? Tonight? Yes, of course. I almost forgot. I'm on my way."

Lisa turned away as if slapped. If ever there was evidence she was a fool for falling for Will, here it was. Yet another woman in his life! Some "Sondra."

"Lisa, it's not what you think."

What a fool she was to trust Will. How idiotic to fall for someone like him; a serial hard case. He might have given up gambling or he might not have. He might have given up alcohol too, for all she knew. But it was perfectly clear he hadn't given up womanizing.

Could she really bear to share Will with every other woman on the planet? What made her imagine she might be any more special than the contessa, or the English twins, or even Mindy for that matter. What did she really know of Will?

He held his hand up, asking her to wait, then pressed the red dot with his thumb.

She'd waited, but only because she had to make her position clear. She owed him that.

"Will, we can't ..." She saw his face fall. "You're doing so well," she said.

"No. Don't you do that." Will sprang back. "Don't you hit me with all that clinician talk. I'm not your client anymore. I'm a free man now. Making my way."

"You are, but I'm not."

"What do you mean? Oh. That man in there. Of course."

"No, no. Not Glen. This is about my profession. I can't be with you for two years. It's unethical. I'll be struck off."

"Who'll know?" he said. "I've always broken rules."

"But I haven't. You go see your 'Sondra.'"

213

"No, Lisa," Will said. He shook his head. "Sondra and me. It's not like that."

Lisa sighed. Of course he'd say that. "Right now, I have to go back to Glen. It's too rude."

She turned and headed back into the pizzeria before she changed her mind and followed Will into his shop or up that flight of stairs.

…

Glen must have guessed something was up. Lisa's cheeks were pink and her eyes were shining. But not for him.

"I've gone ahead and ordered," he said.

"Thank you. So how long have you been team coach, Glen?"

Most people were happy to talk about themselves. Glen was no exception, and the evening passed.

"Won't you let me drop you home, Lisa?"

"I'm fine, thank you, Glen. I've parked my own car just around the corner."

"So maybe you'll join us at training next week?"

"Maybe. Thank you so much again, Glen. 'Night."

"'Night."

…

Next door, grief and frustration roared inside of Will. He just wasn't good enough for her. Lisa didn't want anything to do with him.

He wasn't used to rejection, dammit, especially not from her. They were right for each other. Why couldn't she accept it?

He felt it again, that fury, that white-hot anger that she didn't truly believe he could change. That "boundaries" business? As if he were some kind of wild animal who should be caged behind bars. Not a man. He'd completed his treatment and was as functional now as any other human being.

She didn't trust him.

She could say what she liked about her career and her powers to help him change for the better, but if she didn't believe it? He was truly lost. If she couldn't believe in him, how could he believe in himself?

He hung his head; then took a deep breath, squared his shoulders, and lifted his chin high. He'd show her. She'd known him less than a year. How dare she pass judgment on him! He was Will Huntley; a winner. He'd no longer try his luck at gambling, but he would win Dr Lisa Bakker's respect, alright, and, maybe then, her heart.

He stared at the pizzeria, considered interrupting them again, and changed his mind. Damn Lisa Bakker. He had work to do.

He headed for the library meeting room.

Chapter 24

The big glass door was locked, though there was still a light on upstairs. Will had to message Sondra to come and open it for him.

"You're nearly fifteen minutes late," Sondra said. "I thought you were going to stand me up and let us all down. They're all in there, waiting. Lucky I served cheese and crackers. Hope you've got a good excuse."

"No excuse. I'm sorry. I …"

"There's no time to hear it, whatever it is," Sondra said. "You're on. Right now."

He took a deep breath. He could do this. He strode to the front of the room, turned to face them, pulled out that winning smile and let it widen as he saw it reflected in their own faces.

"Good evening, ladies and gentlemen. My apologies for holding you up."

He sensed their delight in his slightly exotic Aussie accent. This was Will Huntley, a real celebrity, in the flesh, at their meeting. Yes, he could do this.

The small room jostled with local business people, a couple of 'nam vets, some young professionals, and some solid men and women closer to Sondra's vintage, community minded, and more than a little in awe of the fact he was every bit as good looking as the cover of the magazine might suggest.

"I'd like to thank Sondra for inviting me to speak this evening and for gathering all of you, particularly at short notice. She might not have told you she's been a great help to me as I've drawn up the plans to set up the US branch of my family's business right here in your town, Boulder City, which I'm now proud to call my town, too."

216

There was a smattering of applause. They sat back, waiting for him to continue.

"I'm a newcomer, it's true. The newest kid on the block, you might say, but I want to assure you I'm in this for the long haul. Now I understand that some members of your Chamber of Commerce are worried about the town bypass, and of course you all know this place far better than I do. But I want to give you my perspective as an outsider and a newcomer, because I'm *not* worried about it. I see the bypass as a great opportunity."

Some of the audience sat up straighter.

"Sondra might have already told you I've managed to secure a five-year lease on the old travel agency, and I'm working hard to open my new outlet, House of Hearts, in the coming months," said Will. "My new shop will be the first and, for the foreseeable future, the only US branch of the international Huntleys emporium, based in Australia – but it's more than that."

Some members of his audience were hooked already. It was like being back in school or at the pub, cracking a joke. But this was way better.

"Huntleys House of Hearts is not just about romantic hearts," said Will. "It's about healthy hearts. It'll stock a mix of outdoor wear. Let me explain. I'm happy to tell you I'm mighty impressed by your local parks and mountains, including Virgin Peak, and I've just been introduced to the sport of skyrunning. I don't mind telling you people, I'm smitten."

There were some cheers and a "Way to go, Aussie!"

"So what I propose – and I invite you to join me in this – is a brand-new event, a fresh reason for people from all over the world to come here, to Boulder City," Will said. "I want to propose that Huntleys House of Hearts sponsors a new international skyrun, starting here, something like the 'desert to Virgin Peak' skyrun. I'm willing to wager that the media will be interested in me ..." Will paused for the chuckles.

"And will be interested in this event and your beautiful town. We could call it the Black Fire Opal Run. Australia has opals, and Sondra here's been telling me more about your Virgin Valley opals. Maybe we offer a Huntleys black fire opal as a prize."

Will smiled as eyes lit up and people nodded.

"And if you vote for this idea, I'm offering to work with Sondra, your Chamber of Commerce Secretary, and with your events committee, to make this dream a reality."

A few of them leaned forward. Will had captured their interest. He'd been brief but convincing. There'd be something in it for each of them, but a few still sat back, arms folded, frowning.

Sondra spoke up.

"I see you, Lucille and Elsie-May. You're thinking 'What's in this for me?' Well, I'll tell you why our florist and hair salon should care about all these strange runners in our town? And you, LeRoy and all you outfitters and fashionistas. Let's hold a charity ball while we're at it. Really put this town on the map. The Boulder City Black Fire Opal Charity Ball. Any causes you'd like us to support, anyone?"

Will grinned. "Youth mental health; that's one great cause."

Now the whole room was nodding. Sondra swept the mood to a swift, unanimous decision.

"I'd like to move a motion that the events committee investigate creating an international skyrunning competition and charity ball, with Huntleys House of Hearts the major sponsor. Anyone willing to second the motion?"

A dozen hands went up and Will was smiling. With Sondra's assistance, he could do this. Lisa would discover he was here for the long term. Lisa would eat pizza with him yet. Better still, she'd enter his run and support the ball. That would be a dance to remember.

...

That night, in her dreams, Lisa went to Will. As he opened his door to her, the fire in his eyes set her heart racing.

He caught her in his arms and it felt so good, so right. His heartbeat; the shape of his chest; his warmth. Perfect.

What a dream! Their kiss? Pure fireworks, shooting through every part of her body. Her gloom of the past ten days lifted as if the sun had come out.

In her dream, Will drew her into his arms and led her up the staircase one thrilling kiss at a time, stair by stair, up into his bed.

She woke and sat up in bed with a jerk, her heart racing.

After the fourth night of the same dream, Lisa knew she had to do something.

She phoned Jilly.

"Lisa!" said Jilly. "What's up?"

"I know I should ask you about yourself, Jilly, but I really need to talk. A lot's happened."

"Hey, that's okay," Jilly said. "You sound a bit down, Lisa, a bit panicked. That's not like you at all. Come on, out with it. Is Rossco okay?"

"Rossco's back," Lisa said. "Rossco's old and sore but he's okay. He's snoring. But Jilly, Dad died."

"Oh God. You poor thing. That's awful. I'm so sorry. You okay?"

"Yes," said Lisa. "No."

"Do you want me to come to you? Where are you? Are you back in Boulder? Tell me everything."

"Oh, Jilly. Everything was fine. And then I blew it. I don't know who I am anymore. I'm all over the place."

"Well, it's a shock to lose a parent. Talk to me."

As Lisa explained about her father's death, Jilly listened, the weight of grief began to lift, but still Lisa's mood plummeted, the darkness around her heart dragging her down. She could barely speak, but she had to try to explain. Jilly might understand, and there was no one else she could talk to. Rossco always listened, but he never gave advice. She needed Jilly's counsel.

"But there's more, Jilly," Lisa said. "Right before Dad died, before I went to visit him, I almost blew it at work. I'm lucky Dr Peters is so fair. I nearly got myself struck off. Nearly lost my whole career."

"Hey, Lisa! What is this? This does not sound like my sensible friend. I'm the one who takes risks, not you. What happened?"

Lisa explained. As she described Will again and more of his playboy history, Jilly exclaimed. And when Lisa described the way her body was drawn to Will's, and the repeating dream, Jilly gasped.

"Don't make fun of me, Jilly. There's more."

"I'm not making fun of you," said Jilly. "I'm listening. But this Will guy. This is the one who stayed at your house when Rossco was injured, isn't it? This sounds serious."

219

"It is. I have to do that Boundaries course online, which takes six months. But it's worse than that. Dr Peters has laid down the law. Will and I can't see each other for two years!"

Jilly whistled.

"With any other client, that wouldn't be an issue, but did you know Will's setting himself up in Boulder? We'll run into each other all the time. And … Jilly. I just saw him tonight. And all I want to do is to be with him. This guy. I really care about him. I've been fighting my feelings for him from the moment we met. I kept telling myself he was a womanizer, and he is. He sure knows how to flatter. I don't trust him, but he's all I can think about, and I've tried to be so careful!"

"I'm sure you've been careful, Lisa."

"But it's crept up on me, the way I feel about Will. He tells me he loves me, and you know how we empathize with all our clients. We try to stand in their shoes and understand what upsets and motivates them, so we can help. Well, I've seen where Will came from, and his struggles, and I admire the way he seems to be finally taking control of his life. And Jilly … He tells me he wants me to be part of it. Should I defy the two-year ban? Should I give up my career for this man?"

"Lisa, slow down. This is huge. This is big. Don't you dare do anything sudden. You're going to be okay."

"That's why I had to talk to you. I don't want to have this conversation with Dr Peters. Not yet. Not until I know what I'm doing."

There was a silence. Finally Jilly spoke.

"Okay. Okay. Listen up, Lisa, you're a great therapist. I never knew anyone who studied so hard."

"Oh, I'm great at the theory. I just can't trust myself to carry it out."

"Have you actually done anything with this Will?"

"No. I want to and I don't want to. It's killing me. He's probably with someone else now, anyway. Some Sondra. I'm so jealous. I'm an idiot, a mess. He's a clinic client, for God's sake. But I don't want anyone else. When I close my eyes I dream of him. I want him in my life, dammit. Whatever the cost. He's great company. He's fun, he's sexy and he's loving, and all I want is to love him back. I never felt like this about Art."

"Lisa, this is going to be okay." Jilly's tone was professional, but then she went silent.

"Jilly?"

"I'm just thinking," said Jilly. "This could actually be good. Even the Boundaries course."

"How can any of this be good?"

"You've still got your job," Jilly said. "Dr Peters is smart. Because, do you know what? You are going to be a better clinician than ever, Lisa."

"Why's that?"

"Because, for the first time, you're going to really understand temptation, in the same way your clients do. You're going to get really good at impulse recognition and impulse control. Come on. Pull out your strategies, and use them on yourself – the same ones you teach your clients."

"Yes?"

"Distractions, breathing, self-soothing," said Jilly. "Coach yourself. Keep a diary. All that stuff. You know it backwards. So now? Don't just preach it! Practice it. On yourself, kiddo. Day in, day out. You expect your clients to do it, even Will, don't you?"

"Yes," said Lisa. "I do."

"So you need to do this, too, and I'm certain you can. You understand all those different states of mind – emotional and logical. You know how to steer the middle path. Find your wise mind, Lisa. You're the wisest person I've ever met."

"But, Jilly, you're the last person I'd expect to be telling me to keep away from a man. You've been telling me the exact opposite."

"I never encouraged you to date a client. I've known you for years. You're no cheater. It would rip you apart." Jilly went silent, to let her words sink in.

"I told you this was serious," said Lisa. "Go on. I knew I was right to call you, Jilly."

"Well, this two years thing. It won't be that hard, or even that bad. Embrace it, kiddo. And here's why. Two years will give Will time to prove himself; show his true colors. A lot of your clients are great at lying. You've told me so yourself. So, if Will's just a manipulator, you'll have time to see it."

"Yes." Jilly's words made perfect sense. Lisa began to breathe more easily. Her head and heart were lifting. "If Will's still gambling and drinking and womanizing, and he lives in the same town, I'm going to

221

know about it," Lisa said. "But, if he actually builds this business like he says he will, I'll witness that, too."

"And if the two of you actually still want each other after two years is up, there'll be no stopping you!" Jilly's tone was triumphant.

...

Lisa couldn't sleep. Her eyes burned from the computer screen and the online course. At least she'd finally finished the thing; six months of theory she already knew.

She'd taken the evaluation at midnight, determined to be done with it, and printed off the certificate, ready to take into Dr Peters next day for her debrief. She hoped her boss would be happy.

If she'd anticipated a surge of joy at the end of it, she was disappointed. It ticked a box, but it did nothing for her lonely heart, beating there in her chest, still yearning for Will.

Rossco sensed her restlessness. As she tossed and turned, she heard him rise and come across to the side of the bed. When she put out her hand to pat his rough head, he nuzzled it.

"Old boy," she said. "I've been a mess like this before, haven't I?"

Rossco panted in the dark room.

"When I made up my mind to leave Art, you knew, and in time, we left, and we've done alright, haven't we? We'll be okay, I guess."

Thank goodness for Rossco. Her life at the clinic was full of people. But here in her bedroom, she was lonelier than ever. She wanted a partner to share her life with, someone to talk to who answered back, someone who ... No. She couldn't let her imagination go there.

Rossco licked the palm of her hand and sat and settled beside the bed where he began to twitch and snore. Lisa thumped her pillow and turned over and wondered how Will was managing; Will, who could date whom he liked, including someone called Sondra and who knew who else.

...

Dr Peters was pleased with Lisa's certificate.

"Well done," she said. "I had to do that course myself once. Are you doing okay?"

Lisa nodded. She couldn't feign joy. She was functioning. She was turning up, doing her duty, counselling, listening carefully and making suggestions. All her clients made progress as usual.

As the months rolled by, Jilly's predictions came true. Lisa's experience of frustration around her feelings for Will made her more empathetic. She identified with clients more fully when they described their cravings. And when Lisa shared strategies with them for controlling their impulses, she found herself encouraging her own progress.

But in her imagination and her dreams, she ran wild. She would race to Will's corner store, knock on his door and he'd welcome her, kiss her on every step as he led her upstairs to his home above the shop and into his bedroom. Night after night the dream recurred.

When she found her mind straying to the same place during the day, she would use the STOPP skill.

"We 'stop,'" she explained to clients itching to gamble again. "'S' is for 'take a step back.' Observe what's happening inside you and outside of you. Proceed mindfully. And practice your positive self-talk. You can say it with me. 'I don't need to gamble anymore. I don't need to gamble anymore. There are other things to do with my time and money.'

"What things do you like to do?" she would ask them. "What did you enjoy as a child? What do you do to look after yourself, to soothe yourself? Good! Now, let's practice some relaxation."

Lisa's clients made progress, and when she was with them, she didn't have time to think about herself. She loved that about her work, immersing herself in calming their stormy waters, helping them find an even keel, set their sails and steer for their own new destinations.

No other client made her heart race as Will had done. That wasn't why she was there, but it made Will impossible to forget.

No matter how hard she studied her boundaries course, no matter how outstanding her assessment results, it beat in her heart, the song of bad boy Will, with his cheeky eyes and perfect pecs, and the way he'd looked at her as if he really cared about her.

It was after work that time hung heaviest on her hands. After a simple meal, she would lose herself in the labyrinth of social media, and her old routine, of walking Rossco then going for a long run, helped use up the long hours of the evening. The intense exercise helped her sleep, but she knew she was running on auto, going through the motions, her heart nursing itself, deep inside, alone.

One night, in the mirror as she brushed her hair, she saw herself as a therapist might judge her – drab and unhappy and a little bit lost – and she asked herself the same questions. What else could she do instead of moping?

An answer came to her.

…

Marcia's Ballet Studio in Boulder's main street was full of children, little girls in pink leotards, and larger girls, in black, assisting.

Lisa forced herself to turn up that Saturday, even though Jade's studio was in the main street, a few doors down from the pizzeria, within sight of Will's corner.

She tied Rossco's lead to the light pole and went inside. She'd timed her visit for eleven o'clock when a class was ending, mothers chatting at the door, children trailing in and out, and running back to collect a forgotten slipper, concerts being discussed.

Was every small town ballet school the same? There was even a big jar of snakes on the counter, and one of the older girls was selling them, putting them in brown paper bags. It was a step back to simpler times. She found some spare change and stood in the queue. Her mouth watered. She hadn't chewed into a sweet jelly snake in a decade.

Lisa identified Marcia, in her forties and in charge. When the cluster of mothers and daughters had finished their questions and left, Lisa introduced herself.

"Tuesday nights," Marcia said, smiling. "You're so welcome. Warm-ups and flexibility. We'd love to have you. We have fun. The first two sessions are free."

Lisa's heart pattered. She surveyed Marcia's stock and promised herself a purple unitard if she ended up signing up in week three.

"Well done, me," she told Rossco and she untied his lead and headed home.

She stole a glance at Will's corner. Nothing. No light. No action. Windows still covered. He could be in a casino or in Sondra's arms for all Lisa cared. She had to get on with her life.

Chapter 25

Will turned up at Sydney's Kingsford Smith Airport on the first flight of the day, as the summer sky turned bluer by the minute and bright enough to hurt his eyes.

He couldn't believe James was there to greet him, driving his own little red Alfa Romeo.

"What's this?"

"Yeah," said James. "You don't deserve it, Will, but it's what I'd like if I'd just flown for twenty or more hours. Besides, I've been trying to give your Alpha a run at least once a month, like I said I would, and the timing worked out."

"Jesus. You're far too good to me, James."

"Yeah, dead right, I am. But we all want to give you every chance, bro. Nicole's so excited about the US new branch she's cooked dinner for us all tonight."

"What, Nicole? Domesticated?"

"No," said James. "Not totally. Not really. But she's making an effort. Between you and me, I suspect she wants to impress Scottie."

"Well. That only took a decade or more. Scottie'll be pleased."

"They both are. I've never seen Nicole happier."

"And what about you, big brother?"

"What about me?"

"I know we don't ask about Helene anymore …"

"No way."

"So, anyone else? I reckon you're the most eligible of the lot of us. Eldest heir to the Huntley diamond dynasty, and all that."

"Don't tell me about headlines, Aussie playboy," James said. "What was all that, anyway? Gave us a scare, alright. We thought you were back in Jupiter's to blow it all, just as we'd given you the go ahead."

"No," said Will. "Like I told you. I had to test myself at some stage. Maybe the timing wasn't ideal. And I don't mind telling you I came mighty close to having a little spin. Bloody easy to do. I wouldn't be the first."

"So, what stopped you?"

"Look, that clinic is the best thing that ever happened to me. I haven't had a chance to thank mother yet. Too busy making plans."

James was silent as they emerged from the airport tunnel and headed into Rushcutters Bay. Will let the glory of it sink in as they sat at the lights. The giant, deep green fig trees, the flat park, and the forest of yacht masts gently swaying as another ferry went past, awaiting their chance for glory in the next Sydney to Hobart yacht race.

Home. In the olden days, he'd be on his phone by now, trying to work out where the next party would be, or salivating to get to a favorite pub or two. Lately, every spare minute was spent sourcing suppliers for his shop. Today? He was enjoying every moment. He wouldn't be here long, just long enough to check out some Australian outdoor gear suppliers and pick up samples, fine tune the website and the public relations plans for the opening with Nicole, and have some serious financial planning sessions with Scottie and James.

The traffic coming the other way was building up. Nice to have missed rush hour.

"Want a swim?"

"I always want a swim." Will gave his brother a proper smile.

"I've got a coupla towels in the back; spare boardies."

James cut up Ocean Street, giving the engine some throat, and Will felt like they were kids again. He'd love to bring Lisa here one day, out of the desert to coastal Sydney, gleaming harbour and all. The City to Surf Fun Run was in August. She'd love that.

They skirted the junction, and zoomed up Bondi Road, the chimney for the sewerage works like a sentinel from childhood, promising sand and salt.

The surf was shiny and cool, with the sun already starting to sting. Body surfers since before they could remember, the brothers stumbled out of the foam laughing, time and again. For Will, it was like being reborn, washed clean in the froth and surge, the endless drone of the long flight a receding memory.

"Last one," James called out over the roar of the surf. "We've got work to do."

"Sure do."

James took Will back to his apartment to dump his bag and wash off the salt, and they were into Bondi Junction Plaza just as Lorna opened their iconic brass doors, the huge H insignia glinting in the sun like a cliche. Had Huntleys ever looked so good? Will must be getting sentimental.

He ran up all the stairs to Jim's lair, and sprinted across to him like a child, pulling up just before he bowled him over. Was the old man stooping some more? If so, his blue eyes were bright as ever.

"Will, m'boy!"

"Jim. The things I've seen! The places I've been!"

"Hmmph," said Jim. "James tells me you want to settle down."

"A bit. I want to. For once. You saw my business plan?"

"Boulder City, eh? You want to sell my rings?"

"Don't be offended, Jim, but I thought I'd sell something different. Exercise gear. Not that I mightn't need one of your rings someday. Hopefully soon."

"Is that right, young man?"

"Yes. She hasn't said 'yes' yet, not that exact word, but I plan to just keep asking until she's ready. However long it takes." Will went quiet. Serious.

Jim reached out to shake his hand and clap him on the shoulder with his other one.

"Good to hear. I wish you all the best, young Will. If she brings you half the luck and happiness my Eleanor brought me, you'll be a fortunate man alright. Tell me about her."

"I'll bring her here to meet you if I can, Jim. She's tall, serious, and quiet. Unusual choice for me, I know. Lisa has a heart of gold. She helped me turn my life around, that's for sure. That reminds me …"

Will brought the stone out of his pocket. "Ever seen one like this, Jim? I've been polishing it by hand, but I've had a few other things on my plate.

Like opening Huntleys' US branch and planning a world-class skyrunning competition. Reckon we can finish this thing off?"

The stone lay on Will's palm like something alive. Green, yellow and blue lights coruscated. It flashed sparks red as flame.

"Well, isn't that a beauty! I've admired some opals in my time, but this one? Where'd you find it?"

"Nevada. It was just sitting there in the desert, a bit of the way off the road. They call it black fire opal. It's part of my plan now. Huntleys House of Hearts is sponsoring the Black Fire Opal Skyrun!"

Jim raised his eyebrows and took the opal from Will to study it with his loupe.

"You've been up to a few new things yourself, Jim," Will said. "Love that new website. Is that Nicole's work? What's your jewel of the week this week? Can you make it opal? Can you help me with this one? Got any of that polish Nicole told me about? The leather strip? All of that? And look; if we drill a hole just at this end, it should hang quite well to make a pendant. Look at the fire in that, Jim."

"I wouldn't recommend drilling," Jim said. "Opal's tricky. Can be unstable."

"C'mon, just a little hole. It's for someone special. This is for the woman who changed my life. Can we work on it now?"

Will found the drill bit himself, the tiniest one; fitted it into the hand drill, clamped the stone.

"Not too tight, Will. They have minds of their own, these opals."

Will took it carefully, with Jim supervizing. The bit turned in the stone. Splinters of silicon sprayed out like glitter. And then it happened. The top of the stone popped out, leaving a gash.

"Yeah," said Will. "I blew it. You tried to tell me."

"You're not a jeweler if you haven't made some mistakes."

"You're bloody gracious, Jim." Will unwound the clamp, and rubbed the broken edge of the stone with his thumb. Regret ricocheted through him. Why did he always wreck things?

"Wait on, Will," said Jim. "Show me that."

Will handed it over.

Jim put on his eyeglass, turned the stone over, reached for a file without having to look and nudged it into the chip.

Then he pushed the leather and brown powder back to Will.

"You have a bit more polishing to do, but you've still got something there. Something better. Heart shaped. We'll set it. Make it stronger. Ring or pendant? Gold?"

…

Outside in the bright Sydney sunshine, Will squinted at his mobile and tried Lisa's number again.

You've reached Lisa Bakker. Leave a message.

Surely Lisa had replaced her phone by now. Had she got herself another number, a number Mindy hadn't shared with him?

Well, he had plenty on his plate to keep him busy. He'd dropped in on the estate agent to check all was well with the tenant and explore options for selling his apartment down the track; and then turned up for dinner at Nicole's.

His sister had gone to some effort. Will regretted his jetlag. Staying off alcohol had helped, but the long day was taking its toll. Still, it was good to clap eyes on Jim again, this time without the jewelers apron; a rare sight.

Scottie turned up with champagne, and James was there, giving him a bit of a biff on one arm every time he looked like he might yawn.

When James's fiancée, Stella, arrived, Will saw James in a new light, totally attentive to her, their mutual attraction sparkling. James was so proud to introduce her.

"Stella, Will," James said. "Our brother. Been in France and the US. He's back temporarily and has a few plans."

Will saw James bite his tongue, but the warning was there in his eyes. In the bad old days, James would have had to beg him to behave, to not scare away his latest girlfriend, or, worse, steal her. All he did this evening was raise one eyebrow.

James needn't have worried. Stella only had eyes for James. Will envied the way they moved in each other's space, a touch here, a nod there; at ease together.

Lisa's absence was an ache, a missing limb. And he still hadn't even heard from her. One day, though, he promised himself …

They were out on the balcony of Nicole's apartment, the lights of the city like so many extra stars in the humid night. It was beautiful.

"Water for me," Will said.

"Is this the actual Will Huntley?" Scottie asked.

"No. It's his better self," said James, springing to the kitchen for some sparkling mineral water.

"Well, you have to have something sparkling, because Nicole and I have some news."

"News?"

"We're engaged," said Scottie. Nicole took off her apron. and he placed his arm around her, comfortably, happily proud.

"Miracles do happen," Will said.

"Yeah, they do," said Scottie. "I can't work out which is the biggest, Nicole saying yes, or you not drinking."

Nicole looked a little hurt not to be the center of attention.

"It's not about me, mate," said Will. "This is the best news I've heard in years. You and Nicole settling down. Astonishing."

Now she smiled. "You think we're boring, Will."

"I might have thought that once, it's true. But to tell you the truth, I'm envious. You two look truly happy. You too, James and Stella. Sensational! Congratulations!"

They beamed at each other, and everyone clinked glasses, just as James's phone rang.

"Mother! Great timing! Yes, Will got here this morning. No, he's not out at a party. The party's here, at Nicole's. I've got you on speaker, now. Nicole and Scottie have something to say."

"We're engaged, Mother!" said Nicole.

"Oh, Nicole and Scottie, my darlings! Felicitations! You'll have to come to France and meet Emile. And stay here for your honeymoon! Now, Will. Are you being good?"

"Sparkling mineral water, Mother."

"Never!"

"Look, I really need to thank you, Mother," said Will. "I don't care who else hears this. That clinic changed my life. I can't thank you enough. I hate to think where I'd be if you hadn't insisted. And no, let me get in first. That thing about Jupiter's? I suppose you saw it. It was a total beat-up, as usual." Will held up his hand and rushed on.

"It's true I've got my eye on someone from the clinic, but it sure isn't that Mindy or Shelly," Will said. "You're aware of the plans for my US branch? Yes. We're still working out the details. That's why I'm here. How are your plans? I'll race you, then. See which of us can open the first international branch. You know I'll win."

"You always were a winner, darling," Cynthia said. "This all sounds good. We all want you to keep on the right track. We need you to do the right thing, Will. I think this is a good bet this time, don't you?"

"I'm excited, yeah, but not as excited as I am about Nicole and Scottie," Will said. "When's the big date, guys?"

After the meal, Jim went out on the verandah. He looked older, the old limp troubling him more, but he was in great shape for his age – ancient. Will joined him.

They leaned on the railing together, and watched the ferries slip from Watson's Bay to the Quay and lace their way in and out of the bays along the north shore. When the huge Manly ferry glided west towards the bridge, Will spoke.

"You and grandmother," Will said.

"My Eleanor."

"Yeah," said Will. "How many years was it till you got it together?"

"Three years from the moment I first knocked her hat off and we learned each other's names. Four before we were married. Are you thinking of marrying this person you met at the clinic?"

"Yeah," said Will. "But she's disappeared and won't ring me back. Her name's Lisa. She's beautiful, smart, thoughtful, generous, fun. You'd love her."

Jim turned from the view to look at Will. "This the one we fixed that opal for?"

"Yep."

"You young people," Jim said. "I've watched you with those phones. Instant this, and instant that. You've never learned the value of patience. Just because something isn't instant, doesn't mean it isn't worth waiting for. It's not like you've got nothing on your plate already, is it?"

"No, sir. I've got the shop to open, and I'm sponsoring this big skyrun."

"Yes," said Jim. "I waited for Eleanor for three years, and she didn't even know. But I was busy. I told you. All that learning and all that work. I was reinventing myself. Filling up the hollow man. I wanted to be sure I had something to offer her."

231

Will nodded, frowning.

Jim smiled and put a hand on Will's shoulder. "How do you expect those things to happen if you're busy indulging yourself every minute? Quit focusing on what you haven't got and get busy making your future, man. The rest will follow."

Will nodded.

"It's not easy, though, I realize," Jim said. "I remember how it was. I got tired sometimes. Wondered if I was fooling myself; worse, if she'd meet someone else. But hope is always better than despair. You'll look back one day and be glad."

Will glanced at Jim and nodded.

"Look after yourself, young man, and do the right thing, and you and this Lisa will have decades together. You plan your strategy right, get your act together, and the rest will fall into place."

Jim's words helped. If he ached for Lisa, he took action; consulted his "to do" list and worked his way through it. He had to hope she felt the same way.

...

Will arranged to sell his car. With just a few days before he was due to fly back to the US, he took some runs around his old haunts.

He jogged up past the old school, then up the bends of New South Head Road. When he reached the crest of the hill he took in the view of the Sydney Harbour Bridge and Sydney Opera House before plunging down towards the harbor again. A salty plunge in his favorite harbor beach would cool him off. One day he'd do this run with Lisa.

Memories of a hundred parties crowded in his brain as his feet pumped out the distance. As always, homes were being remodelled, rebuilt, bigger than ever, the never-ending renovation circus.

It was three pm. The white vans of plumbers and electricians were leaving as Will took a wind-down lap, up and back along Coolong Road. Soon, traffic flowed back in; expensive four-wheel drives were returning from the school run, some driven by nannies and trophy wives.

A big black car pulled into a driveway in front of him. Will did a double-take, then paused, hands on hips, catching his breath. At the wheel of the latest Audi Q7, the slim, dark-haired woman was familiar. He couldn't quite believe it.

"Hey, Pen!" he said. "You're doing well for yourself."

Her tinted, automatic window slowly lowered. She looked him up. She looked him down. If there was a trace of longing in her eyes, she did her best to hide it. One side of her mouth turned down.

"Pen," said Will. "Did you get my letter? I wrote to apologize. I treated you badly. I didn't know any better back then, but I never meant to hurt you."

She waited.

"I was a jerk," he said.

She nodded but refused to smile. Would she ask him in? Unlikely. She pressed a button on her dashboard. Three children stared at him from the depths of the car, still in their seatbelts in their rumpled school uniforms.

A strange pang of nostalgia swept through Will's chest.

"Who's that, Mummy?" said one.

The big gray gate began to roll open as Pen slid her window closed.

Will overheard her explanation before the window thumped shut.

"Just somebody that I used to know."

Pen accelerated into the driveway and the heavy gate rumbled closed behind them.

There was a hiss. The automatic sprinklers came on and drenched him.

"Ah, Pen," Will said to the gate, wondering if the closed circuit TV camera could pick up his voice as well as his image. "I might have done you wrong when I was too young to know any better, but you've taken your revenge, story after story, and now I've apologized. I don't know what else you want from me. Do you want that reputation? Tough as nails? Is that how you really want to raise those children?"

Still dripping, he stared at the camera, gave her his best smile and blew her a kiss. Pen was as tough as they came. He'd done the right thing finally. Pen could go to hell.

As he jogged on down to the harbor beach, warm Sydney sun on his head and shoulders, Will thought of Lisa, different in every way to cold, vindictive Penny.

He cherished the memory of that day on the couch, in the testing room, when Lisa had almost kissed him.

He remembered gazing into her face as she applied those sticky tabs. He'd feasted on the shape of her eyes, her chin and her lips, so close to

233

his. When he'd caressed her with his own eyes, he was rewarded with a flush of color rising in her cheek.

Did she guess he'd wanted so much more? *Self-control*. The new Will never wanted to scare her away.

He'd wanted her to remember him. Up there on the mountain, they'd started something, hadn't they? Something good.

With Lisa, it wasn't just about sex and his own gratification. He'd wanted to give her pleasure, to show her his appreciation, to make her happy, to *love* her, dammit.

"If you think something, can you make it happen?" he'd asked.

That moment she'd nearly kissed him? It still tempted him, that sweet time bomb; something unfinished, a kiss in store.

Restraint. Maybe there was something to be said for it.

Like never before, Will wanted Lisa.

He could only hope Lisa remembered him.

Chapter 26

That week after ballet, Lisa did a double-take. There were lights on at Will's corner shop, but if Will was back in town, why should she care?

As she prepped for her run over the next few weeks, she looped past his shop. Lights were still on downstairs, but not upstairs. He was working, not entertaining. That was good, but it needn't concern her.

Next evening, Lisa phoned her mother. She'd kept in touch with her more often after her father's death, so she wouldn't feel too alone. This time her mother astonished her.

"Now, Lisa. I've been thinking about coming to see you."

"Really! That's excellent, Mom. That's a great idea. I'd enjoy your company, and I'm sure you'd enjoy the change of scene. When do you arrive? … Tomorrow? But you know I'm going away for a couple of weeks?"

Donna had already bought the ticket, on special.

"Of course you could still come," Lisa said. "You could mind the place for me, look after Rossco. He's still getting better. He'd love your company so much more than going back to the vet … Fantastic. Okay. You've got my address?"

It was a night for phone calls.

"Jilly? What's up?" Lisa had been looking forward to their holiday together. It would be like the old days when they were students, Jilly sharing her wild ideas and experiences as they ate up the miles together. Fun. Free.

"I can't make it, Lisa," Jilly said. "I have to postpone. I'm so sorry. There's too much drama at the office right now."

While Lisa had gone on to become a clinical psychologist, Jilly had specialized in human resources. It was another safe career path. Jilly had picked up an exciting role with a tech start-up in Silicon Valley. It paid well but was demanding.

When Jilly wasn't busy hiring, she was flat out firing, depending on how the venture capital injections were going. It was just the right speed for Jilly, but didn't allow her to plan ahead much.

"I'm so sorry, Lisa," she said. "But you go on and have a ball. Have a holiday romance or three. Pretend you're me. Those Swiss men are gorgeous. And we all know about the French. And those German men. I guarantee they're all taller than you, if that's still your hang-up."

"Thanks, Jilly."

Lisa flew to LA, then across to Geneva. She spent a morning wandering the old city, which was so much older than anything she'd seen in the US, the shops and bridges and lakefront paths picturesque and enticing. The number of watch shops astonished her. Surely there weren't enough wrists for them all.

As she wandered, each fresh reflection of the old buildings in the Lake was mesmerizing. There were even white swans, as pretty as a jigsaw puzzle. As she sat on the edge of the lake and ate an ice cream seven cygnets glided into view, their mother serene.

Lisa wished she had company. She longed to share these joys with someone. It was ten o'clock in the morning. Maybe she should ring Jilly. One o'clock in the morning in California. No, not an option. Besides, she didn't want Jilly to feel left out. What she didn't know wouldn't hurt her.

Lisa's body clock was confused. She studied the surrounding mountains and their reflections. Which actual peak would be Mont Blanc? Her bus wasn't leaving for Chamonix until four pm. She'd simply have to wander.

The dress shops were tempting, the mannequins as tall as she was. She wandered past a lingerie shop that caught her eye, all roses and white ribbons, with silks and bras of every shape and color, so different to the black polyester nightmares she'd ordered online in vain, back in the days of Art.

What could it hurt, to wander in and have a browse and help fill in some time? The shop assistants were attentive. There was even a sports bra, smooth and sleek and supportive, which she should wear on her run. And a bra and pants set, blue-and-white checks. Very girl next door. Sexy girl next door. Very expensive, if she bothered to calculate the exchange rate, which she didn't wish to do. She was having fun.

Delighted with her purchases, she set off again down a laneway, halting. In the reflection of another boutique, she saw herself, in her sensible travel clothes, tight knit leggings and a long t-shirt. Neatish. Ordinary.

Behind her reflection? The red dress of a lifetime. Classic. Chic. Shiny satin. Full skirted. With a low V-neck. She would never wear such a thing to the clinic. Had she lost her mind? She'd already just spent a small fortune on clothes she might never wear.

In a trance, she entered the shop. "Yes, mademoiselle." The Swiss had excellent English. They had it in her size. As she slipped it over her head, it whispered to her. "Yes." And when she saw herself in the mirror, she gasped. Yes indeed.

Lisa refused to consider the price tag. What was a Swiss Franc worth anyway? Apart from Rossco's vet bills, she'd never been extravagant. Just this once …

She twirled. It fitted perfectly. It just needed a slightly lower-cut bra. No matter. She knew exactly where to find one.

Back she went to the lingerie shop, two fancy bags now swinging on her arm, departing it again twenty minutes later with three. Where was sensible, careful Lisa? Was she becoming a "yes, yes, yes" person? It must be the jetlag.

Lisa caught her coach up to Chamonix, winding up and up the mountain, marvelling at the pine trees and steep slopes and tiny stone churches with spires like spindles and cows with cowbells, like jigsaw puzzle scenery.

After settling into her quaint bed and breakfast with flowers in all the window boxes, she wandered through the town. Stone houses, more window boxes, a rushing stream, and plenty of fresh air, even nightingales. She felt like Heidi, excitement simmering inside her from her rash purchases, and for the race ahead.

Next day, the skyrunning crowd was friendly enough, speaking in many languages, comparing their fancy shoes and other running gear. They'd run into each other over the next day or two as they limbered up.

Lisa bought a new CamelBak for water, and some energy drinks. She had to bulk up for the long run ahead. A couple of times, her heart leapt, thinking she recognized Will among the competitors gathering for the race. Each time, she would put on a burst of speed to catch up, only to be disappointed.

On the day of the main competition, the little town pumped with people and bright flags and the media. Will would have loved it.

She admonished herself. This was a perfect holiday. A total indulgence. But even when he was on the other side of the planet, the man invaded her thoughts. They'd run together so well back at Virgin Peak, she wanted him here beside her, drinking in the incredible scenery and the buzz of it all.

It was a crazy wish. He'd proven himself to be untrustworthy. She had no right to feel jealous. He'd never pretended to be anything but a playboy. Her clients' lives were their own.

And if she'd been injured after she let her barriers down that once above his retail venture, that time he'd rushed off after Sondra, more fool her.

Did she regret almost kissing him at the clinic? No. The opposite. She treasured the memory. She'd never felt so cherished in her whole life. He'd treated her like a queen. What had he called her? His Queen of Hearts, as if he worshipped her. It made her smile.

She'd wanted more. Sex. Fun. Joyous sex. Not just sex. Sex with Will.

The larrikin Australian rarely left her mind. Every time she heard an Australian accent, she'd whip around, hoping it was him.

She'd been happy enough before they'd met. But now? He'd forced her to rethink everything in her life. What was she without Will? A clinician. What was she when they were together? *Alive.*

That was it. She knew she could live without Will. But with him? Life would be better.

The race began. She surged forwards with the crowd in a wide bunch at the start. Hyped up racers sprang ahead, while she sprinted past older runners and shorter ones, a great heaving pack of humanity heading up the slopes, squinting at the razor's edge of the mountain against the blue, blue sky.

In the rhythm of the running, in the clarity of the altitude, as her legs pumped and her lungs drew in each breath and let it out, she sifted through her thoughts. Why had she left Art? Because she'd felt nothing. They'd been perfectly civil to each other. But she'd only been half alive. She wanted more joy, more passion and more fun in her life.

When they were together, how did Will make her feel? More joyful. More passionate. More alive. He made her laugh.

More joy, more passion, more fun. Maybe she should look Glen up again. Or at least join the baseball team. But that wasn't the kind of fun she craved.

It became a mantra as she ran, and as she pushed on through the lofty miles, up there in the heavens, along the mountain trail among strangers from all around the world, a new truth grew in her heart, as it entered her lungs and head – *joy, passion, fun.*

Visions of Will stayed with her; Will joking, smiling at her as if he really wanted her and cared about her, Will wanting her. Her vivid dream had become a waking one.

If she kept running away from her feelings for this man, she would have rebuilt her life and hurt her parents for nothing. She might as well have stayed with Art, safe but half dead.

Didn't she deserve a better life? As Will himself had pointed out, "no, no, no" had given her a controlled life, a calm one; but she knew she needed more. She needed excitement. She needed Will.

But how could her silent love ever satisfy him? What if he kept having affairs? Who was Sondra? Could she even trust him with Jilly? He and Jilly were two of a kind. Opening herself up to love could open her to pain.

Besides, the two-year ban was as big as a planet. Heart and lungs burning, legs on fire, Lisa tormented herself.

Well past the wide warm-up miles where the path was grassy and wide, the true ascent began, and runners jostled for position on the narrowing track. Lisa needed to watch her feet to avoid twisting an ankle on the grey rubble, like scales on an enormous dragon. Was she hallucinating? The air was thin up here, at higher than 10,000 feet.

Every man with sunkissed hair and broad shoulders set her on alert. Could it be Will? How she wished he were with her, running easily, as they'd done on their run back in Nevada. She could wish that, couldn't she? It wasn't even about sex, but companionship. She'd done her Boundaries course. She knew the rules.

A dozen Canadians overtook her up the next rise, the gruelling 900-metre section, their accents and cheery red maple leaf unmistakable, emblazoned on the backs of their white jackets.

As the trail narrowed, someone was running right behind her, perfectly in pace, if a tad too close. Was it another Canadian? Should she pull aside to let them pass? It was impossible. The drop beside them was nearly vertical and the steep rock face on the other side unyielding. It was so narrow here she felt like a mountain goat, and was glad she'd trained carefully. There was no choice but to keep pacing it out, lungs burning, for another few hundred yards.

As the trail finally began to widen, she pulled to the right to let her companion pass.

"Lisa," he said.

She knew that voice. Now she truly thought she was dreaming. She slowed right down, stepping further to the side as the trail broadened. She decided to take a breather. The jetlag and altitude were making her crazy. A few sips of water or juice would center her. Maybe she needed a sugar hit.

She stood with her legs apart, head down, calming herself and catching her breath as the cavalcade of other runners headed past, calling to each other in every language.

"Lisa, are you okay?" That Australian accent again. Will's voice. Insane. She squatted, then sat, keeping her head as low as possible, eyes closed, to avoid blacking out. She'd catch her breath and then wait for one of the volunteer guides to help her out. She'd trained as well as she could, but the race was gruelling. Maybe she'd overdone it.

If only Will had been here to run with her. A sob caught in her chest. Why should she be running alone here like this? It was foolish of her. It made her feel vulnerable, even though she was healthy and strong.

A gentle hand touched her shoulder. It was the softest of caresses, the kindness of a stranger. She reached her own hand up and placed it on top, as a gesture of thanks.

As her heart and breathing began to return to normal, she opened her eyes and lifted her head.

He was gazing at her, eyes full of concern.

"Will? It's really you?"

"You've got a bit more colour back now. I was worried about you."

"Will!"

"It's okay. I wasn't sure it was you, either."

Was this a dream? He'd lost the pallor of the clinic. He was healthy, strong and confident, and staring at her, his blue eyes full of concern for her.

Will removed his hand from her shoulder.

"It's okay. I'm not stalking you."

"But …"

"I'm in Europe meeting suppliers. A lot's happened since we last saw each other. I'm sponsoring a skyrun for Boulder City, so I needed to see how the best skyruns operate. Are you feeling better now?"

She nodded slowly. It was cold up here now she'd caught her breath. She wished he'd put his arm around her shoulder.

"It was a longshot you'd be in this race," he said. "Though you did mention you were planning a holiday and I know you love skyrunning."

She nodded again, allowing herself to smile, more than glad to see him.

"You're planning a skyrun for Boulder City? That sounds great, Will!" She needed to keep their conversation general, not personal. If she let him know how delighted she was to see him, how her blood sang in her veins at his touch, she'd be in big trouble.

"You might not believe me," he said. "I know my track record, but I know I'm making progress. This matters to me, Lisa. I want to prove myself to you; to myself and my family, too, but especially to you. I love you."

How she wanted to echo his words. They were right on the tip of her tongue. How simple it would be to pour out her soul to him, up here on the mountain, as strangers from all corners of the world clambered past; to say how much she'd missed him in her life, and how much she'd longed for him to be beside her every step of this race, and in her home, and her bed.

They studied each other. Her eyes drank in the shape of him, as if he were the only peak she wanted to scale, his neck and shoulders and jaw, the breadth of his chest, the tanned arms and hands.

As if reading her thoughts, he brought one hand up to her face and tucked a loose strand of her hair behind her ear. She leaned her cheek into the warmth of it, closing her eyes, and he pushed his fingers back through her hair to cradle her head, bringing his other hand to cup her cheek and jaw.

When he ran one thumb across her lips, she opened her mouth and nipped it. Her eyes sprung open and she locked eyes with his.

"You want me, too," he said, his voice intimate and eyes ablaze with triumph.

Unable to deny it, she let him bring his lips to hers, as he drew her into a hug, his warmth and strength surrounding her.

Her body wanted his. As she started to respond, she wrenched herself away.

"I'm sorry," she said, wiping her lips with the back of her hand. "We can't. I can't."

"I understand," he said. "Dr Peters explained. I shouldn't have done that, but I always want to be with you. Holding back is the hardest thing for me. But we can do this right. The fact that you want me, too? You have no idea how much this means to me," he said, leaping up and hauling her up beside him.

They ran the rest of the race together, and in the chair lift, descending, they pointed out parts of the run like running partners, ignoring the sparks every time they touched. When they alighted, Will took both her hands. She wanted to run her hands up his arms and grab his shoulders and pull him close.

"This is a friendly hug, okay," he said. "No sex. I know the rules. I want to make you happy, Lisa. I want to cherish you, to show you how much I love you. I'm willing to wait for you. And when two years is up, I hope you'll still want me. I need to go get my plane. Just as well. You know where I'd rather be."

Whether or not Will was telling the truth, Lisa's heart sang. Back at the quaint bed and breakfast, with jet lag dragging her down again and after running twelve miles uphill, she slept the sleep of the innocent.

...

Back in Boulder, when Lisa turned up to baseball training, Glen was thrilled. He was keen as a puppy, but it only made Lisa compare him with Will and find him wanting. She felt cruel, but it wasn't thoughts of Glen that kept her awake at night. Bad-boy Huntley. She couldn't get him out of her head.

There'd been no more sign of Will. She'd run past his shop a couple of times, but the windows were still covered in plastic.

"What was that?" Lisa said. "No, thank you, Glen. No pizza tonight. I'm running home. I'm fine. Catch you next week."

Lisa took the long way home, past the old town shops and pizzeria. There was still no sign of Will, as usual. All the windows were still covered. Who knew where he could be? Should she really trust his declaration of love back on Mont Blanc? That was what playboys did. Declare love. He could be blowing about the globe like tumbleweed for all she should care.

...

Lisa and her mother were on the front porch the Saturday morning after Lisa's return.

"Who's that man?" Donna said, as Will ran past and gave Lisa and Donna a wave, as casually as if they'd always been neighbors.

"That's Will. Will Huntley." The shock of recognition rocketed through Lisa's body. She was hot, then cold, then wrestled her mind back in control. So, Will was still around. And on the outside of a casino. Good.

"That man looks familiar."

"He would. He's an international playboy."

"Oh," Donna said. "What's he doing here?"

"We're near Vegas, Mom. There are plenty of famous people here, on and off."

"But he gave us such a friendly wave. It looked like you might know each other. He looks familiar. You're sure he's not an old friend?"

"We do know each other, but we're not seeing each other now. Okay?"

Chapter 27

Will saw Mindy's eyes light up as she buzzed him in the front door of the clinic.

"So good to see you, Will! We've been busier than ever! I think it's because of those photos with you. I kinda got into trouble. Say, how are you doing?"

"Hey, Mindy! How are you? I'd like to make a follow-up appointment with Dr Bakker, please."

"Dr Bakker's busy all day today," said Mindy. "Oh! There's a note here on your file that you're only to see Dr Peters, not Dr Bakker. Your appointment with her is in ten minutes."

"Look, would you please just tell Lisa I'm here?" He gave Mindy a bit of a wink. She smiled.

Had he ever felt so nervous? The opal was heavy in his pocket, glowing like a kaleidoscope, wanting to be admired, awaiting its moment of escape.

Lisa emerged just before eleven am, cool in her white lab coat. She looked annoyed, tight-lipped, glaring at Mindy.

"Mr Huntley?" Lisa said. "You're Dr Peters' client now. I'm sorry I'm unable to help you."

Lisa turned and went back down the corridor. Will raced after her, but hesitated. He didn't want to go back into her consulting room, back where she was the professional and he was the client. They were past that now. This was personal.

The Exit sign glowed at the end of the corridor. Will knew what he had to do. He grabbed Lisa's wrist, gently but firmly, and pulled.

"Come with me outside, Lisa, this way," he said, his voice low and urgent. "This will only take a few moments. I just need to show you something; then I'll leave you alone."

Lisa deactivated the alarm with her keys and pushed open the door. The flood of desert air and wash of light engulfed them both in a bright laneway, the sun high above, the concrete as glary as her white coat.

"Close your eyes," he said. Would she trust him? No matter. He must do this.

He took her hand, opened it gently, her delicate palm upwards. His pulse raced in her orbit, to be so close, to touch her. He reached into his pocket and withdrew the stone. When he'd placed it in her palm, he closed her cool fingers around it.

"Open your eyes, Lisa."

…

Lisa drew her hand away and held the heavy object close. It was warm, warm as Will. As she opened her fingers, the colors of the opal leapt out into the space, reds and greens and blues and golds.

"I found this here," said Will. "In the desert. It was just a rough stone. I've been polishing it for you, to thank you. Well, my grandfather helped me in the end, back in Australia."

Lisa was speechless, transfixed by the fire in the stone.

"Lisa," said Will. "I'm in awe of what you did for me. This is to thank you. You helped me find what was still inside of me. Knocked off all the crud. Found something worthwhile inside."

Lisa was lost for words. Gifts were forbidden. She shouldn't even be out here with Will, alone. It would be more than a year before they could see each other romantically. She knew the rules and she knew how to follow them, even if Will had no respect for them.

"Now go," he said, eyes downcast, as if clouds had passed across the sun. Then he caught her gaze and smiled again. "You need to go back to your work. To your excellent work. Changing lives like mine. But always remember I thank you. You set me free of my old life – back when I was lost and wandering. I love you."

As she pulled open the door, the wash of air conditioning was too cold on her skin. She wanted to put her hand in Will's and run away with him, but she knew she wouldn't. She'd go back to doing what she always did. Following the rules.

"You know I'm there in Boulder," Will said behind her. His voice reverberated through her chest. The whisper of his breath at her neck was delicious.

"For good," Will said. "For you. If you want me. I won't stalk you, but we're great together. I believe in us. And when you're ready, you'll come to me. I'll be there, waiting for my Queen of Hearts."

She twisted back to him, and stared at the pulse in his neck, fighting with herself. If only she were free to throw her arms around him, to brush her lips against his neck, to taste that honey skin.

"We can't accept gifts from clients, Will." Her voice was a monotone, and her words, harsh. He'd obviously gone to a lot of trouble with it. When she opened her fingers, it sparkled between them, this thing with a fire of its own, glittering.

"It was a piece of rubble, Lisa. Worthless. It was just lying in the desert, with a gazillion other neglected bits of dirt. Like I was. A lost human. Till you and Dr Peters healed me. If I was giving a gift I would give this to Dr Peters. This is not really a gift. It's a pebble."

When she returned to her room, walking like a zombie, Lisa told herself that she'd had to give Will those few moments, especially after he'd run with her on Mont Blanc. Accepting small acts of gratitude was part of helping clients to mark the changes in their lives. It validated their progress. Such transactions were a recognition they were successfully transitioning. Gift giving helped them to bring closure to their period of change. It was all about affirming their new selves.

Lisa had a pile of thankyou cards in her bottom drawer. She pulled them out sometimes and read through them all, on those rare bad days when she questioned what she was doing with her life; whether she was really making a difference, or whether she was wasting her time.

She was about to drop Will's stone into the drawer when she changed her mind. It really was far too beautiful to hide away. Heart-shaped. Remarkable. Was that significant?

She kept it in her pocket all day, pulling it out between clients, to dance in the light. Among all the colors was a brilliant red, bright as a flame. No wonder it was called black fire opal. It flashed at her, heavy in her palm, the setting every bit as beautiful. Gold. It was quite heavy. Valuable. More than that. She closed her fingers around it, held it tight. It was precious.

She brought it out in her Friday briefing and tried to give it to Dr Peters.

"Are you seeing Will Huntley?" her boss asked, turning the stone over and over to admire its colors and the workmanship.

"No." Why did her voice come out wistful? "Only when he handed it over."

"Are you seeing anyone else?"

"No," Lisa said. "But Rossco got better."

"Your old dog? Good to hear."

At the close of their meeting, Dr Peters held out the stone to her and pressed it into her palm.

"Lisa," she said, her glance piercing as she dismissed her. "Keep up the good work."

...

The smell of roast beef greeted Lisa when she returned from work that evening.

"Thought you needed some iron, dear," said Donna. "You've been looking a bit pale. Now, look what I've found here."

Donna laid out the local paper on the kitchen bench and pointed to an article. "I thought this might interest you."

"What's that, Mom?"

"A new skyrun, starting right here in Boulder City," Donna said. "That's that thing you do with Jilly isn't it? Look here. 'House of Hearts sponsors Black Opal Skyrun and Charity Ball.'"

Lisa ran to the counter, almost tripping on Rossco. There in the picture was Will, standing tall, his smile as charming as ever. Lisa devoured the caption.

New Boulder City adventure wear outlet House of Hearts founder Will Huntley sponsors new Black Fire Opal Skyrun and Charity Ball.

Lisa leaned against her kitchen counter and read the caption again. Excitement washed through her like a tsunami. She put her head up and smiled.

"Lisa?"

"Thank you, Mom. Very interesting."

247

"He looks like that man who runs past this place sometimes, doesn't he? That handsome one. That must be him, don't you think? Will Huntley."

"Yes."

Lisa's dinner tasted delicious.

…

That evening, Lisa noticed Will's gray jacket hanging on the back of her bedroom door, all stains removed from the evening he'd helped her with Rossco. Good as new. She really should give it back to him; wondered why she'd kept it for so long.

She decided to return it to him that very evening, to thank him again for his kindness in helping her through that awful evening, with Rossco at death's door. Not only might he need it, but wasn't it time she drew a line under their time together and moved on? Completely. For the sake of her career.

So why did she put on a pink shirt that hugged her curves, and retrieve her best jeans, and add a little eyeliner and blush? Not that she needed it. She hadn't felt so alive in weeks. Her reflection showed her eyes shining back at her, and a smile lurking. A real one. She let it out. *Yes!*

"Where are you going, Lisa?" said Donna. "Are you going out with that nice Glen again?"

"No, Mom," said Lisa. "I'm seeing someone totally unsuitable. You wouldn't approve."

"Oh?"

"A former client. Former gambling addict. International playboy. Celebrity bad boy."

"No!"

Was her mother slightly envious, there on the couch, already in her slippers? She put down her romance novel. Rossco snored nearby, twitching in a dream.

"Do I know this man?"

"Possibly. But not like I do."

"Lisa! Should I be worried? Is he dangerous?"

Will's jacket over her arm, Lisa gave her mother a hasty hug. "Very. No, I'm joking! I'm nearly twenty-nine, Mom. And I've got my phone."

"You stay safe! Have *fun*, dear."

Donna's smile was genuine. Had Lisa's father been the stern one? Lisa remembered the first time he'd told her not to turn cartwheels anymore. That summer she'd turned thirteen. He'd said she should be ashamed that her skirts tumbled upside down. That her legs should be covered.

"Yes. Thank you, Mom."

Lisa jogged towards the main street. The light was on in Will's shop.

She'd just tap on the door, and if he didn't answer, she'd hang it on the handle and jog home. That would be best.

The first thing she noticed about Will's shop as she came around the corner was a dog bowl out the front. Filled with water. The windows were still obscured.

She knocked gently. Will pushed open the door, his face alight.

"Lisa!" She loved the way he said her name. "My jacket. I wondered where that went."

"Just dropping it off."

In an old shirt and loose jeans, sleeves rolled up, Will was even better looking than she remembered, if a little dishevelled. Less jaded. More alive. Attentive. A smile so big for her she couldn't help but smile back.

Next door, the pizza place was bouncing, full of people who might recognize her.

She should do this quickly. Just hand it over and go. But she'd come all this way. And she wouldn't be seeing him again after this. Not in any meaningful way. Maybe just passing him in the street now and then.

His eyes lit up. When they sparkled and he smiled at her that way, he was even more attractive. Something inside her went "oh." As if she were a wind-up puppet, and he'd just turned the key.

She forgot what she was doing, the coat still draped across her arm.

"D'you like the dog bowl?" He pointed at it, brim full of water. "Thought you might bring Rossco past now and then. How is he?"

"Better every day, thank you, Will."

He reached for her, touched her arm. She couldn't believe how good it was to see him, stopped herself swooning; remembered the jacket.

As she went to hand it over, Will opened the door wider and ushered her inside.

"Can I show you my shop?" Will said with a note of pride. "Sneak preview."

249

So this was what was behind all the sheets of plastic. The smell of fresh paint. Gleaming cabinets. Old floorboards, sanded and polished. Shoulder level shelves, and hangers on the walls. Enormous screens higher up.

Will flicked a switch and Lisa was transported, as if she were hanging off the edge of Half Dome in Yosemite Valley, the footage breathtaking. On the other wall, someone was snowboarding, the spray so real she almost flinched as it flew towards her.

"Adventure footage," he said. "Like it?"

Lisa nodded, in a daze. This was no shop; it was a destination. Will had something here alright. And she'd worried he was all talk and no action.

He pointed and explained where he was unpacking stock and how he planned to have an exercise bike to measure customers' fitness, but she barely took in his words. She stared around at the interior, then back at him, startling herself to catch her own enthralled expression in one of the mirrors.

"Like it, Lisa? There's no other shop like this for a hundred miles, is there? Maybe anywhere. Stuff's still coming in. Everything from head torches to crampons. I'm still trying to work out whether we stock shoes. Not sure about that. You need so many sizes it's a specialty in itself."

"Shoes …"

"Yeah. Hey, great to see you again, Leese."

He glanced from the half-opened boxes to her, and she shivered as he ran his eyes over her. When his gaze rested on her eyes, flicked to her lips and back with a question, he gave her a smile she'd never noticed before. Candid. Uncalculating. Not the joker, not the flirt. She dodged his eyes, studying instead the shape of him, the set of his shoulders, that chest, the way his veins ran down his forearms to those hands.

Lisa held out Will's jacket again. Sparks flew as their fingers touched, and she snatched her own hands back to her sides. She stepped away from temptation, back towards the door.

"It's wonderful, Will," she said. "Sorry. I've gotta go."

So, it was still there between them; that magnetism. It was undeniable, impossible to ignore, even after all these months. And he'd been true to his word, building a new future for himself. Surely she could begin to let her guard down, to admit to herself how much she admired him; how proud she was of all he had planned and achieved, to concede he was even more attractive than ever; that she might allow herself to dream of him.

...

Will inhaled deeply and smiled as Lisa walked away. He went to his calendar behind the till. Eleven months down. Thirteen to go.

He remembered his trip back to Europe to catch up with his mother and find suppliers, when he'd managed to gain sole US distributorship for three suppliers of technical clothing. What a coup. He'd made some great contacts, suppliers he could approach to sponsor the run. Running into Lisa on Mont Blanc was the icing on the cake, confirming he was on the right path. There was plenty of work to do.

As old Jim had said, if he ploughed into his projects here, he'd have something to offer Lisa when they were free to date. Time was flying. And she was still interested in him. He watched how hard she'd worked to switch on her self-control. It made him smile. It confirmed she was still attracted to him. He loved the way she'd had to hold herself in check, loved everything about her.

And he'd been good. He'd wanted to scoop her up in his arms and carry her upstairs, or maybe make love to her right there on the floor, but had he done that? No. Because he didn't want to ruin her career. He knew what he had to do, and he could trust himself to follow it through.

Will punched both fists in the air, then stooped to empty some more boxes.

Chapter 28

With the clinic busier than ever, Lisa's days flew by. She was grateful to her mother, who'd stayed on, made herself at home in the spare room, kept Rossco company, and prepared meals.

"Let's go out tonight, Lisa, dear," said Donna. "There's free pizza. That new shop's opening, that one on the corner? I found this in the mailbox."

Donna thrust some junk mail under Lisa's nose, an invitation from the House of Hearts.

As Lisa turned it over and over in her hands, her pulse began to race like never before. She checked her watch and dashed to her cupboard where she hauled out her fancy Swiss shopping. Heart pounding, she ripped the tags off the new red bra, then dived into the big bag. Removing the beautiful tissue paper, she slid the red silk dress over her head.

It whispered to her again. "Yes."

Finally, she grabbed the heart-shaped opal on its piece of string, flashing fire.

"You look very nice, dear! Glamorous!"

Lisa and Donna set out, Donna waving at neighbors she hadn't met and those she had, and keeping up a running commentary about the gardens they passed.

The pizza shop was closed for normal business, but next door, Will's shop was ablaze with lights. People arrived from every direction, including news crews. Hundreds of people were gathered on the corner.

The shop appeared to have been wrapped in a huge blue ribbon, lit by spotlights, while the crowd milled outside. Even from a full block away, the display was fascinating, drawing them in, Donna with gusto, and Lisa trailing a little, taking in the scene.

"Oh look, Lisa," said Donna. "There's your friend again, the handsome one. No, wait. No. Yes, there are two of them. Say, is your friend a twin? Come on. Let's take a closer look."

They stood at the edge, towards the back of the crowd. Jeronimo's were serving free pizza, and something was about to happen. Another light blazed, illuminating a small stage and a man in a suit.

"Good evening, ladies and gentlemen. I'm James Huntley the Third, of Huntleys House of Diamonds."

"Ooh," said Donna. "I just love that Australian accent, don't you, Lisa?"

"Shhh, Mom."

"When my brother Will here said he was going to open a branch of Huntleys right here in Boulder City, it was unexpected to say the least, but you people have quite a place here, don't you!"

There was applause and a few cheers.

"Now, Will here, my younger brother, is an unusual man," said James. "He's always pushed the boundaries. Not content to stock jewels for the romantic hearts among us, like our Australian branch, Huntleys House of Diamonds, and our French branch, Huntleys House of Clubs, Will was determined that this American arm, Huntleys House of Hearts, would mainly carry things for what he calls 'healthy hearts' – adventure gear for the great outdoors you have around here."

James held out his arms. "Tell your friends about us," he said. "This store is sure to be a real treasure for your beautiful town. I encourage all of you to come in tonight and browse. Come and see what we have on offer for yourselves and the special people in your lives. But now I'd better move over for Will."

Amid more applause, and strikingly handsome in casual outdoor wear, Will jumped onto the small podium beside James and smiled. A hush came over the crowd. Lisa felt it. This man had a presence. Was he the same Will who'd rescued her pile of spilled folders in reception? That Will had been restless. Bright but aimless. Everywhere and nowhere. This Will had learned to harness all that energy and achieve something. Her heart swelled.

"So good-looking," breathed Donna.

"Mom!"

"Sorry, dear."

"Ladies and gentlemen, I'd like to give a special welcome to each of you, including, for once, the members of the press," said Will as a bunch of cameras flashed and media crews jostled to the front.

"Yes," said Will. "I admit that the media and I haven't always seen eye to eye, but I understand you're just doing your job. And that's why I've invited you. Because not only is there free pizza all round, but for every one of you here tonight, there are opening specials, with ten percent off across the board, and, if you're a Boulder City local, you will always get a ten percent discount, because Boulder City will always have a special place in my heart."

The place erupted. When the cheers died down, Will continued.

"I now have a special announcement, so I hope the media here is paying attention. I now call to the stage a very talented and generous person, whose devotion to Boulder City and the health of the local businesses is unequalled, and who every day gives away her time and expertise for free to people like me, and that woman is none other than Sondra Martin, Secretary of the Boulder City Chamber of Commerce."

Lisa gripped Donna's arm more and more tightly.

When a woman the same age as her mother took the stage, Lisa released her grip.

"Ladies and gentlemen, this young man deserves our congratulations," said Sondra. "I've never witnessed a person work so hard to make their dream a reality. Not only has Will Huntley here transformed our old travel agency into the most extraordinary shop of treasures you've ever imagined – good things for a healthy heart and healthy life – he's been working with our events committee to help plan a new event.

"So stick around a little bit longer, and you reporters, listen up," Sondra said. "Tonight, as well as opening Huntleys House of Hearts, we're announcing the International Boulder City Skyrun and Charity Ball."

Sondra knew how to work a crowd. They whooped and cheered.

"And the prize? You all come in and take a good look at it, won't you? It's a magnificent Nevada Black Fire Opal, set by the founder of Huntleys, Jim Huntley, a master goldsmith back in Sydney, Australia!"

Cameras popped amid cheers and applause, reporters firing questions.

"How many people are you expecting to compete?"

"What's the exact date of the competition?"

"How much are you investing?"

"Why are you doing this?"

"How's the contessa?"

Will took to the stage again. "Thank you, Sondra," he said. "It's now time for us to cut the ribbon and invite the crowd right inside. I'll be glad to take media questions in person right here, beside the door, if you reporters would like personal interviews."

A few more cameras flashed in his face as he posed for the media with a huge smile, framing his shop with his arms.

"But right now, I'd like to welcome Nicole to the stage to cut the ribbon," Will said. "Nicole has made this ceremony possible. She's a key part of our expanding Huntleys global empire."

A woman about Lisa's age stepped up. She wore bright yellow and a big smile, and wielded a huge pair of silver scissors, which flashed in the spotlights as she snipped the blue ribbon. As it fell away, the doors opened, wide and inviting.

She seemed very familiar with Will. A pang of jealousy stabbed Lisa, as she stood in her special red dress, trying to calm her heart.

It was a clear evening, mild with the promise of summer to come, a festival to remember.

"Let's go in, Lisa," said Donna.

Lisa was in a daze. Will had made this happen in less than a year. All this time, while she'd privately feared he was womanizing and gambling again, he must have been working around the clock. His achievement was extraordinary.

"It's very crowded, Mom."

"Nonsense. It's not like you to be shy. I'm going in."

Alone at the edge of the kerb, back from the circle of lights, Lisa let the reality sink in. There were other women in Will's life, and there always would be, but they weren't necessarily rivals for his affection. Sondra. Powerful. Influential. Special alright, but probably not a love interest. Nicole. Who knew?

Besides, Will was still out of bounds to Lisa.

While Donna and the crowd surged inside, Lisa held back in the shadows of the night.

"Lisa." She stiffened at that voice. Every hair on her body was on high alert. Will must have slipped around the edge of the crowd. She felt a hand on her waist, steady, as if it belonged there.

Her red dress swirled as Lisa turned to face Will's warmth. She inhaled, revelling in his proximity.

"I owe you an apology, Will," Lisa said. "About Sondra."

Will laughed out loud, pushing her to arms' distance without letting her go. He seared her with his gaze, down, and up again, his appreciation visceral. She shivered, then met his eyes.

"I owe you congratulations, Lisa," he said.

"Oh?"

"For this," he said. "All of it." The proud sweep of his arm took in the whole scene.

"I don't …"

"Lisa, you made all of this possible," Will said. "You changed me. For the better. For good."

Lisa's body remembered his. It clamoured to be closer. She could barely focus on his words, but when she did, she was ashamed. She'd believed the worst in him, yet he still gave her credit for his own success. This man had a generous spirit.

It took every ounce of willpower not to launch herself at him. She ripped her eyes away from his body and stared at the shopfront instead, anchoring herself to the larger event. Their exchange had to be above board. She would do this right.

"I'd actually like to buy something, Will."

"Yes?"

"A chain, please," she said. "Or a lanyard. Something waterproof, adventure proof. For my beautiful opal."

"Of course. Huntleys can help you. Come this way. You've met James, and now I'd love you to meet the rest of my family, while they're over here."

"Okay. Why, thank you."

His smile was huge. Genuine. It lit her up inside, banished all that lurking loneliness.

Will led her inside and straight to a stylish woman who was ringing up sales at the till while an older man with a beret wrapped up purchases.

"Mother, this is Lisa, the woman I told you about. Lisa, Cynthia."

His mother nodded, her smile polite as Will's was wide; apologetic for the fact she was far too busy to chat right now. "I hope we'll meet again, Lisa."

"And over there, that's Nicole, my sister, and behind her is Scottie, her fiancé. And you remember James?"

Lisa's shoulders dropped a notch with relief and she exhaled as James greeted her with a warm smile and a warmer handshake.

"Lisa! Great to see you again. I'd love you to meet Stella, our chief designer and my fiancée. Stella!" He waved across at a woman about her own age, but she, too, was busy with customers.

Plenty of younger women were looking at Will from everywhere in the shop, but it was Lisa's hand he reached for. She must learn to be content with that, for many months to come. Will pulled her close again, sending her pulse skyrocketing, then ushered her back into the street and away from the lights.

"I've been wanting to talk to you on your own, Lisa, but I've been so busy finding suppliers and setting up the shop, and I realize you're meant to stay away from me," Will said. "I respect that. But you have to understand, I'm still here for you. For *you*, Lisa, and when the time is right, I hope you'll come to me."

Will held her away from him, his hands gentle on her shoulders. He ran his eyes down her body again, then sought her eyes, as serious as he had ever been.

"I'm waiting for you, Lisa Bakker." His voice was quiet but intense, his words for her alone. "You take your commitments seriously, and I respect you for it. One year down. One more to go. We're not there yet, but we're closer every day."

He squeezed her shoulders gently, inhaled and looked to the sky before seeking out her eyes.

"Lisa," he said.

She gave him her full attention.

"I want you to be my wife, to run with me, eat pizza with me, do anything you want with me, any time you like. You don't have to give me an answer

257

yet, but I want you to remember what I told you before I left the clinic. Lisa, I have faith in your powers to guide me towards living a better life. Do you?"

"I do, Will," Lisa said. "You've achieved so much already, and I admire you for it. Congratulations."

"You mean so much to me, Lisa." He brushed her shoulder with his thumb as he dropped one hand to cover his heart.

Lisa could only smile and nod as a therapist might reward a client's progress. To share any indication of how she longed to hold him and return his declarations was strictly forbidden.

...

After that night, every time Lisa saw Will, checking out at the supermarket ahead of her, out for a run in the evening, and once at the post office, Will stopped what he was doing and pointed at his heart. It flipped her own every time. It was all she could do not to mirror the gesture, but to initiate a thing with him, anything more than a friendly smile, would be too risky. To keep her career, she must deny her need to return his love. In her dreams, every barrier dropped away and she was free to love Will fully, wholly, with every part of herself.

Back in daylight, sometimes Lisa would walk her old dog past Will's shop. If he saw her, Will would smile and touch his heart, while Rossco took a drink. Maybe it meant nothing. Maybe all Australians did that. Did she feel sorry for herself?

Once, in the warm sun of a summer's afternoon, Lisa noticed an oval sticker on Will's shopfront. "Proud to support youth mental health services." Now that was worth contemplating. Whether or not Will would keep his word about waiting for her, someone would benefit from his new maturity.

Quietly, barely admitting it to herself, Lisa counted down the days. In the glove compartment of her car, she marked them off with neat little ticks each morning, and as she drove to work, she could only hope Will was doing the same. Her work with addicts reminded her of the temptations that taunted everyone, herself included. She longed to visit Will, to message him, to remind him how much she admired his store and the way his Black Fire Opal Skyrun was taking shape, but the ban on a relationship with him continued.

Colourful banners of multiple sponsors began to appear all over town, along with promotions for the run and ball on social and traditional media. Even Jilly heard of the Black Fire Opal Skyrun and Charity Ball, and asked Lisa if she'd take part.

"Sure," Lisa said. "Join me." What she didn't tell Jilly was there was something significant about the date, burned into her brain. It would be one day short of two years to the dot since Dr Peters imposed the ban on Lisa and Will having a relationship. Midnight after the Black Fire Opal Skyrun would mark the first night of their freedom.

Had Will chosen the date deliberately? As the day drew closer, she began to fret again.

Would Will no longer want her, now that his own life was on a better path? Would being with her remind him of a time he no longer wished to remember? It wouldn't be unusual. Her most successful clients moved on and upwards and away from the support they had once needed. She admired Will, loved his company and longed to be free to truly love him, mind and body, and be fully loved in return.

Lisa was glad when Donna visited her again a few weeks before the race; pleased to be distracted from her worst fears.

Throughout the previous week, lanky runners from all over the world turned up to train on parts of the route. Cafes and Airbnbs were full. Will's shop was doing a roaring trade in running shoes and CamelBaks. The place was bouncing.

Black Fire Opal Skyrun banners in red, green, black and gold now hung all down the main street.

The night before the race, Lisa barely slept, her mind jumping feverishly from the memories of every conversation with Will to all the times they'd touched, desperate for more, but always having to pull away.

Her mind conjured every possible scenario. Furious with herself, she rose at 5am to shower and commence some gentle warm ups.

"Nervous, dear?" Donna said. An early riser, she offered Lisa a cup of tea. Lisa accepted with gratitude.

By the time Jilly arrived in an Uber, Boulder City had been taken over by helicopters and loudspeakers, and police were closing down some of the streets.

There were events for all ages and stages, marshals with iPads and registration tables. Jilly had insisted they sign up for the twenty-miler.

"It's our thing, Lisa," Jilly said, vivacious in a fresh hot pink running outfit. "Starting and ending in your town. Why the long face?"

"What if I run into Will?"

"Of course you'll run into Will. You'll run into Will and so will hundreds of other people. It's perfect!"

"But …"

"Quit worrying, kiddo. I've got your back. Let's do this."

Sure enough, at the start of the race, Will stood, tall and smiling and in control, surrounded by a small and eager pack of reporters, photographers and television crews. Lisa's butterflies accelerated. She grabbed Jilly's arm and squeezed. She'd need to run to settle them down.

"Warm-ups," Jilly said, dancing from the ball of one foot to the other.

"Rossco and I'll watch out for you, girls," Donna said. "Have a lovely run. Good luck!"

Donna waved off Lisa and Jilly at the start and was there again at the finish, as Rossco snuffled up spectators' food scraps.

Jilly and Lisa ran with the pack. Tired and exhilarated they made it to the end.

As Will mounted the stage to greet the tired competitors, Lisa's adrenaline surged.

"Welcome," Will said, handsome in a white House of Hearts t-shirt, the logo clear on his chest.

The crowd cheered.

"We wanted to stage a race, and we did!" Will said. "I'd like to thank all our sponsors, Drake's ice creams, Jeronimo's, the Boulder City Chamber of Commerce, Dream Sneakers, and Jasper and Clay Adventure Jackets."

They cheered again.

"Ladies and gentlemen," said Will. "Let us also thank Sondra Martin, the chair of the organizing committee, and all of the media who have turned up to cover this event, 3EY, Our Sports Network, Nevada News and all of you photographers, videographers and stringers. Welcome everyone!"

More cheers.

"And let's have a round of applause for all our volunteers and the regional police force for keeping our runners safe on the roads." Will gestured to the police chief in uniform, who nodded back with a kind of salute.

"And tonight, I hope you can all join us for the Black Fire Opal Charity Ball. Grand Marshal Fletcher will now announce the winners," Will said.

"That man's looking at you, Lisa," said Donna.

"Shhh, Mom."

He was. Lisa's heart pirouetted. Maybe she shouldn't have raced after all. A few evening runs, occasional baseball and ballet one evening a week were hardly adequate training for a race like this, with so many vertical climbs. All that proper prep, including tapering before the big race, was impossible when you were working full time. Maybe she'd need to visit the medical tent. And there was still the Ball to come. Thank goodness she'd made an appointment at Lucille's to get her hair done, along with half the other runners.

"I think he fancies you," Donna said.

It was true Will kept glancing her way, and when he caught her eye, he smiled, placing his hand on his heart. Even Jilly noticed.

"Lisa!" said Jilly. She elbowed Lisa in the ribs. Lisa patted Rossco's head.

The marshal called out names. Division winners and placegetters took their positions across the stage as Sondra handed the right prizes to the marshal, the crowd cheered and cameras flashed.

Will took the microphone again, congratulating the winners and participants. "It's fantastic to achieve a goal," he said. "It takes planning, and training, and a lot of self-discipline. But I want us to spare a thought for people who, for whatever reason, might have taken a wrong turn at some point in their lives." Members of the press thrust their microphones closer as Will's tone changed. The crowd went quiet.

"It's no secret I've been in the media for different reasons in my life. Now, I'm a proud ambassador for youth mental health services, but it's not about me anymore. I can put you onto some good stories, some stories worth sharing, stories about people overcoming difficult odds and doing great things for others."

There were a couple of thumbs up. The media went wild. Donna went wild.

"What a lovely man," Donna said. As she put her hands to her face in wonder, she inadvertently dropped Rossco's lead. In all the excitement, the old dog slipped away.

When Lisa looked up again, Will was squatting down on the stage, the media still milling as the winners came down the steps and the crowd began to disperse.

Between the heads and shoulders of other runners and their families and friends, Lisa suddenly spotted Rossco, on stage, up there with Will.

She stepped forwards and climbed the steps. As she stooped to retrieve Rossco's lead, Will stood to greet her.

They said each other's names at the same time.

"That's a powerful cause, supporting youth mental health," Lisa said, her admiration genuine. It would be difficult living so close to Will if he no longer wanted to pursue her romantically. But at least if their relationship never progressed, she'd continue to respect the man Will had become, and congratulate him for his achievements. No. She was lying. She wanted far more than that.

"Great cause," he said, eyes warm as he took in Lisa's running outfit and all her curves, though she'd chosen black, so as not to stand out.

"It is." Awkward. Lisa blushed, self conscious to the roots of her hair, damp with perspiration. For a moment she wished she hadn't competed. There was Will, cool, calm and perfectly in control. Of course he wouldn't have run in his own race. Why hadn't she thought of that?

"But if I'd had help back then, I'd never have met you, would I?" he said.

"No. I guess not." It was a fact, an acknowledgement of her role helping him overcome a non-productive period in his life. Nothing more.

Reaching for Rossco's collar, she brushed so close to Will she saw his heart beat under his shirt. She swallowed, tongue tied; awkward as a teenager with a crush.

Donna and Jilly smiled up at them from the foot of the stage as Rossco barked.

When Lisa led Rossco back down the stairs to Donna, Will accompanied her.

"Are you going to introduce us, Lisa?" Jilly asked, only slightly flirty. She held out her hand.

Lisa watched Will like a hawk. He was smooth and charming back, nothing more. Good. Trust her luck Jilly would snaffle him for herself.

Will extended the same charm to Donna.

"Good to see you, Donna," said Will.

"You two know each other?" Lisa said.

"Rossco and I walk past the shop now and then, don't we, old boy? Great job, Will, this amazing race today! And I can't wait for the Ball tonight."

"I had a lot of help, from Sondra and the committee," said Will.

Somehow, Will and Lisa had edged closer together. For all she'd pushed her body to run this race, it was disobeying her now.

Jilly was smiling. "Cute!" she mouthed to Lisa, then raised her eyebrows and cleared her throat.

"Well, Donna and I need to take Rossco home," Jilly said, pulling Donna away with her.

Finally, Lisa found her voice.

"Do you realise the date, Will?" she asked.

"How could I forget it? On reflection, maybe it was a dumb idea, but I needed a distraction, and it's been a good one."

"You needed a distraction?"

"I did. But now I don't."

"You don't." She was lost for words.

"See you at the Ball?"

She nodded and he smiled. If he'd opened his arms to her right then, she would have leaned in and rested her cheek against his chest, there at the beating of his heart. Not yet.

...

Jake's Electrics had gone wild with the lighting. Stepping inside the Art Deco Boulder City Theatre was like entering the heart of a Black Fire Opal.

The place was pumping, the jazz band up on stage providing a range of fast and slow numbers for every taste. Will commanded attention in his white suit, cool and in control, sharing himself around.

In her red dress, Lisa accepted a dance with Glen for old time's sake, then introduced him to Jilly who was having a ball in a shocking pink dress with a jagged hemline, skintight.

"Fantastic way to warm down," she shouted at Lisa above the music. "We should go to dances after every skyrun!"

Lisa was glad to see Donna joining in, and she ran into Sondra near the snack bar.

"Fantastic event today, Sondra," said Lisa. "And tonight. Congratulations."

"Why, thank you," Sondra said. "I don't believe we've met. Local or visitor?"

"I'm local, but I work in Vegas. Lisa Bakker."

"Oh *you're* Dr Lisa Bakker!" said Sondra. "So pleased to meet you. Will thinks the world of you."

"Thank you." Lisa smiled at Sondra as they headed back into the party, but her heart dived again.

If that was the case, why didn't Will dance with her? All evening she was aware of him. He was shaking hands with half the room, laughing and smiling, mingling and mixing, making his way easily among the crowd of locals and strangers, touching a shoulder here, giving a compliment there. That was what playboys did. They were everyone's best friend; no match for a serious, dedicated, lonely therapist. What had she been thinking? What kind of fool was she? She'd waited two years, spent her day running twenty miles and now here she was, feeling sorry for herself in her very best dress.

There was a sheen about Will, and no wonder. In the last two years, he'd built a store from scratch and networked successfully to create something extraordinary for her town. The skyrun was a wild success, a boon for local businesses and enjoyed by all. This charity ball was a triumphant finale, with youth mental health the worthy beneficiary.

When Lisa first met Will, he'd been lost, wasting his many talents. But now? Will was accomplished, widely respected and better looking than ever. No wonder everyone longed to dance with him. Unable to return his interest month after excruciating month, was there any hope for her? Anguish turned and twisted in her stomach.

As the lights dimmed and the band struck up their final number, a slow love song, Lisa lost sight of Will. She was about to retrieve her scarf and head for the door when a strong arm encircled her waist from behind and drew her close.

Gently, Will rocked her body with the beat of the music and she let her shoulders soften. As she leaned against him, Will wrapped his arms around her and squeezed her closer. Her soul soaring, Lisa ran her hands over his and interlaced their fingers, hungry for more of him, and he pressed soft kisses into her neck. Relief rocketed into every part of her. She closed her eyes to blink back tears.

Will held and rocked her to the music like he wanted her, like he cherished her, and when she turned to face him, she melted into him, resting her cheek on that chest as she'd dreamed a thousand times, rediscovering the wonder of his body. Of their own accord, her fingers pressed up and into the texture of his hair, as he found again the curves of her waist and hips and pressed her nearer. As desire surged, together they swayed in a dance she wished would never end.

She searched his eyes. In his gaze, the parade of emotions mirrored her own—wonder, pride, elation, restraint, respect, joy and a flick of mischief. In all the room, in all the world, there was no one she needed more in her life and in her arms. Did Will still want her? He was tender with her, a man in check.

"Let's not waste another moment, Queen of Hearts," said Will as the saxophone let out a final cry and the brush swished on the snare at the stroke of midnight. There, as the crowd dwindled, they pulled each other closer still, and kissed.

"I'm taking your mom home," said Jilly from somewhere nearby.

...

Will led Lisa up the steps to his apartment as she'd dreamed he would, step by step, kiss by kiss.

"I've missed you, Lisa," he said.

At the top, he lifted her in his arms.

A rush. A certainty. Urgent.

"'Yes,' Lisa?"

"Yes." She laughed.

As they hastened to his bed and her dress whispered to the floor, they reached for each other again. Lisa couldn't tell where her own body ended and his began.

265

He said her name like he needed her, like a prayer. "*Lisa.*" Soft fingers ran the trails of her body in wonder, until they both gave in to the urgency of the forces between them, grasping each other close and closer.

Afterwards, Lisa asked him: "Why are you smiling?"

Will held her wrist. Smoothed his thumb up over the bare curve of her arm. "Don't you know?" he asked.

She shook her head.

"Tonight's my first time."

"Well, now. I'm sure that's a lie, Will Huntley." She pushed herself up on one elbow to stare down at him, but he had an answer.

"First time you treated me as your man, and not your client," he said.

"My man."

"I like the sound of that," said Will. "Say it again."

Laughing, Lisa leaned over him, pinned him back against the bed sheets and said it again, between kisses.

"My … man."

If you loved *House of Hearts*, you might enjoy

House of Diamonds

Handsome James Huntley the Third faces a challenge or two at his Bondi Junction jewelry business.

Sparkles fly when newbie jeweller Stella Rhys sets up her home-made jewellery stall outside his shop.

She steals the limelight at his expensive PR stunt, and then she steals his heart.

Instant enemies, and fighting their attraction to each other, Stella and James become entangled in a social media war.

In this "enemies to lovers" romance, **will this dazzling couple ever work out what to do with an engagement ring?**

House of Diamonds is the first volume of Amber Jakeman's fast-paced, heartwarming *House of Jewels* series—with an international flavour—featuring the romantic fortunes of three generations of jewellers; the extended Huntley family. The books may be read in any order.

Praise for *House of Diamonds*

"Stella is an interesting character. Easy to read, feel good book. We need more of these kinds of books. I enjoyed it. I am looking forward to reading the rest of this series." Kris Revson

"Loving House of Diamonds... It's the perfect 'bedtime read'. I really enjoyed it. More publications, please. Please put my name down for Book 2." Annette

"Congratulations on a well crafted and delightful page-turner! The world of jewellery is a splendid backdrop to your romance, as are Sydney Harbour, Bowral and the south of France, with more glimpses of Boulder City perhaps in the eagerly awaited next book. Keep writing!" Sparkle-lover

House of Spades

House of Spades is Volume 3 in the _House of Jewels_ series.

Can love call again later in life? He calls her a trespasser. She calls him a hermit and thief.

Free spirit and serial single Flame Rhys has sworn off love, but try convincing her reclusive neighbor Ross Archer.

Fiery redhead Flame accidentally rekindles the widower's passion for life, for his land and a wife.

But is there more to Flame than meets the eye, as Ross's daughters suspect?

Praise for *House of Spades*

"Your book inspired me to rewild parts of my property."

" ... some delightful insight into the subtropical climate and people of northern New South Wales."

"Flame is awesome."

House of Clubs

Who holds the key to her heart? When stylish Australian widow Cynthia Huntley moves to France and begins to renovate a centuries-old property, she and handsome handyman Émile tussle over a "perfect" chandelier.

Cynthia lets the mysterious yet gallant Émile into her house, but will she let him into her heart?

What is Émile fleeing? And what is worth seeking in life?

As winter closes in, will Cynthia abandon her French adventure? Or can she and Émile claim love again later in life—together?

Praise for *House of Clubs*

"Love this romance. I feel it is the best of this series. Love the ending. And I love how I seem to learn about a certain topic in each of the stories." – Gail

"This book took me to the south of France. There's more to it than meets the eye."

"From the opening paragraph I was hooked and never once during the reading was I disappointed. Well, except maybe when I came to the last page but that was because I did not want the story to end!" Cindy L Spear

Full House

What can you do when you've friend-zoned the one you love?

Nicole Huntley, marketing manager for her family's international jewelry business, froze out family friend Scottie back when they were teenagers.

Now he's the Huntleys' financial advisor. Newly divorced, the affable Scottie needs somewhere to stay. Nicole offers him space, never expecting to fall for him — hard.

But when fate deals the Huntleys a high-stakes fresh hand, "conflict of interest" threatens to shatter her family, destroy their retail empire — and to break her heart.

Get ready for the showdown in *Full House*, Amber Jakeman's latest international heartwarmer in the Huntley House of Jewels saga.

Amber's contemporary love tales — on the sweeter side — may be read in any order.

Amber Jakeman's *House of Jewels* series features the romantic fortunes of the extended Huntley family.
The books may be read in any order.
House of Diamonds
House of Hearts
House of Clubs
House of Spades
Full House

Don't miss out!

Visit www.amberjakeman.com to find out how to order other novels by Amber Jakeman. Sign up to receive occasional email updates.

About the Author

Partial to sunsets, picnics and poetry, feel-good fiction writer Amber Jakeman was a journalist, ghost writer and editor before succumbing to her addiction to uplifting endings.

With readers in more than fifty countries, Amber creates fast-paced heart warmers from her tiny apartment on the edge of Sydney Harbour—historical and contemporary love tales with an international flavor.

When not writing, Amber enjoys time with family and friends, sailing with her husband, travel, walking and savoring other writers' creations.

Amber Jakeman acknowledges Australia's first storytellers and offers respect to Indigenous people past and present and to their descendants.

Visit www.amberjakeman.com to find out how to order other novels by Amber Jakeman, and sign up for occasional updates.

About the Publisher

Lorikeet Press publishes feel-good fiction for readers of all ages. If you enjoy books with uplifting endings, you're in the right place.

Visit www.lorikeetpress.com for more information.

www.ingramcontent.com/pod-product-compliance
Lightning Source LLC
Chambersburg PA
CBHW020356120726
47904CB00002B/588